DI ZHEN

A Thriller

by

Dr. Samuel Grier, Ph.D

© 2009 by Samuel Grier

All rights reserved. Except as permitted under the U.S. Copyright Act of 1976, no part of this publication may be reproduced, distributed, or transmitted in any form or by any means, or stored in a database or retrieval system, without the prior written permission of the author.

Purchased from: **NITWonline.com**

DISCLAIMER: This book is a work of fiction. Elements of the story were either fabricated by the author or based on information obtained in the public domain. Capabilities or processes ascribed to the Central Intelligence Agency, the U.S. military services, the Federal Bureau of Investigation, the Chinese military, Mexican authorities, the U.S. Geological Survey, San Francisco State University, the Epcot Center, or other entities are either a figment of the author's imagination, based on research conducted on the World Wide Web, or based on information in references found in public libraries.

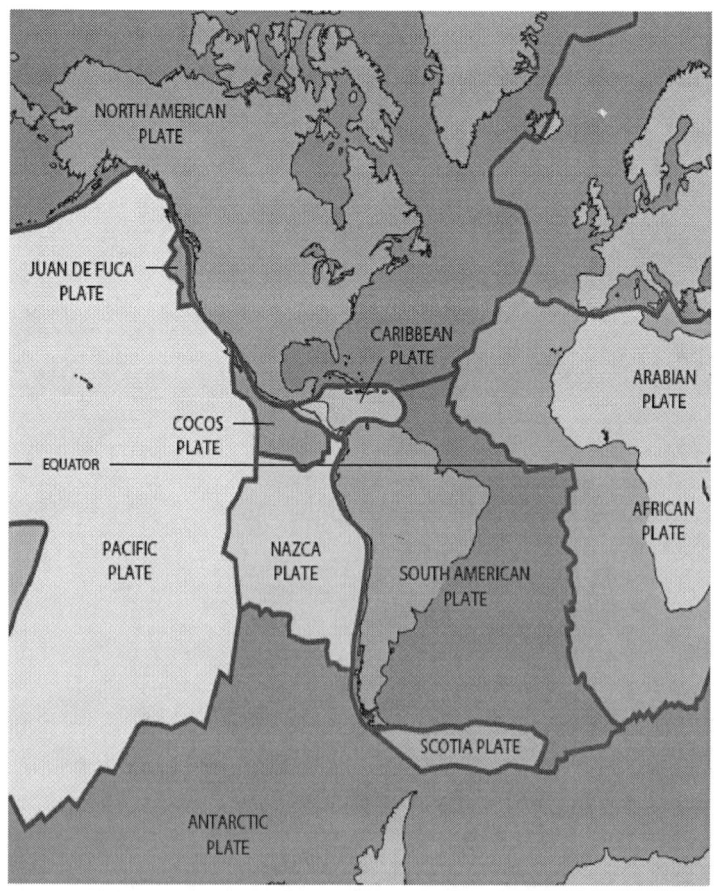

Illustration of Tectonic Plates (Courtesy U.S. Geological Survey)

PROLOGUE

Time: 8:43 AM PST. The streets and narrow lanes were full with the usual rush hour traffic. Pedestrians, mostly tourists, walked casually along the sidewalks toward San Francisco's famed Fisherman's Wharf. Street performers lured passersby in the hope for some loose change, some singing, some standing in costume, others playing musical instruments. A voice practiced opera, the statue of liberty stood proudly in bright silver costume, a saxophone wailed. A light breeze roused the air from its rest, its cool temperature a welcome contrast to the bright sun.

It started as a rapid, buzzing noise, strangely soft, as if the earth, blissfully supine, decided to wake and hum a tune. People on foot were the first to notice. They stopped, turning and asking each other if they felt something, too. Children laughed nervously and squealed at the funny pinpricks that tickled their feet and ran up their legs, some grabbing onto their parents for protection from the phantom force. The statue of liberty was the first to react.

"Earthquake!" he shouted through his mask.

The rest of the would-be musicians and entertainers, veterans of many a quake, picked up the chant.

"Earthquake! Earthquake!"

As if in response to their refrain, the earth began a peculiar jig, that of a drunken pirate spinning on his peg leg, hips rotating obscenely. The rolling motion tossed nearly everyone to the sidewalk. Pedestrians who resisted flailed their arms, teetering precariously, trying to maintain their balance in vain, ultimately tossed disdainfully to the pavement by the triumphant earth. Motorists stopped their cars, their faces wearing unspoken fears.

The rolling motion reached a constant state, first pitching back and forth, and then bouncing up and down. The streetlights and traffic lights swayed as if moved by a great sea wind, and newspaper stands and trash cans leaped from their upright perches to the asphalt. Swimming pools overflowed with miniature tsunamis, the water slapping onto concrete embankments. Bricks and glass rained down from the buildings and onto the sidewalks and streets below, the glass shards imitating first the high notes of a piano and ending their performance with a shattering harmony. Crackling sounds filled the air, the ground moaning haunting sonatas as long, thin fissures fractured the earth.

The calamity lasted for a full two minutes.

***

Professor Beverly Duncan, a seismologist in the Department of Geology at San Francisco State University, sat at her desk on the second floor of the Basic Sciences building that Monday morning, when she felt the tremor and heard a faint growl. She thought it might be the air conditioning, but when the vibration intensified and the buzzing began, her heart found its voice and uttered, "Oh, my God!" Her mind ran while her body crawled. She found her will sheltered under the desk long before the rest of her arrived. As her arm pulled the chair close for protection, books began to fall.

***

The two-storied Oakland freeway was clogged with traffic. As the shaking started, the upper bridge began to sway. Cars screeched to a halt, some thrown into the side rails. Motorists who remembered the quake that collapsed the upper deck during the 1989 World Series, opened their doors and ran or jumped from the lower highway to escape what they perceived as certain death, some injuring themselves as caution was cast aside. But the shaking did not change its timing or direction, and this time the structure held.

***

The shaking lessened in frequency and intensity. The earth drifted slowly back into a fitful sleep. Small rumbles lightly jostled the city, but the tossing and turning subsided. Beverly Duncan crawled from under her desk and struggled to her feet, gravity doing its best to keep her pinned to the floor. Just for an instant she admitted that her weight's burden had prevented a quick escape, and she vowed, "I will lose it!" She surveyed broken bookshelves and scattered books, but it was the shattered vase and divided daisies that released her tears. As they rolled down her cheeks, Bev felt a surge of energy. She sensed renewal.

The blinking monitor on her desk caught her attention and pushed her tears away, and Beverly was suddenly back to work. She opened her Internet browser and logged onto the worldwide earthquake locator, which tracked events across the globe in real time. There it was. Location: West Coast, United States. Time: 1643 Z. Magnitude: 7.1. The coordinates of the earthquake's origin were listed. Her surroundings told her the epicenter had been somewhere well outside the city.

CHAPTER 1

Rick Starr sat in his office cubicle, carefully folding a paper airplane he was about to launch across the room when Central Intelligence Agency Director John Renoir walked in. John Renoir — long-time political appointee in a variety of appointments and now the new chief of the Agency — shook his head when he saw the paper plane. "I'm glad to see we don't overwork you guys."

Rick grinned. "Hey, this is an important test I'm about to perform."

"Right." Renoir threw a packet of papers on Rick's desk. "Take a look at these. I need an answer right away." He turned back as he left and pointed his finger in Rick's direction. "And I need the right answer. Even I know this doesn't look good."

Picking up the packet, Rick set it on his lap. He put his feet on the desk and leaned back, casually leafing through the pages. He considered John Renoir a good boss, and with a distinguished name like Renoir — he pronounced it distinctly when he introduced himself, "Name's Ren-wahr, John Ren-wahr." — that alone was almost reason enough to be head of the Agency. He was easygoing, but tough when he had to be. Congress liked him because he did not know how to tap dance. But Rick knew what made John Renoir truly effective was that he could make more decisions in an hour than most people could make in a week.

The cover sheet on the package was labeled TOP SECRET ESI — extra sensitive information. It would be a security violation for almost everyone else in the office if they even touched the packet of papers. He held the cover sheet for a moment, reveling in the privilege of holding something this sensitive, of this magnitude. That the United States of America — history's most powerful nation — would trust him to make judgments about issues of the greatest concern to the country and its president sobered him. The exhilaration of being one of the first, and sometimes one of the few people to review certain highly-classified information, thrilled him. Although he would have denied it had someone asked, reading documents like this gave him a sense of importance, even power.

The first page was a satellite photo. It took Rick a moment to get oriented. The coast of China. South of Beijing, it looked like. He turned on his desk lamp and held the photo in the light. It was a military installation, a harbor. *Must be Xiamen. Right across the Formosa Strait from Taiwan.* He had seen plenty of photos of Xiamen before. It was always a hub of activity, and this picture was not any different. The second page was another satellite photo. *Yes, also Xiamen. But the harbor is more than just busy...it's full of ships and boats...seem to be neatly parked across the harbor...and the military base close by is choked with vehicles and soldiers. The place is a blender of activity. Hmmm, date is today's. What's the date on the other photo? Three months ago.*

The subsequent pages detailed a timeline of number of ships, number of soldiers, and number of trucks and other heavy equipment. The figures steadily increased and finally reached critical mass to where the Pentagon's early warning indicators went yellow all at once. He stood up and looked over the top of his cubicle, searching for his boss. Renoir was behind the glass partition, back in his office. Rick marched past John Renoir's secretary. He dropped the packet back onto his boss' desk. "Isn't it obvious?"

Renoir stared at Rick. "So tell me. What is it?"

"An invasion force."

"An invasion force? Why would the Chinese be putting together an invasion force? Who are they gonna invade?"

Rick shrugged. "Well, if they were actually going to invade

someone, my guess is they'd do what they've been threatening to do for as long as I can remember."

"You mean attack Taiwan? What for?"

"Reunification. What else?"

"They'd have to be crazy. Every time China talks about using force to reunify, the international community goes nuts."

"Let's face it, you and I think like Americans," Rick said, walking over behind his boss and picking up the first satellite photo. "Think like an Asian. Think Chinese, center of the universe kinda stuff. The rest of the world is uncivilized. Oh, yeah, China uses countries in the West as trading partners, and they buy oil from OPEC and anyone else they can. But it's utilitarian. One of the reasons they're so difficult to deal with in the Security Council is that compromise with the rest of us uncivilized Barbarians doesn't make sense to them.

"Our support for Taiwan is interference in their internal affairs." Rick walked backed to the front of Renoir's desk.

"That harbor is Xiamen, only 200 kilometers across the Formosa Strait. See those landing craft? I think the Chinese have only a few hundred, and there must be nearly a hundred in the south of the harbor."

Renoir squinted at the photo. "Invasion force? Pentagon only just noticed this stuff last week."

Rick shrugged. "I don't think they're gathering for a Church picnic. Don't forget they've got a thousand short range ballistic missiles along the coast north of Xiamen. This stuff could be a follow-on force, or maybe it's part of a mop-up operation. But there are some other things we could check to see if there's really something to all this. 'Course, China could be testing to see if our support for Taiwan is what we say it is. See how our new president reacts when they push a little."

Renoir looked up at Rick. "If what you say is true, this is more like a shove than a push. President's proved he can be tough. Look what he did just to get elected." John Renoir stood up and yelled out to his secretary. "Liz! Get Carlson and Davis and tell them to meet me in the War Room!" He walked toward the door. "C'mon with me." Renoir leaned forward slightly, as if a weight sitting on his shoulders just got heavier. Rick had seen it before. People like John Renoir bent at the waist when they walked, and it was difficult to keep pace with them.

They went together down the hall to the War Room, where satellite images could be viewed in real-time. The United States recently placed an experimental satellite in geosynchronous orbit at an altitude of 35,800 kilometers over Shanghai. It was experimental because its optics were comprised of "nanosats", miniature satellites whose multiple likenesses melded into a single composite image with the same fidelity as a satellite in polar orbit at a much lower altitude of 600 kilometers. And while a satellite in polar orbit circles the earth repeatedly and guarantees a brief view of almost any point on the globe at the same time once a day, a geosynchronous orbit, or stationary orbit as it is also called, offers the capability to view forty percent of the earth's surface twenty-four seven, which in this instance included activities at Xiamen.

"Push this president?" asked Renoir to no one and everyone. "Wait till the president shoves back," he growled.

Rick smiled to himself, careful not to let the amusement register on his face. He had witnessed power politics many times, and it could get ugly. The president would have to be tough, or the outcome of this shoving match could be a disaster. The Chinese were masters at detecting the slightest hesitation and then exploiting it. They often seemed oblivious to realpolitik when it suited their purposes.

***

Fifty feet in the air in an observation tower overlooking California's San Fernando Valley. Feet perched atop the desk. The aroma of fresh coffee finding its way to every corner of the room. Classical music in the background, the sound softly wafting through the air. *Mmmmm, this is good.* Marlimae Cooper — Marly for short, Coop to her friends — born and raised in the Colorado Rockies, was in her element. Her two-year old Western Highland Terrier, Benny, lay on the floor, happily chewing a small rawhide bone next to her chair. Sunlight peeked over the horizon and shined through the windows, the entire valley floor glistening in the early morning light. Marly squinted her eyes, drinking in the sight of the day coming to life. *California isn't Colorado, but it's close enough for now.* She leaned back and tilted her chair on two legs.

Marly's mother, Trudy, had vacationed in Colorado with her family when growing up. She decided to attend college in Denver and met Marly's father while she was a student. He was a cowboy from nearby Littleton, she an Easterner from New York. Trudy fell in love with her future husband's rugged good looks and casual approach to life. She loved his bronco riding and shared his enthusiasm for wild western rodeos, which in those days were sprinkled throughout Denver. He was a cowboy who thrived in the Colorado Rockies, and Trudy thought that she could be content living out West for the rest of her life with a man who had no equal. But she discovered that her New York roots ran deep.

She chose for her daughter the name of her own great grandmother Marlimae, a New York debutante, in the hope that the name would somehow magically transform Marly into an Easterner by virtue of its origin. But the magic never worked.

As far back as Marly could remember, she rode horses. At thirteen, her parents bought her a quarter-horse named Nugget, a gelding Palomino graced with a striking light colored mane. The family lived near the Englewood reservoir before the area was built up, and Marly spent countless hours riding through the fields and along the dirt roads behind their small ranch. She barrel raced all through school in rodeo competitions, usually finishing in the top three but not winning enough to think about going national. Nugget was a dozen years old when she left home and went off to school, and while she continued to ride sporadically in college, horseback riding drifted off to a past life and became only an occasional diversion.

Marly also hiked all along Colorado's Front Range, and the yearning in her for mountain living could not be quenched. She spent a summer in Omaha, Nebraska, with cousins and felt like she was suffocating on the prairies in the muggy, thick air. The stickiness of her clothes, the difficulty breathing she experienced, all were signs to her that she had to get back to her mountains. Her soul had fused with the West, and it caused a restlessness, a sense of longing to be outdoors in nature.

Although the Cooper family went every summer to the family estate in upper New York, daughter Marly was always ready to return home. Trudy finally accepted that Marly would never share her love for the East. Marlimae grew up in the West and would spend her life there, having inherited her father's deep affection — or was it an addiction — for the Rocky Mountains.

Marly's uncle had been caught in the great Alaska earthquake of 1964. His harrowing stories of the ground shaking for over seven minutes, the earth rising and falling as if it were liquid rather than solid, scared and exhilarated her at the same time. It made her want to learn everything she could about earthquakes. Her interest culminated in winning first prize at the state science fair in Colorado as a high school senior with her project on the great San Francisco earthquake of 1906.

She went to college with the goal of someday becoming a seismologist, and she earned her Bachelors degree from Colorado State University in Fort Collins and received her Master's and Ph.D. in Geology from the University of Colorado in Boulder. When she finally began searching for employment after graduation, she was confronted with the reality that there was not a significant demand for seismologists in Colorado. She reluctantly sought opportunities outside the state, but only those that could satisfy her craving for mountains, blue sky and dry air, and she was now an Associate Professor of Geology at San Francisco State University. Recognized internationally as one of the foremost experts on the San Andreas Fault, she spent her time outside the classroom doing hands-on fieldwork in the more remote areas that sat on the Fault, and she loved it.

Today she and her dog Benny would trek through the valley and record readings from a portion of the U.S. Geological Survey's alignment array residing on the San Andreas Fault. There was a series of creep meters that ran alongside for several kilometers, and their readings were recorded monthly. Creep meters did exactly what their name implied: They measured ground creep, a cable spanning the fault attached to a gauge designed to record even the slightest movement. If one side of the fault shifted in relation to the other, the alignment array would detect the change. The San Francisco earthquake in 1906 revealed a significant amount of ground surface displacement, and it was believed that the stress preceding an earthquake might produce measurable distortion of the earth's surface. When the associated stress from the distortion was suddenly released, the resulting rebound could cause an earthquake.

After today's stroll through the Valley, Marly would return to her office and check the public worldwide earthquake locator on the Internet to see if anything noteworthy happened while she was incommunicado. Since the Locator came on-line in late 1994 and with the placement of towers in the San Francisco Bay Region that used the Global Positioning System to make precise measurements of the earth's surface, tracking earthquake activity was effortless. The locator recorded the origin, magnitude, and time of every earthquake in the world. The vast amount of data changed constantly, and most of it sparked little interest.

Marly found that being a seismologist was an emotional roller coaster. There was occasional, intensely personal arousal that only the prospect of a major earthquake could generate, followed by long periods of boredom. There was nothing more that a seismologist wanted than to be part of a team assigned to cover a great quake — an earthquake that registers 8.0 or higher on the Richter Scale. The problem with a quake of that magnitude was the death and mayhem that would accompany it, and hence the emotional turmoil. Who wanted death and mayhem? Certainly not Marly. But the exhilaration she relished came with the thought of witnessing and analyzing the causes of the "Big One".

Second best was accurately forecasting that an earthquake was imminent and in the process saving tens of thousands, or even hundreds of thousands of lives. Marly's conscience told her that she could only hope for second best, and it was this motivation that drove her to be part of the team that closely watched the alignment array along the San Andreas.

The real truth, of course, is that a seismologist gets to have it both ways.

***

Rick Starr walked into the War Room behind his boss. The latest in high-tech wizardry, from here one could control which objects U.S. satellites orbiting the earth looked at, and then view the imagery in real-time. The Agency paid millions to put the facility together, its funding hidden deep within the Federal Budget. It took nearly two years to build and was equipped with a trio of large flat screens — each a full twenty-five feet diagonally — that showed even the finest details projected onto them. John Renoir walked over to a phone and picked up the receiver. "Bring up number seven on screen one." Seven was the experimental satellite in stationary orbit over Shanghai that could also be made to look at Xiamen. In walked Larry Davis followed by Denise Carlson. Davis and Carlson were CIA analysts with expertise in the region, but they lacked the coveted adjective *senior* before their job titles. They were part of a recent series of successful investigations, and although relatively new to the business, they both proved they could find and follow a scent.

"Sit down," said Renoir, more of an order than an invitation.

The three complied by sitting on a long couch facing the flat screens. Renoir sat at the left end of the sofa next to Rick. A picture appeared. Renoir picked up a controller.

"We need to go south," said Rick.

Renoir pushed the button on the remote. The lens slowly panned down the coast until Xiamen sat in the middle of the image. Renoir looked at Rick.

"A little farther south," Rick said. The lens continued its pan of the China coast. "That's good." The image on the large flat screen showed another military installation south of Xiamen and a road connecting the two.

"Zoom in on the road."

The lens slowly zoomed in on the road and the very north end of the military installation. "Hold it."

Renoir set the remote down. "What are we looking for?"

Rick did not reply. He only watched the screen. A moment later, a convoy of two large passenger trucks, loaded with what looked like soldiers, left the installation and took the road heading north. The trucks were army green and typical of an era long past. The Chinese still produced trucks for its armed forces using designs inherited from the former Soviet Union decades earlier, and watching Chinese army maneuvers often looked like a Hollywood World War Two reenactment.

Innovation had always been imported. Only now was innovation becoming something to be cultivated rather than feared in the People's Republic, but the advent of new ideas was limited to the military and business sectors.

The convoy passed out of view. Rick still said nothing, and Renoir sighed. He was told by some of his colleagues that spooks — a term he generously applied to everyone that worked for the Agency — were an odd breed, and he certainly did not have reason to disagree. He crossed his arms and continued watching, looking for what he did not know.

John Renoir was fifty-nine years old. Despite appointments to positions in three different administrations, he always harbored a desire to get into the intelligence business. He was responsible for the deployment of a number of space intelligence assets as a young researcher, and their capabilities and potential for gathering information fascinated him. His rise to senior management in the defense sector and the recent election of a long time friend to the White House gave him the opportunity to lobby for the job of CIA Director. However, he sometimes wondered about the wisdom of his choice, particularly when he was overwhelmed by all the information the U.S. tracked and accumulated. There were experts in every area, so that helped. But he found that understanding the big picture and making an intelligent assessment of events took both time and an excess of smarts. And although he earned his Ph.D. in physics from Princeton when he was only twenty-five years old, every once in awhile even he felt that he was not up to the task of properly absorbing and analyzing what was available. As he watched the image, another convoy appeared on the road.

Rick finally spoke. "This is a base with the Chinese equivalent of the U.S. Marine Corps. If trucks filled with soldiers have been going from here to Xiamen, it probably confirms the Chinese are putting together what looks like an invasion force." He looked at Renoir. "We should take a look at our imagery from, oh, let's say the last four months to see what it shows."

Renoir did not hesitate. "Carlson, get on it." She got up without a word and left the room. Renoir looked at Rick. "What else?"

"Four things. Dongshan Island is located across the Formosa Strait from Taiwan. It's been used for large-scale military exercises in the past. The Pentagon can tell us if there are amphibious landing craft, tanks, armored vehicles or anything else that could be used for an amphibious assault. Second, we should check the airbase closest to Xiamen to see what their air force is doing. Third, we should assess how far from the strait their navy is. They've been building more submarines the last couple of years than the rest of the world combined. If their navy and subs are all close by it could be significant. And finally, we should check for diplomatic activities in the U.S."

"What kind of activities?" asked Renoir.

Rick moved his head from one shoulder to the other as he was thinking. "Something different from the usual trade delegations and university students. Anything that can't be explained without a closer look."

"What are we looking for?"

Rick rested his chin on his fist. "We should see if the Chinese are planning to pull a trigger."

"Pull a trigger?" It was the first time Renoir heard the term.

"Yeah," said Rick. "See if they plan to do something that would give them an excuse to make a move on Taiwan."

"You're kidding. Like what?"

"Like blowing up their embassy in Washington and blaming it on the Taiwanese." said Rick.

Renoir gaped. "So we should check for activities in Washington?"

"No. Too obvious. We should look for something subtle, clever, hard to detect. Something that requires serious digging."

"Why just the U.S.? How about Europe?"

"If you want maximum impact and coverage, you do your dirty work in America." Rick thought for a moment. "Short of invading Taiwan, damage in the United States, even a little, would give the Chinese leadership immense satisfaction."

Davis was up and out of his seat. He was an Asian-American, a second generation immigrant from Taiwan. "I'll look at Dongshan, the airbases and their navy, and I'll get Joe Craxton in the computer information systems section to see if the intelligence database shows whether the maniacs are up to any unusual activities."

"Maniacs?" Rick asked without thinking. He looked up at his colleague. "Is that supposed to mean something?"

"On Taiwan, we call Chinese officials on the mainland maniacs." He smiled. "Main-land. Main-iacs. It's a joke." He shrugged and left the room.

"What else?" asked Renoir.

"We should let the Chinese know we're aware of their activities and let them react. Their reaction might tell us more about their intentions than anything else."

"What do you think they'll say?"

"My guess is they'll claim it's all for a military exercise."

"Do you really think this buildup is to push the president?"

"I don't know," said Rick. "Chinese foreign policy is usually characterized by the proverb 'Kill the chicken to scare the monkey', and I don't see any dead chickens lying around."

"Yeah," said Renoir, "there's just one pissed off monkey." He scowled.

"Technologically, China's armed forces are inferior to those of Taiwan, but numerically they're far superior. Maybe that's why they're being discreet. They want to even the odds by taking advantage of their numbers, which could mean they're serious." Rick rubbed his chin. "If this isn't handled right, it's hard to say where it could lead."

Renoir bit his lower lip. "OK. I'm gonna sit on this until you guys get back to me. I need to know as much as you can find out before I raise it with the SecDef and ask him to take this to the president."

***

Marly Cooper poured herself a small cup of extra-strong coffee, espresso style, and added milk and sugar. The Italians would call it a *macchiato*. Drinking coffee brought a special pleasure that only real coffee drinkers could appreciate, and she considered herself a real coffee drinker. Tea had its place if you had a cold or upset stomach, but it was weak, pale and tasteless in comparison. Herbal tea did not register on her personal Richter scale of beverages. And decaffeinated coffee? A sin of untold proportions that should have condemned its creator to the lowest depths of Dante's inferno. The caffeine in coffee raised her heartbeat, activated the muscles in her legs and arms, and prepared her psyche for the day. All in all, one of God's small treats for people to enjoy before they began their daily toil.

Looking across the valley, Marly watched the sun rise above the horizon. The emotion she felt as the sun flashed red and slowly turned orange as it climbed into the sky reinforced her belief that being a professor and seismologist was right for her.

But she also knew that her lifestyle of chasing after what often seemed like plumes of dandelion seeds scattering in the wind, was not going to help her meet someone she could share her life with and start the family she wanted one day. Her sister Marilyn was five years her junior, and she already had two kids. Marly was aware that she was becoming jealous of her sibling. Always the high achiever and the recipient of all the recognition and praise when they were growing up, it was Marilyn who now saw much more of her parents and who with her children was the object of their adoration.

Marly's childhood had been carefree, even idyllic, and she was becoming anxious to recapture the feelings of security and serenity that were part of her makeup for such a large part of her life. Feelings that she believed only marriage could provide.

There were boyfriends growing up. Lots of them. High school brought her the first love of her life. Anthony — he insisted on being called Anthony and corrected anyone who tried to call him Tony — was an Italian boy whose parents moved up to Littleton from Trinidad. His skin was olive colored, his hair blue black. He had a heavier beard than the other boys and was much more masculine than his peers. The height of their romance was to sneak kisses, or *baci* as he called them, everywhere and anywhere. But Anthony had to compete with Nugget and barrel racing and Cooper family trips to New York, and the relationship remained innocent.

College brought a series of boys, and she was convinced she loved each of them madly. Graduate school brought only one, another "rock head" as the geology students called themselves. But in the end he was, well, boring, and the relationship was short-lived. Instead, Marly buried herself in her studies and relentlessly hiked the Front Range, mostly as part of her graduate research.

Since joining the faculty of the university, there had been no one. Lots of girlfriends, lots of male acquaintances, but none that piqued her interest. As much as she hated to admit her own sexist feelings, she wanted a husband — the right one, of course — and that was the problem. The older she got, the longer her list of required attributes for the final guy in her life grew. At age thirty-two, her biological clock was ticking, no matter what the magazines said about women having babies happily in their forties. She found herself having thoughts of a squandered youth by not already having children. Besides, wouldn't it be grand to share everything she knew about earthquakes with her own kids, just like her uncle had, and put the college classroom in the rear view mirror for awhile?

With the last sip of her coffee, Marly set her cup down. She arrived late yesterday and spent the night in the tower to get an early start, so she might as well get on with it. "Well, Benny, shall we get started? Otherwise, we'll be here all day and won't make it to the office this afternoon."

After rinsing her coffee cup and turning off the stereo, Marly slipped Benny into her backpack. She zipped it so that only his head protruded from its top and pulled the pack onto her shoulders. She opened the door to the tower, turned around, and climbed down the ladder with the dog panting happily, his head bobbing up and down like the clown in a large Jack in the Box. She slipped off the pack and released Benny, who began running circles around his owner as she turned off the gas-powered electric generator.

Marly walked down the hill through bushes and over loose rocks, with Benny close behind. The rocks on the game trail made a familiar scrunching sound as her Klondikes pressed them into the earth. Wearing shorts and a loose denim top, sleeves rolled up, the slow trek gave the sun time to work on her face, arms and legs. *A wonderful feeling, the warm sun.* She looked up into the blue sky and breathed deeply. The loneliness that haunted her lately suddenly returned. As if he could read her mind, Benny gave a small bark. "Yes, Benny, I know you're here. You're such great company." Marly stooped and rubbed his head and ears. His fur felt good to her hands. "If only you could talk to me."

With only a clipboard, a pencil and a bottle of water, Marly's backpack was almost weightless. But she wanted to have her hands free in case she lost her balance on the loose rocks and needed to catch herself. She deftly worked her way down the hill to the first meter of the alignment array. She read the gauge, wrote the reading down on her clipboard, and compared the reading to what was written only a month before. She decided she must have misread it.

Marly stooped and read the gauge again. *Nope, that's right. Hmmm. Maybe the previous reading on the paper was wrong, a miss-mark. Did the last person juxtapose the first two digits?* She watched Benny mark a large cactus. "Come on, Benny, we've got to keep going."

A half-hour later, they approached the second meter in the array. Marly stooped and read it. *Now this is weird.* She took the palm of her hand and straightened her hair by pushing it back and down to her neck, glancing at the gauge again and then back at the sheet of paper. The gauge was registering a full twelve centimeters difference from the previous month's reading. The last meter had shown a nine-centimeter difference, and she had never seen a change of even a fraction of a centimeter before, without some type of major earthquake activity. *Does this mean the digits weren't switched, after all?* She looked at the initials at the bottom of the page to see who took the previous readings. *JT. Julie, and Julie's a freak when it comes to data. She wouldn't make the same mistake twice, would she?* Marly recorded the new reading. She could feel the goose bumps on her arms, even in the hot sun. She put all thoughts out of her mind and ran down the hill, nearly tripping on some small dry shrubs, but never slowing down. *Gotta get to the next meter.*

Benny could barely keep up with her.

There it is. Marly slowed her pace and approached the meter cautiously. She took her time, hesitating. *If the numbers match the ones from a month ago, it probably means Julie messed up.* She pulled the protective cover from the meter and leaned over to read the gauge. She caught her breath. Not nine centimeters or even twelve, but fourteen. *Fourteen centimeters. More than five inches difference between this gauge's reading and the value in last month's report!*

***

Rick sat in his cubicle. Larry Davis ran up to his desk. "You're not gonna believe this. They pulled a switch."

Rick sat back. "What do you mean? What'd they switch?"

"They usually keep Finbacks at the airbase closest to Xiamen," said Davis. Rick stared at him, waiting. "The base is full of Leopards. Finbacks are for air superiority. The Leopard is not only their top-of-the-line fighter, but its primary role is ground attack."

"How'd they do that?"

"Both planes train in the same areas. We think they did simultaneous exercises and when they landed, they traded places."

Rick nodded. "They knew we'd eventually discover the switch, but it's interesting they wanted to have things in place before we noticed. Still no dead chickens, though."

"What'd you say?"

"Nothing. Just talking to myself."

"There's more," Davis continued. "Dongshan island is crawling with military equipment and amphibious craft. All operational submarines have left port, and their entire navy is less than two days sail from the strait."

Rick shook his head. "What's your assessment?" Rick looked at Davis to let him know his question was sincere.

"An invasion of Taiwan is too far-fetched for me," Davis said. "Anytime the Mainlanders push, the Islanders push back. I think it's like you said. They're testing the president to see how he reacts and whether we still have the same commitment to Taiwan. Maybe they think we're overextended with Afghanistan, or just plain tired from the Iraq war."

Rick nodded. "Anything on the diplomatic front that's out of the ordinary?"

"I'm checking with Joe Craxton on that next. He's supposed to be doing a search of the database."

***

Marly Cooper checked the rest of the alignment array's meters on her list. One gauge read over twenty centimeters higher than its last reading. *All of them are high. All of them!*

She was breathless when she got back to the tower. Benny was unhappy that he did not get to do his leisurely sniff and pee routine, and he barked to show his displeasure. But Marly was now on a mission. She had to get back and check the remote readings from the remainder of the alignment array to see if they registered change, too. *Is this a local phenomenon or did it cover the whole of the valley?* She shoved Benny into the back and leapt into her SUV.

CHAPTER 2

Marly Cooper parked her jeep and jumped from the driver's seat. Benny followed close behind. She grabbed her backpack from the floor of the truck and walked briskly into the building that housed the Geology Department. She no sooner opened the door when Beverly Duncan came running up.

"Coop, where the heck have you been?"

"Right where I was supposed to be — reading the alignment array. You won't believe what I found."

"The meters showed a change, a big one."

Marly's mouth dropped open. "Yeah, but how did..."

"Wait till you see what we've got. Yesterday we got hit with a seven pointer. The whole San Francisco area is affected. Every single instrument. Tilt meters, strain meters, creep meters, GPS shows they all changed, too," said Beverly.

"We had an E-Q?"

"Yeah. No major damage, but we've got lots of minor events, more than I've seen recorded after an earthquake since I got here. Everything is going crazy."

"You said a seven pointer? I didn't feel a thing in the valley."

"The phone is ringing like it's Easter at the Vatican. Everyone that watches the USGS website has noticed the big shifts. They're asking if they're for real, and you're standing here telling me they are."

***

Rick, Davis, Carlson, and Joe Craxton sat at a table. "OK, Joe, what do you have?" asked Rick.

"Well," said Craxton. "First, we got four Chinese trawlers in the South Pacific off the coast of Peru and Chile. Then we got two more trawlers off the east coast of Panama, waiting to head through the Canal. Then we got..."

"Whoa, Joe," said Denise Carlson. "What are you doing? We said we wanted unusual activities that were occurring in and around the United States."

"No, that's not what Larry said. He said unusual activities in America. So I put the word America into the system, and this is what I got outta the database."

"North America, you idiot," said Carlson. "Not Latin America or South America. North America."

"Hey guys," intervened Rick. "Knock it off. Just the United States for now, Joe."

Craxton flashed a dirty look at Carlson. The two dated for over a year and then broke up. Ever since the breakup, Denise took every chance she could to make Joe look like a fool, and there was plenty of opportunity.

"I got a group of students..."

"No student stuff, either, Joe," said Rick.

"OK. Just so you know, there are hundreds of activities planned this year in the United States, but only three that we think warrant further investigation. The rest are pretty standard stuff."

Rick nodded. "Fine. Let's hear them."

"There's a delegation of twenty officials arriving at the United Nations in New York. We've done an analysis on the list of names, and five of 'em we've never seen before. I've asked the INS to take a look at the list and let me know what they think."

"Larry, you take that one and push Immigration and Naturalization hard. These days their morale is in the toilet, and we can't afford a screw-up by those guys. We need a solid answer." Davis nodded and headed out the door.

Craxton continued. "The second is a group that got visas to join a tour that's going to the Epcot Center at Disney World."

Carlson laughed. "Why Disney World?"

"Because there's an exhibition put on by the Taiwanese at Epcot during that time, and the tour specifically mentions the exhibit as part of its itinerary."

Rick and Carlson looked at each other, nodding. "Not a slam dunk, but it's worth a look. Take it, Denise," said Rick.

"Got it." She was up and out of the room before Rick finished his sentence.

"The third?" sighed Rick.

"Four Chinese professors are attending an annual conference on earthquakes at San Francisco State University in a couple weeks."

"Why should we look at that? I thought I said no university visits."

"You said student stuff. These guys are professors. You got two of 'em visiting California every couple weeks since January. One week here, one week back in China, one week here. Hell, that kind of travel would kill anybody. About the time you got rid of the jetlag you'd be flying again. Seems almost like they're coming over to the states to get something and taking it back to China. I figure the Chinese government must be paying for all this travel, too, 'cause it ain't exactly cheap."

"The government's paying for their travel is probably not so strange. But that is a lot of back and forth." Rick rubbed his chin. "Earthquakes? When was the last time China had a major earthquake?" Craxton shrugged.

Rick nodded. "I think it was during the seventies. And we just had something in California yesterday, didn't we? OK, I'll take it. Thanks, Joe."

***

Marly and Beverly scanned the data. The entire San Francisco Bay region, both east and west of the San Andreas Fault, seemed to have slipped to the north.

"What do you think, Bev? How can both the North American and Pacific plates be moving north? The North American plate usually goes south. I'm surprised the creep meters caught the change."

"It is odd. It's usually the Pacific Plate that slips, and even then it's a creep of about two inches a year in the areas of the Andreas that aren't locked together. We've seen six inches lately, and the adjacent plates are moving pretty much in tandem. Like you say, it's kinda strange."

"Maybe Reid's elastic rebound theory can explain it," said Marly.

"All I have to say is that it's perfect timing for our conference. We could be witnessing geological change in real time, and this might be leading up to a major E-Q."

Marly nodded. "What does the computer simulation show?"

"Actually," said Beverly, "the computer models are having trouble making sense of the data. So Ralph's working on them to see what he can do. We've got no precedent."

The Geology Department secretary, Sherry Grant, walked into the room. "Hey, Coop, you've got a phone call."

"I'm busy."

"Don't you even want to know who it is?" teased Beverly. "Maybe your destiny is beckoning."

"Right. Sorry, Sherry. Everybody in town has been calling. No more calls."

"The guy's from Washington and says it's urgent. He won't take 'no' for an answer."

Marly turned in her seat and looked at Sherry. "What? You mean I've been ordered to answer the phone?"

Sherry raised her eyebrows and gave her an "I'm just doing my job" look.

Marly got up from her chair. "I'll be right back. I don't know who this turkey thinks he is."

Marly picked up the receiver. "Doctor Cooper here."

"Doctor Cooper, your secretary told me that you're very busy, but

I sincerely appreciate your taking my call."

Some of the anger subsided. "That's OK. How can I help?"

"My name is Rick Starr, and I work for the government in Washington. I'm responsible for looking into activities associated with China, and I see that you've got four people from mainland China coming to your conference on earthquakes."

"I don't know exactly how many are coming, but that sounds right. They typically send a pretty big group to the annual conference, and they've had a delegation coming to the University every month since I've been here."

"Which was when?"

"When what?"

"When did you arrive at the University?"

"Oh," said Marly, becoming distracted and distinctly uninterested in the caller's questions. "About six years ago."

"Can you tell me how many people visit and who the point of contact is?"

"Uh, listen," said Marly, "can you call me back some other time, like week after next maybe? I'm really busy right now." She hung up the phone, shaking her head. The phone rang. She looked at Sherry. "If that's for me, I just left." She walked out of the room.

***

Rick hung up the phone. He could not get Doctor Cooper back on the line.

"So what's up?" asked Renoir. "Got anything?"

"We've got a couple of things we're looking at in New York and Orlando. I may have to go to San Francisco tomorrow."

"Why, what's going on?"

"Don't know," said Rick. "Just a hunch, I guess."

Denise Carlson walked into the room. "According to the State Department, the people on the tour to the Epcot Center are all officials or military officers. Young guys, six of them, and apparently they're being met at the airport by their embassy. Not something they do for normal tourists."

"OK," said Rick. "Get some help from the FBI to intercept and shadow them. I have a contact for you if you need it. I want to know who meets them, where they go, where they stay, and whether or not they're carrying metal. Get a Mandarin Chinese linguist and get authorization using the Patriot Act for a national security tap on any cell phones they might use. You'll need NSA to help you with decryption."

"Do we consider these guys terrorists?" asked Carlson.

"Worse," said Rick.

"Got it." Carlson left the room.

Renoir looked at Rick. "That doesn't sound good."

Rick nodded. "This is probably the best lead we've got, but I'm having trouble figuring out how this could be a trigger."

Carlson came back in. "There was a message on my desk from the State Department, and I think we've got something. The vice president of Taiwan will be at the exhibit the same time the tour is there."

"I'm not having trouble anymore," said Rick. "I want the FBI on this one all the way."

"Already got it rolling," said Carlson.

"I think you should brief SecDef now," Rick said to Renoir. "There's evidence that China may be putting together an invasion force capable of causing significant trouble and could — with the emphasis on could — pull a trigger down in Florida that would give them an opportunity to use it. The president needs to have a plan, and he's got less than a week to get the right people to help him put it together."

Renoir nodded. "OK. Get me a package that I can give to the secretary before I brief him." He looked at Rick, holding his gaze as he spoke. "You're thinking they might try to harm the Taiwanese vice president?"

Rick nodded slowly. "It sure seems to be a possibility. But if that's the plan, they're counting on the Taiwanese to overreact and do something stupid. It doesn't pass the 'really good idea' test as far as I'm concerned, but I don't think we can rule it out."

***

"You're going where tomorrow?" asked Denise Carlson.

"San Francisco. I can't get anyone to talk to me on the phone, so I need to go there in person," said Rick.

"But you can't walk out now. World War Three could be just around the corner. You know that Renoir won't want you gone."

"I'll be there when he talks to the SecDef this evening. Besides, you'll be here. You can handle it, and you know more about the Florida operation than I do. I should be back right after the tour group arrives in-country."

"Doesn't matter. You're the senior analyst. Why do you need to go to San Francisco, anyway? This Florida thing is what we're looking for, isn't it?"

Rick looked at Carlson. "Florida is my first choice. But my intuition screeches at me every time I think about dropping this earthquake thing. China's been sending a delegation to San Francisco every month for the last six years, and Craxton told me two of them have been coming every couple weeks since January."

Carlson shrugged. "Maybe they like sourdough bread. And if they've been visiting San Francisco for six years, why is it suddenly suspicious? I'd agree with you if the visits began six months ago, but six years?"

Rick nodded his head in seeming agreement. "That's why it's an issue. Why are they visiting so often all of a sudden, and why always the same person at the same university? Academics usually like as much input they can get from as many sources as they can."

"Isn't Orlando a more tempting target? You know, *carpe diem*? Besides, what harm can they do studying earthquakes?"

"That was my first thought, too, but the Chinese don't act impulsively. They plan carefully, and they think long term. They may pass up what you and I consider golden opportunities because they haven't prepared adequately. Their focus is on grand strategy, not tactics."

Carlson returned Rick's nod. "OK, but I'll be surprised if Renoir lets you go."

***

"What'd he want?" asked Beverly.

"Who?" asked Marly.

"The guy who just called. Are you all right?"

"Yeah, I'm OK. He was asking questions about people visiting the University, but they didn't have anything to do with me. So I hung up."

Beverly raised her eyebrows. "Why'd you do that? For someone who says she's getting lonely, you sure don't act like it. Maybe he was cute."

Marly rolled her eyes. "He didn't sound cute. And you need to quit trying to match me up with every guy who just happens to get my phone number. If I'm going to leap off a cliff and really love someone — someone to whom I offer my very soul." Marly began speaking dramatically and held out her arm. "Well, then it needs to be the right person. Someone that I choose because..."

"...because he's a hunk!" said Beverly.

"A rich hunk!" Marly added.

The two women laughed.

"How's the conference coming, anyway?"

"It's going to be huge," said Marly. "Over five hundred participants. Greece and Turkey are big players because of the earthquakes a couple years ago. Even got a few last 'minute-ers' because of the earthquake yesterday. Should be a good one, and you're the star of the program."

***

Beverly Duncan was Marly Cooper's best friend. Since Coop's first day at SFSU, they spent at least a part of every workday together. Beverly arrived the year before and made not a single friend that year. As the university's first female seismologist there were no natural female associates to claim as acquaintances, much less friends. Most of the women professors were too feminist for her taste, anyway. And the men on the faculty tended to be older and married, gay, or young and immature. Coop brought a welcome breath of fresh air.

The daughter of a diplomat, Beverly lived in Belgium from the time she was five years old until she graduated from high school. She had a bright smile, dimples and beautiful blonde hair. But the earthquake had reminded her that, even after countless diets and New Year's Resolutions, her weight was still an issue. She felt shapeless and unattractive.

Living in Belgium, where it was customary to be greeted with a kiss on the cheek by your peers at the beginning of the day and when you saw each other for the last time at day's end, being overweight was not the obstacle to acceptance many young girls experienced in the United States.

So it was a shock when she came to the States to go to college, where she was avoided meticulously by the popular crowd on campus. She noticed that boys never stared at her as they did other girls. She wondered if the sight of her even registered in their brains. In the end, her suspicions were true: She was invisible to members of the opposite sex. Except when Marly Cooper was around. Coop was a looker and attracted men, lots of them, and Beverly was always included in the conversations — and Coop never seemed to mind. Coop was indeed a wonderful person, a best friend. And she had earned Beverly Duncan's undying loyalty.

***

When Marly opened the door to her apartment, Benny scurried into the kitchen and sat expectantly next to his food dish. Marly followed. "OK, OK, I get the message." She reached down and rubbed Benny's ears, but his hunger was greater than his need for affection. He whined.

"That bad, huh?" She laughed and stood up. She pulled a twenty-five pound bag of dried dog food from the cupboard — it was almost empty — and dumped the contents into the dog's bowl until pieces spilled over the sides. Benny sat impatiently, looking up at his master.

Marly waited for a moment and then gave the release command. "OK, Benny. OK."

The small dog attacked his bowl. Marly emptied his water dish and filled it with fresh water. "There you are, little guy. Now if only my dinner was as easy."

She threw the bag of dog food back into the cupboard and spied a box of Grape-nuts. She reached in and grabbed it. *Natural wheat and barley cereal, 98 percent fat free, high in fiber, and no preservatives. Not to mention that it provides twelve essential vitamins and minerals and requires absolutely no cooking. Perfect.* She pulled a bowl from another cupboard, a spoon from a drawer, and flipped open the refrigerator. Grabbing a carton of milk and closing the refrigerator door with her knee, Marly carried the small load out to her tiny living room and set it down on the coffee table. Plopping herself onto the adjacent dark green leather sofa, she settled in for another solitary dinner. Food had turned into fuel, so it really did not matter that she always ate alone, she told herself. *Besides, it doesn't have any taste.*

Picking up the remote control from the sofa's armrest and punching on the television, she juggled her bowl, filled it with Grape-nuts and leaned back to watch the local news.

The news anchorwoman looked seriously into the camera. "The president today announced that China is amassing troops, amphibious landing craft, airplanes and ships in the Formosa Strait and has asked for an explanation. Thus far there has been no comment from the Chinese government." The anchorwoman turned to her colleague.

"The president has also released some satellite photos, hasn't he, Hal, to substantiate the charges?"

"Sure has, Donna." A black and white satellite photo of the harbor at Xiamen appeared on the screen between the two news anchors. "These photos show that a harbor, just across the Formosa Strait from Taiwan, is filled with landing craft and other vessels that the president has claimed could be used as part of an invasion force."

The anchorwoman turned back toward the camera, her face filling the screen. "The president has stated that any attempt by China to attack Taiwan will be met with the full force of the United States armed forces. He has directed the carrier battle group, USS Harry Truman, to sail immediately to the area. The Truman should arrive there in about five days." She turned back toward her co-anchor.

"Hal, what's the reaction in Taiwan? Do we know yet?"

"Sure do, Donna. The Taiwanese say they'll resist any attempted invasion by China. They say that unification isn't the only principle at stake in cross-strait relations and that as a democratic state, the people of Taiwan will decide if and when reunification will occur. They say that reunification must be agreed on by both sides and that the terms for reunification, including using force, cannot be dictated by China."

"Does this mean the reason China would invade Taiwan is to reunify the two countries?"

"That's what the White House is saying, Donna," replied Hal.

Marly stopped chewing. Maybe this was why the guy from Washington called and was so interested in her conference. But what did a couple professors attending a conference in San Francisco have to do with an invasion of Taiwan? *Typical government overreaction.* She took two chews and then stopped. *Maybe the guy calling her was from the CIA, like Alec Baldwin in the Hunt for Red October. Wow. OK, next time I'll take his call.* The telephone rang. She set her bowl of cereal down, muted the TV, and walked over to her phone. The handset was a large model of a volcano with a flashing LCD and lava spewing down its sides. The caller ID showed the number as "Private".

"Hello?"

"Doctor Cooper? This is Rick Starr again."

It's the guy that called me at work, Marly thought. "Don't you know what time it is? Don't you have a life?" She wanted to make it clear she was unhappy. "I have an unlisted phone number, you know."

"Yes, I know. But this is a matter of national security, and I need to talk to you. I'll be flying into San Francisco tomorrow and wondered when we could meet."

"Meet? I'm very busy tomorrow."

Rick cut her off. "I'm available any time. Lunch. Dinner. After dinner. Middle of the night. I need only an hour or so of your time. It's important."

"I just heard on the news that China might invade Taiwan. Is that what this is about?"

"Yes."

"Is that all, yes? Can't you tell me more? Maybe then I'll be more cooperative."

Rick sighed. *Why are women always so impolite to me? I thought pheromones couldn't travel over the phone.* "We don't know whether or not China really plans to invade Taiwan. China might simply be trying to be provocative. But to be safe, we're looking at anything involving the Chinese that might be a little — well, for lack of a better word, unusual."

"Is interest in earthquakes considered unusual by the United States government?"

"By itself of course not. But there are other factors we're aware of that make it worth investigating."

"Who do you work for? The CIA?"

Silence. "Yes, that's right. The Central Intelligence Agency."

Marly smiled to herself. "OK. I like to eat lunch at a place just outside the north end of the University campus here in San Francisco. Manuel's. Mexican food. Can you meet me there?"

"What time?"

"Twelve sharp."

"I'll be there. Early, even," said Rick.

Marly set the phone down into its cradle and walked slowly back into the living room. She flipped the television channel over to CNN, and the possible invasion was its top story. She turned the sound back on and listened to the commentators. "The president has scheduled a press briefing for eight o'clock this evening, and we'll be covering it right here on CNN."

Whoa, this is serious business, and I'm going to be part of it, helping the president of the United States of America determine whether or not China really plans to invade Taiwan. First an earthquake and now I'm talking to the CIA. Any more excitement, and I'll have to buy a fun meter to measure it all.

***

John Renoir was having a fit. "What do you mean he went to San Francisco?"

Denise Carlson shrugged her shoulders. "He said he told you he was going."

"He told me he might go. If he'd asked, I would have said no!"

Which is precisely why he didn't ask, Carlson thought to herself. She shrugged her shoulders again. "I'm prepared to take over until he gets back tomorrow night."

Renoir did not answer right away. He just glared at Carlson. "He better be back tomorrow night."

***

Rick Starr leaned back in his airline seat and closed his eyes as the plane reached cruising altitude. He thought back to the conversation he had the night before with Dr. Cooper. He did not wear a watch, so he rarely knew what time it was, and he certainly did not have a life. Was it so obvious, even to someone three thousand miles away?

Rick Starr was half Italian. His father had been in the United States Air Force stationed in Naples, Italy, and he encountered a beautiful Italian girl who captivated him from the moment they first met. She learned English in school, and when Rick's dad was involved in a car accident with an Italian driver who ran a red light, she came to his rescue and translated. A brief and intense courtship was followed by marriage, and the pair moved back to the United States at the end of his father's military tour.

Rick remembered his mother fondly, who died of lung cancer a year ago. A typical Italian, his mother smoked heavily, but she never tried to defend her addiction. She said that she did not want her children adopting that "filthy Italian habit". Her favorite joke was that an Italian breakfast consisted of an espresso and a pack of cigarettes. It was not so funny after she was diagnosed as terminal.

His mother returned only very occasionally to Italy after her marriage, adopting her new country and becoming a naturalized citizen. While she gave up her Italian citizenship, she kept her love for things Italian. On summer evenings, it was not uncommon for his parents to sit outside in their backyard with a bottle of red wine, a bowl of olives, and a large hunk of *Parmigiano Reggiano*. His mother smoked constantly and laughed incessantly, slipping occasionally into Italian to tell her children, her *bambini*, how much she loved them. Her hair was long and dark, her skin perpetually tanned, her eyes green. Everyone thought it strange that his mother had green eyes. But Rick went back to Naples a number of times on his own, and most of the women in his mother's family had dark green eyes that captured men as easily as a Venus fly trap ensnared insects.

It was Naples that almost kept Rick from becoming part of the CIA, where a background investigation uncovered that his mother had relatives in the Camorra, the local mafia. And it was the dark green eyes of a young Neapolitan that lured him into marriage while still in college — a union that would last a tempestuous decade before ending in divorce. But that was all very long ago.

It was a whirlwind at work recently. Promotion to senior analyst came almost immediately upon Rick's return from an extended vacation.

The scope of his new responsibilities overseeing the CIA's China portfolio brought new energy and required different thinking.

China was remaking history. Its swift economic expansion and growing nationalism stood in stark contrast to European economic stagnation, multilateralism, and rapidly changing demographics. And while Europe's birthrate was far below replacement and was leading to a continent of elderly retirees, China's colossal population was expected to grow to one and a half billion before finally hitting a plateau. Every other year China's population was increasing at a rate equal to all the inhabitants of Canada.

China doubled the world's labor pool when it plunged into the global marketplace, and it was expected that half the cars on the planet would eventually be owned by Chinese drivers. China was proving that size matters.

Rick found the Asian mindset fascinating, and he was intrigued by the patient and deliberate approach that the Chinese generally brought to security issues. But there was something strange about this particular instance. Rather than the normal confrontational approach used to advance its foreign policy, China was acting quietly, even surreptitiously. He usually did not have to search for the "dead chickens", and that worried him.

The mixed signals made him uncomfortable and were why the attendance of a couple Chinese scholars at an earthquake conference grabbed his attention. He checked the Internet for information, and China's last major earthquake was in 1977. Over 250,000 people were killed, so it was reasonable the Chinese would be attending conferences where earthquakes were the theme. He also discovered that more people were killed in China in a 1556 earthquake — over 800,000 — than in any other in recorded history. A quick Google search turned up the Chinese pinyin for earthquake: *di zhen*. He wondered if there was a way to predict earthquakes. He'd have to ask the professor in California if that could be a reason for the interest of Chinese scholars.

Rick tilted his seat back slightly. He could feel his mind, weary from all the recent activity, slowly drifting to a quieter dimension. He did not resist.

***

Marly was having a raucous day at the office. The instruments that registered movement in the San Francisco region were showing more change taking place — another two inches — and it was unclear how long the shifting could continue without causing an earthquake that might do real damage. California senators and congressmen started questioning whether the Federal Emergency Management Agency was prepared to respond if a major earthquake were to occur in the state. "It appears that FEMA is no better prepared to respond to a major earthquake in California than it was when Katrina hit New Orleans and wiped out the city," asserted the state's senior senator.

Minor tremors between 3.0 and 4.0 on the Richter scale were now taking place with regularity. Even longtime Bay Area residents were nervous and voicing their concern. Gaining the attention of earthquake experts was the simultaneous movement in the same direction of the northeast side of the Pacific tectonic plate and the southwest corner of the North American tectonic plate. Previous recordings showed the plates always moving in opposite directions.

Reporters called Marly's office non-stop, and the saga of the "shifting ground" was vying for top story with the possible Chinese invasion of Taiwan.

Nostradamus predictions were trotted out by the tabloids, and unscrupulous televangelists were urging Californians to repent and send money, or face God's wrath.

San Francisco residents, even business owners, departed for long vacations. One estimate put the number of those abandoning the city at well over ten thousand. Illegal immigrants were stopping short of San Diego, and the number of illegals re-crossing the border back into Mexico exceeded the dribble of humanity still willing to come north.

The mayor called for calm and encouraged people not to leave the city out of unwarranted fear. He drew parallels with what happened to the population of New Orleans in the aftermath of Hurricane Katrina, suggesting that people in San Francisco were "better than their Louisiana counterparts", which began a war of words between the two cities' mayors.

Beverly Duncan was asked to appear on local television stations and take interviews with people like Larry King on CNN and Bill O'Reilly on Fox News. Marly was happy to pass on the interviews that she considered part of the entertainment business, and concentrated on scientific inquiries.

The frenetic activity surrounding the fear of the "big one" was what Marly yearned for her entire life, and she was not about to shirk any of the fallout. She patiently answered reporters' questions when they called or interviewed her. Some of her academic colleagues who hired themselves out as talking heads were making wild claims and offering expertise they did not possess. She tried her best to remedy the damage caused by the misinformation they presented.

"No one knows if another earthquake is imminent or not," she would state, and she refused to speculate. "There's no way to know if there will be an earthquake of any real magnitude anytime soon. We need to continue to monitor the situation. We are trying to develop a working computer model with the help of experts from the U.S. Geological Survey. As soon as we know more specifics, it is our intention to tell the public." And so it went until lunch.

Marly left the office a little later than planned. She took a moment to check her makeup and hair in the ladies' bathroom mirror — makeup that she usually did not bother with. Having no interest in analyzing why she was taking time she did not normally devote to vanity, she was conscious enough of it to acknowledge that it was true. She would be a few minutes late for her appointment — she assured herself it was an appointment despite the odd sensations she was feeling — at Manuel's with Rick Starr, the CIA man.

CHAPTER 3

Rick Starr entered the nearly full parking lot in his rental car, ten minutes early. Manuel's looked like a hole in the wall from the outside, but people were stacked up waiting to get in. It appeared to have just opened, and the seating already looked like it was going fast. Rick got into the line that snaked its way up to a large reception desk just inside the door and searched for a woman that looked like what, a typical professor? He figured she'd be by herself, but none of the women in line were alone. *She must not be here yet.* With one or two exceptions, the crowd was mostly students: young, tanned, and carrying book bags. *Mexican food. Corona beer. What a life.*

***

Marly pulled into a slot near the back of the parking lot and walked quickly to the front of the restaurant. *Five minutes late.* The line to get in was short. *Good. We won't have to wait long.* She was nervous. *What the heck is wrong with me? Must have spent too much time talking about all this guy-stuff with Bev.* She looked at the men waiting in line to see if there was a CIA type.

Just in front of an Italian guy dressed in a polo shirt and jeans — dating Anthony had made her keenly aware of the "Italian look" — was a man in a suit wearing a power tie. Had to be him. Feeling confident, Marly walked over to introduce herself.

***

Rick caught sight of the woman to his right. She was medium height, striking in appearance, and wearing dark slacks and a white blouse with the top two buttons unbuttoned. Her short dark hair blew lightly in the breeze. Rick saw that she was making a beeline for the gentleman in front of him.

***

Marly walked up to the man wearing the tie. "Hi, I'm Doctor Cooper."

The man was surprised. "Hello, Doctor Cooper, I'm Harvey Ghent. Do we know each other?"

Marly blushed. "I'm sorry. I mean I'm not sorry, but I thought that you were someone I was supposed to meet here for lunch today."

Rick smiled. "Doctor Cooper." Marly turned to face the man to her left. "I'm Rick Starr." Rick extended his right hand.

"Oh, hello, Mister Starr." Marly took Rick's hand and turned back toward the man in the suit. "I'm sorry, but this is my date." She blushed. "I mean, my appointment."

The man nodded and smiled.

"It's a blind date," Rick said to the man. "We've talked on the phone. But not a lot." He turned toward Marly, and she gave him a funny look. "I'm not helping, am I?"

Harvey Ghent laughed, smiled, and turned back to face the front of the line.

Rick spoke again. "It's a pleasure to meet you, Doctor Cooper. Would you please call me Rick?"

"Of course. And would you please call me, uh..." Marly did not know if she wanted him to call her Marly or Coop. Rick leaned forward slightly waiting to hear her name. "Call me Marly."

"Marly. That's a great name," he said, thinking it sounded like a name you'd give to your dog. "I like that name. Marly, I mean." Rick smiled his nicest smile.

"Have you been waiting long?"

"No," said Rick. "Just a couple minutes, and it looks like we'll be seated in a moment. I know you're busy, and I appreciate your carving time out of your schedule to meet me. It really is important."

"It's actually no problem, and I'm sorry for my impatience. Like most people, I think I'm busier than everyone else. I'm glad we could arrange a time that's convenient for both of us."

"I have a lot of questions. I have to confess I don't know much about earthquakes."

"So what's going on with the invasion thing? Any more news?"

"None so far. The Chinese are playing coy. It's a strange situation. The Chinese leadership usually makes it clear what they want — they even make it a point to be over the top. This time they may be hiding something. That's why I came to San Francisco."

"What do you think they're hiding?"

"I don't know," said Rick. "But it means that I need to look at asymmetric approaches and talk to people like you. I guess I'm saying I need more time to figure it out."

"Has anyone ever told you that you look like the Italian singer Andrea Bocelli?" Marly asked.

Rick looked into Marly's eyes, noticing tiny creases just above her cheeks when she smiled. "You know, you're the second person to tell me that. I still haven't listened to any of his music, but it's on my list of things to do."

Marly held his gaze and felt like Rick was peering into her soul. "You just have to get one of his CDs. He's amazing."

A young woman walked up. "Two?" she asked. Rick nodded.

"This way, please," the young lady said, grabbing a couple of menus.

"The food must be good."

"The best," Marly said. "I eat lunch here every chance I get, and I've never gotten tired of it."

The hostess led them to a small table next to a window, and they sat down. "The chicken burrito, Christmas style, will not only clear your sinuses and make your nose run, it'll put hair on your chest," said Marly.

"Sounds like a winner," laughed Rick.

The waiter walked over to their table. "Can I get you a drink?"

"We're ready to order," said Marly. The waiter pulled out his pad and pen. "I'll have your chicken burrito Christmas style and a Coke, please."

The waiter turned to Rick.

"Same for me."

The waiter gave a curt thank you and left.

"That was easy," said Rick.

"And our food will get here fast." Marly paused. "You know, you're not what I was expecting, being from the CIA."

Rick laughed. "You mean no suit and tie? I thought since I was away from the office that I'd go casual." He smiled again. "Of course, I could return the compliment and say that you don't exactly fit my idea of what a woman college professor is supposed to look like, either."

"What am I supposed to look like?"

"For sure I thought you'd be older."

"How old do you think I am?"

"Twenty-nine?"

"Close enough. What else?"

"Grumpy look. No makeup. Frumpy." Marly's frown brought a disarming smile to his face to show he was only kidding.

"You have a nice smile. Your wife is lucky."

Rick was puzzled for a moment and then realized she must have noticed the wedding band on his finger. "Thank you, but I'm not married."

Now it was Marly's turn to be confused. "But you're wearing a wedding ring."

"Yeah, it's kind of complicated. I got divorced and haven't ever really gotten back into the dating scene." He frowned.

"I'm sorry about your divorce."

"No, it's OK. It's been ten years. One of those things in life you read about and see happen to other people, but never want or expect to happen to you."

"Ten years is a long time to play it safe. To be still wearing your wedding ring, I mean."

Rick gave a shy laugh. "Yeah, when you say it like that it makes it sound weird, doesn't it? I guess it's a defense mechanism that I've gotten used to."

Marly could feel her personal interest in Rick Starr waning. She vowed she would never marry a divorced man. She knew all the statistics. A second marriage had less chance of success than a first. Patterns were already developed and were brought into the second marriage, creating all the same troubles that plagued the original. She wanted to start out married life with someone who had never been there before. Otherwise, where was the adventure?

"Are you all right?" asked Rick, noticing Marly's blank look.

"Sure," lied Marly.

The waiter interrupted their conversation with the Cokes.

"If you're ready," said Marly, "maybe we should start with your questions."

"OK, let's see, we can do that." Rick pulled a folded piece of paper from his pocket and a small digital voice recorder. "Do you mind if I record our interview? I don't have to if you're uncomfortable, but it would help me. I won't have to take notes."

Marly had been letting journalists tape their conversations with her recently, and she was used to the request. "Sure."

Rick spoke in monologue, giving the date, time, and place of the interview, followed by his and Marly's names. "My first question," continued Rick, "is how many Chinese scholars visit SFSU every month, and who it is that they come to see? What do they do while they're here?"

"After we spoke I talked with my colleague, Doctor Chen, who's a naturalized citizen from China, by the way. He hosts a small delegation from the Chinese mainland. Usually three or four people, usually once a month, and they do fieldwork. He shows them where we record measurements to watch for crustal deformation and what kind of instruments we use to measure it."

"You say crustal deformation. What exactly is that?"

"Crustal deformation is a measured change in the earth's surface, or in technical terms the earth's crust. That's what we're seeing right now, for example, here in California. There is movement of almost a foot in some places."

"A foot? Twelve inches doesn't sound like very much to me."

"In the world of tectonics, it's enormous. In the Bay area, we see changes of maybe two inches a year. Recent measurements are over five times that much, and they're occurring in a fraction of the time."

Rick paused while he referred to his paper. "Can you predict when, or where, an earthquake will occur?"

"No, and this is an important point. No one can predict exactly when or where there will be an earthquake. We don't know how to do that. We're still trying to figure out how earthquakes happen. I mean, we understand the mechanics for the most part. Earthquakes happen when the earth's tectonic plates shift. But we have no reliable way to predict when or exactly where. Having said that, we can forecast when an earthquake might occur. For example, we're forecasting a major earthquake in the San Francisco Bay region sometime in the next forty years."

"What do you mean by a major earthquake, and when you forecast an earthquake do you mean that you'll have one in exactly forty years, or about forty years? What is it that you're saying?"

"A strong earthquake measures between 6.0 and 6.9 on the Richter scale, a major earthquake is between 7.0 and 7.9, and a great quake would register 8.0 or more. As for the forecast period, we're saying the probability of an earthquake increases over time, until it becomes one hundred percent by the end of the forecast period. Data shows that major earthquakes around fault lines happen about every one hundred and fifty years. Since the last great earthquake in San Francisco was in 1906, it's believed that we're not due for another one for a few more decades."

"Is there much difference between a 7.0 and an 8.0 on the Richter scale? What does it mean to say 'major' versus 'great'?"

"Each number on the Richter scale is an order of magnitude greater than the previous number. That means that a major earthquake can be ten times as powerful as a strong earthquake, and a great earthquake can be up to ten times more powerful than a major earthquake. If you do some quick math, a great earthquake has the potential to be one hundred times more powerful than a strong one."

"I didn't know that. So it sounds like a 7.0 is a whole lot worse than a 6.0."

"Right. The San Francisco earthquake of 1906 was estimated to be an 8.25. That means it packed over twenty-two times as much force as the 1989 world series earthquake here in San Francisco, which was a 6.9. The 1906 earthquake killed seven hundred people and did a few million dollars worth of damage. The '89 earthquake killed sixty-three people, injured almost 4,000, left another 10,000 homeless and did $13 billion in property damage. The difference in damage, of course, mostly reflected the level of economic development of the region."

Rick paused again. "But you had an earthquake last week that registered over a 7.0, and I hardly heard anything about it."

"That's because the epicenter of the quake was well away from any population centers, and there wasn't any significant damage to the city proper. We say in a case like this that the intensity of the earthquake in San Francisco was low."

"What if California had another earthquake like it did in — when did you say, 1906? What would happen?"

"Well," said Marly, "the 1906 earthquake caused the San Andreas Fault to slip as much as fifteen feet along a 270 mile segment from south of San Jose, through San Francisco, up to Cape Mendocino. If that happened again, the effects would be devastating."

"How devastating?"

Marly shook her head. "Try to imagine an earthquake twenty-two times worse than the one in 1989. Maybe tens, even hundreds of thousands of people killed and injured. For sure hundreds of billions of dollars in property damage. Perhaps a million people left homeless. Water tables affected, which could lead to agricultural ruin. California produces 13% of the U.S. gross domestic product. The destruction in the state would be unimaginable."

Rick leaned forward. "So an earthquake of that magnitude, it doesn't sound like California could cope with the damage by itself."

Marly shook her head again. "It would be like a whirlpool and suck in the whole country."

Rick leaned back. "Is it possible that your Chinese colleague has learned how to predict when and where an earthquake might occur?"

"Doctor Chen?" Marly shook her head. "I don't see how he could. And if he did, for sure he'd want to tell the world." She shook her head again. "There's no research I know of that claims an earthquake can be predicted accurately, and I read all the journals."

"Could someone stop an earthquake if they knew it was imminent?"

"No, that's the frustrating part. Even if you could predict earthquakes, you couldn't stop them. Take what we're seeing now. We know this activity is likely to cause a major event sometime in the future. Maybe sooner rather than later. But when and exactly where, we don't know. And we couldn't prevent it, even if we knew for sure."

"You mentioned tectonic plates. What are they? Are they part of the continental shelf?"

"Actually, yes. Scientists believe that 225 million years ago there was only one super continent in the world, Pangaea. The theory is that Pangaea broke apart into fourteen tectonic plates that are pretty much in constant motion. We call that motion continental drift."

"That's Biblical, you know," said Rick.

"What's Biblical?"

"The Bible says that the continents were once joined together in a single landmass."

"I didn't know that."

The waiter came with their food. Rick turned off the recorder.

***

"Any word on the New York crowd?" asked Renoir.

Carlson shook her head. "Not yet. Immigration says the visit is routine. We've asked them to canvas the list, anyway. I've told them we need them to give us their assessment in writing, and we need it fast."

"And?"

"They promised they would no later than close of business tomorrow."

"What about Orlando?"

"We've got the FBI team in place. The delegation from China going on the tour arrives tomorrow. We've got the phone taps, the metal detectors, and the photo team briefed and ready to go. We should have a complete data dump after they arrive: who, what's been said in anticipation of their arrival, and what they're carrying in the way of protection."

"OK. We still can't get the Chinese government to respond and tell us what the hell they're doing, and the Pentagon is going nuts. The SecDef's guys want more than the two carrier battle groups that have been authorized to go to the area, but the president wants to wait until the Chinese react. This is giving me ulcers. When's Starr getting back?"

"Tomorrow night. He leaves San Francisco at two o'clock and should get in at seven thirty or so."

***

"When is your conference?" asked Rick.

"Week after next. Everyone arrives Wednesday for registration, and the presentations begin Thursday," said Marly.

"Are there any presentations that I could watch and understand?"

"Sure. My colleague is giving the first talk, and she'll be discussing the changes that have been taking place here in the Bay area. It's going to be a great kickoff and should generate lots of interest and debate."

"Sounds good. Any others?"

"You know," said Marly, "you might want to hear this guy from the U.S. Geological Survey, who's researching Coulomb stress transfer."

Rick laughed. "Sounds like a psychological problem."

Marly laughed, too. "It does, doesn't it?"

"Is it something I could understand?"

"Actually, the concept is simple, and the presentation includes lots of visual aids. So it's pretty easy to follow. He and his colleagues were actually able to predict the general area where, and to some extent when, earthquakes occurred in Turkey. They're trying to help develop the computer model for what's happening in the Bay area."

Rick put his fork down. "How does it work, this coolin' stress transfer?"

Marly laughed. "I said C-o-u-l-o-m-b stress transfer. The idea is that every time there's an earthquake, the stress that led to the earthquake is transferred someplace else. Computer models have been developed to calculate the stresses, and like I said they've actually had some pretty good luck. Of course, we all get excited when someone seems to be able to predict an earthquake. The problem is that no one can do it consistently."

"OK, that sounds like one I should see. Any others?"

"We always have one presentation at the end of the first day to discuss current trends. We do an analysis of the earthquakes that have occurred over the past year and talk about patterns, magnitudes, number of events, and anything unusual. It just so happens that I'll be giving that talk. I'm still collecting data, and this weekend I'll run the data on computer models to identify..." Marly watched Rick sitting, his chin cupped in his hands, watching her every word, following her every movement. "I feel like you're watching me too carefully, Rick Starr. You make me feel like I'm sitting under a microscope. Is that part of your CIA training? Are you wondering if you can believe what I'm telling you?"

Rick dropped his hands and shrugged. "I can tell why you're a professor. I wish I'd had a professor like you in college. You have a way of making a topic really interesting."

"Really? If only my students were as enthusiastic." Marly put her fork down and cupped her own chin in her hands, staring back. "Are you sure you can't sing?"

"Positive. If I sang, you'd sue me for damages."

Marly laughed gently and sat back. "I don't think I'm hungry anymore."

"Me, neither," said Rick. "Do you mind if we finish our session?"

"Ask away."

Rick started his tape recorder again. "I just have a couple more questions. Let's see. How many earthquakes are there in the world each year? Ten? Twenty?"

Marly laughed again. "Actually, you probably don't read about many more than that. But worldwide, on average, there's an earthquake every thirty seconds. Most of them are small, of course. Ones that nobody ever feels."

Rick was surprised. "You're kidding. That's what, almost three thousand earthquakes a day? That's pretty amazing." He fumbled with his paper. "Have the number and frequency of earthquakes been increasing over time?"

"No. We're just doing a better job of detecting them. We've got over four thousand seismograph stations around the world, and the data they generate is sent automatically to the worldwide earthquake locator on the Internet."

"You mean I could look at data measured by seismograph stations around the world on the Internet?" asked Rick.

"Sure. Anybody can."

Rick shook his head. "Wow. OK. One more question. In which part of the world do most earthquakes occur?"

"That's an easy one, but I think you're trying to stump me."

Rick gave Marly a look of mock horror.

"That's OK," said Marly. "I'll answer it for you. The Pacific Ocean. Most earthquakes happen in the circum-Pacific seismic belt. About sixty percent."

Rick turned off the recorder. "Thanks, Doctor Cooper. If I can be serious for a moment, you've been a great help. I can tell that you're a real mover and shaker in the earthquake world. Not just a major mover and shaker, but a great mover and shaker."

***

John Renoir looked at Denise Carlson. "What did you say?"

"They're flat out denying it. China is saying the photos we released are phonies, that we doctored them."

Renoir looked at Carlson, unable to formulate an intelligent question. "Could you say that again? You mean the Chinese are denying that they have anything out of the ordinary in the Formosa Strait?"

"That sums it up nicely, and I'd guess more than half the world believes them. Our own media isn't helping, either, asking the president whether he has independent confirmation. We've gone to the Western European Union's satellite center in Madrid, but they don't have anything that's anywhere near China. So it's our word against the Chinese, and they're winning the P-R game. They're claiming we're attempting to turn world opinion against them and undermine their relations with Taiwan."

"So what now? Do we have other intelligence we can exploit? How about humint? Can someone on the ground get us pictures?"

Carlson nodded. "It's risky, but if this is important enough, they'll deliver. We should probably get an assessment of what they can do for us before risking exposure."

"Go ahead and start the assessment process. What's the Pentagon doing?"

"They're getting together a series of photos showing the entire build-up from start to finish. This could be a tough one."

"Call Starr. I want him back, and I want him back now. Send a plane for him if he can't get a commercial flight."

Renoir was pulling out all the stops. Carlson could see that he was flailing. The Chinese had the upper hand, and he knew it — and what was worse, they knew it.

***

Rick's cell phone rang. He pulled it from his pocket. "Starr here."

"Rick, Denise. Making any progress out there?"

Rick looked at Marly Cooper. "Yeah, I'm making great progress. Most of my questions are answered, but I'll have to come back to San Francisco week after next before I'm satisfied there's nothing going on."

"You should probably discuss that with Renoir. Have you been following the news, by the way?"

"Not really, why?"

"The whole thing is off the hook. The Chinese reaction has been to deny everything. Now we're having to scramble because complete denial was never anticipated."

Rick switched the phone to his other ear. "What do they say is our motive?"

"They're claiming we're manufacturing the whole crisis. That we're trying to destabilize relations between them and the Taiwanese. They may not need a trigger if the dialogue keeps escalating like this."

Rick nodded. "Anything on New York or Orlando?"

Denise shook her head. "New York looks like a non-starter. Nothing more on Orlando yet. We've got everything prepared for the group's arrival tomorrow."

"OK. I'll try to catch a flight back tonight."

"I've already called the airlines, and there's nothing available. Everyone is booking flights out of San Francisco and Oakland because of the earthquakes out there. We've got a plane coming from Travis Air Force Base to pick you up. It'll be at the airport in an hour. Renoir wants you here, pronto. He's starting to get nervous."

"OK. An hour's about right. I'll leave *subito*." Rick closed his cell phone and returned his attention to Doctor Cooper. "That was the office. I've got to get back sooner than expected, but you've already answered my questions. I still want to come back to see those presentations we talked about, so can you reserve a place for me?"

Marly smiled, but was distant. "Sure."

Rick gave a shy look. "Is it possible that I might have an escort? Maybe you could act as a point of contact for me?"

"Of course," Marly said, wondering if Rick would be attracted to Beverly but already knowing the answer.

Rick could sense the growing distance between himself and the professor. "Well," he finished the conversation, "you've been very kind with your time."

CHAPTER 4

The Air Force C-21 touched down gently on the runway at Andrews Air Force Base. Rick was tired. He had not been able to give his visit to California — or Doctor Marly Cooper — a moment's thought. When he got to the airport, he was met by an Air Force officer with a swath of classified papers accompanied by an armed guard. All were labeled Top Secret, although after he read them he wondered why. The documents were inputs, solicited from experts around the world, by the National Security Council on China's motive for its actions. He spent the entire flight reading them. Rick thanked the pilot as he deplaned, and he was not surprised to see Denise Carlson standing there waiting for him.

"Did you get through all that paperwork?" asked Carlson.

Rick shook his head. "Barely. A lot of stuff, but most of it isn't helpful. The experts are missing the point. Who cares why China might want to invade Taiwan? Or whether they're too integrated with the West for it even to be a possibility? Any one of us can speculate about that. I want to know why the Chinese are taking such pains to act covertly. Are they really serious this time? And if they are, why this particular moment, and what would give them the political cover they need to do something?"

Carlson nodded her head as he talked. "I hope you're not tired, at least not too tired." She looked at Rick, and he sighed, giving her a "of course I'm tired" look. "We've got a meeting with Renoir at the office. Something else has come up."

"I knew you weren't meeting me because you called me back early. What is it?"

"I can't tell you, because I don't know, either. Joe phoned me just before you landed, and John has called a meeting and wants both you and me there. So believe it or not, I came here because I knew your car was at Dulles and that you'd need a ride."

"Yeah, well thanks," said Rick. They walked slowly across the tarmac.

"How was your trip to San Francisco? Maybe I should go with you next time."

"Nice try, Denise. Renoir isn't going to let both of us out of his sight, and you're the stuckee."

"I know. I was just doin' some California dreamin'."

Rick looked over at Denise Carlson. Her break-up with Joe Craxton had been hard on her. The two of them dated for over a year, and she wanted more from their relationship — marriage — but Joe was not ready for a commitment. Divorced, he said he was not interested in going through all that marriage crap again. Although Rick appreciated Joe's feelings because of his own experience, Joe and Denise made a good team. He even told Joe. It seemed to be another sad episode in the continuing saga of intimacy in the new Millennium.

Divorce. Taking its toll on its victims, leaving lonely people and shallow relationships in its wake. When a new relationship gets too deep for one of its victims, the fear of drowning sets in. In desperation one of the parties breaks free — leaving the other alone, to drown again in the waters that require two to navigate and survive. Rick knew all too well the wounds that divorce inflicted on a couple. He still wore his wedding ring, his fear of another relationship so great. Married for ten years, divorced for ten years. He had not given any of this much thought for the last several years, until the beautiful Doctor Marly asked about his wife.

Denise returned Rick's look and smiled. Rick smiled back.

"You're a jewel, Denise. A real jewel."

***

Doctor Marly Cooper returned to the office after her lunch with Rick Starr. Beverly Duncan was waiting.

"Well, don't keep me in suspense! Did he look like James Bond?" Beverly asked.

"Not at all. He was completely un-cool. Just an ordinary guy who happens to be an analyst with the CIA. He's divorced, and you know that doesn't work for me."

"That's no fun. Good thing you won't see him again, huh?"

"Oh, he's coming to the conference." Marly nodded her head to and fro. "And actually, he's kind of handsome. An Italian. Someone I felt comfortable with, like we had been friends for a long time. But the divorce thing." She looked at her best friend. "He's going to arrive the first day. He wants an escort. I'll introduce you."

Beverly's eyes lit up. "He's coming to the conference? The first day? And he's Italian?"

"Don't get your hopes up. He wears his wedding ring even though he's been divorced forever."

Beverly suddenly frowned. "And he works for the CIA. He's probably boring and conservative and sexist. You and I don't exactly believe in staying home and baking brownies — at least not yet."

Marly shrugged. "How do you know he wouldn't stay home and bake brownies for you, Bev?"

Beverly shook her head. "Let's not go there. Mister Mom's not my type."

"You know, Bev, you've never told me about 'your type'. What are you looking for in a man?"

"Well, I have to say I'm not very particular. It's not like I've got a stick hanging in the closet to fight off a bunch of hunky guys trying to break down my door and ravage my body. But if you're serious, most important? I'd have to say a sense of humor."

***

Rick Starr, Denise Carlson, Larry Davis and Joe Craxton sat around a table with John Renoir. "OK, Joe, show us what you got and what you think it is."

"The Chinese moved their top of the line ground attack aircraft, the Flying Leopard, from near Beijing to an airbase outside Xiamen. But they have something else there I didn't recognize. It wasn't a Finback or a Fantan, so I called a buddy at the Pentagon who works foreign sales and sent him a picture of it." He looked around the table at each person, savoring the aroma of suspense that he perceived was filling the room. His colleagues waited impatiently for him to continue.

"It's an F-10." He waited for the inevitable question. He suspected that Rick was the only one who would know what he was talking about.

"OK, dipstick, so it's an F-10," said Carlson. "Are you going to tell us what that means, or do we have to do a brain extraction to get the information? Assuming we could locate your brain, of course."

Renoir had not heard Carlson's sarcasm before, and he looked at her and then back at Craxton. Craxton pretended to laugh.

"That's pretty funny, Denise." He pretended to laugh some more, snorting for effect. "You are one witty little wench."

Rick could sense Renoir's discomfort. "OK, guys, we've been entertained enough. Look, Joe, you've done a great job uncovering this thing. But we've all had a long day, and once you explain to us what you've found, we can go home and try to get some sleep before everyone starts tossing hand grenades our way tomorrow."

"We've caught some pictures of the F-10 by satellite, but it's typically been at night or early morning. We suspected the Chinese had about a dozen prototypes, and the rumor was there were problems with production." He paused again. "There are forty aircraft on the ramp, and they appear to be fully operational."

"You'll have to excuse my ignorance, but is this a significant development?" asked Renoir

Rick turned to answer. "The F-10 is programmed to be China's multi-role fighter, with about the same capability as the F-16. In fact, they developed it in part by 'borrowing' an F-16 from Pakistan. The radar and the engine were designed by the Russians. It's been designated the Qian Shi-10, which means it's an attack aircraft. They also got a lot of technical help from the Israelis. A high performance aircraft like this is unexpected."

"How could they build an airplane we don't know about when we've got satellites watching everything they do twenty-four hours a day? And why are the Israelis helping the Chinese?"

"Getting information twenty-four hours a day is part of the problem," said Craxton. "It's information overload. Turns out the Chinese were building the F-10s at an old Finback production facility, and after a close review of previous photos..." Craxton paused. "Let me back up for a second. When the planes we thought were Finbacks rolled off the assembly line, they were wheeled into hangars and left there. No one questioned why the planes never flew, because apparently it's not unusual for planes to be parked on the flight line for long periods of time." He shook his head. "These guys were clever. They only moved the F-10s in bad weather, and they had the aircraft wrapped in tarps when they were towed. It was low tech, but it worked."

"Tarps? They covered the jets in tarps when they towed them on the flight line, and we didn't wonder why? Do we cover our planes in tarps? I don't think so," Renoir said, answering his own question.

"The analysts thought it was quirky at the time, but they didn't look deeper. It was only after I asked the question that they took a hard look," said Craxton. "They screwed up."

Renoir sat back. "Does the SecDef know about this?"

Craxton shook his head. "Not yet. I wanted to brief you before I sent it over."

Renoir looked at the group, but he turned his gaze to Rick. "Tomorrow at sixteen hundred the president will meet with the SecDef, the joint chiefs, and me. Rick, I want you there." He looked at the group again. "Find the trigger before that meeting."

***

Rick was in at 6:00 AM, and the office was already buzzing. The six men arriving from China for the Epcot tour were due in at 9:00. After spending the night ruminating about all the damage they might do, Rick's recommendation would be to detain them for violating customs — they'd probably have to invent something, but in this case anything would do — and send them home. No sense in even giving them a shot at pulling the trigger.

Denise Carlson was busy in her office. When she saw Rick, she waved him in. "We've got something from the intel shop. It's a little peculiar." She handed him a list of names.

"Last name on the list of the group arriving today." She leaned in and pointed her finger at the paper she put in Rick's hand. "It's native Taiwanese instead of Han. Intel thinks it's a midlevel bureaucrat from Taiwan's ministry of defense who defected to the mainland."

Rick held the list. "A defector? There must be a hundred thousand Taiwanese going back and forth to the mainland, either working or running a business. Some of the men have two wives. Defecting almost doesn't make sense anymore. And a midlevel bureaucrat from the MOD probably wouldn't have much value. As a mole, maybe. Hmmm. This could be an interesting development, but it won't matter. I want Customs to intercept these guys and get them on the first plane back to China."

Carlson was puzzled. "I thought we were going to track them."

Rick shook his head. "I don't think we can afford to let them into the country. Not the way things are developing."

Carlson nodded. "OK. You want me to check with Renoir first?"

"Is he in?"

"No."

"Then we'll just tell him. Go ahead and give the order to Customs, and tell them to let us know when they have the group in custody."

***

Marly pulled the data from the worldwide earthquake locator and loaded it into her computer. She only had to click on the continental plate or plates she wanted information for, and Java loaded the applicable data into her database. Another click would start an animation showing all the EQs on the plates in question.

Marly clicked on the Pacific and North American plates, and the Java program stated its readiness to port the data. But before starting the download, she paused, remembering her conversation with Rick Starr and the mention of Coulomb stress transfer. She clicked on Cocos and Nazca, the two small tectonic plates to the east of the Pacific plate and just south of the North American plate.

Her plan was to review when and where earthquakes occurred over the past six months. She set up the animation program so it would show earthquake activity on each of the plates, while speeding up the time sequence. That would let her watch where and in which relative order earthquakes, above some threshold that she selected, occurred on and around the plates. She chose magnitude 4.0 so the majority of earthquakes during the six months would be "dropped". *Was there something significant happening on a particular segment of any of the plates that might explain the movement in the Bay Area?* Marly could feel the goose bumps tingling on her arms.

***

It was 7:45 AM. Rick stretched and yawned at his desk. He was watching Fox News on his computer monitor. An announcement that China's president would be visiting Mexico — Mexico, for God's sake — at the same time the tour group was in-country sent chills down his spine. He sprinted for Renoir's office. Renoir had just walked in and the look on Rick's face told him to expect bad news. "What?"

"Fox News just announced that China's president will be in Mexico City during the same period that the tour group is in the states."

"The Chinese are visiting Mexico? That's a new one."

"The timing is definitely odd, but it could be important."

Renoir prepared for the worst. "OK, tell me."

"The intelligence division thinks that one member of the tour group from China that's coming in could be a defector from Taiwan. We thought that was strange, but maybe it makes sense.

"What if the Chinese make an attempt on the life of the Taiwanese vice president, but they don't get the reaction they want?"

Renoir was shaking his head. "You don't think this other guy might try to assassinate the Chinese president?"

Rick nodded.

Renoir shook his head. "When someone defects, don't they want to live in the country they're defecting to? I mean, why would this guy want to do this? Is it just a coincidence he's part of this tour?"

"Maybe it's not him. Maybe it's another guy using his name."

"So you're saying he's part of a bigger plan? That the president of China is in on the plot? And he actually agreed to getting assassinated?"

"Maybe there's an agreement not to try too hard, or maybe it's a plan designed to fail. Maybe he doesn't know about it. But if this defector from Taiwan were even to make an attempt on the life of China's president, they could claim he was encouraged to defect."

"Of course," said Renoir, "why they sent him to the United States in the first place would be irrelevant."

"Even worse, they could claim that we set up the defection, invited him to visit the U.S., and put him up to it."

"And give them a reason to do what they want." Renoir finished Rick's thought. "What are we waiting for? Let's pick the bastard up when he arrives."

Rick nodded. "I've already told Denise to have Customs intercept the entire group. To not even let them into the country."

"Right. Get a car to take us to the airport. Where's Carlson? I want her along. I want this finished before we meet with the president this afternoon."

***

Marly watched the animation. There were 7,000 earthquakes a year with a magnitude of 4.0 or higher, and she'd be watching over half of them. As the animation progressed, she watched each week of the past six months tick off at the top of the screen. The earthquake patterns were random and dispersed across the plates, until week seventeen. A series of earthquakes, all below a magnitude of 4.5, appeared around the Nazca plate off South America. The last six weeks showed there were exactly 48 earthquakes of nearly the same magnitude, all along the edge of the plate — and they always occurred in pairs, symmetrically and on opposite sides. This was activity consistent with careful planning, and inconsistent — or at least highly unusual — with Mother Nature. Embedded among the thousands of earthquakes, the events normally would not be noticed, and she considered that she might be imagining the pattern. But when she isolated the Nazca plate and reran the animation sequence for the last six weeks, sure enough, there they were. Not only were they symmetrical, but they occurred at regular intervals.

She wondered about Coulomb stress transfer. Maybe it was the Nazca plate that was destabilizing. Maybe the stress associated with this bizarre series of events was being transferred through the Cocos plate up to the Pacific and North American plates. She'd have to show this to Beverly and Ralph Thiele, her colleague at the Geological Survey.

***

Renoir, Rick, and Carlson walked into the airport. They headed for the Customs office, near baggage claim at the international terminal. Carlson led the way.

They walked in, and a group of men and women dressed in green "bags" that looked like Air Force flight suits, stopped their conversation. "Yo, Denise," said one of the men. "What brings you here?"

"Hey, Marvin. We're here to join up with your people intercepting the Chinese group."

"I called and left you a message on your cell phone. They arrived yesterday."

Carlson pulled out her phone. She had forgotten to turn the ringer back on after their meeting the night before. She let her mind parse the statement just made by Marvin. "What do you mean they arrived yesterday? They're supposed to get here today at 9 o'clock."

"I know that's what you said. But we checked the passport computer when they didn't show up on the manifest of this morning's flight. They came in last night."

Renoir interrupted. "How's that possible? Don't they have to have visas?"

"Sure," Marvin said. "But the visas are for a one-time visit. It doesn't specify when they have to arrive. It only says they can't arrive after a certain date."

"Where's the FBI?" asked Rick.

"Search me," said Marvin. "Were they supposed to be here?"

"I told them we didn't need them anymore," said Carlson. "Since you said Customs would detain the group, I called FBI and pulled them off the case."

Rick looked at John Renoir and back at Denise. "Call the Bureau and tell them we need to pick the group up again. Let 'em know we've got a major problem, and alert them to the visit of China's president in Mexico. We need to make sure nothing happens to either the vice president of Taiwan or the Chinese president."

Carlson punched up a number on her cell phone and put it to her ear. "Al, this is Denise. We screwed up. We need you back on the case...yeah, the group from China. Turns out they came in yesterday." She nodded. "Yeah, doing the obvious was unexpected. Hey, one more thing. China's president is showing up in Mexico." She listened to the voice at the other end. "Yeah, we need you to take a look at that, too." Another pause. "OK, got it. Call as soon as you get something."

Carlson hung up and frowned. "They said it's going to be like looking for a needle in a haystack. They'll cover the Chinese embassy, check local hotels, a couple of safe houses they know the Chinese stash people, and watch to see if the group shows up for the tour." She dropped her arm by her side. "It isn't looking good."

Renoir was beside himself. "This is great." He looked at Rick. "How could this happen?"

Rick shook his head. "We assumed they'd show up as planned, and it was a bad assumption."

"That's all you can say? It was a bad assumption? China might invade Taiwan at any moment, and all you can say is that we made a bad assumption? Is that what I tell the president this afternoon?"

Rick sighed. "I think you tell the president the FBI is staking out the primary targets."

"I'm sure the president will want to know why we didn't take these guys into custody when they arrived," said Renoir.

"Then we'll just have to tell him they arrived ahead of schedule. The good news is we've probably figured out how they hope to justify their actions."

Renoir shook his head. "You don't know the president like I do. He'll rip your lips off if you give him a lame excuse like that."

"So let him rip. It's the best we can do for the moment. Even if we had grabbed them, it wouldn't change the facts. The U.S. still needs to prepare a plan for worst case. Trigger or no trigger, China may still launch an invasion of Taiwan."

Renoir nodded. "OK. Denise, you follow up with the FBI. Rick, you'll need to help me prepare for the meeting with the president this afternoon. I think this is going to be one ugly baby — ugly enough to break a mother's heart."

***

The White House situation room bristled with activity. Rick recognized the chairman of the joint chiefs and the service chiefs. Also present were the secretary of defense, secretary of state, the president's national security advisor, and the president's chief of staff. Noticeably absent was the vice president, who was off in California covering a fundraising event the president had to drop at the last moment. It was too important to be ignored, so he sent the first lady and the vice to cover for him. Politics never stopped, even during a national crisis.

They gathered around a large conference table. The president's press secretary walked into the room.

"Gentlemen, the President." In walked the president of the United States. He walked with assurance and purpose. There was no doubt that this man was in charge. *Maybe he would rip their lips off, after all*, thought Rick.

"Thank you, Katarina. Have a seat, gentlemen." The president took a sip of coffee from the cup that awaited him at his seat. "OK, Christopher," the president said to his national security advisor. "What have you got?"

"Sir, we've got the Chinese spring-loaded to launch an invasion. All their subs are in the Strait, the rest of their navy is within two days sail, and they've got over 300 aircraft — forty of which are top-of-the-line, fourth generation fighter-bombers we didn't even know they had — standing by on something akin to alert. They've also got some two hundred landing craft and enough marines at Xiamen to ruin anyone's day. To sum it up, we got a fox lickin' his chops outside the hen house." Christopher Bennett was a thirty-something Wunderkind.

"All right, Christopher. John, you have anything to add to that assessment?"

"No, sir," said Renoir.

"Randy," the president said to his secretary of state, "what's the political situation? Is China's leadership still denying everything?"

"Yes, sir. They're claiming we're making it up — that the photos we released are fakes. It looks like that's going to be the line they take until it's to their advantage to say otherwise."

"When do we think that'll be?"

"Don't know, sir. For now, we're looking like the bad guys, and as long as that music continues to play in the international media I suspect they won't change their strategy. BBC and Al Jazeera make it sound like we're the ones with the problem. The BBC is trying to get an invitation to Xiamen so they can see what's really going on, but the Chinese are stalling. You'd think that would tell them something."

"Jack, what about our response?" The president directed the question to his secretary of defense.

"We've got the aircraft carrier Truman three days out. I've asked the Chief of Naval Operations to get another two carrier battle groups ready to deploy, but he's having trouble spinning up the force."

The president looked at his CNO. "What's the problem, Charlie?"

"No problem, sir. It's just that we've been caught at a bad time. The JFK and the Stennis are the only two other carrier battle groups we've got right now. The Stennis is on its maiden deployment, and the skipper says his crew isn't combat ready."

"You agree with that, Jack?"

"Sir, Charlie says the captain of the Stennis is one of his best. I think we have to take his word for it," said the defense secretary.

The president interrupted. "We've got an international crisis, and you're saying a response isn't possible because a new carrier lacks a little training? I don't think so." He glared at the chairman of the joint chiefs. "What do you think, Dan?"

The chairman squirmed. "Well, sir, it could be dangerous if the crew isn't combat ready. The American people won't be happy with unnecessary casualties."

The president shook his head. "It'll be a lot more dangerous if we don't show up when the bully is pushing our friends around on the playground." He looked back at the CNO. "Fire the skipper, and find someone who can handle the job."

"Sir, I don't know that we need to fire him..."

"Relieve him, Charlie," shot back the president. "Either you do it or I'll personally fire him. I want him replaced, and I want that boat on its way to Formosa in twenty-four hours, combat ready or not."

The president turned his gaze away from the CNO, making it clear the conversation was over. "What else are we doing, Jack?"

"Well, sir, we recommend you authorize a call-up of the Reserves. Voluntary for the moment. We've got virtually all our attack subs preparing to leave port. Our plan is to keep two back on each coast. The Air Force will beef up its presence in Okinawa and Korea, although the Okinawans are giving us one heck of a time at Kadena. Local governor says he believes the Chinese version of what's going on."

"What's the bottom line?" asked the president.

No one at the table volunteered an answer immediately. Christopher Bennett finally spoke. "Taiwan is going to get its ass kicked from one side of the island to the other if the Chinese decide to launch an invasion and we don't intervene."

"And if we do?"

The chairman of the joint chiefs spoke up. "Sir, it's going to be all-out war. The carriers are too vulnerable to place directly in the line of attack, so we'll park them on the back side of Formosa. Once military action is imminent, we'll use Tomahawks to crater the runways near Xiamen to keep most their aircraft from getting off the ground. Navy will launch off the carriers and nail any planes lucky enough to get airborne, before they get to altitude. Subs will be in place in the Strait to clear out anything that decides to make its way to the island, and the Aegis will be there to help with missile defense. Air Force fighters will be hooked up to tankers and flying air superiority. We should be able to eliminate most of their landing craft before they ever hit the shore." The Chairman nodded his head. "We need time to get everyone where they're supposed to be, but we're moving out. If you're asking who's going to win this thing, there is no doubt."

Christopher Bennett spoke again. "We should expect China to launch upwards of a thousand short range attack missiles before they start the operation. Without us in place, Taiwan could have enough scorched metal on the island to manufacture paper clips for the rest of the world for decades."

The president shook his head. "What about casualties? Any estimates?"

The chairman frowned. "There'll be tens of thousands dead on Taiwan, potentially lots of civilians. It's irrational for the Chinese to attack cities and the economy, since ostensibly they want Taiwan's economic power. But if they decide to do it anyway, the entire island becomes one big target. As far as our forces go, we expect minimum losses."

"OK. So what's the chance they'll really launch an invasion? What are you guys thinking?"

Christopher Bennett spoke once again. "If they find a good enough excuse, we think the chances are pretty good."

The president did not hide his annoyance. "The Chinese need a reason to invade Taiwan? We can't even get them to admit they've got their entire armed forces geared up for an invasion. Why would they need an excuse?"

Bennett spoke again. "We think they're looking for international support, and they'll only get that if it looks like they were provoked. By legitimizing their actions, they hope to marginalize us and our role."

"What kind of excuse are you guys thinking? Give me an example. CIA, talk to me."

"Well," said John Renoir, "just as one example, they could blow up their own embassy in Washington and claim the Taiwanese did it."

"Fair enough," said the president. "Now tell me something realistic."

"Sir," said Renoir, "I have with me one of my senior analysts, Rick Starr, who's an expert on the region. He can brief you on what we think might be one way the Chinese could trigger an invasion."

The president leaned back in his chair and looked at Rick, waiting.

"Good afternoon, sir. When this whole thing kicked off, we began looking into activities involving the Chinese that might provide them justification — in their eyes, obviously — to invade Taiwan. We've settled on two simultaneous activities, both involving a group of Chinese tourists scheduled to join a tour on Monday to go to the Epcot Center..."

"At Disney World?" asked the president.

"That's right, sir. Disney World." The president sighed audibly. Rick continued. "During the time their tour takes place, the vice president of Taiwan will be present at an exhibit at Epcot." He tried to judge the president's reaction without success. "Fox News announced that China's president will visit Mexico City, coincidentally at the same time the tour is at Disney World."

"Yes, I know," said the president.

"We learned this morning that one of the group is a Taiwanese defector." He paused. "We believe that two individuals from this group could attempt a pair of assassinations. The first involving the vice president of Taiwan while he's at the Epcot Center, and the second the Chinese president in Mexico."

The president did not hide his surprise. "You think a Chinese tourist will try to assassinate China's president?"

"Sir, we think the defector might try. And tourist was a poor choice of words on my part. The group consists of government and military officials. Young ones."

"When does the group arrive?"

"It was scheduled to arrive this morning."

"It seems to me the answer is easy. Pick up the group, and the plan is a bust."

"Yes, sir, we thought of that," said Rick. "But instead of arriving this morning as planned, they arrived last night."

The president raised his eyebrows, but did not say anything immediately. "So what you're saying is that it's too late. You didn't think about the possibility they would arrive early, and now they're already here."

"Yes, sir," said Rick. *Here it comes*, he thought, involuntarily touching his lips.

"And I assume you're also going to tell me that you have no idea where they've gone."

"That's correct, sir."

The president leaned forward again and looked around the table. "I'm not convinced that China actually plans to launch an invasion, or if they do that they need an excuse to attack. I think all this could be because there's a new guy sitting in this chair — a test of our nation's resolve under the leadership of a new president.

"Let's refine our military strategy. Jack, you'll need to brief all of us again tomorrow on our response. Christopher, both you and Jack need to provide more details on how the Chinese and Taiwanese forces match up."

The president paused and shook his head. He appeared to be thinking out loud. "I'm not sure we have enough information to make an accurate judgment of China's intentions, although CIA's assessment is worrisome."

The president stood up, and everyone stood with him. "Thank you, gentlemen, ladies. See you back here tomorrow, same place, same time." He looked at Renoir. "John, you need to keep us informed as the situations at Epcot and Mexico City develop. I don't want to be blindsided by CNN or Fox News."

"Yes, Mister President," Renoir replied.

CHAPTER 5

Marly Cooper sat with her colleagues Ralph Thiele and Beverly Duncan as they watched the animation sequence for the third time. Thiele shook his head. "This is definitely not natural."

Beverly shook her head. "I'm not convinced that it couldn't be something organic, maybe a reaction to forces in the earth's core. Or maybe the plate is destabilizing in a way that's developing a kind of slow motion harmonic wave. Sort of like a bridge that's getting ready to collapse. What do you think, Coop?"

"I have to agree with Ralph. It's too symmetrical, too regular. Take a closer look: Every other pair of earthquakes occurs on a line exactly perpendicular to the previous pair." She shook her head. "But if it's not a natural phenomenon, what is it and what's causing it?" Marly dropped her hands to her lap. "You know, the guy from the CIA who interviewed me was asking if the Chinese had discovered a way to predict earthquakes. I wonder if they discovered this before we did and have been studying it already."

"If every big earthquake was preceded by this kind of activity, all of us could predict them." Thiele shrugged his shoulders. "And there's no way to be sure that this kind of activity is necessarily going to lead to anything. Did you check to see if this has happened in the past?"

"I went back to the very beginning since you guys began recording data at the Geological Survey. As far as I can tell, this is the first time in recorded history that any kind of regular, symmetrical pattern like this has occurred on the planet."

"So what do we do? How do we find out if these earthquakes are environmental or not?" asked Beverly.

"I don't know that we can. Let's watch the plate and see if it continues," said Thiele. "In the meantime, I'll check with a couple of my colleagues to see what they think. Maybe the Navy is up to something, and we don't know about it."

"It's gotta be organic," said Beverly. "Even with the symmetry. Anything else is too far-fetched."

***

Rick looked at Carlson. "Are they sure?"

"That's what they said. Six guys in a large white van, accompanied by a couple of embassy personnel, have left the compound. They appear to be headed to the Disney tour offices," said Carlson.

"We should tell John."

The two of them walked toward the office of John Renoir. His secretary pointed with her head to guide the two familiar visitors to their destination. Renoir looked up when they walked in.

Rick raised his left arm and pointed his index finger toward Denise to indicate that she should do the talking.

"I just received a call from the FBI. Six men have left the Chinese embassy." Renoir got a puzzled look on his face. "Looks like they're headed for the Disney offices to join the tour going to Orlando."

"This is a surprise." He looked at Rick. "What do you think?"

Rick shook his head. "It's definitely unexpected. I think we should bag these bozos."

"Send them home?"

"Or at least confine them to their embassy until the two targets have left the hemisphere."

"OK," said Renoir. "Do it."

"I'd like to be there with Denise when the FBI picks them up," said Rick.

"No objection from me. Where do they plan to take them into custody?"

"I don't see why we should intervene while they're in transit. We'll pick them up after they get to Disney."

"Right. Just make sure they don't disappear again."

"You better tell the president's chief of staff," said Rick. "Confining these guys to the Embassy could create an international incident. The president may have to respond to this one personally."

***

Denise Carlson and Rick Starr drove up to the offices of Disney Tours. Waiting outside, and sitting in a parked car with three other agents, was Al Dennison. Denise and Rick had barely stepped from their car when Dennison walked up.

"Hey Al, great day, huh?" asked Carlson, nodding to him.

Dennison grunted. "They're inside with an escort. Young girl who doesn't look old enough to drive." An empty white van was parked at the curb.

"I'm surprised this is turning out to be so easy," said Rick.

"You're one lucky sonofagun. We might never have found these guys if they had split up," said Dennison.

The warm sun was shining brightly. Rick lifted his hand in a salute to shield his eyes and sighed. The warmth felt good. "I'm not complaining." He looked at Carlson, who gave him a thumbs-up. "OK, we're all set."

Dennison pointed his right index finger in the air and spun it rapidly, giving the ready signal to the waiting agents. They stepped out of their parked vehicle and entered Disney Tours. Rick, Denise Carlson, and Al Dennison followed.

"FBI, ma'am," said the lead agent to the startled travel guide. He looked at the young female escort from the Chinese embassy and flashed his badge. "Are you in charge of these gentlemen?"

"I'm their interpreter, and I'm escorting them on their tour to Disney World," the woman replied. She held her arm out in the direction of her colleague. "Mister Sing is the driver and will return to the embassy."

"I'm sorry, ma'am, but we'll need you and all these gentlemen to get back into your van and return to your embassy. We've been directed to restrict them to the embassy premises." Rick noticed that one of the men stepped in the direction of the door. When no one moved, he stepped back. Rick looked around to see if anyone else noticed.

The escort became aggressive. "You know that this action will be protested by our ambassador?"

"Yes, ma'am," replied the agent. "Your ambassador is welcome to call the State Department for an explanation. The United States secretary of state is expecting his call."

***

Marly reviewed the data again, and two more earthquakes — once again symmetrical and on opposite sides — took place around the Nazca plate in the last twelve hours. She noticed that the arcs between the various pairs of earthquakes that already occurred were more or less equidistant between adjacent events. *Why didn't I notice that earlier?* she wondered. *Symmetrical events that occur in pairs that are coordinated almost perfectly in both time and space.* She estimated that two more pairs of events, two to three days apart, would make the arcs all the same length and complete the circle. Her eyes grew wide. If she was right, in four to six days the entire perimeter of the Nazca plate would have been subject to a series of earthquakes, all between 4.0 and 4.5 on the Richter scale, all spaced equally apart.

***

"This is weird stuff," said Thiele in response to the latest pair of events. "I've talked with several of my colleagues at USGS, and they all agree. Something's going on down there."

"What could it be?" asked Marly.

Thiele shook his head. "It sounds outrageous, but someone, or something, seems to be messing with the Nazca plate. And we just had another three-inch slip to the north at the same time as this last pair of earthquakes."

"Beverly?" asked Marly.

Beverly was nodding. "How about the guy from the CIA? Can you call him?"

"I don't know his phone number. I only know his name."

"So call the CIA and ask for him."

"Yeah, right. What do I say? 'Hi, this is a seismologist from California, and I need to talk to this guy who came out to see me last week. I have no idea where he works, and I don't know his phone number. Oh, and by the way, will you please connect me to his office?'"

"Sounds like it's worth a try," said Thiele, ignoring her sarcasm. "He has access to the kinds of resources we need if we're going to figure this out anytime soon. We sure don't."

"Maybe we do," said Beverly. "What if we were to contact a salvage company to take a look at the ocean floor around these underwater earthquakes? Like the guys who recovered artifacts from the Titanic?"

"Who's gonna pay for that? Besides, it would take weeks, probably months, to get something like that set up," said Thiele.

"And if these earthquakes will completely encircle the Nazca plate in a couple days, then something, maybe something really big, could happen," said Marly.

"That's why," said Thiele, "we need to get the government involved. If this guy from the CIA thinks it's important, I'll bet he can get resources lined up and moving a lot sooner and faster than we ever could." He gave a laugh. "Besides, who else other than the U.S. government can afford to contract someone with a submarine to take part in what might be nothing more than a scavenger hunt on the bottom of the Pacific Ocean?"

***

"I have a bad feeling about this," said Rick to Denise Carlson after they climbed back into their car.

"About what?"

"Something's not right. It was too easy."

"What do you mean?"

"Did you notice the one guy who stepped toward the door when the agent said they all needed to get back into their van?"

"You think he was going to run?"

"No."

Carlson shook her head. "What's your point?"

"The group had an interpreter, which implies to me that no one spoke English, at least not very well — which is what you'd probably expect from a group of young soldiers and bureaucrats."

"So? Maybe the guy speaks a little English. Maybe he watches American movies on TV. Besides, you don't have to speak a lot of English to figure out what big men in dark suits carrying badges means."

Rick drummed his knee with his fingers. "Yeah, you're probably right." He slapped his knee and looked at Carlson. "Or maybe he'd been briefed that we might show up. Did you collect their passports?"

"Al did."

"When we drop them off at the embassy, I want the passports. Give me your cell phone." Carlson handed Rick her phone. "Joe? Rick here. I want you to call the airport and get yesterday's tapes from their security cameras. I want to see a tape that shows me the group from China that arrived yesterday...sometime in the evening, probably...yeah, tell them to get the tape and have it waiting for us at Customs so we can look at it. Denise and I'll be there in about an hour." He punched off the phone and handed it back to Carlson. "Call Al and tell him I want him to meet us at the airport with the passports after he drops the group off." He looked over at Carlson. "Let's go to the airport now. I don't want anyone telling us we have to wait to see those tapes."

"What are you thinking?" asked Carlson.

"I think they pulled another switch on us. I'll bet you a hundred dollars the faces on the security tape don't match the faces in the group we just picked up."

***

"Yes, ma'am, Rick Star. I think his name is spelled s-t-a-r. He said he worked for the CIA, and he came out to California to ask me some questions about earthquakes."

The operator at the Pentagon rolled her eyes. She looked at her colleague sitting next to her and put her phone on mute. "I tell you, the stories we get. Some guy says he's from the CIA — how can this woman believe a line like that — and now she's calling here trying to find him."

Her fellow operator shook her head in sympathy. "Poor girl. Take the message. Give her a little hope."

The woman shook her head and punched her phone off mute. "Honey, did your friend say he worked here at the Pentagon?"

"He didn't tell me where he worked, just that he was from the CIA."

"Uh-huh. OK, honey, give me your message again, and I'll try to find him for you."

***

Al Dennison walked into the room. Rick and Denise Carlson were watching a tape showing a group of people walking out of an arrival gate and down the concourse of the airport. Rick turned around, and Dennison handed him the passports and six photos.

"We already had pictures of the six guys on the tape. After you called me, I compared the pictures with the passports." Dennison raised his chin toward the video. "What do you think?"

"We think at least two, maybe three don't match up," Rick replied.

"Our guess is that three of them don't fit."

"Hi, Al," said Carlson. "Long time no see," she joked, and he shook her hand and kissed her cheek.

"Run it again from the beginning, and freeze-frame each face."

The technician stopped the tape when the first person in the group appeared. Rick found a matching passport. "Does this look like the same guy to you?"

Carlson and Dennison looked at the passport picture and then at the face on the screen. "Could be," said Dennison.

"Yeah," said Carlson, poking her colleague in the side. "It's the same guy."

The technician moved to the second face, with the same conversation taking place.

The third face led to a different conclusion. "I think it's significant that the guys who have disappeared weren't the first ones off the plane.

That tells me their exit was choreographed." He shuffled through the passports again, looking at the pictures. "I can't find this guy." Carlson and Dennison confirmed Rick's assessment. The same was true for the fourth and fifth faces. The sixth matched.

"So there are three of them that are no longer with the group," said Rick.

"I thought there would be one for Orlando and one for Mexico." said Carlson. "You think there's a backup?"

"I don't think we're that lucky."

"What do you mean?"

Rick frowned. "There's probably a third target."

Now it was Dennison's turn to frown. "A third target? We'll never get protection to the target in time if you don't tell us who it is, and soon."

"So there's a safety valve," said Carlson. She looked at Rick. "Do you have anyone in mind?"

Rick shook his head. "The only other prominent Chinese official I can think of is their representative to the United Nations, and of course Taiwan isn't a member of the UN."

"How about kids of important officials? Maybe we need to look at students from China and Taiwan," said Carlson.

"I doubt that would be sufficient to justify a war. I'm not even sure that doing something to China's UN representative is enough justification, but it's all I can think of for the moment." Rick looked at Denise. "How about if you generate a list of all the prominent officials in the U.S. from China and Taiwan? And for the sake of completeness, let's also generate a list of all prominent naturalized citizens and any dissidents who might be over here, for whatever reason." He rubbed his chin. "Can you think of any other group we should consider?"

Carlson shrugged. "How about athletes? Should I check if there are any here, either from Taiwan or China?"

"Can't hurt," said Rick.

Al Dennison spoke up. "We've got our guys in place in Orlando, and there's another team on its way to Mexico City. That's the best we can do for now. Call us when you get the drop on your third target."

***

"Did you get through?" asked Beverly.

"I left a message. They said they had to find him," said Marly.

"Find him? How many people in the CIA have a name like Rick Star?"

"I don't know," said Marly. "Maybe it's not his real name. Maybe it's a fake name for when he talks to regular people."

"Ooooh, I never thought of that," said Beverly, shaking her head. "I'm beginning to feel like we're part of a Tom Clancy novel."

***

News flash, conveyed by a young woman with jet black hair and bright red lipstick. "This story has just come in. Police now estimate the number of people, who have either left the Bay Area or who have plane reservations to depart in the next two weeks, has surpassed 50,000 and is still growing. Arriving commercial jets are virtually empty. The mayor has appealed again for calm, criticizing small business owners who appear to have closed their doors. He called for them to remain in San Francisco and reopen their stores, or face the loss of their operating licenses. A number of businesses are complaining that not only are employees quitting without notice, but that there aren't any customers, either. A franchise owner for Taco Bell says the local neighborhood where his restaurant is located is a ghost town and that even the homeless have taken flight."

"Is the governor involved?" asked a large face that suddenly appeared to her left from off screen.

"Not yet. He's appealed for calm, too, but he's remaining neutral. He says he knows that people are following their conscience."

"A good political answer. Fifty thousand?" The face whistled. "We now return you to our regularly scheduled programs…"

***

"China's UN representative is out of the country? Did you turn up any other names?" asked Rick.

Carlson shook her head. "Only diplomats from China and Taiwan here in Washington. What do you think about them as targets?"

Rick sighed. "Could be, but I'm skeptical. They just don't have the visibility. What about naturalized citizens or dissidents?"

"We do have several dissidents in the country, but none with ties to Taiwan. As far as naturalized citizens, no one seems to stand out. We did get the name of the professor in California that you mentioned — the colleague of Earthquake Girl in San Francisco."

"Earthquake Girl?" asked Rick. "How'd you come up with that?"

Carlson shrugged. "I don't know. She likes earthquakes, I guess."

Rick shook his head. "Let's think about the Chinese professor for a moment. He's been meeting with three or four visitors a month from mainland China for the past six years, and he's been showing them how to detect whether or not the earth's surface is changing, how it looks when there's going to be an earthquake." Rick raised his eyebrows. "What if he showed his visitors something that could indicate a giant earthquake was about to happen sometime soon, really soon? Maybe they wouldn't want him telling anybody that."

"So the professor isn't a trigger, he's a threat. Knows something they don't want him divulging." Carlson frowned. "But what's this got to do with the primary targets?"

"Good question. But what if there was a major earthquake — no, a great earthquake? So big that it killed and injured hundreds of thousands of people, left millions homeless, and caused property damage in the hundreds of billions of dollars? Would the United States be so overwhelmed by what happened that it could not — or maybe would not — even try to respond to an attack on Taiwan? Remember what happened after bin Laden's thugs hijacked the airliners and crashed them into the World Trade Center and the Pentagon? It took President Bush twelve hours to get back to Washington, and he had to overrule his security detail to get to the White House to make a speech from the Oval Office. How long would it take us to respond if half the state of California was instantaneously whacked?"

"I thought you said that no one could predict when there's going to be an earthquake."

"What if they could? What if the two assassination attempts are the bait, and the earthquake is the trigger that causes us to retreat? Doctor

Cooper says that 13% of the U.S. gross domestic product is produced by California. Guess who has over a trillion dollars in U.S. securities? What if we defaulted on our loans to China because California imploded? What if the conditions the Chinese set for delaying payment included staying out of Taiwan?"

"So the third guy missing from the tour group goes after the professor because he told his government something terrible is about to happen in California."

"Not just terrible, but catastrophic. Why don't you contact Dennison and tell him to put someone on the professor? Tell him it's a guess, but it's the best we can do for now."

Carlson left the room. Rick walked to his desk and sat down. He pulled out the phone number for Doctor Marly Cooper's office. It was late. *Now what did I do with her home phone number?*

***

Marly was exhausted. She slowly opened the door to her apartment, and it was all she could do to pet Benny, who was starving for affection. She had spent the last two days almost exclusively at work, and she felt guilty about leaving him home alone. The earthquake data she was looking at consumed her, and now Doctor Chen called with news of his sudden return to China because his mother had a stroke. He was expected to give one of the keynote presentations at her conference, and she was scrambling to find a replacement. It was too much for one day. "OK, Benny, let's get you some dinner, you little hound dog you." She scratched his ears, and he wagged his tail and whined with pleasure.

She pulled out Benny's large bag of dog food, but it was empty. "Doggone it, Benny, we're out of food." She breathed in deeply and let the air in her lungs out slowly. "OK, we'll go for a quick walk and pick up a new bag." She grabbed Benny's leash, which made his tail wag all the harder, his whine turning into a bark. "Yeah, yeah, Benny."

The phone rang. Marly ignored it.

***

Rick hung up the phone. No luck finding Doctor Cooper, either at work or home. He left a message on her work voicemail to call him.

***

The three men, all Asian, sat quietly on the Washington metro. It was a time of day when the trains were nearly empty, and each occupied a separate seat. The tracks created a whirring sound as the car sped along. To the casual observer, their departures were random occurrences along the route from Washington to Dale City. Each left the train at a different stop, where a rental car was waiting. All had a different mission, a different set of instructions, known only to them.

Ling Mao's job was benign. He would pick Doctor Chen up at his residence in San Francisco and take him to Mexico, where they would catch a flight back to China. Doctor Chen's days in America were over. It was time to return home.

***

Lead agent Tom Dorley had worked for the Bureau for twenty-four years. With a reputation for aggressive leadership, it was no surprise that he found himself in charge of the detail assigned to protect Taiwan's vice president. He fanned his team out across the area surrounding the Taiwanese exhibit at the Epcot Center. This was going to be tough. There were nearly fifty people, all in costume, who were part of the display, and it would not be hard for someone of Asian descent to enter the exhibit undetected.

Dorley made each member of his team responsible for a subset of the employees participating in the exhibit. In the morning when the display opened and the employees arrived, the team member responsible for his subset gave a verbal OK over the radio to confirm a positive ID. If anyone unexpected showed up, he had two "rovers" ready to do an intercept, one from the front and one unseen from behind. The others were spring-loaded to assist if there was any trouble. The employee entrance to the exhibit area was closed off after opening hours, and he and his team switched their focus from filtering employees to watching tourists for suspicious activity. Epcot set up a metal detector at the entrance to the exhibit, and he manned it with several agents to prevent any reckless assassination attempts. Two agents of Asian-American descent, dressed as if they were part of the exhibit, were stationed ten feet inside the barrier surrounding the display, directly down in front of the platform holding the vice president.

The vice president would be on-scene this afternoon and all day tomorrow. Dorley's team members would have the procedure down pat by the time he arrived. One agent was assigned to remain behind the vice president, albeit out of sight, the entire time he was present. Her job was to whisk him to safety — there was a panic room underneath the exhibit — at the first sign of trouble.

It was set to be a day full of boredom punctuated by a single burst of violence. Dorley and his team had to keep their minds focused over the course of the next two days. He called for a check-in, and each agent responded according to plan. Now it was just a matter of waiting. For who or for what, he did not know. Success would be measured by the absence of excitement, and he was determined to keep this show unexciting.

***

Kam Fong was sick from the tension that possessed him during the flight to Mexico City and the subsequent ride from the airport to his hotel. To come this far and possibly be intercepted before having a chance to begin his mission was a thought that had made him physically ill. He tried to calm himself and sat quietly in the corner of his hotel room, a refuge on the edge of the noisy downtown arranged on his behalf by a local contact. At his feet was a large briefcase containing a vest lined with enough plastic explosive to level a small building. Wearing it, he had only to get within a few yards of his objective. Pulling the small lanyard protruding from the lower left of the vest would instantaneously project his target, all passers-by, and himself into legend — never to be forgotten at what would become a critical juncture of history, a historic moment of epic proportions and epic consequences.

Ever since he defected from Taiwan in protest of his country's refusal to negotiate with the mainland to create a single China, his hosts had isolated him. Placed under house arrest in a small studio apartment, they worked to convince him to become a martyr. He was angry at what he thought was a strange request. "I am only thirty years old. I did not choose to come to China so I could kill myself." But they were persistent. And patient. They kept asking him if he wanted to see the two Chinas reunited.

"How?" he kept asking, but they would not answer. They kept insisting that he could not be trusted with the how if he did not agree to the what.

Fong's grandparents were among six million native Taiwanese living on the island of Formosa when two million Nationalists, under the leadership of Chiang Kai-shek, arrived in 1949. The Nationalists fled China following their defeat by Communist forces under Mao Tse-tung. They believed that they would eventually return with Chiang Kai-shek to the mainland to overthrow the Communists and rule a single China. The Nationalists used this myth, as Fong called it, as a pretext to oppress the native populations and to confiscate property.

During the notorious Kaohsiung Incident in 1979 when native

Taiwanese protestors marching for democracy became the victims of rioters, Fong's grandfather was severely beaten along with other protest leaders and died from his injuries. This incident galvanized Taiwanese natives into political activism, and Fong's parents helped found the then-illegal Democratic Progressive Party and were vocal supporters of the political opposition when it finally swept into power in 2000. His grandmother, however, never recovered from her husband's death. She "adopted" Fong from birth as her favorite and taught him to loathe the Nationalists and never forget what happened. She died a hollow, bitter and angry woman, never seeing the election that finally ended Nationalist rule.

Unlike his parents who supported an independent Taiwan and a new identity for its people, Fong began to view reunification as not only positive but necessary if the Kuomintang, the political party of the Nationalists, was to be finally crushed and disbanded. And although most of the population opposed unification with the mainland, Fong longed for it. He believed that the reunification of Taiwan with the People's Republic was the only way to avenge his grandfather's untimely death. He joined the Taiwanese Ministry of Defense with hopes of rising to a level where he could affect policy, but it did not happen. His aspirations far exceeded his average abilities. Stalling early in his career as one of thousands of midlevel managers in the oversized Taiwanese bureaucracy, he eventually concluded that defecting was his only hope of making the change for which he longed. He was sure that mainland China would welcome his help to build a strategy for reunification.

Fong adamantly refused at first to talk about martyrdom. He did not like the suicide bombers who were terrorizing the Jews in Israel. He detested the 9/11 killers and those who were now murdering people indiscriminately in the Middle East and elsewhere. And then there were the London bombers. Despicable, all of them, crazy, immoral dupes; robots. There was no other explanation for such extreme acts of violence, and he would have no part of it.

When his new benefactors reminded him of the Japanese kamikaze and how they gave their lives willingly in defense of Japan, Fong remained unmoved. He told them, "Even the kamikaze wore uniforms and flew military aircraft. It would be dishonorable for me to pretend that I am a civilian and perform the actions of a soldier. It is dishonorable to kill women and children."

"What if we gave you a uniform?" they asked.

"It still would not matter. People like you, people like bin Laden, you don't die for your cause. You find people like me to die in your place."

The next day he was introduced to the Chinese president.

***

Fong checked the piece of paper that had been waiting for him in his room. The day after tomorrow, China's president would arrive for a reception at the city mayor's residence. There the president would greet the crowd, a spontaneous gathering about which no one would know. But he knew exactly where the president would be, and he would be in the crowd's front row. Just before the reception ended, when the crowd was at its largest, the president would walk up to him, take his hand, and Fong would pull the lanyard. The western media would do the rest.

Their simultaneous deaths would be the catalysts for reunification and in turn lead to the demise of the Kuomintang.

When he met with the Chinese president, and the president assured Fong of his own willingness to die for their common cause, Fong finally agreed to give his life in honor of the memory of his grandfather.

***

John Kale, traveling with his team of three other agents, put his magazine down as the plane settled onto the runway in Mexico City. He and his team received authorization from the Mexican government to be part of the protection team covering the Chinese president. They were given a peripheral role that did not afford them much control, but they would be allowed in the Chinese leader's presence for his public appearances. Kale hoped that would be enough. He looked at his watch. Fatigue was clawing at his body, and he consciously shook it off. Almost dark, they'd have only tomorrow to survey the areas where the president would be exposed to someone who might want to harm his person.

***

Rupert Budowski sat in his car reading the newspaper across the street from the modest home of Doctor Kim Chen, who lived alone. His job was to watch the house and report any suspicious activity. He yawned. Another no-brainer. This guy was not going anywhere except bed.

His Styrofoam coffee cup was empty. He looked at the house. All was quiet. Time to get a refill. He started his car and pulled quietly away from the curb. He'd only be a minute.

***

From his bedroom window Doctor Chen watched the car that had been sitting in front of his house for several hours drive away. Who was watching? Did someone know about their plan? His bags were packed, and he wondered if he should tell anyone. No. That might delay his departure. *It is time to go home, and that is all that matters.*

CHAPTER 6

Marly walked into her apartment. She set the five-pound bag of dog food heavily onto the counter as Benny barked happily, doing a dance around her ankles. "OK, OK, Benny. You've got to cool it. I'm pooped tonight, all right?" She leaned over to pick up his empty bowl, when the phone rang. *Determined little telemarketer at the other end.*

"Hello?" She braced herself for a sales pitch.

"Doctor Cooper?" It was Rick Starr.

"So you got my message? I was beginning to think they'd never get it to you."

"Message? I never got a message," said Rick.

"Well, I didn't have your phone number, so I called the Pentagon and asked them to have you call me."

Rick laughed. "You called the Pentagon?"

"What's so funny?"

"I don't work at the Pentagon. The CIA offices are outside of Washington."

"Oh. It might have helped if you'd left me a way to contact you, you know."

Rick sighed. "You're right. With the phone call summoning me back to Washington, and since we made plans for me to come back to San Francisco, anyway, and I had your phone numbers." His voice trailed off. "I guess I didn't think about it, which is just an excuse, of course." Rick knew he should have given her a number where she could contact him. "I messed up. I'm sorry."

Marly's energy was rebounding. Benny sat expectantly, looking up at her. "Listen, I've got to feed my dog. Wait fifteen seconds, and I'll be right back." She put the receiver down and walked into the kitchen. She filled the dog bowl with food and set it on the floor. Benny sat patiently.

"OK, Benny. OK."

Marly picked up the phone. "I'm back."

"Listen, how about if I go first?" asked Rick. "It's about Doctor Chen. We're concerned about his safety because of his close association with the Chinese delegations visiting the United States."

"Really? It's interesting you'd mention him. Doctor Chen called me today and said his mother had a stroke. He's flying back to China tomorrow to see her for a couple weeks. He was supposed to be one of the keynote speakers at my conference, and it's going to be tough to find a replacement."

"He's going back to China? Tomorrow?"

"Yeah, that's what he told me."

Rick was puzzled. *What did this mean? Was Chen not in danger? Was he not the third target? Was the timing unfortunate or suspicious?* "I have to say I'm surprised at the sudden tragedy, especially with so much else going on already."

Marly just listened, anxious to change the subject. "Well, I don't know what to say. Doctor Chen is a nice man, so it doesn't surprise me that he's going home under the circumstances."

"How old is Chen?"

"I don't know," said Marly. "Maybe fifty, maybe fifty-five. Why?"

"Has he been back to China before? I mean, since he was naturalized?"

"I don't think so."

"So this is the first time he'll have seen his mother in how many years?"

"At least eight, I suppose. I vaguely recall someone saying he's been at the University eight years."

Rick nodded. *Enough for now.* "OK. What was it you wanted to tell me?"

"We've discovered earthquakes in the Pacific Ocean that we think are related. They seem to be causing some kind of strange phenomena involving one of the smaller tectonic plates off the coast of South America." Marly wondered if she could explain it over the phone in a way that Rick might understand.

"What earthquakes are you talking about?"

"It's something you need to see for yourself. Can you come back to San Francisco?"

"I could probably come on the week-end. We've got some important work going on right now, and I can't break away."

"I don't think it can wait. Something big could happen. Well, I don't really know if something will happen. But I'm convinced you need to see this now, not later. It's important."

Rick was going to say no, but decided against it. "OK. I'll be there tomorrow. I'll call you just before I leave Washington. Does that work?"

Marly nodded. The relief she felt surprised her. *Probably the tension from all this commotion.* "OK. I'll pick you up at the airport."

***

John Renoir was livid. "Absolutely not! The president is expecting us to meet with him — the real, no kiddin' President of the United States of America — POTUS — and you're not going to run off to San Francisco just 'cause you've got a hunch about something."

"But it's more than a hunch. My contact is convinced it's important. If the Chinese have learned how to predict earthquakes and we have a massive earthquake in California, the United States might not be able to respond to an invasion of Taiwan even if the president wants to." Rick pushed his boss hard. "Besides, this Professor Chen thing, his mother being sick and all. It sounds suspicious. I think he knows something and is trying to leave the country before he gets caught. We need to be thorough and follow every lead. We need to check this out." He could sense Renoir was relenting.

Denise Carlson watched and marveled at Rick's salesmanship. She shook her head and spoke up. "I think he needs to go."

Renoir gave her a dirty look. "You better be available on your mobile phone every minute you're away from Washington," he said, pointing at Rick's nose with his finger as he spoke.

"Yes, sir, I'll do even better than that. I'll be available every second."

Renoir shook his head. "Don't get smart with me. You're pressing your luck." He looked at Carlson. "Set up Air Force transport, and I want it to wait for him." He turned his attention back to Rick. "Not one minute longer in San Francisco than absolutely necessary."

"Got it. Not even a..." Rick caught himself. Renoir was not smiling.

***

Tom Dorley watched Epcot close the employee entrance. "Time to go into phase two," he instructed his team. They repositioned themselves to observe the arriving crowds. More than half the tourists pouring into the exhibit were of Asian descent. Any one of them could be the bad guy.

"Watch carefully, boys. Sue Lee, are you in position?"

Sue Lee Morrison nodded. "I'm directly behind where His Excellency will stand, and I have a two-seventy of the area. Only thing I can't observe is an approach directly from the front."

"Ten-four," said Dorley. "The approach is our problem. You just worry about what you can see."

***

Having driven non-stop from Washington, Foo Yung pulled into the large parking lot surrounding Disney World. He paid five dollars to the parking attendant, who had a Chinese face like his own. He greeted the attendant in Chinese, but the blank stare told him he was wasting his breath. His smile turned into a scowl, and he chose a space close to the exit. He checked the ceramic gun that had been hiding under the seat of the rental car, loaded with six plastic bullets. The gun could kill a man at ten meters. Beyond that, the bullets might break ribs or fracture bones. Getting close to his target would be essential for a successful kill.

Foo Yung knew that gaining access to the heavily guarded vice president would be difficult. But he also knew that surprise and speed were potent allies capable of confusing an adversary and throwing him off balance, the ensuing shock of a successful "hit" crucial for a getaway afterward. His instructions were to make an attempt this afternoon — the attempt more important than the result — his only requirement being to let the world know that he intended to assassinate the Taiwanese vice president. But he decided that he would succeed and return home. After all, it was not enough to be part of history. One had to survive history if one was to savor the notoriety promised by such a daring act.

Recruited for this task because he was the national Wing Chun Kung Fu champion, Foo Yung was in superb physical condition and extremely disciplined. His mind was keen and quick. Looking for weakness was an instinct. He lived to fight, and he had never met a man he could not vanquish. Fate was also at work: Foo Yung spoke English reasonably well and with an American accent, the result of teaching U.S. embassy personnel interested in learning martial arts. And he was married to the daughter of a Communist Party member, an honor that only sixty-nine million Chinese enjoyed. His father-in-law had appealed to his vanity, his conceit, that he was the only one who could execute this crucial task for his nation. The flattery worked, and Foo Yung was in America to fulfill what he knew was his personal destiny.

He was assured by his father-in-law that his wife and family would be cared for if anything happened to him. His wife would work a government job and follow her father into the Party. His son would study at a university in Europe. The plan for his eventual return to China should he survive was simple enough: U.S. extradition to Taiwan, and then a prisoner trade with the Chinese mainland. The timeframe involved in the process was less clear.

When captured, he was to say that his actions were designed to ensure the future of his country and that of its errant child, Taiwan, through reunification.

Foo Yung entered Disney World, returning the artificial smiles of the almost giddy employees. *The entrance fee is astronomical. I could live a month on this back home.* He paid with the hundred dollar bill he found in the ashtray of his rental car. Abundant excess was everywhere.

There it was: a sign to the Epcot Center. He began his journey — a journey put into motion by Fate herself — a journey into history.

***

Ling Mao flew from Washington National airport non-stop to San Francisco. Driving a dark blue Ford, he would be at Doctor Chen's in a little over an hour. He had called ahead before he caught his plane, and the doctor was already packed and waiting. They would drive straight through to the Mexican border and proceed to the airport at Mexicali as the first stop of the long trek home.

***

A Disney triumph, the Epcot Center was a place of marvel. Magnificent displays, futuristic and prehistoric creatures sharing the same space, technological gadgets beckoning to the curious. Off to the side of the entrance stood the Taiwanese display, teeming with activity and showing off the beauty of Asian culture. Foo Yung watched for just a moment, observing the metal detector that security walked everyone through before they approached the exhibit. He absentmindedly touched the pocket sewn into his undershirt that held his ceramic weapon. He looked to the right of the exhibit and noted several people taking more than a casual interest in each person passing through the metal detector. He looked to the far left. It was the same there, too. The exhibit was surrounded by people protecting the vice president — people waiting, looking for him.

So probably I won't survive, after all. Fate has decided that my destiny ends here. He let himself feel regret for only a moment.

Foo Yung walked casually toward the other exhibits, all the while observing the procedures used by the security personnel manning the metal detector.

***

A Boy Scout leader led his troop into the Epcot Center. "Stay together, boys!" he commanded to little avail. This was Troop 79, Orlando, a proud gathering of mostly Asian-Americans, some of Taiwanese descent. He led the way to the metal detector. "This way, Troop 79! This way! C'mon, boys, over here now! Turn off the music and take those ear plugs out so you can hear me. Stop texting! The exhibit is over here!" Twenty-three boys strong, Troop 79 began the process of going through the metal detector. A second scoutmaster lagged behind.

Another crowd of tourists followed close behind, led by a man with dark, intense eyes. He seemed to look beyond the boys in front of him, his attention riveted on the platform where the Taiwanese vice president now stood, smiling broadly and waving to the crowd. The man tapped the shoulder of the scoutmaster waiting with the scouts to go through the metal detector. The scoutmaster turned to face him.

"I was a Boy Scout myself many years ago. I was wondering if I could borrow your hat for a few minutes while I get my picture taken up near the exhibit with a friend. Would you mind?" He smiled sheepishly, doing his best to look obsequious.

The scoutmaster smiled back. "Of course not. Here, take my scarf, too. Might as well look authentic."

Foo Yung's smile broadened. "You are too kind. Thank you. I will return them to you as soon as I am finished." He placed the hat on his head and tied the scarf around his neck.

***

Tom Dorley watched the group of Boy Scouts coming through the metal detector. The three photos he and his team were given to identify the possible suspects were grainy, and it was grueling duty to peruse each and every person entering the exhibit area. He knew his people were probably not as sharp as they were at the start of the day and could use a short respite. "OK, team, here come the Boy Scouts. Take a breather. We've still got a long day ahead of us." He ordered the agents at the metal detector to let the Boy Scouts in and to hold off on admitting others for five minutes.

One of the men standing inside the barrier, down in front of the platform holding the vice president, looked at his colleague. "I gotta take a leak. I'll be right back."

"Don't take too long," the other replied. "I hafta go, too."

***

Foo Yung stepped up into the group of scouts after walking through the metal detector. "Excuse me, boys. I'm going to go ahead of you, if you don't mind. My friend is waiting up by the exhibit for me. Excuse me, boys, can you let me through? Thanks." He adjusted the scarf around his neck and the hat on his head. He did not have a brown shirt on like the rest of the scouts, but the hat and scarf had the desired effect: The boys moved aside to let him through.

***

Agent Dave Brown, arms crossed, stood idly at the entrance to the exhibit, watching the Boy Scouts move through the metal detector. He thought back to his own youth when he was a scout like these boys, going places to earn merit badges and seeing things he might otherwise never have had the chance to experience.

He tried to listen to the conversations. What do boys talk about nowadays, anyway? Girls? Cars? Sports? Computers? He wanted to eavesdrop on the conversation of the two boys nearest him, but there was too much noise. Their iPods and cell phones were like physical appendages, and the boys reluctantly placed them on the conveyor belt that took them through the x-ray machine.

Agent Brown casually looked over his shoulder at the scoutmaster that had gone through the metal detector, but was now walking briskly toward the exhibit. The hat was too large for his head, and he was wearing a blue long-sleeved shirt. The scouts and their troop leaders were all wearing brown short-sleeved shirts and stood waiting in a group. He scanned the exhibit area to see if anyone was taking note of the man's approach. Brown's colleagues were laughing, talking — even Agent Dorley was looking back at the exhibit, searching for Sue Lee. No one was watching. There was a wall of boys between him and the man in the hat and scarf, and he knew he could never reach him. He called out, but his voice was drowned out by the crowd. He hit his mike. "Boy Scouts. Check out the Boy Scouts!"

The reaction was immediate. The agents turned their attention to the metal detector to see Dave Brown waving both arms over his head.

"Talk to us, Dave. What are we looking for? What do you see?" Agent Dorley instinctively reached for his weapon and removed it from his shoulder holster.

***

Foo Yung noticed the simultaneous movement and sudden attentiveness of the people that had been watching the crowd when he first arrived. There were three people to his left and four to his right, all frantically scanning the area, looking for something, anything, looking for him. What Foo Yung did not notice before was the man dressed as if he was part of the exhibit, about ten feet or so inside the barrier —

directly in his path and who was now clearly on the alert. He glanced over his shoulder to see what all of them were staring at and saw a security guard waving and pointing in his direction.

Time stands still when Destiny beckons. Foo Yung broke into a sprint and with an effortless leap was inside the short barrier surrounding the exhibit. He trained for months in preparation for this moment, and the thrill of combat propelled him forward to the prize that stood on the platform. The Boy Scout hat he was wearing flew from his head. He caught the eyes of the man standing just inside the barrier — *yes, his eyes are searching for me.* Before the agent could react to Yung's rapid approach, Yung slammed the tips of his fingers, wrist locked, into his throat. The man gasped and fell backwards, groping at his neck, trying to breathe through his shattered trachea.

Yung raced past two startled adolescents and reached inside his shirt for his weapon. He grasped the grip of the gun, still racing for his target: the man with the smile waving to the Boy Scouts. His target would soon be in lethal range. All he needed was an unobstructed shot. He pulled his weapon from its hiding place and slipped his right index finger over the trigger.

Fate opened the way and Destiny awaited him.

***

Sue Lee Morrison was behind and slightly below the vice president. She scanned the crowd, but was not in position to see the man in the front of the exhibit racing up towards the platform where the vice president stood. She continued to survey the group of Scouts, but saw nothing out of the ordinary. She called into her radio, "I don't see anything. Do we have a delta-five or not?"

Tom Dorley answered immediately, his attention on the man sprinting toward the vice president. "Sue Lee, he's coming up from the front of the platform. The front of the platform! Get the vice president into the safe room, now!"

But it was too late. He watched the man leap with what seemed like superhuman strength onto the stage where the vice president was standing, take two quick shots at pointblank range that sent the vice president toppling backwards, and then leap off the back of the platform and knock a surprised Sue Lee to the floor. Dorley watched helplessly as the assassin fired two more rounds into his colleague. Dorley raised his pistol to shoot, but the mob of young people now panicking and running aimlessly across the exhibit area made a clear shot impossible. The assassin hit the door at the back of the exhibit at full speed, shoving it open with a bang, and disappeared into the sunlight.

***

Foo Yung could feel his body tense as he timed his leap onto the platform. He put his weight on his right foot and pushed off, sensing that the vice president was taking notice of his approach. The smile left his victim's face, hands rising in an effort to protect himself as Yung landed on the platform. Yung fired two quick shots, spinning to the right, placing his hand on the railing surrounding the platform, and pushing himself up and into the air. He cart wheeled and landed on the balls of his feet at a dead run and slammed into — *what, a woman?* She was carrying a weapon, and it went spinning off to the side as she fell to the floor. Taking no chances that she might recover, Yung fired two more quick shots and began his sprint once again for the door at the back of the Center. He heard no shots other than his own, and when he pushed on the door it flung open and threw him into a small alley leading away from the exhibit. Time seemed to begin again and, the sun bright, he squinted. Yung tossed his pistol into the bushes that lined the alley and began the journey to safety. He slowed to a fast walk, and he blended with the swirling throng of bodies at the end of the alley.

***

Agent Dave Brown watched the scene in horror, and when the killer leapt off the platform, Brown raced for the front door. He expected the shooter to flee the park, and he would try to head him off. Meanwhile, Tom Dorley and several other agents went out the back. One agent stopped at the platform where the vice president and Sue Lee were lying, calling for an ambulance on his cell phone.

Agent Brown put the palm of his hand around the grip of his pistol as he left the building. The crowd outside was enormous, and it was nearly impossible to distinguish faces among the ocean of bobbing heads. He looked across the crowd, searching for the closest exit where he figured a killer might try to take flight — one that offered the means for quick escape. Epcot security guards and Florida state police raced past him in the direction of the exhibit, and he could hear the approaching siren of a fire truck.

Scanning the crowd methodically, not knowing what he expected to see, Agent Brown was resigned to the likelihood that the assassin would make a successful escape. *But what's that?* An Asian man wearing a long-sleeved blue shirt with a Boy Scout scarf around his neck was moving quickly toward the exit. *It's him!*

***

Foo Yung was sweating hard, his shirt stained wet from the exertion, but he could see the exit just ahead. He wiped his brow, his muscles tensed in anticipation for the sprint that would set him free just beyond the gate. He smiled, never hearing or feeling the bullet that struck his right side, collapsing his lungs instantly and sending him unconscious to the concrete.

***

Agent Brown aimed his pistol at the fugitive. When he had a clear shot, he took it, firing at the right side of the suspect's chest.

Agent Dorley and the rest of his team turned and headed in the direction of the sound and the panicking crowd, the air filled with screams. They arrived to find Agent Brown standing over the fallen assassin.

***

Renoir sat with Carlson, Davis, and Craxton. "OK, what have we got?"

Denise Carlson thumbed through the stack of papers sitting in front of her. "It looks like the assassin got through to his target at Epcot. The vice president is in the hospital in critical condition, shot with plastic bullets from a ceramic gun."

"Plastic bullets?" asked Davis. "Unbelievable."

"We also have an FBI agent in the hospital with two bullet wounds, in guarded condition. And, we have the assassin himself in custody, also in critical condition. Turns out his name is Foo Yung."

Renoir looked at Carlson. "Foo Yung?"

Craxton and Davis could not help themselves and began to snicker.

"The vice president of Taiwan was shot by somebody whose name is on the takeout menu at Peking Sam's?" Renoir shook his head. "OK, what else?"

"We've got four agents in Mexico City, and we've got one agent in tow behind Doctor Chen. Chen's supposed to fly to China tomorrow and was picked up at his house by somebody who we're guessing matches one of the missing suspects. But if Chen's flying back to China, he's not flying out of San Francisco. They appear to be heading south, currently on a beeline to Mexico."

"So two bad guys down, one to go." Renoir sat back wearily.

"I don't think four FBI agents are going to be enough to protect the Chinese president," Carlson continued. "We had eleven of the best in Orlando, and it sounds like the guy walked right past everybody and practically strolled up to his target."

Davis shook his head. "That's all our Mexican contacts will allow. They say they're in charge of security and that they're doing us a favor by letting our guys tag along."

Renoir rubbed his eyes. "OK, Joe, what's in the news?"

"Everything's going China's way. Taiwan is mobilizing its forces against the State Department's advice. They're convinced after what happened in Orlando that the Chinese are going to attack." Joe looked around the table. "Taiwan is reaching a state of near hysteria. Virtually every commercial flight leaving the country is full. It'll take months to empty the waiting lists as they exist now, but that's not stopping people from trying to get off the island. The United Nations Security Council has called for a meeting to discuss the rising tensions, but China refuses to sanction it, saying they'll veto anything the United States attempts to do on behalf of its illegitimate partner. Satellite photos show Taiwan's military is standing up everything they've got."

"What does China say about the assassination attempt?"

Joe shook his head. "Nothing. They say their guy who came into the states is being detained at their embassy and that this guy Foo Yung was never part of the tour group."

Renoir looked around the table. "What's the assessment? What's our next step?"

Carlson spoke. "If China's president is killed, we've got the ingredients for a major conflagration. We estimate that Taiwan's forces will be mobilized completely within a week, and we know that China has its military poised to strike."

Renoir wrinkled his brow. "Why, if China is going to invade, would they let Taiwan mobilize? Wouldn't it be a heck of a lot easier if Taiwan wasn't ready for an attack?"

"I think it's like Rick says," said Carlson. "It won't matter as long as the U.S. military doesn't get involved."

"But we are involved. Three carrier battle groups are in the Strait or on their way. No one's gonna change that."

Carlson nodded. "You're right, for the moment. But remember why Rick said he had to go back to San Francisco. He's worried the Chinese may have learned how to predict earthquakes, and he thinks they might know that something big is about to hit California. If a large earthquake rocks the West Coast, Rick thinks public opinion would demand that we leave Formosa to take care of Americans. Not to mention that half the ships in the Formosa Strait are from southern California, and the crews would want to get back to their families."

Davis spoke up. "And without us there, maybe China won't have to take military action. Maybe they'll negotiate the arrangement they haven't been able to get up to now: immediate and unconditional reunification."

CHAPTER 7

John Kale spent the majority of his time in Mexico. The chaos and laid back culture synched with his character. Unattached and always available, he spoke Spanish reasonably well, loved the food, and had numerous friends and acquaintances. He knew Mexico City intimately, and he was the Bureau's first choice for jobs requiring cooperation with the police.

His team walked carefully through the areas where the Chinese president would visit. With one exception, the route provided adequate protection. They returned to police headquarters where their point of contact, Juan Miguel Gonzales, was waiting. Kale had worked with Gonzales before, and he was one of the relatively competent members of the city police force.

"Señor Kale," Gonzales said, "how was your trip?"

"Very good, Miguel. Your man here," Kale pointed to the young man standing next to him, "was kind enough to take us along the route planned for the president's visit."

"Yes, and what do you think?"

"Other than the reception at the mayor's house, we're pretty happy. We think where you plan to hold the reception is too open and too exposed. We especially don't like that you plan to let the Chinese president stand in plain view, waving to the crowd like a rock star with a bunch of fans in the audience."

Gonzales laughed. "Señor Kale, my friend. You know that the president's presence at the mayor's house will be a complete surprise, so we are not worried. No one will even know that he is coming. It will be a nice opportunity for Mexicans to see China's president. Besides," he said winking, "Mexico City is a safe place, and we must show the world that we are a civilized society."

Kale knew that he would get nowhere with the Mexican authorities. Nonetheless, he felt obliged to voice his concerns, and perhaps Gonzales would take precautions at the mayor's house based upon his team's assessment. "Of course, Miguel, of course." He found it within himself to conjure up a polite laugh and returned his host's smile.

***

Rick Starr stepped out of the Air Force C-21 with his one piece of carry-on luggage and was escorted to a door that would take him to the main concourse of the airport terminal. There, dressed in a black t-shirt and tan Capri's, her hair swept back, her skin perfectly tanned — or so it seemed to Rick — was Doctor Marly Cooper, waiting for him. *I could get to like San Francisco.*

***

Marly Cooper watched as passengers walked through the large exit leading from the gate area. When Rick emerged, she found herself suddenly feeling warm. Dressed in a dark green polo shirt and khakis, a day's growth of beard, his black hair combed straight back, Rick Starr looked very Italian and a little lost.

***

Rick walked up to Marly and shook her hand. "It's awfully nice of you to meet me at the airport."

"If I'm going to drag you three thousand miles across the country, it's the least I can do."

"Have you had a good day? Any luck replacing Doctor Chen?"

Marly was surprised he would remember what she thought she only mentioned in passing. "Yes, as a matter of fact, I have." She looked at Rick, and his expression told her that he was enjoying her company.

"So you found something significant. Something you think I should see," Rick said, steering their conversation to business.

"Yes. I'm hoping that you can help us find the resources to investigate a very unusual and what we believe to be unnatural phenomenon."

Rick raised his eyebrows. "What do you mean by unnatural?"

Marly shook her head. "You need to see it for yourself. That's why I asked you to come right away."

"Oh, and here I thought it was because you wanted to have lunch with me at Manuel's again."

***

John Kale was on the phone with his boss.

"OK, John, what's your prognosis? What does the director tell the president?" His boss was referring to Alex Petrosvilli, Director of the Bureau.

"China's president is toast. Getting to him would be a cakewalk. If someone wants to take him out, he's a gone-er — with a capital G."

There was a discernible groan at the other end of the line. Kale spoke again. "OK, it's not quite that bad. The authorities are counting on the fact that no one has been informed of the president's route, unless you count the several hundred underpaid police officers who are supposed to protect him. Even if all those guys do their job, once the president begins his trip, a Luddite could figure out which direction he's gonna go next."

"OK, I hear you. But for the record, what do I tell the director?"

Kale hesitated before he spoke. "Tell him to assume worst case."

***

Rick Starr kneeled and watched as Doctor Marly Cooper expertly worked her computer. He put his hand gently on her shoulder and rested his elbow on her desk. Marly's fingers ran across the keyboard effortlessly, and he looked with fascination as an animation showing what looked like a map of the world, subdivided into a series of large areas outlined in red, filled the screen.

"It's here," said Marly, pointing to the computer monitor, the largest that Rick had ever seen on a desktop. The world map was labeled with the various tectonic plates. "This tectonic plate," she pointed to the Nazca plate, "is technically part of the Pacific plate, and it's subducted under the South American plate." She ran her finger up and down the red boundary line separating the Nazca and South American plates.

"You've lost me on that one," said Rick.

"By subducted, I mean that it's pushed itself up underneath the South American plate. Because the density of an oceanic plate is greater than the density of a continental plate, the oceanic plate goes underneath, which causes a disturbance in the upper plate, in this case showing itself in the formation of the Andes Mountains."

"Oh, I see. And does subduction cause earthquakes?"

"It can," said Marly, "and it also causes volcanic activity when the subducted plate becomes deep enough. Since we see a significant level of volcanic activity in the Andes, we can assume that the subduction has progressed substantially. It may even be that whatever is bothering the Nazca plate is contributing to the recent volcanic activity there." She circled the Nazca plate with her finger for emphasis. "This is where the disturbances I told you about are happening."

Rick nodded. "Let me make sure I'm getting it. What you're saying is that you have this tectonic plate — the Nazca, which is really part of the Pacific plate, but in fact it's sort of separate..." Marly nodded to show that he had it right so far. "...and the Nazca plate is slipping underneath the South American plate..." Marly nodded again. "...and it's this plate..." He pointed to the Nazca, "...that has some sort of strange activity affecting it. Something unnatural that you're going to show me."

"Exactly," said Marly. "Now watch. I'm going to take you through the last four months of earthquake activity in this area." She typed on her keyboard, and the animation on the screen came to life.

Rick watched carefully, Marly sitting silently. Little red explosions blipped on the screen every time an earthquake of four or higher was recorded. The computer's clock clicked off in increments of fifteen minutes, and on average there was a red blip for every two to four clicks. The blips were randomly dispersed across the area on the screen, when a pair of red blips occurred almost simultaneously at the north and south ends of the Nazca plate, followed by a second pair on the east and west sides. He continued to watch, and the pairs of earthquakes, at regular intervals, slowly worked their way counterclockwise — equidistant from the adjacent pair — around the plate.

Rick looked at Marly. "Are you referring to the pairs of earthquakes on the perimeter of the Nazca plate?"

"Yes," said Marly. "Watch what happens when I isolate on those events. I'll have the timing data print with them."

The screen cleared, and Marly reran the sequence, beginning two months and a week ago. Pairs of earthquakes painted themselves on the screen, almost precisely on the red boundary line that made up the Nazca plate. "Today there are 25 pairs. I estimate that 27 pairs will complete the circle." Marly pointed to the numbers next to the red blips on the screen. "The earthquakes appear every two to three days. That means three to five days until what I don't know. But with events in the Bay Area seemingly occurring in response to these disturbances and maybe as a result of Coulomb stress transfer, if things continue..." She looked at Rick. "My colleagues and I don't think these are the work of Mother Nature."

"But you said they're earthquakes."

"I know I said that." She shook her head. "But it made me think about what you said. That maybe the Chinese have discovered something we don't know, about when and where an earthquake might occur. Maybe they saw this, this whatever it is."

Rick dropped his gaze to the floor. "So you're saying that these earthquakes could really be a disturbance of some kind, like a bomb?"

Marly shook her head. "A bomb, no. The international community monitors the nuclear test ban treaty with the international monitoring system, and it can detect explosions anywhere, even underwater. We hear depth charges going off during naval exercises. We can even hear whales sing. So not a bomb. But maybe something else?"

Rick stared at the Nazca plate on the screen for a full minute. "Have you ever changed a flat tire?"

"Sure," Marly said. "When you're a working girl who lives alone, you learn all that stuff."

"So tell me how you loosen the bolts on a tire that you want to remove from your car."

"You pick a bolt and loosen it. Then you go to the one on the opposite side and loosen it. And then..." Marly's voice dropped off. "I don't see what you're getting at."

"What if you wanted to loosen a tectonic plate so that it might move and cause a major earthquake, like in California? You could begin with a series of, let's call them disturbances for the moment, around the perimeter of a nearby tectonic plate, big enough that they cause the tectonic plate to shift." Rick looked at Marly. "You mentioned Coulomb stress transfer, how the stress from a disturbance in one area like down here, could be transferred and cause stress to build up here." Rick pointed first to the Nazca plate, then the Cocos plate, and finally at the San Francisco Bay region.

"Joe said something about some Chinese trawlers, four of them off the coast of Chile." Rick nodded his head. "And something about two more going through the Panama Canal. But that would have been days ago." He pulled out his cell phone and punched up a preset. "But how could they?" He did not even know how to finish the thought that provoked the question.

***

Ling Mao pulled into the line of cars waiting to go into Baja California. Doctor Chen was asleep. They'd be at the airport in Mexicali in a few hours, where they'd catch a plane to Guadalajara.

Agent Rupert Budowski pulled into line, a dozen or so vehicles behind the rental car carrying Doctor Chen. He dialed up his point of contact at the Bureau. "They're going into Baja. Am I supposed to let them continue across the border?"

"Direction's still the same, Rupe. Follow 'em till they get where they're goin'. Then call us."

"OK, but once they get across the border, it makes stopping them a lot harder because we've got to deal with the Mexicans."

"I know, but nothin's changed."

"All right. You'll need to get me across the border as soon as they go in. Otherwise, I'll never be able to keep up with them. The line's a mile long tonight — literally."

"No problema, man. I'm on the horn now with the Border Patrol. I'll have 'em push you through as soon as your buddy is on the other side."

"Ten-four," replied Budowski.

***

Joe Craxton sat at the table with Larry Davis and Denise Carlson. The cell phone in Joe Craxton's pocket rang. "Craxton here."

"Joe, this is Rick."

"Hey, Ricky baby." He smiled at his colleagues. "You better get back here soon, buddy. We just got word that the Chinese president's gonna be made into chop suey."

Rick heard the comment, but it did not register. "Yeah, great. Listen, remember those trawlers off South America you talked about when this whole thing first broke?"

"Oh, yeah. Some Chinese trawlers. What about them?"

"I need you to get me more information. Like what they're doing, how long they've been there, their current location. Routine stuff, but thorough."

"OK, I can do that. When do you need it for?"

"Now," said Rick. "I need it right away."

"I'll do it as soon as I'm finished with Larry and Denise..."

"Now," said Rick again. "Later won't cut it. Call me back in half an hour on my cellular with what you've got. Let me talk to Denise."

Craxton handed the phone to Carlson. "Gotta go. Rick needs something and wants to talk to you."

"What's up?"

"Two things. Doctor Cooper says that Chen told her his mother had a stroke and plans to fly back to China. Tell the FBI to intercept and pick him up. We've got a major problem back here in California, and I think Doctor Chen knows about it. I also need the information on the trawlers that Joe's going to get for me, and I need it yesterday. Can you get Larry to help him?"

"Can do." Carlson pointed at Larry Davis and then with her thumb in the direction where Craxton went.

Davis nodded and got up to find his colleague.

"What's this about the Chinese president?" asked Rick.

"Bureau says he's an easy target."

Rick nodded his head at the news. "Tell Renoir I'll be on my way back to D.C. after Joe calls and that I'm pretty sure I know what's going on out here in California. Not only that, it's a lot worse than we thought. We're going to need help from the big dogs on this one."

***

Rupert Budowski watched the car with Doctor Chen pass through the large gate leading into Mexico. He waited patiently for the Border Patrol, but the wait was not long. A man, dressed in dark green, approached his car and waved his arm to indicate that he should pull out of line and drive up to the gate.

***

Ralph Thiele and Beverly Duncan introduced themselves.

"I love Italian men," said Beverly, smiling. Rick nodded and smiled back. Beverly committed to a diet the day the earthquake hit, and the weight she was losing was already apparent. She was wearing makeup, too, the first time ever that Marly knew of. She felt a tinge of jealousy. *Ridiculous. He's divorced, anyway.*

"Beverly," said Marly. She cleared her throat.

"What? I'm just having some fun." Rick laughed and grinned. Marly frowned.

"What do you think?" asked Thiele. "Are you going to be able to get someone down there?"

"Down there? You mean on the bottom of the ocean?"

"Yeah. We need a submarine, one that's used to salvage ships." Thiele gave a diving motion with his hand. "I don't think these things are just earthquakes."

"What do you think they are?" asked Rick.

"I don't know. But to cause an earthquake that registers a four on the Richter, they've gotta be big."

"Like nuclear big?"

"Yeah," said Thiele, mulling over Rick's words. "Yeah, like a nuke. But these have to be real earthquakes. If someone was setting off nukes, we'd know it."

"I'm confused," said Rick. "They're either earthquakes or they're not. You're saying they are, but that they don't really act like they would if they were a natural phenomenon."

"If it makes you feel any better, we're confused, too," answered Thiele.

"Tell me," said Rick. "Is it theoretically possible that a tectonic plate could be loosened enough to make it drift and then crash into another plate, which could cause an earthquake someplace else? Or maybe cause a shift like you guys are seeing out here?"

"I don't think it's just theoretically possible, it's happening. After the last pair of earthquakes on the Nazca plate, we had an event north of the Bay Area in the wine country that registered over a five, plus another slip of almost three inches. We're going to get a massive earthquake if this keeps up. And we haven't even talked about tsunamis."

Rick's cellular rang. "OK, hold it." Rick looked at Marly. "Can you plot a couple of points for me on your monitor?"

"Sure."

"All right, Joe, give 'em to me." He passed the first set of coordinates to Marly. They plotted out just north of the latest red blip on the northwest side of the plate. "The second?" They plotted out just south of the blip on the southeast side. The third and fourth set of coordinates indicated the other trawlers were already in position where one might expect the next pair of earthquakes to occur.

"How long have they been in the general area?" He put his thumb up and nodded at his three colleagues. "Four months? What about the two trawlers that were waiting to get through the canal?" Rick paused. "One's still waiting? Where's the other one?" Rick read a set of coordinates to Marly, and she plotted it. "What else can you tell me about the trawlers?" He got a puzzled look on his face.

"They're whaling ships? I thought the Japanese and Norwegians hunted whales." He shook his head. "OK. Good job. I'm heading for the airport."

Rick closed his cell phone and shook his head. "They're whaling ships."

"Makes sense," said Thiele.

"It does?" asked Rick. "Why would you say that?"

"They have a big hold in the middle of the ship where they can pull in a whale for processing." He shrugged his shoulders. "It's also the right size for a small submarine. The trawlers could be ferrying small subs, and if they're deep sea submersibles, maybe the subs are involved somehow."

Rick shook his head. "That's an amazing theory." He looked at Marly and Beverly. "Can you actually see where the tectonic plates come together? On the ocean floor, I mean?"

"We can see where they come together at the San Andreas Fault.

So in general, the answer is yes."

"Does your monitoring system that listens for explosions ever go down for maintenance?" Rick looked at Thiele.

Thiele shrugged. "I suppose. But it's twenty-four seven, and I can't imagine it's ever down for more than a few hours at a time."

"Can you check it out?" asked Rick. "Like now?" He handed Thiele his cell phone.

"Let me call my office. They'll have to get some phone numbers for me." He left the room.

"All this theory seems to have been substantiated by Doctor Chen."

"Doctor Chen?" asked Marly. "Why Doctor Chen?"

"It's my guess that Doctor Chen has been in on this since the beginning. He's been the source of the expertise, convincing his colleagues that this stuff you're just finding out is possible." Rick looked at Marly. "Suddenly having a sick mother that requires him to return to China is too much of a coincidence. I've ordered the FBI to pick Chen up for questioning."

"But he's a naturalized citizen," protested Marly.

"Clearly not because he loves America," said Rick.

"How are you going to stop this?" asked Beverly. She pointed at the computer monitor. "It looks like two of the whaling ships are already in position to do more damage, and the other two are on the move."

"I don't know. What would you recommend?"

"We talked about it before you got here, and like Ralph said, we thought that salvage subs would be the way to go. But after this discussion, what good would they do? What do you think, Coop?"

"I think we need to do something about the trawlers."

"Maybe we take out the trawlers with the subs in them," said Rick, more to himself than the others.

Thiele walked back into the room, shaking his head. "This is odd. I just got word that the IMS has had connectivity problems with the Pacific hydrophones for the last three months. The lines have been going up and down, and no one has figured out why."

"The IMS?" Rick frowned.

"The international monitoring system," said Thiele. "It's been deaf for most of the last three months."

"So this means that someone could be exploding nuclear weapons on the ocean floor, and your system wouldn't hear them?"

Thiele rubbed his chin and thought for a moment. "I guess so."

Rick nodded. "They've been tickling the dragon's tail, and no one has heard a thing."

***

It was a madhouse. Rick landed and was met by John Renoir. Based on Rick's assessment of events in California, Renoir asked the secretary of defense to call an emergency meeting in the White House situation room. The national security advisor, the secretary of state, the FBI director, the military service chiefs, Renoir and Rick would be there. The meeting would begin at 2:00 AM. If justified, the president would be summoned.

Rick cringed at the thought of trying to explain to the group what he observed with Marly Cooper and her colleagues. He was sure that even if he could get everyone in the meeting to understand what he said, they still would not believe him. Now he wished he had Doctor Cooper along. "John, this isn't going to work. What I saw is too hard to explain without the animation."

"So draw a picture," said Renoir.

"OK. I'll draw a picture." Rick did not think it was a good time to tell Renoir that he almost failed art class in high school.

The secretary of defense called the meeting to order. "John asked me to call this meeting because of information his people have uncovered in California." The group turned toward Renoir, who smiled and nodded confidently. Rick's stomach tightened at the thought of speaking to this group of men. *What if the president wants to hear the explanation? Will I get my lips ripped off this time?*

"I have with me senior analyst Rick Starr, an expert on China, who was with us a few days ago when the whole Formosa affair was taking shape." The group turned its attention to Rick. He managed a weak smile. "At that time, we were concerned about identifying the triggers that might set off a Chinese invasion of Taiwan. Since then, the vice president of Taiwan has been shot by someone who we believe was brought into the United States by the Chinese.

"The shooting, in combination with our reporting on China's forces in Xiamen, has led Taiwan to declare a state of national emergency. They're mobilizing everything they've got, but as you well know, without our help they have little chance against a conventional attack from the mainland.

"Meanwhile, the Chinese president is in Mexico, and Alex — I don't pretend to speak for you — but our understanding is that your assessment of the situation in Mexico is that the president may be at significant risk." The FBI director nodded.

"We are now convinced that a second suspect — the defector from Taiwan who you remember we identified at our last meeting — will try to assassinate the Chinese president."

"You seem to be implying that China wants this defector to succeed," said the national security advisor.

"We believe he will make an attempt. We are skeptical he will succeed, but we have no way of knowing." Renoir waited for another question, but the group was quiet.

"Our analysis is that China will use the attempt on the life of its president to establish justification for invading Taiwan. The problem with this strategy is the presence of the United States military in the Formosa Strait. Our president has responded with a show of force that clearly indicates U.S. determination to ensure the continued independence of Taipei." He paused to give the group a moment to digest his words.

"To summarize, the Chinese leadership will have the motive to invade but no opportunity. If the threat of invasion is going to get them what they want, the U.S. military presence in the region has to be eliminated." He paused and then spoke slowly and deliberately. "We believe we have discovered how China plans to make our forces withdraw, without firing a single shot." Leaning over toward Rick Renoir whispered, "OK, it's over to you. You better be convincing." Rick looked back at Renoir swallowing, obviously nervous. "Draw a picture!" Renoir growled.

Rick Starr stood up to address the group. "It isn't going to be easy for me to explain what's causing the earthquakes in California. It's actually a fantastic story, and you need to understand that three of the foremost experts in the world on plate tectonics and the San Andreas Fault are the ones who made the discovery." Rick cleared his throat.

"A quick science lesson." He took a large piece of paper lying in the middle of the table and drew a circle. He drew a rough outline of the continents inside the circle. "This is a map of the earth. The earth's crust is not a single entity, but is actually made up of fourteen or so separate pieces, called tectonic plates. These plates float on top of the earth's core, which is made up of molten rock." Using dotted lines, Rick drew from memory the Pacific plate, the Nazca plate to its east, the Cocos plate just above the Nazca plate, and finally the North American plate.

"Each tectonic plate moves independently of the others. The plates might move apart, they might slide parallel to one another, or they might collide. This movement causes earthquakes." He looked at the group around the table. All of them were looking at his piece of paper.

"We believe that China is setting off a series of nuclear explosions around one of the plates." The entire group, all at once, looked at him. "The international underwater monitoring system uses hydrophones to monitor the nuclear test ban treaty." Rick chose his next words carefully. "The system has been intermittent for at least three months. In other words, the international monitoring system is deaf. There have been over fifty nuclear explosions in the Pacific Ocean, and the international community has not heard a thing." Rick looked at the faces in the group to gauge their reactions. Every expression was perfectly immobile. *Obviously the result of much practice*, thought Rick.

"The worldwide earthquake locator has recorded 25 separate pairs of earthquakes, all between 4 and 4.5 on the Richter scale, on the perimeter of this plate here." He pointed to the Nazca plate. "The seismologists believe that these earthquakes are causing stress, which is being transferred as a result of this plate moving." Rick pointed to the

Cocos plate. "The stress is accumulating on the San Andreas Fault in the San Francisco Bay area." He moved his finger up the paper to show how the stress might move from south to north. "When the stress finally releases, it will generate a massive and devastating earthquake."

"Whoa, whoa," interrupted the chairman of the joint chiefs. "How can the Chinese be involved?" He looked at the chief of naval operations. "Charlie, have you got reports of Chinese activity?"

The CNO shook his head. "Nothing's been reported to me."

"They're not using military hardware," Rick said. "They're using whaling ships that sailed through the Panama Canal. We believe the trawlers are hiding deep sea submersibles capable of planting nuclear bombs on the ocean floor between adjacent tectonic plates."

***

It's "Good Morning America" in downtown New York City. An attractive blonde fills the screen, reading from her teleprompter. "People continue to flee the Bay Area in growing numbers. In response to the demand for more seats, United, American and Delta airlines have increased the number of outbound flights and the capacity of their planes from both the San Francisco and Oakland airports. San Francisco's mayor has complained to California's congressional delegation about the airlines openly exploiting people's fears, and he has asked the city council to deny the airlines' request for additional flights. The mayor has again appealed to locals to refrain from leaving the city, but his appeal is falling on deaf ears. As more small businesses close temporarily for lack of employees and shoppers, the city's mayor has called for people from outside the region to consider a move to San Francisco. The governor, meanwhile, continues to support the rights of California citizens to follow their conscience." She turned to her colleague. "For more on this growing controversy, we go to Dave at the airport. Dave, what's this about the governor planning a trip out here to the east coast?"

CHAPTER 8

The group stood as the president walked in, dressed in a richly textured maroon bathrobe with the presidential seal over his left breast pocket. His casual dress was in direct contrast to the rest of the group, outfitted in dark suits and "Class A" uniforms, all with ties. "Sit down, gentlemen." The president sat at the head of the table and took a long drink of coffee from a cup placed at his seat. "I trust this is important, given the time of day." He held out his wrist and looked at his watch for effect. It was 3 AM. He took another swallow, set his coffee cup down and looked at the group, waiting for someone to begin.

"Mister President," started John Renoir. "CIA believes we have critical information that requires your immediate attention. If you agree with our assessment, we're asking your authorization to take appropriate action without further delay."

The president was silent.

Renoir repeated his analysis of events in Orlando and Mexico, and then turned the floor over to Rick.

"Mister President, we believe we have credible evidence showing that China is responsible for the events in San Francisco."

"You mean the earthquakes," the president said more than asked.

"That's right, sir. We believe that China, using small submarines housed in whaling ships off the coast of South America, is detonating nuclear bombs on the ocean floor with the intent of destabilizing the North American tectonic plate and ultimately causing an earthquake that will decimate California." Rick went through the identical explanation that he gave a half-hour earlier.

The president listened intently, his face registering amazement more than outrage. He leaned forward with his elbows on the table, hands folded, brow furrowed. "If this is true, it's quite extraordinary." He looked straight at Rick. "You're sure this is what's happening?" He gave a questioning look to Renoir.

"As sure as we can be under the circumstances."

"What does that mean? You're ninety-five percent sure? Ninety percent?"

"Sir, it's difficult to assign a probability. What we are saying is that the preponderance of evidence supports our assessment, and each new piece of evidence substantiates it further."

"Do you have independent confirmation from intel sources?"

"No, sir. Our humint sources have turned up nothing."

"Maybe there's nothing to turn up." The president sat back in his chair and crossed his arms. "If there is an earthquake, what would be the consequences?"

Rick spoke again. "My colleagues in San Francisco estimate that a great earthquake would cause tens of thousands of dead and injured, hundreds of billions in property damage, and millions left homeless. It has the potential to alter the underground water tables of the state of California and destroy its agriculture. With California producing over 10% of the U.S. gross domestic product and China holding a trillion dollars in treasury bills, we could find ourselves defaulting and negotiating a financial settlement with the very people who caused the catastrophe.

"An earthquake like this will create a disaster that exceeds the country's capacity to respond domestically or to sustain its foreign policy commitments. We believe that China's primary intent is to so overwhelm the United States that we will have no choice but to abandon the defense of Taiwan. This in turn presents them the opportunity to reunify the two Chinas, using force if necessary."

"All this is for reunification?"

"If it's an accurate assessment, it's much more than that," said the secretary of state. "It's energy. It's Central Asia. It's the Shanghai Cooperation Organization. China is all over Africa. South America. They still have the world's third largest economy, even with the global economic meltdown. This not only generates physical tectonic change, but it completely reorganizes the political geostrategic landscape — literally in the span of a few hours."

"If they TKO the American economy," added the national security advisor, "it means even more chaos. I'm sure the European Union would love nothing better than to see the euro become the number one global currency, or to combine it with the dollar in some way. And to prevent a complete collapse of the world economy they'd move fast with the support of all the big nations — China and Russia in particular. And maybe even us because we wouldn't be able to offer any alternative and would need the stability to recover."

"But they're integrating with the West," protested the president. "We buy more stuff from China than anybody else in the world. They signed an agreement with India to cooperate on energy. In ten years, 200 million Chinese will be morbidly obese. That's about as western as you can get. I am having great difficulty believing that this is China's intention, even with the evidence you've presented."

"This operation has been in motion for at least six years," said Rick. "The security is so tight, it's assessed as the work of a very select few in the government and the military."

"Do they even have enough nukes to do this? They used over fifty already? How many nuclear weapons does China have?" asked the president.

"Our estimates put the number at about two hundred," said Renoir. "And they're building more as fast as they can."

"All right. Let's assume for a moment that everything you just said is true. What is it you're asking me to do?"

Rick looked over at Renoir and then back at the president. "We need to stop the trawlers that house the submarines. The ones that are now moving into position, we need to keep them from delivering their payloads." He paused to let the president assimilate his meaning.

The president leaned forward again. "You're saying that we should sink them? Are they in international waters?"

"That would be an act of war," said the SecDef. "How can we be sure that this half-baked theory is even true? I mean, it's a science fiction story that we need time to check out."

"We don't have to sink them," said Rick, raising his finger to get the president's attention again. "We just need to disable them, make them dead in the water." He looked at the chief of naval operations. "To use nautical terminology." He looked back at the president. "We believe the submarines themselves are deep sea submersibles, which are small and have limited range. Without the trawlers, they can't get to their targets. As far as checking the story out, the consequences are too great to wait. We need to take decisive action, and quickly." Rick impulsively pounded the table with his fist to emphasize his point, startling the president and causing a secret service agent in the room to step forward. Renoir buried his face in his hands.

"That's awfully easy for you to say, what's your name, Mister

Starr?" asked the president.

Rick did not back down. "Yes, sir, you're right. It is easy for me to say. But I have seen the evidence firsthand, and I am convinced that my colleagues are right."

The president looked at his joint chiefs. "OK, gentlemen, if we decide to act as recommended by CIA, what can we do? What are the options?" He looked at his secretary of defense. "Jack, is there some way to disable the trawlers without sinking them?"

The SecDef turned to the CNO for an answer.

"I'll have to see if there's some way that our subs can torpedo the ships carefully. And I don't know how long it will take to get a sub into position. Where did you say the trawlers are? Off South America? There are only two attack submarines left on the West coast. We have half a dozen or so tied up doing oil security, and the rest we sent to Asia."

The Air Force chief of staff spoke up. "We've got harpoon missiles we can use to disable the ships. I suspect that we could reduce the weapon yields to where they wouldn't — to the best we could determine, anyway — where they would not sink the trawlers." He looked at the president. "Using B-52 aircraft we could have bombs on target in 24 hours best case, 48 hours max."

"That sounds like the best option for now," said the president. He addressed his secretary of defense again. "I want you to consult with the attorney general for a finding on whether or not China's actions and our response constitute an act of war, and I want this all done without any fanfare or leaks to the press. God only knows what CNN or Fox News would do with this. If what CIA says is true, I don't think we're going to get a lot of protest from the Chinese, even if we sink their ships. So let's get this cranked up and get a plan into place." He turned his attention to the Air Force chief of staff. "Jerry, I want this done quietly. Use your best. One crew, one plane if possible."

"Yes, sir. I've already got in mind the unit that we'll use. It's one of the best."

"You didn't hear me, Jerry. I didn't say 'one of the best'. I said 'the best'."

"Yes, sir," replied the Air Force chief. "I was trying to be modest. It's my best."

"This is no time for modesty. If we're gonna kick ass, then I want to do it wearing steel tipped boots."

The president stood up, and the group stood with him. "We meet again this afternoon in twelve hours. I want a full report of where we are and what we plan to do. I also want a clearer picture of what CIA showed me this morning before I make a final decision." He looked at the group. "And the next time we meet at 3 AM, I expect all of you to be dressed appropriately!"

Rick was elated, but he did not show it. He was convinced there would be a decision to take action, and although it might not necessarily prevent an invasion of Taiwan, it would save American lives, protect the already struggling American economy, and keep America's military presence in the Formosa Strait a factor in China's calculus.

***

Marly Cooper plotted the coordinates of the trawlers as they were passed to her by Joe Craxton. Rick swore her and her colleagues to secrecy and she felt, for the first time, the thrill of being part of a surreptitious plan to thwart bad people who wanted to do bad things. *This could be addictive*, she thought.

Two trawlers were already in position over the edge of the Nazca plate, and she expected that there would be two events shortly. They could not stop this pair of explosions, she knew, but maybe the next. Marly also plotted the coordinates of the trawler that came through the Panama Canal on the previous day, as well as a sixth trawler which just entered the Canal. She pondered why the first trawler that came through the Canal headed south.

***

Federal agent Rupert Budowski answered his ringing cell phone. "Rupe here."

"Rupe, this is Howey. Where ya at?"

"Oh, about forty miles on the other side of the border. I think that these guys are headin' to Mexicali, my guess'd be to catch a plane. Why, something change?"

"Yep. Just got the call that we're to pick your two boys up. We're in touch with the Mexican authorities tryin' to arrange some help. Plan is that they'll stop 'em, and you'll cuff 'em and bring 'em back home. Think you can handle it?"

"Sounds pretty routine. You think the Mex's will be that cooperative? That hasn't always been my experience, you know."

"We've told 'em this one is national security stuff, and they've agreed to cooperate. I'll give ya a call when we hear back where they're gonna stop 'em."

Budowski sighed. "OK, Howey. Just keep me posted. Meanwhile, I'll keep my distance and stay out o' sight."

***

The White House situation room was full. People Rick had never seen before crowded in. He wondered if the president's directive for "no leaks to the press" could hold up in a mob like this. He was seated in the chair next to the one John Renoir would occupy, who was over talking to the secretary of defense. Unhappy and showing it, the SecDef still was not convinced they had enough evidence to proceed as Rick proposed.

The president walked in. He was wearing his maroon bathrobe from the night before, and even the normally staid faces of the group registered their surprise. The president shed his robe at his chair, revealing a dark pinstriped suit. "You guys aren't very good at following orders." Everyone laughed.

The president sat down and motioned for the group to sit with him. He looked around the table, nodding and smiling at people he recognized. "OK, Jack," he directed his comment to the SecDef, "what have you got to report?"

"Well, sir," he began, "I'm still not convinced that we have enough evidence to warrant action, and neither does the attorney general."

"Why isn't he here?" interrupted the president.

"Sir, he's going to try to come later. He's been delayed."

"OK. Go on."

"Sir, the attorney general says that firing on the Chinese trawlers would unequivocally be an act of war."

"What did he say about the possible nukes China is setting off and the effect that they're having on the California coast? What was his assessment of that?"

"He said that the nuke business is a violation of the nuclear test ban treaty, but since China has never signed it — and for that matter neither have we — it's nasty business, but not an act of war. I didn't talk to him about California."

The president did not hesitate to show his annoyance. "Jack, that's the most important question. China may have already committed an act of war by attempting to destabilize the North American continent."

"Sir, I don't think we've established that yet."

"Jack, I think you're the only one at this table convinced that it's out of the realm of the possible."

"Mister President," said the SecDef, his voice becoming more deliberate and emphatic, "I've conferred with the experts on my staff, and they tell me that there has never been a single reported case where a nuclear explosion has caused an earthquake. Never."

"Sir," Rick Starr interrupted the president. The president looked down the table.

"What?" he barked.

John Renoir tried to make himself smaller.

Rick did not let the president's tone of voice cower him. *After all, didn't he just ask me what I want to say?* "Sir, this morning we've had two more simultaneous explosions as predicted, on the Nazca plate, each just under 4.5 magnitude on the Richter scale, and two of the Chinese trawlers were at those exact coordinates just hours before they occurred. The result has been another three-inch shift to the north of the entire San Francisco Bay Area. We believe that this latest pair of seismic events confirms our assessment."

"John?" the president asked Renoir. "You still believe this assessment is accurate?"

Renoir looked up. "Yes, sir, and we have the pictures you asked for that show exactly what happened, when it happened, and where it happened." He looked over at the SecDef. "I'm more convinced than ever that our assessment is on the mark."

"All right. I am inclined to believe, no matter how extraordinary or irrational its actions may seem, that China is involved in events on the floor of the Pacific Ocean, and I'm ready to take action." The president looked directly at his SecDef. "Having said that, Jack, what are the options?"

The SecDef made it clear that he was not pleased. "We've got three attack subs on their way to South American waters, the two we held back and a third that we diverted from Formosa. All three are days out. The quickest response is to use an Air Force B-52 bomber carrying harpoon missiles. We asked engineers to lower the yields on the missiles as you directed, and we loaded eight harpoons into a B-52 at Fairchild Air Force Base, Washington. The plane's crew is standing by. They are the best and most experienced aircrew the Air Force has available.

"The plan is to launch the plane and have the crew open a sealed flight plan once airborne. They will be met by tankers and air refueled off the coast of southern California. They will then fly their mission and fire one harpoon, two if necessary, at each trawler with the intent to disable the rudder system. They will be met by two tankers en route back to the United States for another air refueling. After landing at Fairchild, we will debrief the crew. The mission is classified Top Secret." He took a deep breath. "Our subs will continue their journey to the south for follow-up operations if needed."

"I thought there were six trawlers."

"Yes, sir," said Rick. "We'll intercept and quarantine the sixth as it exits the Panama Canal, and we're currently tracking the fifth, which is heading south. It's unclear whether these ships are related to the other four."

"OK," said the president. "When do we launch the B-52?"

"Sir, we suggest that the crew launches so they arrive at their first target when it's dark," said the Air Force chief of staff. "We believe it's best they fly the attack portion of the mission under cover of darkness."

"Agreed. What time will I be briefed on the mission's success?"

"Sir," said the SecDef. "We ought to have the results no later than ten hundred tomorrow. I suggest we convene at noon for a full mission debrief."

The president stood up, and the rest of the room stood with him. "If anything goes wrong on this mission, if the pilot sneezes when he's firing his missiles, I want to know. And I don't want to hear a word about any of this from the media."

"Sir," said the Air Force chief. "The entire mission will be flown comm-out. Not a single radio transmission will take place once the aircraft departs the runway, until it's back in the traffic pattern at Fairchild."

"Fine. I leave the details to you. I just want to know that the results were 100% successful."

"Sir, normally..." began the Air Force chief.

"I don't want normally!" snapped the president. "I want perfect! If this crew can't deliver, get me one that can. We won't have a second chance to fly this mission." He looked around the table. "See you tomorrow at noon."

***

Marly Cooper plotted the latest position of the trawlers. They showed one pair departed the location of the most recent detonations, and the other two were moving into place for the very last pair of events. *What was Rick up to? Why didn't he call?*

She plotted the coordinates of the ship sailing to the south. She drew a line from the previous set of coordinates through the current ones and projected its course down to the Antarctic. The line went straight through the upper left corner of the lower right panhandle of the Nazca plate. She cocked her head to one side and stared blankly at the computer monitor's screen. The phone rang.

"This is Doctor Cooper."

"Marly?"

It was Rick. "I was getting worried. What happened?"

"Good news. The president has ordered the military to stop the trawlers."

"What do you mean? Sink them? What about the submarines?"

"I can't really tell you," said Rick. "Just trust me when I say that by tomorrow morning, China won't be nuking the bottom of the ocean any longer."

"OK," said Marly. "But the course of the trawler heading south bothers me. Its track takes it right through a funny place on the Nazca plate."

"Funny? What do you mean?"

"I don't know what I mean. It just seems odd that its course would take it precisely, and I mean exactly, through the very corner of the panhandle of the plate." Marly ran her finger over the display on the screen. She could feel goose bumps forming on her arms. "I wish you were here," she blurted. "I mean, I think you should see this in person. It's too hard to explain over the phone."

"I should be there in a day or so. You can show me what you have, and maybe we can determine if its actions are related to the others."

Rick hung up the phone. He noticed that he felt energized after talking with Marly.

***

Agent Rupert Budowski looked up ahead at the flashing blue and red lights. He watched the car carrying Doctor Chen slow down, its brake lights filling the late afternoon dusk. There were three police cars, the *Federales*, blocking both lanes, stopping cars and checking their occupants. Budowski pulled out his cell phone and dialed his contact.

"Howey, this is Rupe. It looks like the Mex's got a roadblock set up to corral Doctor Chen just down the road from my location. Have you gotten a call?"

"You gotta be kiddin'. No, they never called. Stay on the line, and I'll find out what's goin' on."

***

Ling Mao slowed as he approached the flashing lights and pulled into the line of waiting cars. He noted that there were three cars and six officers.

Doctor Chen woke up when the car stopped. "What is the problem?" he asked in English.

Ling Mao shook his head. He wondered for a moment if the police were looking for them. *It is not possible.* Still, he felt for the Uzi under the front seat, and he positioned it where he could get to it quickly.

***

"Rupe?"

"Yeah, Howey, I gotcha. Go ahead."

"The Mex's say they don't know what this roadblock is about. They say they're still working your case and will get back to me when they have something set up."

"OK, Howey. But it looks kinda strange. They look like they're searching for someone. You sure you spoke to the right people?"

"Ten-four on that, Rupe. Hang loose. I'll get back to you."

"Ten-four, Howey. Talk to you later." He hung up his cellular, knowing that the Mexican police set up random roadblocks for any number of reasons, including looking for drugs and fugitives. He decided he better be ready to intervene.

***

Lieutenant Colonel Rich Ellis sat in base operations with his crew at Fairchild Air Force Base, Washington. They were waiting for the operations group commander, Colonel Steve Rader, to brief them on why they were called to report to the flight line with their flying gear. Lieutenant Colonel Ellis was old enough to have sat alert during the Cold War in the early days of his flying career, waiting to take off and obliterate the Soviet Union at a moment's notice, but he had never been part of a short-notice mission like this. He watched his gunner buy candy bars from the vending machine and stuff them into the leg pockets of his flight suit. They all suspected this flight would be a long one, since the flight kitchen provided them with two box lunches each. It was clear they would be flying, but strange they were not asked to plan the mission. Maybe that was next. In walked Colonel Rader, alone.

"Rich, how ya doin'?" asked the operations group commander.

"Great, Colonel Rader. How are you?" He looked past the colonel for his squadron commander.

"Doin' good, doin' good. Got your whole crew here?" He looked around the room and counted five more crew members before taking the young lieutenant colonel by the arm and pulling him over to one side.

"Yes, sir. We're all here and ready to do our mission planning. I've asked the radar nav to get charts for worldwide coverage, so we're pretty much ready for anything."

"There won't be any mission planning, Rich."

Ellis let the surprise show on his face. "Sir, the regs require all flights to be planned by the crews that are going to fly them." He was telling the colonel the obvious, but as the senior B-52 pilot on the base and chief of standardization and evaluation, he felt he needed to quote the flying regulations.

"I know, Rich. But this mission is classified Top Secret, and the only three people who know that are you, me and the wing commander. That's why no one else is here to send you off. The flight's been planned in Washington by someone a lot higher up in the food chain than you and me, and all I have for you is a sealed envelope. The only one who's seen the contents of this package is the wing commander, and he's been called to Washington to debrief the secretary of defense after you guys get back." He handed Ellis a thick, sealed manila folder. "The entire mission is in here. Maps are included, but you better take those charts your radar nav picked up in case you need them. I don't know what this is about, but it's important."

Lieutenant Colonel Ellis took the folder, turning it over in his hand. "Can we open it and get our bearings before takeoff?"

"No. You're going to take off and fly the Spokane Two departure. Once airborne, you'll go comm-out and remain comm-out until you get back here and request entry to the traffic pattern. Your navigators can open the package on climb-out and direct you to the proper altitude and heading. You'll use SATCOM with encrypted text to report your progress to me here in the command post. I've been told that you have complete authority to do whatever's required to complete the mission, including deviating from the flight plan. You'll have a special squawk for your transponder to give you priority handling by air traffic control."

"Sir, I thought you said we were going to be comm-out."

"You are. I'm just telling you that with the squawk you'll be using, ATC will get everyone and everything out of your way."

"Sir, is there a chance that we might not make it back?"

"Rich, I've told you everything I know about the mission. You've been chosen because you and your crew are the best. So do us proud."

"Sir, can we call our wives?"

"No. I'll do that. From here on out, you're on mission. The crew bus is outside waiting to take you to the aircraft." He put his arm around Ellis and escorted him back to where the rest of his crew waited. "I tried to put myself on the flight with you, but they said under no circumstances would anyone other than the crew be present on the plane." He turned to face the pilot. "Brief your crew at the aircraft. You've got an hour and a half before takeoff, so you need to get on the stick. I know that we've loaded harpoons on board, but that's all I know. I don't know what you'll be doin' with 'em, but I suspect that you'll be shooting something. Good luck." He shook Ellis's hand.

Ellis looked at the colonel. "Thanks, Colonel. We won't let you down." He picked up his flight gear. "Let's go, guys!" he shouted to his crew. "Crew bus is waiting outside!"

The crew's radar navigator, Lieutenant Colonel Tom Wilkie, walked up. "Hello, Colonel Rader. Aren't we gonna plan this thing, Rich?"

"Nope. We'll talk about what we're doing once we get out to the aircraft. Let's get everyone on the bus. C'mon, Chief, we're runnin' late. Let's get our stuff loaded."

Colonel Rader stepped outside and watched the crew board the bus. Lieutenant Colonel Rich Ellis sat in the front seat and returned the colonel's eye contact, nodding. As the bus pulled away from the curb, Colonel Rader saluted his younger counterpart.

Lieutenant Colonel Ellis returned the salute. His hands trembled.

CHAPTER 9

The aircraft commander, pilot, navigator, radar navigator, gunner, and weapons systems officer headed for the parking location occupied by the Boeing B-52 Flying Stratofortress. The crew did not indulge in its normal puerile antics, but instead rode to the plane in silence, digesting the hard reality that this mission would be operational. Lieutenant Colonel Rich Ellis, the aircraft commander, was the most somber of the group, knowing the mission was classified and appeared to involve actual combat. The rest of the crew could only guess at the importance of the flight.

Ellis sat deep in thought, his mind on his wife Mary Lou and events of the morning. He got up early as usual. He intended to climb back into bed before his wife awoke, but she got up before he expected and got the kids off to school early. "Will you go back to bed with me?" he asked, after the last of their clan went out the door.

"No," she answered. "I'm up for the day."

He sighed. It had been weeks since they had sex, and his wife was avoiding him. From his point of view, this minor episode marked one more incident of rejection, another missed opportunity to build the kind of intimacy that he craved, all the while refusing to acknowledge the kind of intimacy that his wife longed for. He found himself thinking of sex all the time, and he did not like some of the thoughts that were creeping into his mind. He knew that his wife was not happy with their relationship, but having even that knowledge did not slow the downward spiral that engulfed it. They subsequently argued, and he left without a good-bye, welcoming the unexpected call to report to base operations with his flying gear.

But this mission? Classified and with live harpoons? This is more than I need right now. Damn it, Mary Lou. Why so much conflict? What are the chances we won't see each other again to make things right? Ellis had similar doubts about returning home before he went to the Gulf back in 1991 and again in 2003. He shook his head, trying to make the thoughts of disaster go away. He was glad he would soon have other things to worry about. Urgent things to occupy his mind, leaving little room or time to concern himself with anything other than "the mission".

"OK, guys, listen up," Ellis said. "Our flight today is classified Top Secret. I don't know much about it other than we'll be comm-out from after takeoff until it's over and we're back in the traffic pattern. We'll have a special squawk with ATC that pretty much lets us do whatever we want. We have live harpoons on board." He paused to see his crew's reaction. They were all stone-faced. "We're gonna fly the Spokane Two departure, and once we're airborne, Tom, you and Bob will need to open the mission package." He tossed the envelope given to him by Colonel Rader over to his radar navigator. "You'll tell the rest of us where we're going and why we're being sent off on short notice with so little information. Colonel Rader says we can't open the package until after we're airborne." He took note of the questioning look on Tom Wilkie's face and shook his head. "He said don't open it, so we won't."

"Colonel," said the gunner, "if this mission is so flippin' important, why didn't anybody come see us off? Where's the wing king? Where's the squadron commander? Shouldn't your wives been told?"

"Since we're in complaining mode, I don't like flying when we haven't mission planned," chipped in the radar navigator. "Ever since a Fairchild crew went down in Arizona back in the eighties while flying low level, every flight's supposed to be completely planned. Besides, I don't like us not being prepared for what's ahead. How are we going to drop live harpoons when we don't even know where we're going?"

"Sounds cool to me," said Jimmy Blase the pilot, who would fly the right seat up front with Ellis. "This is why I joined the Air Force. Heck with the mission planning. Let's just go out and do our thing..."

"All right," Ellis cut in. "I'm not happy that we're not planning this mission, either, but Jimmy's got the right attitude. We've flown together a hundred times, we've flown harpoon sorties at least a dozen times, and there's not much that we haven't seen. We were chosen for this mission because we're the best crew on the base, and I think we're the best in the Air Force. As for anybody sending us off, the mission's classified. The wing commander is in Washington with the politicians, and the squadron commander doesn't even know that we've been tasked to fly. The only one who knows about the mission is Colonel Rader, and even he doesn't know the details. So relax. Let's do our jobs like we always do, and everything's going to be fine." He looked out the window and spoke quietly under his breath. "Just fine, Mary Lou, just fine. I'll be back home soon, and we can work on our problems."

"You better quit talkin' to yoreself, Colonel, or I'll have to report you to mental health so they can pull you offa the personnel reliability program," said the gunner.

"OK, Chief, you do that, and I'll let 'em know about all the beer you drink after every flight," replied the colonel.

"Hey, flyin' with the likes o' you guys would make any truly sober individual drink to excess."

"I'll drink to that," laughed Jimmy Blase.

The weapons systems officer, or "wizzo" as he was called, had picked up the secrets bag and thumbed through the list of call signs for the day. "I hope it's an omen. Our call sign for this mission is 'Paydirt'."

***

Ling Mao watched the car in front of him closely. The driver handed the police officer what appeared to be the car registration. The officer looked at it briefly, handed it back, then waved him through.

Perhaps the police are looking for a stolen car, he thought. He glanced down to make sure the Uzi was not visible and pulled the rental contract from the glove compartment. Doctor Chen followed Ling Mao's look downward, and he saw the weapon for the first time. The expression on his face spoke for him. "Don't worry. I won't use it unless I have to," Ling Mao said in Chinese.

Ling Mao was assigned to the Chinese embassy in Mexico City for two years and spoke perfect Spanish. He was familiar with the arbitrary nature of street justice in Mexico, and he would be ready to deal with any renegade police officers swiftly and without hesitation. His assignment was to return Doctor Chen safely home, and he would let no one get in the way.

***

The B-52 crew on flight "Paydirt-zero-two" went through its preflight checklists. Rich Ellis completed the outside walk-around, ensuring that everything on the plane was normal and in operating order. He preferred to say that things were in order rather than that they appeared normal. The BUFF, short for Big Ugly Fat Fella, was such an odd-looking airplane that there was little normal about it. Its long fuselage of almost 160 feet was too thin, its drooping wings that spanned 185 feet while hanging over forty feet from the top of its fuselage to the ground were too wide, its vertical tail was too tall, and its horizontal stabilizer was too broad. Eight engines hung in pairs of two under the wings. Its appearance was that of a gangly adolescent that had not grown into its limbs. The plane was the workhorse of the Vietnam War and the Cold War. There were only fifty-six left on active duty out of the original 744 that were built. Some aircrew members in the seventies had declared the B-52 unsafe to fly and yet here he was thirty years later, still flying the same airframe. It was spooky to be piloting a plane that was more than half a century old. He gave a last look and then stooped over, climbing up into and through the hold that led to the cockpit.

The pilots and gunner sat in the cockpit, while the two navigators and the electronic warfare officer sat downstairs. The gunner used to sit in the tail of the airplane with his guns, but the G and H models of the B-52 gave the gunner remote access to his weapons from the cockpit and a view of the airspace behind the plane through a camera. Crewmembers in the cockpit ejected up and out the top of the plane in the event of an emergency, while the three navigators ejected downward. The ejection sequence was an odd arrangement, but one that made sense when the aircraft was first designed in the 1950s as a high-altitude bomber.

Jimmy Blase sat in the right seat, going through the checklist that would place all the plane's switches into the correct position for the preflight. He came to the standardization and evaluation branch just a year ago, but he was the best right-seater that Ellis had ever flown with. Ellis climbed into his seat and pulled open the left-side window to let in some air. The two pilots went through their preflight together quickly and flawlessly.

It was a clear day with cool temperatures, so the takeoff data was uncomplicated. The plane's computer calculated the takeoff numbers and Ellis turned S-1, referred to as the "go/no-go" speed, and the "rotate" speed over in his mind to make sure they stuck. He was surprised the plane did not have a full load of JP-4 onboard. That meant a reduced-thrust takeoff, and he suspected they would be meeting a tanker shortly after getting airborne. He listened to the radio to see if there was a tanker crew preflighting, but they were the only plane on the flight line actively preparing to fly. Either he guessed wrong and this would be a very short flight, or the tanker would be coming out of another location. Given the mission was classified, he supposed it was the latter.

"Checklist complete," said the pilot into his interphone. "Standing by for engine start."

"Roger that," replied Ellis.

"Gunner's checklist complete, Colonel."

"Copy, Chief. How are the rest of you guys doing?"

***

Ling Mao pulled his car up to where the police officer was standing. The officer appeared surprised to find two Asians on the road to Mexicali. "Give me your registration," he demanded in English.

Ling Mao handed him the rental contract. "This is a rental car," he replied in Spanish. "We picked it up in California. We have authorization from the rental company to drive into Mexico."

"You'll have to get out of your car," the officer said, switching to Spanish.

"Why?" asked Ling Mao. "We are merely passing through the area. I work at the Chinese embassy in Mexico City, and I can show you our papers if you like." He was given diplomatic passports for both Chen and himself.

The officer was undeterred. "Señor, you will have to get out of your car. We need to search it."

"I demand to speak to your supervisor."

The officer laughed. "I have no supervisor. I am the *jefe* here, and I said to get out of your car." He touched the handle of his pistol with his right hand, still holding the rental contract, and motioned to one of the other officers behind him to come over to the vehicle.

Doctor Chen was getting visibly nervous. Ling Mao put his hand on Chen's arm to calm him. "We are not getting out of the car," Ling Mao said emphatically to the police officer. "You will have to call your station chief and ask him to come here. Only then will we cooperate."

***

Agent Rupert Budowski could see that things were not going well for Doctor Chen. He dialed up his contact. "Howey, this is Rupe. We've got problems. This area is known for runnin' drugs, and the Mex's don't seem too happy to see a couple of Chinese boys in a fancy car. It looks like there's going to be trouble. Can you intervene somehow?"

"You gotta be kiddin'. It would be hard enough in the states to find someone to call. To intervene down there would be nothing short of a miracle. Aren't you able to do something?"

Budowski swore under his breath. "I don't like this ad hoc stuff, Howey. I told you guys we'd have problems once we crossed the border. I'll try to take Chen and his driver into custody now. This isn't going to be easy, you know."

"I know," said Howey. "Give it a whirl. If it don't work out, we'll get 'em farther down the road."

Agent Budowski got out of his car and called out to the police officer standing at the window of Ling Mao's vehicle. "Officer," he called in Spanish to get his attention. The officer turned. Budowski flashed his badge. "I'm an FBI agent from the United States. Can I talk to you for a moment about the men in that car?"

***

Ling Mao looked into his rearview mirror when the officer turned to his right, and he saw the man in the car behind him stand up and hold something out for the officer to see. The man was talking, but Ling Mao could not hear his voice, and he did not like it when the police officer walked away from his car to speak with him.

"They know," said Chen, who had turned and was looking out the back window. "That man was waiting out in front of my house in his car when you picked me up."

Mao stared at the mirror intently, watching the men talk. He turned his attention to the second police officer standing by his window, who was gazing absentmindedly at the car behind them. In a single motion, Ling Mao had the Uzi out and pointed at the man's chest. He pulled the trigger and released it quickly. Three bullets leaped from the Uzi's barrel and drove the officer to the ground. Ling Mao slammed the accelerator to the floor, tires squealing, slicing his way between the two police cars parked in front of them. The car fishtailed, but quickly straightened. No one returned fire. Doctor Chen looked back. Mass confusion filled their wake.

"How will we get back to China now? Everyone will be looking for us!" said Doctor Chen in Chinese. He switched to English. "You should not have brought that weapon with you."

Ling Mao did not answer. He pulled a cellular phone from his pocket and dialed up the Chinese embassy in Mexico City. "We can't drive to Mexicali. Our escorts will have to meet us outside the city limits and take us in. We've run into trouble, and the police will be looking for us." He listened for a moment. "We have a rental car, and the authorities kept the contract…yes, I know the place. OK, they should flash their lights to identify themselves."

***

Agent Rupert Budowski looked over upon hearing the burst of shots from what sounded like a machine gun, coming from the car that held Doctor Chen and his driver. He watched the police officer standing by the driver's window collapse to the ground clutching his side, the others nearby leaping to the pavement to avoid the same fate. Car wheels shrieked, and the vehicle containing Doctor Chen wove its way between two parked police cars and fled into the increasingly gray weather. Budowski stood dumbfounded. The police officer talking to him ran to his fallen colleague. Budowski dialed up his point of contact.

"Howey, Rupe here. We have a situation…yeah, a really big problem."

***

The crew called its checklists complete. "How long till takeoff?" Ellis asked his navigator on interphone.

"Thirty minutes."

"Roger copy. 'Engine start' checklist."

The pilot switched on the rotating beacons to alert the flight line that they were about to fire up the engines. "Ground, Paydirt-zero-two starting engines," he called into his radio.

"Roger, zero-two, call ready to taxi," replied the ground controller.

"Zero-two wilco."

"Crew chief, this is the aircraft commander," Ellis said into his interphone. "We're ready to start engines."

"Roger, sir," the crew chief replied in a muffled voice, his mouth encompassed by the rounded cup designed to minimize engine noise. "You're cleared on number eight."

Ellis and his right-seater started the aircraft's eight engines. All systems were go. The pilot brought the generators on-line, and Ellis cleared the crew chief to remove external power from the aircraft.

"Sir, you want me to pull the pins on the harpoons?"

Ellis cringed at his mistake. "You got ahead of me, sir," said Jimmy Blase.

"Roger, pull the pins," Ellis said. Pulling the pins would arm the ship-killers. They were ready to rock and roll.

"Got 'em, sir," said the crew chief. "You're cleared to close the bomb bay doors. I'm going off interphone."

"Roger that. I owe you one."

"Anytime you wanna buy me a beer, sir, I'll be around." His interphone clicked off.

"Bomb bay doors," read Captain Blase, continuing the checklist.

"Close," said Ellis. The pilot flipped a switch, and the doors thumped closed.

"Engine start checklist complete."

"Taxi checklist," said Ellis.

Blase keyed his radio. "Ground, Paydirt-zero-two requesting taxi to runway two-three."

"Roger zero-two, you're cleared to taxi as requested. Hold short of the runway."

"Zero-two wilco." Blase looked at his aircraft commander and keyed his interphone. "Crew, we're cleared to taxi to runway two-three."

Ellis gave a thumbs-up to the crew chief, who ran under the plane and pulled the wheel chocks. The crew chief ran out to the front of the plane and signaled the aircraft commander that he was cleared to begin his taxi. The giant B-52, its wingspan so large that small landing gear were attached to the end of the wings so they would not scrape the tarmac, pulled out of parking straight ahead and turned to the right at the taxiway. The crew chief stood and saluted. Ellis returned his salute, and the crew chief pointed down the taxiway. Ellis gave him another thumbs-up. "All right, guys, this is it," he said on interphone. "Say something now, or forever hold your peace. We're on our way, and there ain't no turning back."

The gunner ripped open the wrapper of one of his candy bars. "Don't worry, Colonel. This mission is gonna be a regular *tour de force*. I can feel it. We're all gonna be heroes by the time we hit the traffic pattern."

"A *tour de force*?" laughed Blase. "You sound like a cultured human being, Chief. I thought you enlisted guys avoided culture."

"Culture's my middle name, Cap'n," replied the gunner, "with a capital K. I can order a beer and ask where the bathroom is in a dozen foreign languages."

***

Two of the *Federales* jumped into their police cruiser, turned on its top lights, and sped away after their unseen quarry. Agent Budowski climbed tiredly back into his car and followed. Having lost the element of surprise, the operation was degenerating into a goose chase. Budowski grew up on a farm, and he knew way too much about chasing geese to like it. He hung up on his point of contact.

***

"Paydirt, this is Romeo."

The pilots looked to their left. Romeo was the call sign for the supervisor of flying, and he was calling for permission to take a last-minute look at the plane and check for loose panels, dripping fluids, or smoke coming from the aircraft or its engines. Romeo would be another aircraft commander, who shared intimate familiarity with the outside of the aircraft and its many peculiarities.

"Roger, Romeo," said Lieutenant Colonel Ellis. "You're cleared in for a quick look. We're in a hurry."

"Roger. This will only take a second."

"Two minutes till takeoff," said the navigator on interphone.

"Stand by," replied the aircraft commander. He watched Romeo's truck circle the front of the plane from left to right.

He disappeared behind the plane and pulled up a moment later just ahead of the left wing. He gave Ellis a thumbs-up. "You look good, zero-two. Go ahead and get outta here."

"Thanks, Romeo. See you when we get back." Ellis switched to interphone. "Takeoff checklist."

"Ground, Paydirt-zero-two going to tower." Jimmy Blase switched the radio frequency to channel two. "Tower, Paydirt-zero-two requesting clearance for on-time takeoff."

"Roger, zero-two, Tower. Taxi into position and hold for clearance." Ellis taxied the BUFF onto the runway, the "twelve thousand foot remaining" marker off to the right. Fifteen seconds passed. "Zero-two, you are cleared for immediate takeoff, Spokane Two departure. Contact ATC after airborne. Good luck."

"Zero-two wilco, tower. See you guys later." Jimmy Blase

switched to interphone. "Landing lights."

"On."

"Flaps coming to twenty. Sir, I'll take the throttles."

"Roger."

"Takeoff checklist complete."

"Roger. Say S-1 and rotate speeds."

***

Colonel Steve Rader watched the B-52 as it sped down the runway. It never rotated, instead lifting off the runway nose-down, the only airplane in the world to take off with a negative flight attitude. The aerodynamics worked, but they broke all the rules, and it took practice getting used to. The Buff, its drooping wings giving it the appearance of a giant eagle, raised its flaps and gear and slowly climbed into the sky. The colonel watched until he lost the plane in the haze. "Good luck, Ellis. I pray that this mission is a complete and uneventful success." He impulsively saluted and turned to go to the command post, where he'd follow the flight with the help of air traffic control. It would be a long night.

***

Tom Wilkie tore open the manila package containing their flight plan. He scanned the list of waypoints, headings and altitudes. "OK, crew, we're climbing to flight level two-eight-zero, and after the Spokane Two departure we'll be turning to heading one-seven-zero. Pilot, set squawk to one-one-one-one. Air traffic control frequency is two-three-three-point-five."

Jimmy Blase set the squawk and ATC frequency and spoke into the radio. "Spokane departure, this is Paydirt-zero-two. We've set squawk to one-one-one-one, and we're going comm-out at this time. See you later."

"Roger, zero-two. Understand comm-out. Monitor Guard. We've got a good squawk. Good luck."

"Wilco and thanks. Zero-two out."

"Crew," said the pilot into his interphone, "we've gone comm-out and will monitor Guard frequency for the rest of the flight." Guard was the designation for the standard military frequency 243.0, monitored by all U.S. military aircraft around the world, as well as air traffic controllers. It was meant for emergency voice traffic and gave assurance that all military aircraft in the same line of sight vicinity could communicate with each other.

"Crew," said the radar navigator. "I'm looking at this flight plan. We've got a refueling down off the coast of southern California, and then..." There was a long pause, as Tom Wilkie perused the flight plan. "Wizzo, you better get over here and take a look at this. The pucker factor's gonna be off the scale on this one, boys, big time." He spoke under his breath, mumbling incoherently.

***

Agent Rupert Budowski did not like driving fast, anyway, and this chase was proving dangerous. He could feel his car complaining around every curve, and the steering wheel fought the sharp turns and narrow roads. He went just fast enough to keep the flashing red lights of the police cruiser in sight. It would not be difficult to lose Doctor Chen's car out here in the desert. There were any of a thousand places where they could pull off the road. He was certain the driver with Doctor Chen was a professional, and he was not counting on a stupid mistake.

Budowski touched the map on the passenger's seat. He could not read it now, but touching it seemed to bring back its details. *The road we're on leads to only one place: Mexicali. So what's the plan now? How will he fly out of Mexico? Why would the driver shoot a police officer and make Chen the object of a manhunt?* Budowski had to think for only a moment. *Chen won't be going through normal commercial channels. A charter will fly the doc home.* He dialed up his point of contact. *Maybe this chase ain't over, after all.*

***

"OK, Nav," said Ellis. "Don't keep the rest of us in suspense. What are you mumbling about?"

Tom Wilkie keyed his mike. "After we refuel with the two tankers — and we take on all the gas we can — we're flying down to the coast off South America. We've been given four sets of coordinates, and that's it. Let me read you what it says. 'Crew has four targets with coordinates of,' and it gives the coordinates of the targets as of 1800 zulu today. 'The crew is to determine optimum target sequence and strike each target vessel with at least one harpoon missile in the aft section. If the crew determines that a single harpoon does not disable the ship such that it is set adrift, the crew is authorized to fire a second missile, also to the aft section. The yields of the harpoons on board have been reduced by engineers to significantly damage, but not sink the target vessels. The crew will note the coordinates of each target vessel and assess its respective damage.'"

"Does it say why we're shooting harpoons at these guys and who they are?"

"I'm looking...here it is. 'Target vessels are Chinese trawlers suspected of housing deep sea submersibles and potentially contain nuclear weapons on board.' Whoa! 'Although a defensive response is not anticipated, the crew should take every appropriate precaution when striking the targets.' That's it."

"Wow! We're going to war!" Captain Jimmy Blase could not hide his enthusiasm.

Ellis collected his thoughts. "OK, Wizzo, you better get with the navigators and figure out the target sequence. And we're supposed to hit the target vessels in the aft section. Can we even do that, Wiz?"

The crew's weapons systems officer, Charlie Macklin, keyed his mike and gave a "yahoo" into the interphone that blew everyone's ears out.

"Doggone it, Cap'n Mac," complained the gunner.

Macklin was a Texas boy through and through, and he wore his accent proudly. "Boys, this is gonna be just like huntin' possums back home. We're gonna line up on 'em from behind, at about a thirty-degree angle, and we're gonna pop 'em before they even know what hit 'em. And are you askin' if we can smack 'em in their butt crack? It'll be easier than pullin' a greased string from a monkey's be-hind."

Ellis smiled, looked over at his pilot and shook his head. "OK, Mac, just make it happen. Sequence them 'possums, and Jimmy and I'll get this sucker oriented so we're coming in from be-hind. But you'll have to take it from there. I don't want to try a night visual."

"Gotcha covered, Rich," replied Macklin. Macklin and Wilkie began to work the details, setting up offsets for their approach to the trawlers and defining the parameters for the strike.

Meanwhile, the navigator plotted the course to the refueling track. "Come right heading one-niner-three," he called.

"One-niner-three," repeated Ellis. He turned the knob on the console clockwise and the autopilot, which he had engaged at level off, responded effortlessly. The plane banked slightly right and leveled out as it reached the desired heading. The navigator watched his compass to confirm that the pilot followed his direction.

"We'll be refueling with two tankers at flight level two-seven-zero. Call signs are Mug-one-one and Mug-one-two...they're coming out of March Air Force Base. A couple reserve crews."

"Copy," said Ellis.

***

"Yeah," said Howey, "the Mexican authorities are all over the airport. These boys won't be gettin' through, charter or no charter."

"Why don't I share your confidence, Howey?" asked Agent Budowski. "And what are the Mex's doing in case the doc and his escort decide to alter their departure point?"

"They're setting up checkpoints."

"I sure haven't seen any, and I'm almost to Mexicali." He sighed. "Keep me in the loop, Howey. If I see anything, I'll get back to you."

"OK, Rupe. Meanwhile, I'll tell the national security whiz kids what's happenin'. They probably won't be too happy 'bout all this."

"Well, tell them we aren't happy, either."

CHAPTER 10

Lieutenant Colonel Rich Ellis idly perused the engine instruments, and each was within normal range. He scanned the altitude, attitude, airspeed, directional and vertical velocity indicators — called a crosscheck in the pilot vernacular — to ensure that the autopilot was doing its job. All was well. He watched his right-seater check the aircraft's refueling system and configure the fuel panel for air refueling. He knew that his navigator was busy searching the radar for the two tankers and that the radar navigator and wizzo would be working on how best to strike their targets. The gunner, on the other hand, was napping. With head back and mouth open — the oxygen mask hanging loosely from one side of his helmet and resting against his cheek — he was in la-la land. Ellis managed a smile.

Flying comm-out made the cockpit quieter than usual. The Guard channel was mostly silent, but it was reassuring knowing that someone was always just a radio call away. The air refueling would also be comm-out, something they had not practiced in awhile. But air refueling was so routine that it did not worry Ellis. If the tanker crew did its job, and he suspected it was going to be one of the most experienced under the circumstances, the rendezvous would be uneventful, and he and the right-seater would easily get the BUFF into position behind the tanker to take on fuel. They'd have the system set to full open to suck in so much JP-4 that the weight of the fully-loaded aircraft could be sustained only while airborne — landing would collapse the landing gear. It would be a sight: two Boeing KC-135 Stratotankers, each in turn hooked by its boom to a B-52 whose wings would be flapping plus or minus fifteen feet from centerline. The B-52 would be tucked behind the tankers in an imaginary four-by-six foot box less than eighteen feet away, all while the planes flew at over 300 miles per hour. The United States had the largest and most capable air refueling fleet in the world, and today would prove its value once again.

He heard ATC, broadcasting on Guard for their benefit, clear another plane out of their flight path. "United forty-three, you have a B-52 aircraft at your two o'clock, altitude two-eight-zero."

Ellis leaned back in his seat as best he could and tried to relax. In another fifteen minutes, there would be a blitz of activity to coordinate the refueling rendezvous. He let his thoughts drift back to when he and Mary Lou and the kids first arrived in Spokane.

Spokane was a fun time for the family. They had arrived from Grand Forks Air Force Base after a three-year tour, not exactly one of the world's garden spots. Hard winters, antiquated and crowded base housing, and not a tree in sight. The joke was that the telephone pole was the state tree of North Dakota. Although the squadron was "tight" because everyone lived on base and socialized often together, the environment was bleak. After closing Loring Air Force Base in Maine, and Kincheloe and K.I. Sawyer in northern Michigan, Grand Forks and its sibling Minot were the last of the northern tier bases that were once the mainstay of the old Strategic Air Command. The end of the Cold War led to the closing of the northern linchpins in its wake, a relief to most Air Force families but a severe economic blow to the surrounding communities. To fill one pilot slot at Loring Air Force Base — located on the Canadian border in the very north of Maine and ten miles north of Caribou, the northeastern-most city in the United States — six pilots would submit their paperwork to resign from the service. It was an expensive proposition that the Air Force was only too happy to jettison once the world changed with the fall of the Berlin Wall in 1989.

Spokane, on the other hand, had a population of just under 200,000, with a prosperous downtown and the feel of a small community. It had everything anyone could want, but without the big city problems.

The Ellis family lived in the northwest part of the city. They opted for the newer suburbs rather than the old South Hill or the Valley, and it turned out to be a good choice. People in Spokane were down-to-earth, and they readily welcomed military people into their neighborhoods. It was a short thirty-five minute commute to work each morning, and the base itself was well taken care of and well supported by the Air Force. A Washington National Guard unit shared the base's real estate, adding to its popularity in the local community.

The kids loved their new school, and Mary Lou enjoyed the neighbors. It was a tonic for their marriage: a new house, a new dog, a friendly neighborhood, a good school. For awhile life seemed good. But surroundings go only so far for solving family problems, and the dissatisfaction associated with Air Force life began to resurface shortly after their arrival in the Northwest. When the kids spent their days at home, his wife did not mind the constant moving and the busy life of a fulltime mom. But now with empty days and little of a challenging nature to fill them, she began to complain of the constant moving, of living in places like the barren plains of North Dakota. She wanted to go back to college either to update her skills or to learn a new profession. She had lived her life for her husband's Air Force career, and she was growing weary of it. He expected to go to a squadron commander's job next, his early selection for full bird colonel already in motion. They were anticipating another assignment only twenty short months after arriving in Spokane. Life was getting complicated, and he did not know what to do about it.

"Crew, I have the tankers. They're at a hundred miles. Rich, you need to descend to flight level two-five-zero for the rendezvous. Tankers are at two-seven-oh."

Ellis sat up in his seat. "Roger, Nav, descending to flight level two-five-zero. I'm going manual." He reached up and gently switched off the autopilot. This autopilot trimmed the aircraft for level flight better than most, and he smoothly lowered the nose of the plane and applied forward trim to take the pressure off the wheel. The navigator watched his altimeter, the plane in a slow descent, to confirm the pilot's response.

"Crew, A-R checklist," called Ellis into his interphone. "Wake up, Chief, the tankers are up ahead, and we need the gas." The gunner stirred in his seat and hooked up the loose side of his oxygen mask.

"Roger, Colonel, I'm on. I wasn't asleep. I was just checkin' my eyelids for holes."

***

Ling Mao pulled off to the right, reversing direction on the shoulder of the highway and driving behind a large rock formation.

Doctor Chen looked across at the man who so easily shot the police officer and realized that the abstract had become real. He had put into motion that which might kill tens or even hundreds of thousands of people, people no different from the man shot less than an hour earlier. He wondered at the ease with which death embraced its victims. And yet he could not find it within himself to feel remorse.

The police car, top lights blazing, raced by. The fact that it did not hesitate in its pursuit of the unseen made it clear their vehicle was not noticed. Moments later, a second car, the one with the man that tried to intervene back at the roadblock, also passed. Ling Mao waited patiently. One minute, two, then three. Satisfied that no one else was following, he turned on the car's headlights in the fading light and took the dirt road off to his left. There he would rendezvous with others that he knew at the embassy, people who would see that he and his precious cargo made it safely out of Mexico and home to China.

"It won't be long, now," Ling Mao said in Chinese to his charge. "We will soon be on our way."

"Yes," replied Chen in English. He caught himself and switched to Chinese. "I want to go home where I can be free from the noise of mobile telephones and the sounds of traffic jams. Where age is accorded honor and wisdom respected. Where youth possess humility. Where I can walk in safety wherever I go, in slippers that caress my feet and in a robe that rests lightly upon my shoulders." He spoke English again, slowly. "Home, yes home — to my China."

Ling Mao looked over at Chen and wondered how long it had been since the old man visited the mainland. A fourth of a billion Chinese did not have access to potable water, and nearly half a billion were subject to terrible pollution. Living in Shanghai was akin to smoking two packs of cigarettes a day. One hundred and fifty million Chinese were homeless, and a third of a billion were expected to migrate to the already overcrowded cities in the next two decades. There were more than two hundred protests across the country every day, and hundreds of millions of mobile phones guaranteed that there was never any peace or quiet anywhere. Privacy was not an option in China, and after living in the West as he had, it was difficult for Ling Mao to return home. He suspected this old man would have problems adjusting culturally as well — he just did not realize it yet. At least Chinese kids were still relatively civil, but Ling Mao suspected even that would not last in a globalized world. Differences these days between young and old people had more to do with generations and technology than cultures.

***

Marly plotted the course of the fifth trawler. Its heading did not change. True to geometry, that the shortest distance between two points was a straight line, the trawler did not deviate from the direct course that would take it to the armpit of the southeastern panhandle of the Nazca plate — a place that offered the leverage one needed to rotate an object lying loosely on its foundation. The fact that this ship, too, was a trawler that could contain small submersibles made her expect the worst. And the ship was less than three days out from its destination.

She was unsure if they could keep their activities secret for another three days. The university reluctantly closed the lab at Rick's request to all but the three of them: herself, Beverly, and Ralph. She asked Rick if they needed a guard, but he insisted that to keep people from becoming suspicious, they should keep the lab locked and only say that they were doing experiments that required it to be closed for the week.

She looked at the topography of the Nazca plate and decided that she could test her theory about the trawler. There was another short panhandle at the northwest corner of the plate, opposite from the first. If the sixth trawler headed for this area after it departed the Panama Canal, then she would know that the two ships intended to plant their cargo on the ocean floor at opposite ends of the plate and with simultaneous explosions try to rotate the Nazca plate like a top. Even the slightest jar would press the Cocos plate into the North American plate, with a result she was not sure she wanted to contemplate. She could feel the goose bumps tingle on her arms. She needed to talk to Rick Starr.

***

Renoir groaned.

Rick shook his head. "It's not fatal. They're just trying to get Chen out of the country before we connect him to the trauma. If they pick him up, fine, if not then it really doesn't make much difference. I was just told by intel that humint sources claim he was a member of the Communist party. If true, that's another indicator that Chen's guilty. Of course, it would be nice to have confirmation that we're correct — assuming that he would talk."

"You're right that it doesn't really matter operationally," said Renoir. "But he deserves to be caught so that we can hold him accountable." He looked at Rick. "The guy should hang."

Denise Carlson sighed. "The Bureau thinks they might still be able to intercept him at the airport. They don't expect him to fly commercially, so they're looking at charters and private planes. It'll be tough to fly him out undetected."

Renoir gave a short laugh. "In Mexico, all things are possible. Money doesn't just talk, it shouts — and people don't just listen, they obey."

***

"Tankers are turning," called the navigator. "They're at five miles. We should be at two miles after they complete the turn."

"Roger," replied Ellis. "I've got the tankers in sight. Open the receptacle door, Pilot."

"Copy and wilco," replied Jimmy Blase. A small door slid back on the top of the plane behind the cockpit, revealing the receptacle. "A-R Checklist complete."

The two pilots watched the tankers roll out. Ellis stabilized his speed to match that of the lead plane. "We're at one mile, crew," called Ellis into the interphone. "Departing two-five-zero for two-six-five."

Lieutenant Colonel Rich Ellis pulled behind the first tanker as he had hundreds of times before on other missions. He paused five hundred feet below the KC-135 and a half-mile in trail. The boom was lowered by the tanker's boom operator, the signal that the bomber was cleared in to air refuel. "Departing two-six-five for two-seven-oh, crew." He paused at a hundred feet in trail, the boom now fully extended and beckoning the BUFF forward.

Ellis pulled into position beneath the aircraft that loomed large in his windshield. The tanker's boom operator, visible through a thick Plexiglas window as he lay on a wooden platform in the rear of the tanker, effortlessly plugged the hydraulic boom into the bomber's receptacle. Once the boom was in, a series of green lights under the KC-

135 lit up and visually informed the bomber pilot of his position in relation to the tanker.

Jimmy Blase opened up the valves on the fuel panel, and gas began pouring into the body tanks at the rate of over a thousand gallons a minute. In fifteen minutes they'd take on a hundred thousand pounds of fuel, over sixteen thousand gallons of JP-4. The tanker continued in position like a rock, and Ellis easily kept the large bomber in perfect trail. As the fuel gauge registered just over 100,000 pounds of fuel transferred, the flow stopped, and the boom retracted. Ellis slowly descended to 500 feet below the lead aircraft. He looked to his side, turning a degree and a half to the right and pulling the throttles back slightly. The second KC-135 was a mile to the right and 500 feet higher than the first. Ellis corrected his heading back to centerline and slid flawlessly behind the second tanker. The plane's boom operator lowered its boom, and Jimmy Blase configured the fuel panel once again for the remaining fuel. This time they expected 125,000 pounds. "Moving in," Ellis called into interphone, pushing up the throttles to add power.

The second tanker did not appear to be flying on autopilot, and its pilot was over-controlling the plane. Rather than making smooth attitude corrections and letting his altitude vary gently, the pilot was trying to maintain the refueling altitude precisely by making short, abrupt adjustments. It made holding position more difficult for Ellis, but he had flown so many refuelings and had such a command of flying that he made even the difficult task of staying behind this tanker appear easy. The twenty minutes or so passed quickly and without incident, but Ellis was still happy to get off the boom.

"Post A-R checklist," Ellis called into the interphone. Jimmy Blase reconfigured the fuel panel, and the navigator plotted the next heading.

"In another thirty seconds, crew, we'll be at the end of the air refueling track, and we'll be turning right to heading two-five-five. Radar nav says that heading will take us to our first target, which is 900 miles out. Flying time is eighty-four minutes."

"Roger, Nav," replied Ellis. "OK, Mac, let's start talkin' about how we're going to hit that first trawler — altitude, airspeed, approach angle and post-attack damage assessment."

"Gotcha, Rich. It'll be dark in less than an hour, and you'll be goin' to night vision goggles to make your approach. We'll descend to 5000 feet starting 250 miles out. Once you get on heading and airspeed behind the target, the radar nav and I'll take over. We'll turn him into road kill before he even knows we're there. I'm planning a hundred-mile approach at a thousand feet with a drop thirty miles from the target. You'll swing right and climb to 10,000 feet for the damage assessment. You ought to get broadside to the trawler about the same time the harpoon nails him."

***

"You say you're sure that the fifth trawler's destination is the southern panhandle of the Nazca plate? But you want to confirm your suspicion by letting the last trawler leave the Panama Canal and see where it turns before it's intercepted?" Rick paused. "I don't know if I have the authority to delay the intercept, but I'll try. So you think it's going to turn to the southwest and drive to where there's a second panhandle?"

"Right," said Marly. "They're going to do just like you said when you change a flat tire. I'm betting they plan to give the plate a good kick now that it's loose, with a couple of simultaneous explosions from opposite corners." It was Marly's turn to pause. "Rick, this time they could go really big, way beyond a 4.0 on the Richter because they don't have to hide their intentions anymore. It might not only cause a great quake up in California, but it could cause a tsunami near the Nazca plate with the potential to swamp Mexico and South America. The one that hit Indonesia and killed 225,000 people was caused by a 9.0 earthquake. If these explosions cause one that's anywhere near that high, who knows what could happen?"

Rick shuddered. "You'd make a good analyst, Marly. I'll do everything I can to let the last trawler make its turn, and I'll tell my boss that we have to stop the fifth one, too. Good work. Let me know if something changes. Otherwise, I'm going to run with what you've given me."

"Rick," Marly said. "I was thinking. Shouldn't we tell someone here in the Bay Area that something really bad might happen so we can evacuate the city?"

Rick paused before he spoke. "If something bad happens, will it affect only San Francisco?"

Marly knew what Rick was going to say. "No. Even though we only measure the effects here in the Bay Area, an earthquake like we're talking about will affect the entire west coast."

"So to be safe the entire West Coast of the United States with a population of nearly fifty million people would have to leave their homes and head east?"

"Just thought I'd ask."

"Do you want to leave San Francisco?"

"No. I wasn't thinking of myself."

"We won't let the trawler leaving the Panama Canal get to the other corner of the Nazca plate. We're stopping the first four trawlers from doing any more damage. And we'll do everything we can to stop the last one from arriving at its destination."

***

Two hundred and fifty miles out from his target, B-52 aircraft commander Rich Ellis pulled back the throttles and lowered the nose of the giant plane. "Descending to five thousand feet, crew. Let's go to night vision goggles in the cockpit. Chief, how about closing the cockpit door so we don't get our night vision messed up by the 'gators downstairs? You guys still got those neon lights on?"

"Closin' the door, Colonel," replied the gunner.

"I've got the trawler heading directly west," said the radar navigator, ignoring the aircraft commander's ribbing.

"Let's come to heading two-six-five."

"Roger," said Ellis. "Passing flight level one-eight-zero, crew. What's the altimeter setting, Nav?"

"Go ahead and set two-eight-eight-zero. We've got perfect weather out here tonight."

"Perfect weather. I like it. Maybe Paydirt was an omen just like you said, Wizzo." The gunner grinned into his oxygen mask.

"Come to heading two-five-five, Rich. Wind's changin' a little down here."

"Roger," said Ellis. "Passing ten thousand feet, airspeed checks below two-fifty."

"Now to heading two-six-oh. We're back on course. Trawler's up ahead at just over a hundred miles."

Ellis turned the large bomber for their final approach to the target.

He saw lights in the distance, a dim green glow.

"Slow to two-twenty, Rich, and open the bomb bay doors," said the radar navigator. "We're at a hundred miles."

The right-seater raised the red switch-guard and moved the switch that would expose the contents of the plane's lower fuselage.

"Roger, and I'm level at five thousand."

"Roger. Start your descent now to a thousand feet and come right to heading two-seven-zero."

"Take the throttles, Jimmy. OK, Wizzo, you're cleared to fire up the harpoons."

"Roger roger," said Macklin. "Radar's primed. I'll be droppin' a 'poon at thirty miles, plus or minus."

"Rich," the radar nav interrupted. "Let's come right heading two-seven-two."

"Right two-seven-two, and I'm passing three thousand for one thousand."

"Roger, Rich. We're at eighty miles."

"Eighty miles. I've got the trawler in sight. He's a bright green tonight. Passing two for a thousand feet. Got a lock-on yet, Wizzo?"

"I had a lock at a hundred miles. That's one big sucker out there. He's gonna be tough to miss."

The giant B-52 leveled off a thousand feet above the water. Designed by Boeing engineers on the back of an envelope during a flight to the nation's capital and originally built for high-altitude bombing, the Stratofortress was an aerospace marvel. After the Soviets built missiles that could shoot aircraft down at high altitude, the B-52 adopted low-altitude, high-speed penetration tactics that would let it approach its targets with complete surprise. Never intended to fly close to the earth's surface at high speeds, it nevertheless performed its mission admirably and with surprising agility. It now skated effortlessly across the water.

"Fifty miles, Rich. Come to heading two-six-nine."

"Heading two-six-nine. We're at a thousand feet, two hundred and twenty knots. Still gonna pickle at thirty miles, Wizzo?"

"Thirty-one, Rich, thirty-one. This baby is dyin' to get started. You should hear it buzz in the headset. Sounds like a four-fifty-four under the hood of an old Chevy Corvette — just singin' away, waitin' to rocket outta the chocks."

"Man, that trawler is one big enchilada, ain't it? Why's it so lit up? You'd think they was playin' basketball on the deck or somethin'," said the gunner, peering out the front windscreen. "They're cryin' out for some negative attention."

"Last correction. Come right to two-seven-one and hold it."

"Two-seven-one."

"One minute to pickle," called the wizzo.

"All this talk 'bout pickles is makin' me hungry," said the gunner. "Think I'll have me another candy bar. I'm workin' up a big appetite sittin' here listenin' to you guys."

***

Ling Mao pulled into the flat, open area surrounded by jagged rock formations. He parked in one corner, the darkness enveloping them. He silenced the car's headlights, waiting for the signal that would liberate them from their pursuers.

Doctor Chen closed his eyes. He felt very tired, as if the memory of eight years of life in exile were descending upon him all at once. He wondered if he would ever get home. Despite the confidence possessed by the younger man sitting next to him, Doctor Chen doubted that he would leave North America. But no matter. He volunteered to be part of the historic forces that would reunite the motherland with her prodigal son, and he did not regret his decision. It was worth even the price of never seeing his loved ones again. He decided to try to sleep. He suspected that it would be an especially long night, regardless of its outcome.

***

"Pickle," said the wizzo. "Climb to ten thousand feet, come right five degrees. Maintain airspeed."

"Harpoon's away, Wiz," said Jimmy Blase. The missile dropped to just above the water, its jet propulsion system coming to life as it drifted slowly down toward the sea. It sped away from the bomber at near supersonic speed. "That's one fast whale killer. I've never seen a live launch before."

"I've popped a few," said Ellis. "They're pretty wicked."

"You guys know that big suppository you're about to plant up the ass o' that trawler cost over half a million dollars?" asked the gunner.

"Back left five degrees, Rich," called the navigator.

Ellis turned the plane, the aircraft in a steep climb with its engines at full thrust. "Well, Chief, the taxpayers are sure gonna get their money's worth tonight. I have the feeling the missile we just fired is going to do a lot more damage than half o' mil. I copied you, Nav, left five degrees, and I'm leveling at ten thousand." Ellis looked over to his left. "Target's directly left. I'll keep it in sight until the harpoon..." Ellis' words were cut short as the harpoon struck its target, a large green flash in his night vision goggles indicating that the missile found its mark. "It's a hit, Wiz, smack dab in the derriere."

The wounded ship took an immediate hard right. The Buff's crew watched, the ship slowing in a constant right turn, seemingly unable to alter its course. "I think we've set her adrift, boys. OK, Nav, find me target number two. Mission accomplished on number one. Good job, Mac."

"I tole you boys this would be a *tour de force*...I told ya. Not bad for a Texan, Cap'n Mac. You raised the Lone Star state a whole notch in my eyes. Not hard, of course, when you're number fifty outta fifty."

"So who's last now, Chief?" asked Jimmy Blase.

"Whaddaya mean?"

"If Texas went up a notch to forty-nine, someone else is number fifty now, right?"

"Oh, yeah. I see what you mean. Hafta be Massachusetts. Yep, KK-land for sure."

"KK-land? What's the KK stand for?"

"Kennedy and Kerry."

"You are one redneck S-O-B, aren't you, Chief?"

"Redneck for sure, Pilot, but S-O-B, no way."

"I think we need to have an indaba, Chief," said Jimmy Blase.

"An inda-what?"

"It's part of my heritage, Chief. Black history. You need to look it up in the dictionary."

"I don't even own a dictionary, Pilot, and I ain't never heard no African-American friend o' mine use language like that. You better start speakin' English if you want enlisted people to understand you, Cap'n."

***

Kam Fong, alone in Mexico City and anxious now to avenge his grandfather's death, laid his head on the pillow. He knew that he would not sleep, but he could rest. He would spend his last night awake, listening to the sounds of the night, the sounds of the city.

Tonight was the before. Tomorrow night, when he was in the afterlife with his grandparents, would be the after. He could not wait to tell his grandmother the good news.

***

Marly Cooper shut off the computer. She let herself go limp and sighed. Sticking her head in the door was Beverly Duncan. "Goin' home? It's awfully late, you know. Even those of us who have been charged with saving the world need sleep."

"I'm done. And I'm exhausted. You want to come over to my place and have a glass of wine? All this stress is too much for me."

"Of course. How's our secret agent doing? Are they fixing this mess you've discovered? I sure haven't heard anything in the news."

"Everything they can, and Rick's getting back to me tomorrow first thing." She shook her head. "It's hard to believe this is really happening. Doctor Chen couldn't possibly be responsible for trying to kill thousands of people." She sighed. "Do you think we should tell someone so they can at least evacuate the cities? I know we can't evacuate the entire west coast."

"Coop, we've already told everyone that we think this could erupt into something big. Every plane leaving the airport is full. A lot of the businesses here and in Oakland are closed. Tourism is dead. People who want are evacuating on their own, and they're doing it in a way that no one's getting hurt.

"I've said in interviews the entire state and possibly even the entire West Coast could be affected, but the reaction from most people is skepticism. People are just too used to hearing fortune tellers cry wolf." Beverly paused and looked at her friend closely. "Are you getting scared? Do you think we should leave, too, or cancel our conference?"

Marly returned her friend's look and smiled. "We can always cancel our conference at the last minute. And I'd never run. I'd rather die first."

"Me, too."

Marly rested her elbows on her knees. "It just seems that we should be doing more. Maybe we need to say that a great quake followed by a monster tsunami is about to happen in three days."

"Then we'd sound like doomsday nuts. And we need to realize that this isn't just for the short-term, you know? Even if the Chinese never do another thing, we could be living with the effects of this stuff for decades, maybe centuries. How long do we tell people they should stay out of the area? The stress that's built up will eventually be released, and then whammo."

"The elastic rebound theory," Marly finished Beverly's thought. "So we'll probably get a chance to save the world again."

"Like a friend of mine once said, 'You know, you never know.'"

"Now that sounds like an intelligent friend."

Beverly laughed. "It makes sense if you think about it, and I'm sure after a few glasses of wine that it will make perfect sense!"

Marly returned her laugh. "Let's go. Race you to the parking lot."

***

Rick Starr looked at John Renoir. "Thanks, John, for taking care of Doctor Cooper's request."

Renoir shook his head. "It wasn't easy convincing the Navy to let a ship carrying nukes escape. They'll give the ship two hours, and then they pounce. It was the best I could do."

"I think it'll be enough," said Rick. "We just need an initial heading. Then we'll know." Renoir nodded tiredly. "And once we know, we'll have to start ginning up a mission to take out the fifth trawler that's on its way south to the Nazca plate."

"What do you propose?" asked Renoir.

"Another Air Force B-52 gets my vote. What do you think?"

"Sounds right to me, as long as there's good news tomorrow. If not, you might have to come up with something else."

CHAPTER 11

Pandemonium engulfed the Shanghai. One of the largest and most modern whaling trawlers in the world, it had been hit by a large object that shattered the rear of the ship. The explosion was negligible, but the damage substantial nonetheless. The rudder hung from its supports, the ship's propellers were bent and jammed, and the engines stalled when the propellers ground to a halt, sucking in thousands of gallons of ocean that now flooded the bilge pumps and filled the aft of the ship with smoke. The two small submarines in the ship's interior that were tethered to the sides of the hold overturned and were bobbing like corks.

Sirens sounded, voices shrieked, and the ship's radio operator called MAYDAY repeatedly. It did not yet occur to anyone that the ship might have been intentionally struck by an unseen enemy. The roar of jet engines off to the starboard side were lost in the cacophony of sounds that filled the night air.

***

"Turn left heading zero-niner-zero. Second target is about a thousand miles and ninety minutes away."

"Turning left to zero-nine-zero. Say altitude."

"Two-five-zero."

"Thanks, Nav. Crew, climbing to flight level two-five-oh." The B-52 and its crew climbed up and away from the ship far below. Lieutenant Colonel Rich Ellis took one last look through his night vision goggles. A bright florescent green, probably fire, was getting brighter and lit the water around the trawler. He shook his head. "OK, Wizzo, one down and three to go. Let's make 'em all as painless as this one."

***

Black engulfed the night. Ling Mao could not see the car that he knew to be directly in front of him — he could hear only the quiet of its engine. The car flashed its lights, and he turned on his parking lights. The other car's headlights suddenly quenched the darkness and turned in his direction. Doctor Chen awoke as the headlights of the oncoming vehicle filled the night. Ling Mao held up his arm to shield his eyes.

"They're here," said Ling Mao. "They're here to take us to your aircraft." There was a split second of disorientation on the part of the waking Doctor Chen, as he tried to listen in English but heard only Chinese.

***

"What's the plan, guys?"

"Radar nav's gonna take you about twenty-five miles east of the target, Rich. Target is heading north, so you'll be dropping to five thousand feet again and driving south another hundred miles or so. Then you'll be turning back north and we'll fly the same track, a hundred mile approach with a thirty mile drop at a thousand feet. It'll be another kiddie ride at Six Flags. You'll love it, I promise."

"This is almost too easy, Wizzo. Can't we do something to make the ride a little more excitin'?" asked the gunner. "I don't even know why they made me come along."

"This is as exciting as it gets, Chief," said the wizzo. "Once you get a horse galloping, you don't feel the bumps no more, and we're gallopin' now, Chief, we're gallopin' now."

***

Doctor Chen and his driver stepped out of their vehicle and climbed into the waiting limousine. Chen's bags were loaded into the trunk. The limo was black with dark tinted windows and equipped with two tan leather bucket seats by the rear doors. There was a large center area with a table surrounded by four more chairs. Seated in two of the chairs were men from the embassy in Mexico City. Tucked into the frame of the car on either side were soft drinks and a small bucket of ice.

"Nice car," said Ling Mao, who climbed in and twisted the top off a bottle of soda. "How you guys been?" he asked in Spanish.

"We're surviving," one of the men replied, also in Spanish.

"We can't go to Mexicali," said the other. "We're going to have to go to a private airfield thirty miles south of the city. It's the only way we can be sure that your cargo will not be detained."

Ling Mao repeated the words in Chinese. Doctor Chen just nodded. He knew that circumstances were becoming complicated, and he understood the dilemma facing his escorts. He smiled to assure them that he was not upset with the new plan.

***

The B-52 started its descent, the target off in the distance to its right. Without external lights and the moon waning, the bomber swooped like a large phantom descending to capture its unsuspecting prey below. Red lights shining dimly in the cockpit and the soft whine of its idling engines were the only clue that the colossal jet was a manmade object and not some primordial flying creature that arose from out of the past. The large trawler shone a bright green in the pilots' night vision goggles, an easy target for the Big Ugly Fat Fella.

"Got a visual on the target, Wizzo," said Ellis. "I'll roll out at a hundred miles and five thousand feet, ready to rock n' roll. Keep an eye on my attitude and altitude, Jimmy. I'll be making a visual turn and descent."

***

The limousine sped along the highway that ran outside of Mexicali. With its diplomatic license plates, the vehicle was waved through the roadblocks set up to apprehend Doctor Chen.

The ride was smooth. No one talked, everyone's thoughts leaping ahead to where they would find a plane waiting to take them to Guadalajara. At Guadalajara, Doctor Chen would be given a passport with a different name and board a Chinese airliner. He would be safe from scrutiny and quietly ferried home.

***

The B-52, winging its way to its target, rolled out smoothly above the glistening water. "Five thousand feet, guys," Ellis called into his interphone.

"Roger," replied Tom Wilkie, the radar navigator. "You're just outside a hundred miles. Go ahead and descend to a thousand feet. We can start our approach here. Turn to heading three-five-four."

"Heading three-five-four, departing five thousand feet for one thousand. Keep me straight, Jimmy," Ellis repeated, "it's dark out here."

The sky was overcast, and a light rain fell. Vertigo, when the visual loss of the horizon fatally succumbs to the misleading perceptions caused by the flow of fluid in the human ear canal, was the bane of many inexperienced pilots not trained to trust their flight instruments. Vertigo's spell killed young JFK and his wife on a dark night near Martha's Vineyard when he insisted on flying using visual flight rules. Jimmy Blase kept his eyes glued to the blue and orange attitude indicator and the radio altimeter's red needle, which told him whether the wings of the giant B-52 were level and what altitude they were flying above the water. Although the pressure altitude read a thousand feet, the radio altimeter showed they were only 800 feet above the ocean's waves.

"Leveling at a thousand feet, airspeed two-twenty, heading three-five-four. Standing by for your direction, Tom. When you gonna pickle, Wizzo?"

"This time pickle'll be at thirty-three miles."

"Go ahead and come right to heading three-five-six," called the radar navigator. "We're drifting a little bit left."

"Yeah, there he is. I got the target locked in. This boy is gonna be dog paddlin' like an old turkey, real soon," said the wizzo.

"Climbout's the same — five degrees right and ten thousand feet."

The bomber, weighing almost two hundred tons, skimmed through the humid air just above the surface of the ocean, virtually invisible. Only the thunder of its engines betrayed its presence and by the time they were heard by the intended victim, the BUFF would be making its escape.

***

"Bomb's away, crew," called the wizzo. The harpoon dropped from the B-52, its insides catching fire and sending the missile hurtling toward its target. The crew watched it accelerate, an inanimate object come to life to devour its quarry. Lieutenant Colonel Rich Ellis pushed the throttles to full thrust and yanked the nose up and to the right. He leveled the wings and began to lower the nose.

"Leveling at ten thousand feet, crew." Ellis looked left and watched for the bright green flash. The ship seemed to lurch at the harpoon's impact, and the first flash was followed by another. "I think we have a secondary explosion. These guys may be in trouble." He turned the airplane to the left. The gunner and the pilot both strained to look out the aircraft commander's window. "Maybe we need to call someone and let them know there's a problem here."

"No can do, Rich. Our directive says comm-out, no exceptions," said the radar navigator. "I can put it in the encrypted SATCOM message, though. I can at least do that."

"OK, guess there's nothing else we can do here. Where to next? I'm getting tired. Jimmy, you take the controls." Lieutenant Colonel Rich Ellis looked down at the ship. Another bright green flash told him that this ship was more than set adrift. "I think you need to log this one as potentially sunk, Tom. I just saw another explosion."

"Roger, Rich. Number one trawler adrift, number two sunk."

***

A naval flag officer and a captain in uniform stood in the office of a nondescript building in Beijing, reading the urgent message. "It's a second MAYDAY," said the captain. "Both ships say the same thing. There was an impact in the ship's stern, which caused them to lose control of the vessel. The first ship now reports hearing the sound of a jet aircraft just after it was struck."

The admiral's face lost its color. "The Americans," he whispered hoarsely. "They are attacking our ships. They know..." He raced to his desk and picked up the phone. He spoke as soon as someone picked up at the other end. "The Americans are attacking the trawlers...yes, I am certain." There was a pause. "The first trawler reported hearing the sound of jet engines just after impact. They are striking from the air."

Another pause. "Yes, sir. I will have a message sent immediately."

***

Doctor Chen looked out the dark window of the limousine as it sped along. He watched boulders and cacti, lit by the car headlights, flutter by. He wondered at Western ways: fast cars, bright lights, constant commotion, tumultuous and profane conversation, and the corrupting, pervasive influence of Hollywood and the music industry. It took a long time to adjust to the pace of life in America, and yet it seemed that he arrived here only a few days ago. He wondered if he would miss this country that he came to admire begrudgingly, mostly because of the quality of its university education system. He realized that his own country discouraged innovative thinking and open-mindedness, and he decided that he would do his best to change the way he taught his classes. Tolerance for other views. Innovation. Initiative. Out-of-the-box thinking. Old ideas for America, but new and radical novelties for China.

The only time he felt elation away from the college environment was when he took trips into the American wilderness. He visited Colorado's Rocky Mountain National Park, Wyoming's Yellowstone Park, and Arizona's Grand Canyon. These were some of the earth's masterpieces — God's country as Americans called them in their usually naïve fashion — stark rock formations, majestic wildlife, radiant blue skies.

He let his mind drift back to the present, the darkness outside consuming everything, swallowing the passing ground and rocks with its deep gullet.

Suddenly, the darkness exploded. Up ahead, surrounded by bright lights powered by generators, was a Lear jet. Its engines whining, splitting the quiet, it was waiting for its cargo. Informed that Doctor Chen was only minutes away, the crew had prepared for his arrival.

Once onboard, Doctor Chen would be lifted into the sky and propelled one step closer to home.

Doctor Chen heard Chinese and found that he could not understand. His look told his escort he was confused, and Ling Mao repeated what he said once more. "Doctor Chen, it is time. This is our plane. We are going home."

This time Doctor Chen smiled and nodded. "I am ready."

Ling Mao wrinkled his brow, puzzled. Why did this old man keep speaking English?

***

The B-52 continued its journey to the third target.

"Where'd you go on vacation, Cap'n Mac?" asked the gunner.

"Went to Europe, Chief, to a place called Slovenia," replied Captain Charlie Macklin.

"You mean like Czech-o-slovenia?"

"Nice try, Chief. You're thinking Czechoslovakia, which broke up into two separate countries. Slovenia is a small place just northeast of Italy. Used to be part of Yugoslavia before it busted up into a million pieces. We operated out of a little resort called Lake Bled and went to the capital Ljubljana, which is real pretty. Kinda provincial, Chief, although I doubt you know what that means. Then we went to Lipizza where they breed the Lipizzaner stallions."

"I know what provincial means, Cap'n. I did graduate from elementary school, you know."

"Hey," said Jimmy Blase. "Are the Lipizzaners the horses that were in the Sound of Music?"

"Right," said Macklin. "They have Lipizzaners in Austria, too. They train 'em at the famous Spanish Riding School in Vienna, but the stallions are the national symbol of Slovenia where many of them are bred. They're beautiful animals. In fact, the horses are born black and slowly turn white as they get older, until they're pure white when they're adults."

"Hey, just like Michael Jackson!" exclaimed the gunner.

The gunner's comment was met with thunderous silence. "You know, Chief," said Jimmy Blase, "if you weren't such a redneck, I'd turn you in for being a bigot."

"Hey, Cap'n, I didn't say nothin' that wadn't true."

"He has some kind of skin condition, you know," said Macklin.

"Time to start your descent, Rich," the radar navigator called into the interphone. "I hate to interrupt what is clearly a deeply intellectual conversation, but the trawler's at two hundred fifty miles directly off the nose of the aircraft."

"Descent checklist," Rich Ellis called in response to the prodding. "Descending to five thousand feet, crew. Jimmy, I'll take the controls back now." He placed his right hand on the eight throttles that controlled engine thrust. Pulling the throttles back to idle, he lowered the nose of the aircraft smoothly to maintain airspeed. The B-52, like a giant falcon, entered the dive that would lead to its prey — a slow moving vessel of steel that could not avoid by maneuver the fate that was about to befall it. Ellis looked out onto the horizon to see the florescent green light of the ship that should have been visibly floating on the ocean's surface — but there was only darkness. "I don't have a visual, Tom. You got the target on radar?"

"Sure do, Rich. You ought to see something any second."

Ellis strained to see. "There's nothing down there. Nope, I don't have a tally on the bogey."

The pilot and gunner joined the aircraft commander and peered out the front windshield. "There's nothin' but black out there, awright," said the gunner.

"Hang on. I'll be right up. Charlie, you watch the radar. He's at 150 miles at twelve o'clock." Tom Wilkie unstrapped his shoulder harness and lapbelt and laid them neatly to the side. He inserted the metal safety pin into the lower left side of his ejection seat and stood up, beginning the short journey from the radar navigator's station to the cockpit. He climbed up and stood behind the jump seat position between the two pilots, letting his eyes adjust to the environment and then peering out into the darkness. Nothing. Only the night.

"What's this? You think they know we're coming? You think the other ships called somebody after they got hit?" asked the gunner.

"Maybe they heard the MAYDAY calls," said Jimmy Blase. "Maybe after the second MAYDAY, they know we're on to 'em."

"We're a thousands miles from the other targets," said the radar navigator. "Even with a MAYDAY, what are the chances a whaler crew would do something like this on their own? Someone sent them a message. Told 'em we're coming and that they'd better turn out the lights."

"Well," said Ellis. "If they think that turning their lights off is gonna make any difference, they've got a big surprise coming. OK, guys, I'm leveling at five thousand feet."

"You think we need to take any precautions?" asked the radar navigator.

"I don't know what a trawler could do to us," said Ellis, "and I wouldn't know what to do about it, anyway. It's not like they're gonna shoot at us thirty miles off their stern or give chase after we pound 'em."

"Maybe they could hit us with a handheld missile or somethin'," offered the gunner.

"Chief, you gotta see what you're gonna shoot, and I don't think they're going to see a thing," said Ellis. "We're making an over-the-horizon shot, and we're gonna smoke 'em. They're not gonna even know what hit 'em, just like the others didn't know."

"Go ahead and drop to a thousand feet, Rich," said the wizzo, "and we'll begin our approach."

The B-52 slowly descended to a thousand feet. The radio altimeter read just over 900. The water was smooth like slick, shiny black marble.

"A hunnerd miles to the target. Release will be at thirty."

"Climbout instructions remain the same," called the navigator.

Tom Wilkie strained to get a visual on their target. He finally shook his head. "I can't see a thing. You guys see anything in your night vision goggles?" His question was met by silence. He shook his head again, and he patted the aircraft commander on the shoulder. "Keep looking, Rich. He's out there, you just can't see him yet." He turned away and began the descent back downstairs. Instead of going to his seat, however, he stood behind the wizzo and watched the target in the radar. "Fifty miles, crew," the wizzo called.

"Roger, fifty miles," said Ellis, "and I've finally got a tally on the target. It ain't much, but I think I've got 'em. You can run, boys, and you can even turn out the lights, but you can't hide from the law."

"You tell 'em, Colonel," said the gunner. "We're talkin' truth, justice and American firepower."

"Forty miles," called the wizzo. "Thirty-five…thirty-two…and pickle. Begin your climbout."

Rich Ellis watched the harpoon leap from the Buff and begin its sprint to the trawler. Jimmy Blase looked down at the engine instruments and pushed up the throttles for the climbout. The gunner sat back in his chair, wishing he could smoke a cigar.

***

It lasted for only the smallest part of a second, but the blinding white light that suddenly filled the cockpit of the B-52 was ferocious enough to cause both pairs of night vision goggles worn by the pilots to go black — and suddenly neither could see. The pilots were unaware of the bright flash that caused what they thought was a malfunction, but which in reality were the night vision goggles' auto-shutoff mechanisms protecting their eyes from the brilliant light. As if on cue, both pilots removed their goggles.

"My goggles quit working," said Rich Ellis.

"Me, too," said Jimmy Blase.

"Hey, Chief," said Ellis. "We're gonna need you to check the circuit breakers. I think we've had a malfunction." He impulsively checked to see if the goggles were still plugged into his console. He looked out the windscreen into the darkness to see if he could reacquire the target. The loss of their night vision goggles distracted them, and they were now less than ten miles to the trawler.

The pilot turned his attention back to setting the throttles for climbout. "Sir, we need to begin our climb."

***

The gunner, who closed his eyes after the harpoon was launched, felt the white flash even with his eyes closed. "What the hell was that?" he called into the interphone. "Did you guys see that?" He turned his head and looked back behind him to see if the light emanated from somewhere inside the plane. Both pilots removed their night vision goggles, and neither pilot knew what the gunner was talking about. "You want me to check the circuit breakers?"

The pilots went back to flying the plane and did not respond to his question. Not that it would have mattered, for a second flash — this one with twice the brilliance of the first — filled the cockpit and destroyed the unprotected retinas of Lieutenant Colonel Rich Ellis. His vision disintegrated instantaneously into complete blackness, and he attempted in vain to reach up and cover his eyes, the signal from his brain never reaching his arm, the thought seemingly suspended in transit. His nervous system plunged into an epileptic fit, a victim of the dazzling burst of white light.

Jimmy Blase, his eyes on the throttles, caught the flash indirectly. But it still did its work. The pilot could not see, and his brain was filled with excruciating pain and his ears with a screeching sound that was intolerable.

***

As the throttles advanced, the engines wound up. Tom Wilkie held on to the wizzo's chair in anticipation of the climbout.

***

The gunner, startled by the second flash, turned his gaze back to the front and saw the aircraft commander's body convulsing, his arms hanging loosely by his sides. The pilot was screaming, his hands over his earphones. The gunner watched in horror as the nose of the airplane pitched up in response to the increased engine thrust and the plane, now flying without a pilot at the controls, began a slow right turn. The right wing began to drop, the plane setting itself up for an eventual spiral into the ocean. The altimeter read 2400 feet.

***

The plane's abrupt pitch up threw Lieutenant Colonel Tom Wilkie into the air backwards against the bulkhead behind the wizzo's station. He never felt the floor as it reached up and yanked him down forcefully into a horizontal position, driving his mind to a place familiar only to the unconscious.

***

The navigator, who had been casually monitoring the inertial navigation system and the altimeter, watched helplessly as the papers on both his desk and the radar navigator's flew into the air. "What the hell's going on up there? Rich? Jimmy?" He reached for the arming handles on his ejection seat and for a moment wondered if he should eject from the airplane. He saw that their altitude was decreasing, and if it got much lower, ejection would be impossible.

***

The B-52 gunner, veteran of nearly a thousand sorties, unstrapped and struggled out of his chair, leaning forward toward the pilots' positions. "Pilot," he shouted into the interphone. "Hit the autopilot. Hit the autopilot!"

But Jimmy Blase could not hear. A loud screeching noise still filled his ears, and his eyes burned with a searing white light.

The gunner fell onto his right side as the plane's wing continued to drop. He watched the altimeter start to unwind, the nose-up trim for level flight unable to counter the downward forces. He could see the pilot's attitude indicator showing an increasingly steep bank. Another few seconds, and the airplane would be in a flight attitude from which it could not recover.

The gunner began to sing the National Anthem. "Oh-oh, say can you see..." He put his hand underneath his body and with superhuman effort, pushed himself into a crouch and leaped forward. "...by the dawn's early light..." He landed on his feet and thrust himself upwards into a standing position. "...what so proudly we hailed..." He leaned over the throttle quadrant, reached up and pulled the small bar directly above the three silver autopilot switches, engaging the three axes of the autopilot simultaneously. "...at the twilight's last..." The aircraft response was immediate: the nose of the airplane abruptly pulled up and assumed level flight, and the wings of the giant B-52 jerked themselves into a position parallel to the water. The gunner engaged the autopilot altitude control switch just before he was lifted off his feet—"...gleam-innng!..." and was thrown to the left side of the aircraft, collapsing to the floor. He tried to pull himself up, but gravity pinned him to the flight deck. "...whose broad stripes and bright stars, and to hell with the rest," he sang.

The aircraft, its throttles set at near maximum thrust, caused the autopilot to begin trimming the plane nose down. It was only a matter of time until the thrust of the eight engines would exceed the trim authority of the horizontal stabilizer. The gunner crawled once more toward the console that separated the pilots' seats. He yelled into the interphone again. "The throttles, Pilot, the throttles!"

This time the pilot heard, although his head was still filled with the screeching wail of a banshee. He reached a trembling left hand over to the throttles and pulled them back slightly. It would not be enough to prevent catastrophe had things progressed to their logical conclusion, but it was enough to allow the gunner to reach the front of the cockpit again and pull the engine throttles back to where the autopilot could maintain level flight.

The airframe of the giant B-52 heaved a sigh of relief, and the gunner let his head fall tiredly to the floor. He slowly lifted his eyes and looked at the pair of pilots. The aircraft commander was no longer moving, pressed back into his seat with his arms dangling lifelessly. Jimmy Blase, although no longer screaming, continued to writhe in his seat. "There's nobody flying the airplane," the gunner called into the interphone. "Both pilots are down. I got the autopilot engaged, but there ain't no crew left." He looked at the aircraft commander again. "There ain't nobody to fly the plane 'cept the autopilot."

***

The harpoon hit its target and exploded, rupturing the outer hull. A second explosion rocked the ship's aft and sent metal flying into the air, just as the now-pilotless B-52 passed overhead at barely a thousand feet above the water. Shrapnel tore into the plane's outer skin on its left wing and sank deep into its number three engine. The rapidly spinning blades of the number three engine splintered, shelling out the engine's insides and destroying its sister engine hanging next to it. Had the number one and two engines on the outside of the wing failed instead, the torque caused by the thrust imbalance would have sent the aircraft into a horrendous sideslip and plunged it into the black liquid below. Instead, the plane swerved left for only a moment until the autopilot compensated for the lack of thrust on the aircraft's left side.

"We lost engines three and four!" called the gunner.

Captain Jimmy Blase, feeling the motion and acting on instinct that comes only after much practice of aircrew emergency procedures, pulled back the throttles for engines five and six on the opposite side of the plane to reduce the asymmetric thrust. He advanced the four outer engines and pulled the throttles for the failed engines back to the shutoff position. The aircraft resumed flight, oblivious to the fate of its pilots.

"Colonel Ellis?" Jimmy Blase called into the interphone.

"He's unconscious, Cap'n," said the gunner. "It's just you, me and the autopilot."

"You've got to be my eyes, Chief," said Jimmy Blase. "I can't see."

"OK, I can do that."

"Look at the engine instruments. Is the fire light on for engine three or four?"

The gunner looked closely at the instruments for each engine. He had never noticed the small bands of green on the gauges before. The dials were all "in the green". For the first time, he understood the term he heard pilots use hundreds of times. "No fire lights. Everything's in the green, Pilot."

Jimmy Blase sat back in his seat. He thought that he could see a little. The screeching noise in his ears was nearly gone. He had to collect his thoughts fast, and more than that, he could not panic. "You've got to help Colonel Ellis, Chief. Do you know what's wrong with him?"

***

Captain Charlie Macklin peered over his shoulder. The radar navigator lay motionless on the floor. He looked back at the navigator, who was unstrapping from his seat. The navigator returned his look. "I'll help Colonel Wilkie. You take the navigation."

Charlie Macklin looked at the heading displayed by the global positioning system that would take them to their next waypoint. "Come right to heading two-eight-one, Jimmy."

Jimmy Blase reached over to the knob that would tell the autopilot to turn the plane. "Chief, this knob I've got my hand on directs the autopilot to turn the plane. I'm going to turn it to the right. You tell me just before the heading indicator reaches two-eight-one."

The gunner stared at the aircraft's avionics until he found the compass. "OK, Cap'n, I got it. You can start yer turn."

"Charlie," said the pilot, "we'll need to tie the autopilot into the GPS and let it fly the flight plan until I get my vision back."

***

Mary Lou Ellis awoke with a start. She clutched at her throat, which seemed to have partially closed. She caught her breath and thrust open her eyes. It was dark. She turned her head to read the digital clock: 3 AM. She let her head sink into the pillow and felt the bed push up against her body.

Mary Lou was unable to fall asleep that night, upset with the day's events. She argued with her husband, Rich, and he stomped out of the house angrily after receiving a phone call to report to base operations. In all the years of their Air Force career, this was a first: Rich did not call to say good-bye prior to takeoff. Even when TDY, he sent a quick text message saying that he loved her and the kids and would do his best to be safe. Instead, Colonel Rader called her several hours later to say that her husband was flying an important short-notice mission and was not returning until the next day.

When then-second lieutenant Rich Ellis was called to fly combat missions in the 1991 Gulf War, the Ellis children were frightened that their father might be killed in combat. Ellis and his wife told their children that of course he would return, and to make sure, Dad would take one of their mother's shoes with him. He promised to take the shoe on every flight — he eventually flew twenty-six sorties into Iraq and Kuwait — and when he returned that he would put it on Mom's foot like he was the handsome prince and their mother Cinderella.

When he finally came home and his family met him on the ramp at the air base, the first thing Rich Ellis did after hugging his family was to put the shoe he took with him onto his wife's foot. His children squealed with delight. This rite became a tradition of sorts. Thereafter, Rich Ellis snuck into the bedroom of one of his kids before every flight and took a shoe. And after every flight when he returned home, he'd put the shoe onto the foot of the child to which it belonged. It was not unusual for one of the kids to wake up with a shoe on his foot, the one that Rich Ellis took with him on his airplane.

Mary Lou was panicked. She slipped out of bed and inspected the closet of each of their children. Every closet contained only pairs of shoes. None was missing. In the midst of their anger, her husband had forgotten to take a shoe. She clutched her throat again, once more feeling like she was choking. Why was she so frightened, so upset? She vowed never to send her husband off to fly again after an argument. It was all so foolish, so incidental to the gift of life and the togetherness of family. She realized that in her own frustration to carve a life and identity separate from her husband and children, she was beginning to take them for granted. She willed away the fear that gripped her and walked downstairs to the kitchen. She put a glass of cool water to her lips and felt it wash her throat. She set the glass onto the counter and slowly retreated to bed.

But sleep would not come, an ache in her chest keeping her awake. She lay there, remembering the life she had together with her husband, from when they first met until their argument that morning. She prayed away the ache, but her pillow was replete with tears.

CHAPTER 12

Doctor Chen stooped to enter the door at the back of the Lear jet. Twelve small seats, six on each side of the aircraft separated by a narrow aisle, filled the small fuselage. A man stood in the aisle to Chen's right as he walked in, and nodded respectfully.

"Doctor Chen, it is an honor," the man said in Chinese.

Chen looked at the man and returned his nod. "The honor is mine," he replied. He became conscious of which language he was speaking now. America and the English language were no longer necessary, and he willfully abandoned them both. He nodded again. "Yes, the honor is all mine."

The man held out his hand and beckoned him to turn toward the front of the plane. Chen looked to his left and saw that one seat was prepared with a pillow and a blanket. He walked to it and sat down gently. The leather cover with its thick padding felt good. Ling Mao followed him and took a seat closer to the front. He spoke with the man, who in turn walked up and into the cockpit. The door of the plane closed a moment later, and the loud whining of the engines became a dull whir. Doctor Chen put his head back and closed his eyes. Was he really leaving the United States after so many years? Would he truly make it home? He did not let himself believe that it was possible.

***

"What's my altimeter reading, Chief?" asked Jimmy Blase.

"It says thirteen hundred."

"How much fuel do we have?"

The gunner looked at the giant fuel panel. Jimmy Blase could feel him hesitating. "It's the big dial. It should say total next to it."

The gunner found it. "Ninety-four thousand."

"How about airspeed? What's the airspeed indicator reading?"

"It reads two-forty-five."

"What about the weather? Any weather out there, Nav?"

Macklin checked his radar. "I've got it on full tilt...it's hard to say. Nothin's called for from what I can tell in the flight plan, and I can't see anything."

"What about it, Chief? You see anything out there?"

The gunner looked out into the darkness. The sky was no longer overcast, and a small moon flung its dim light across the water. Stars lit the night sky. "Looks clear and a million to me."

"OK," said Jimmy Blase. "The plane's flyin' and everything seems OK. We've gotta attend to Colonel Ellis. How's Colonel Wilkie?"

The navigator spoke into the interphone. "I think he's got a concussion. There's a lot of blood back here, and he's got a bad gash. He's not responding to anything I say. I think we should break open the first aid kit and see if there's some smelling salts."

"Sounds like a good idea, Nav. You guys got a kit down there with you, right?"

Robert T. Mueller III looked at the bulkhead behind him. A gray first aid kit hung on the wall next to a flashlight and a crash axe. "Yeah, we got one."

The gunner, meanwhile, began to look after the aircraft commander. He installed the metal safety pin into Lieutenant Colonel Ellis' ejection seat, unhooked Ellis' lapbelt and lifted the shoulder straps away from his chest. He released the four metal lanyards that attached him to his parachute. He raised the aircraft commander's chair to full up and lowered its back as far as it would go. He hooked his arms under Ellis' armpits and heaved him from his seat. Jimmy Blase guarded the throttles and the knob of the autopilot as Ellis' feet dragged behind him and across the controls. Ellis was dead weight, and he did not move. The gunner laid him down at the back of the cockpit. He felt for a pulse, and it was rapid and weak. "I think the Colonel's got a problem. His heart is beatin' like a machine gun, and he's not breathin' too good. I think he might be goin' into shock or somethin'."

***

Sleep remained elusive. Mary Lou Ellis climbed tiredly from bed, wracked with anguish. Knowing that Rich needed her — she did not know how she knew or why he needed her — she felt helpless. She walked downstairs and dropped heavily to the living room couch, unable to cry anymore. Falling back, her head on the armrest, she stretched her feet across the couch's cushions. Eyes open, she looked at the ceiling. It stared back.

***

Colonel Steve Rader turned to the major sitting next to him. "Anything yet on the third target?"

"Nothing yet, Colonel. They're only a little late with their report. Maybe they're out of range of the SATCOM."

Colonel Rader nodded, looking at the clock. He decided to get another cup of coffee. He flew many a mission over the water, and it could be a lonely place.

***

The navigator broke open the tube of smelling salts and held it under Tom Wilkie's nose. He stirred, but would not wake. The pungent smell of salts filled the navigator's nostrils. He tried again. "C'mon, Colonel, this is good for you. Wake up!" Still the colonel did not respond, his head turning away from the sharp smell, his eyes remaining closed.

"Colonel Wilkie won't come to. He's probably got a concussion for sure. I'd guess a bad one."

"OK, Bob, I hear ya," said Jimmy Blase. "Rich is in pretty bad shape, too. You got any adrenaline in that kit back there?"

"No, there's nothing like that." The navigator fumbled through the rest of the first aid kit. "Just lots of bandages...more smelling salts...scissors and...let's see, some ointment or something."

"I think there's adrenaline in our survival kit," offered Charlie Macklin. "I sorta remember when we went through the contents in a training class, that we had adrenaline. No one knew what it was for. They said to use it if you were really hurt bad, or if you got shot or stung by bees or bitten by a snake."

"OK, Chief, I want you to open Colonel Ellis' survival kit and find the adrenaline."

"Got it, Cap'n." He grabbed the parachute from the aircraft commander's seat and detached the survival kit. He grabbed a thumb-sized ring tab and pulled. The kit exploded, the tightly compressed arctic sleeping bag leaping from inside the green canvas. The chief yanked the bag out, exposing the rest of the contents. He took a pocket flashlight from his flight suit and shined it on the various items, looking carefully until he found a small red plastic box with a white label that read

"Adrenaline, syringe with". He popped open the box and found the syringe, its cylinder square instead of round.

"I found the adrenaline, Cap'n, but I ain't never given no shot to nobody."

"No one can help you, Chief. Colonel Ellis needs the shot, and you've gotta give it to him."

The gunner sighed. He pulled a piece of paper from the box and read its directions into the interphone. "This thing says to hold the syringe upward and push the injector until liquid comes through the needle. Then I'm supposed to inject half the contents of the syringe by pushing the injector to the stop. If more adrenaline is needed, I'm supposed to twist the injector a quarter turn and inject the rest. That's it. So what do you think? Should I give all the adrenaline to the Colonel, or only half?"

"Give him both hits. It sounds like he needs it," said Jimmy Blase.

The gunner clumsily followed the directions, pulling up the sleeve of Ellis' flight suit and pressing the syringe's needle into his forearm. The gunner pushed the plunger to its stop, turned the plunger a quarter turn, and emptied the syringe with another push. He pulled the needle out and felt Ellis' pulse. It became more pronounced and then slowed. "It worked! The Colonel's heart is beatin' regular-like."

"OK, Chief!" said the pilot. "Good work. Go ahead and try to make him comfortable as best you can. I need you up here with me."

"What happened to you guys up there, anyway?" asked the wizzo.

"We got hit with a bright light of some kind," Blase said. "It was unbelievable."

"It sounds like it was a laser," said Charlie Macklin. "They must have hit us with a laser."

"They hit us twice," said the gunner. "After the first flash, the pilots took off their goggles. Then we got smacked again, and it was like someone neutered the neighbor's cat with a sledge hammer."

"They probably blasted us with a flippin' laser," said Macklin again, agitated. He looked into the weapons scope at his firing station. "I knew that's what happened. My equipment looks like a piece of two-week old fried chicken from Popeye's. I can't fire any more harpoons. They hosed us. They knew exactly what they were doing. We're done."

"Done?" asked Jimmy Blase. "Whattaya mean we're done? Don't we have anything else we can hit them with?"

"I got some chaff," said the wizzo. "Want me to hit 'em with some chaff? Radar's still good, so we can fly to the trawler and all wave as we go by. Flip 'em the big bird to let them know we mean business."

"C'mon, Charlie, you're not helping me here."

"How much gas we got?" asked the navigator, who was back in his seat. "You guys gonna stay at this altitude and airspeed? We're never gonna reach the last target, anyway, flying down here."

"How much gas we got left now, Chief?"

The gunner looked at the fuel panel. "Just under ninety thousand."

"How far to the target, Nav?"

"At this altitude and airspeed, about three and a half hours."

"How much gas is each engine burning, Chief?"

The gunner looked carefully at each engine. "It looks like just over three thousand pounds an hour for each engine."

"OK," said the pilot. "That's three thousand times six engines…so we're burning about eighteen thousand pounds per hour…times three is fifty-four…and another half hour makes sixty-three. So ninety minus sixty-three means that we'll have twenty-seven thousand pounds of fuel left after we hit the last target if we stay at this altitude. And since I can't see, I want to stay down here at least until we hit the trawler. Then we should be able to climb to altitude."

"We're already a thousand miles from the coast, Pilot," said the navigator. "If we go for the last target, we'll be over fifteen hundred miles out, and there's nothin' but water out here in case you didn't notice."

"And don't forget I can't fire any more missiles," said the wizzo. "The whole system looks like a piece of beef jerky. You're not going to be hitting anything."

"How about the guns, Chief?"

"What about 'em, Cap'n?"

"Are they loaded? Do we have ammo on board?"

"'Course we do."

"Then that's what we'll do. We fly over the target, and the gunner will fill the backend of the next trawler with lead until it's disabled. He can even try to hit the subs that are inside the ship."

Robert Mueller held his head in his hands. He looked at the wizzo, who was updating the system for the next waypoint. He never really wanted to join the Air Force. His father, a wealthy businessman, insisted that he go out and do something completely unrelated to the family business before he'd make him an executive in the company. He had done every job in the business when he was growing up and expected to walk into a VP job after college. OK, maybe he did not work as hard in school as he could have. Maybe he goofed off a little on the job. His father said that he needed more perspective, more maturity, before he would be accepted by the Board of Directors in a key role. But he was aware that it was really his father who wanted him to do something else. His father would not admit it, but Robert knew. So even though he was confident that he was more than ready to become someone important in the business, Robert went into the Air Force. *Well, Dad*, he thought, *I hope you're happy. So much for maturity. I'm not even going to make it through the night.*

"Listen, guys," Mueller said into his interphone. "This is nuts. Nowhere in this directive does it say that we're supposed to fly ourselves into the drink. So why are we even thinking of doing this? If we're gonna make it home, and I think all of us are in agreement that we want to make it home, then we need to head for shore — and we need to get going in that direction now. We don't have the fuel to strike another target and still make it someplace where we can land, and you heard Charlie. We can't fire our missiles and besides, we've stopped three of the trawlers, which is probably better than anyone expected." The navigator was shaking. "Pilot, even if you climb to altitude after hitting the last target, we're still gonna be almost a thousand miles from the coast when we run out of gas. We're gonna be like a bunch of clams at a clambake — sitting in a bucket of hot water with no place to go but down the hatch."

"Maybe we could call for the tankers to meet us out over the water," suggested the wizzo.

"That's a good idea, Charlie, but right now, I can't see a thing. So even if we had tankers, I probably couldn't refuel."

"But maybe your eyes will get better. Maybe we should plan that you'll be able to see well enough by the time we meet up with the tankers."

"I am not for this plan you guys are cooking up," said the navigator, raising his voice. "You think you're fixing lasagna, but all you're fixin' is a bunch of spaghetti. We've got a pilot who might die, and we've got a radar navigator who's got a concussion and needs a doctor. We can't fire any more missiles. You can't fly this airplane with only four people. We've got every reason to abort the mission and go home — now!" He crossed his arms for emphasis.

"What's the difference between lasagna and spaghetti, Nav? I'm not sure I get your point," said the gunner.

Captain Jimmy Blase leaned back in his seat and forced himself to relax. His parachute, full of tightly packed nylon that would support his weight should he need to eject, offered little comfort as a backrest. He tried to gauge the consequences of continuing the mission. *I sure wish I could ask Colonel Ellis what we should do.* He blinked. He thought he could see a blurry light.

***

Kam Fong listened to the noises of the night. Screaming sirens, a television turned too loud across the hall, a woman coughing next door. He heard the bathroom faucet dripping and the clock next to his bed clicking silently in his mind with each passing minute. Every sound was magnified, his senses never clearer than at this moment. *This must be what it's like when one knows he is seeing or hearing something that he will never see or hear again.* He closed his eyes and tried to picture the sounds that he heard. His mind cooperated, and his brain filled with images. He would not let his thoughts wander to the tomorrow. Tomorrow would be here soon enough, and it was the night that satiated his senses.

***

Captain Robert Mueller spoke again. "Didn't you guys hear me? We're gonna die if we continue the mission. This is suicide, and I didn't sign up for a suicide mission. What we're doing is immoral. It's like making ourselves into kamikazes."

"OK," said Jimmy Blase. "Let's take a vote on whether to continue the mission. There's only four of us. If it's a tie, then I make the final decision. Agreed?"

"I don't know," said Mueller.

"Then I'll make the decision without taking a vote."

"OK, OK. Let's vote and see where it gets us."

"All right. Bob, since you're the one who's most against flying the rest of the mission, you speak first."

"OK. My thinking's like this. First, we can't shoot any more harpoons. Charlie says his equipment's shot. And I say the guns on this junk heap aren't good enough to take out a trawler. They're made for shooting down airplanes — small fighters, for Heaven's sake — they're not for sinking ships that weigh half as much as Rhode Island. Besides, the guns were put back into commission just for this flight, so how do we even know they work? Second, Jimmy can't see, and if he can't see then he can't refuel. That means if we decide to do this insane thing you guys are suggesting, we're gonna be stranded like a couple of toads at a frog fry." Mueller had not strapped himself back into his seat and was nervously shaking his legs and tapping the nav's table with the eraser on his plastic pencil while he spoke. "And third, let's say that Jimmy does get his sight back. Who's to say that he'll even be able to refuel if we get the tankers out here to meet us? You got to admit, Jimmy, there have been a couple o' times you haven't been able to fly worth a damn, and you couldn't stay on the boom long enough to get any gas, much less to save our lives. How are we supposed to depend on you to get us home?"

"You're burning your bridges, Bob."

"Sometimes the truth is like pigeon stains, Jimmy. You can scrape 'em off, but they're still gonna stink. I'm being dead honest because I don't wanna be a dead liar. So that's what I think. We've done the best we can. Heck, the Navy dropped a spy plane into China, and they brought the crew home, gave them all medals and treated them like heroes. We've done our job, we have two people injured, and I think we deserve medals, too. And we can't get our medals if we're served up as fish food in the middle of the ocean."

"OK," said the pilot. "We have one vote to go home. Who's next? Charlie?"

"I agree with Bob. I think we have to take care of the wounded. Rich is almost dead, and Colonel Wilkie is out cold. I can't fire any more missiles, and I don't think our guns are going to do anything to that trawler other than make some loud plinking sounds on its hull. And if they're waiting for us like the last trawler, who knows what they'll pull out of their bag of tricks? Maybe this time they'll fry us with some other kind of whacko device we don't know about. I think we could be dying for nothin', and while I'm not afraid to die, I don't believe in dying for no good reason. And I don't think the Air Force wants us to die for nothin' either, although I could be wrong, I suppose."

"So we have two votes to abort the mission. OK, Chief, what do you think?"

"I'm not ready to decide yet, Cap'n. What do you want to do?"

"For me, it's a matter of duty and honor. We were given a mission to fly, and I think we're still mission-capable. I think it's our obligation to do everything we can to complete the mission, even if it means being stranded in the middle of the Pacific Ocean with hardly any possibility of getting home. And this isn't a suicide mission. We've still got a chance to call the tankers and refuel. My eyes are getting better.

"When I signed on the dotted line, I knew there'd be times like this, and I'm ready to pay the price if it comes to that."

"You're an idiot, Jimmy!" shouted the navigator into the interphone. "You think we're gonna be heroes if we complete this mission? They'll hang a plaque in our memory on the wall at base ops that no one will ever read. And when the building is torn down, the plaque will go in the garbage. I think we need to go home. Any other decision is a bunch of crap."

"You already had your turn, Bob, and now it's the Chief's. The vote's two to one. If he says we go home, we go home. If he says we go for it, we go for it. So tell us, Chief. What are we gonna do?"

"Well, I gotta agree with the two navigators that I think completing the mission is a pretty stupid idea. But then, I also gotta agree with you, Cap'n, that we've been given somethin' to do, and we're supposed to do it even when the odds ain't good. And by God, as patriots serving our country in the world's greatest Air Force, we oughta do it."

"What are you saying, Chief? Are we going home or not?" asked the navigator. "The real question is, 'Are you volunteering to commit suicide?'"

"I'm still thinkin', but I suppose if someone paid me enough money to make it worth my while, I might consider it."

"Chief, you're an imbecile."

"You gotta hurry up, Chief, or we might as well just keep going because by the time you make up your mind, we'll be out of gas, anyway," said the wizzo.

"Give him a second," said the pilot. "This is probably the first time a Chief has had the final say on what a B-52 is going to do. So take your time, Chief, but we do need you to decide pretty quick."

"I think I'm ready," said the gunner. "I vote that we fly to the last trawler and blast those Commies outta the water using the tail gun."

"You shtupidblitheringenlistedswine!" shouted the navigator incoherently, his words unintelligible to the rest of the crew. He leapt from his seat and ran to the bulkhead, nearly falling over the unconscious radar navigator. He pulled the crash axe from the wall and turned to face Charlie Macklin, who was staring at him.

***

Robert Mueller III looked at the navigation equipment sitting on his console. *If I destroy our equipment, we can't fly to the last trawler. We'll have to turn back east and fly until we hit the coast, and then we can bail out and be picked up by a boatload of fishermen, or an oil tanker or something.* He looked at the console of Charlie Macklin, where there was a duplicate set of avionics that could also take them to the trawler. *Both sets of equipment have to be destroyed if we're going to go home.* He raised the crash axe and sprinted for the inertial navigation system on Macklin's desk.

***

Charlie Macklin watched Mueller yank the crash axe from the wall. His eyes bulging from his head, Macklin thought that Mueller looked like the utility man that was electrocuted in front of his house when he was a small boy. The man had fallen to the ground at the end of their driveway, and Macklin clearly remembered two things about the incident: the smoke that radiated from the man's head, and his bulging eyes. Eyes that nearly came out of their sockets from the shock of ten thousand volts.

"Bob?" But Mueller appeared to occupy a parallel universe and did not answer. "Bob?" he repeated.

When Mueller raised the crash axe and started running toward him, Macklin knew that Mueller's brain was no longer in charge of his body. It was Mueller or him, and he unstrapped from his seat and stood to face the deranged being charging in his direction.

**

Onboard the whaling trawler Mao Tse-tung, the Chinese naval captain stood reading the message handed him by his executive officer. "Bring the crews of the submarines to me. I need to speak with them," the captain said. His tone was harsh. He had been against this operation from the beginning, and he vented his feelings to others in his chain of command who he thought should have known better. He believed the potential consequences of their actions if they were ever found out would far exceed any reward. This fetish for reunification, when the process was already unquestionably underway both economically and culturally, displayed a lack of strategic perspective. *We're becoming Westernized, even in our thinking. If Sun Tzu were present, he would mock us.*

In an act designed to make him prove his loyalty, his military superiors assigned him to command one of the four ships that would break the will of the United States.

He was not surprised that the Americans were now attacking.

Six men stood at attention, uniforms immaculate, ramrod straight. "Gentlemen," the captain began. "We are at a crossroads. I have been honest with you from the beginning and told you why we are on this mission — that we are the catalyst that will reunite the Motherland with Formosa. It has been your honored task to lay on the bottom of the Pacific Ocean the weapons of reunification, and you are being called to do it again."

He paused before saying more. "But this time, you may also be called to offer the ultimate sacrifice to our great country and its people." He looked at the face of each man, one at a time. Not one of them flinched. None of them showed any emotion. "The Americans will attack us with their bomber aircraft within the hour. We cannot make our last position before they strike, so you must leave us sooner than planned and proceed to the final target area." He paused once more. "The target area is still six hours away, and there is insufficient power in your batteries for you to reach your target and return to the ship after you accomplish your vital task. You will have to surface, far away from our position. The submarines are not designed for the open ocean, and there are no emergency locator beacons on the submarines for security reasons. The chances of your being discovered are small. All this I tell you so that you are fully aware of what it will mean for you to go on this mission."

The captain walked from one end of the line to the other, again taking in the expression of each man. "I will not order you to go. Instead, I leave it to your personal sense of honor. You may excuse yourself from the mission by stepping forward." No one moved. The captain was greatly saddened by the dedication of the group, their willingness to die so readily for a lost cause. He said next what they expected to hear.

"I knew that the men serving under my command were deserving of their country's trust to complete this crucial assignment. The weapons are being loaded now as I address you, and the submarines will be ready in thirty minutes. You may write a letter to your parents and families, telling them of your decision to accept this great honor. We will as a nation venerate your heroic efforts for all eternity. You have my esteemed admiration for your courage. Go in peace, my friends."

The executive officer dismissed the six men, who left without a word. The captain turned to his executive officer. "The weapons' yields must be increased to their maximums. Beijing has ordered us to take full advantage of this last opportunity before we are attacked by our adversaries."

The executive officer saluted. He looked at the captain and hesitated, as if to say something. The captain nodded his head in silent reply to the unspoken question, and the executive officer left quickly to do the captain's bidding.

***

Colonel Steve Rader set his coffee cup down. The sound of ceramic striking wood echoed in the command post. "Send a message to the crew. I want to know if those guys are still out there."

"Sir," said the major. "We're only supposed to contact the crew in the gravest of circumstances."

"They're over an hour late reporting in. We don't know if they've been shot down, if they ran out of gas, or if they're just plain lost. I'd say that any one of those possibilities are pretty grave circumstances. Send an encoded message on SATCOM and find out what the hell is going on." He turned to a female captain sitting close by. "Call ATC and see what they know about the plane."

"Yes, sir," said the captain.

Colonel Rader looked around the command post. No one seemed to be concerned. No sense of urgency, no sense that something might be askew. Efficient technocrats functioning flawlessly without thinking. *I just don't fit in this Air Force anymore*, he thought to himself.

***

Doctor Chen watched the ground fall quickly away from the Lear jet, which was rapidly climbing into the dark sky. He closed his eyes yet again, and this time sleep came easily.

***

Captain Charlie Macklin stepped to the side of his station as Captain Robert Mueller arrived, crash axe raised and screaming. He gave Mueller a shove as the crash axe smashed into his navigation equipment. Mueller fell to the right, carrying the axe with him in his right hand. Spinning in the direction of his left shoulder, he slammed into Macklin's ejection seat, the crash axe having arrived there first. The axe, a double-edged stainless steel wonder designed for cutting easily through the aluminum skin of airplanes for quick escape in the event of an emergency, sliced just as easily through the flight suit and flesh of Robert Mueller. He released the handle of the axe and put his hand to his thigh where one edge of the axe was buried. He looked over his shoulder back at Charlie Macklin, who was leaning over, his hands on his knees, and staring.

"Charlie," Mueller called. "Charlie…" Mueller felt lightheaded and pulled the axe from his rapidly hemorrhaging leg. There was no pain, only red wet goo soaking into his flight suit.

CHAPTER 13

The captain of the Mao Tse-tung stood looking over the side of his ship. He ordered the outside lights turned off and, except for the glow of an almost spent cigarette, he was camouflaged against the blackness. He wore a round hat with a jet-black bill, and his uniform was crisp white and freshly pressed. Two small boards, each black with four gold stripes, perched on his shoulders. He was dressed in full formal attire, as if a parade of sailors might appear on deck at any moment. His executive officer approached him with a salute, which the captain tiredly returned.

"Captain, the submarines have left for the ocean floor." His executive officer paused and searched the face of his commanding officer. "They will run out of oxygen in an hour at a depth of over 10,000 feet, and the crews will never have the opportunity to plant their weapons." His voice quivered slightly.

The captain held up his hand. "Do not tell me any more details. When our superiors ask me why the weapons were never delivered, I must be able to answer them truthfully that I do not know."

"Why did you have me increase the weapons to their maximum yields, when the submarines will never reach their destination?"

"I did not want to disobey orders. I can say that I obeyed my orders completely, that it was the crews of the submarines put onto my ship that failed their mission."

The executive officer looked at his mentor, waiting for him to say more. But the captain only gazed out to sea. He took another drag from his cigarette and tossed it overboard. The executive officer broke the silence. "When will the Americans attack us?"

"Soon," said the captain. "You can tell the crew to turn out the lights on the interior of the ship, but it won't matter. The Americans have night vision devices and the best radars in the world."

"Shall we resist?"

"Of course," was the reply. The captain turned and faced his faithful protégé. He extended his arms and put his hands on the other officer's shoulders. "It is our duty to resist the enemy when we are able, and we must always do our duty."

***

Rick arrived at the office. "Joe, did you get the coordinates of the trawler?"

"Just like you asked, Rick. Every half-hour from when it left the Panama Canal until the Navy picked 'em up."

"Thanks. I'll give Doctor Cooper a call. She's been waiting for these so she can plot the trawler's course." He took the sheet from his colleague and looked at the numbers. He gave Joe a pair of pats on his arm. "Yeah, she'll be happy all right."

"Not gonna deliver them in person?"

Rick turned to look at Joe. "Why would I do that?"

Joe laughed and winked. "Rick, I think when it comes to personal stuff, you fool yourself a lot." He turned and walked away. "Just thought you might want to give them to her personally, but then, what do I know?"

Rick shook his head and watched Joe until he disappeared from sight. He walked to his desk and checked the time on his computer. Eight thirty. *That makes it five thirty in California*, he thought. *Hmmm.*

She'd want me to call her, even if it was middle of the night. He picked up the receiver and dialed Doctor Cooper's apartment.

"Hello?" said a voice that seemed to come from far away.

"Marly? This is Rick. Did I wake you?"

A pause. "Yeah. What time is it?"

"I think it's five thirty your time. Shall I call back later?"

"No," Marly said. "I couldn't sleep last night worrying about all this stuff. Guess I finally fell asleep, though." She reached for the clock on her nightstand and looked at the numbers. She struggled to clear her head.

"I have the coordinates of the trawler that you wanted so you could plot where it was going."

Marly pushed herself up in bed and brushed her hand through her hair. Her nightgown pulled to one side, and she tried to make herself comfortable by lifting her body and shifting her weight. It did not help. The grogginess would not leave her. "Can you fax the coordinates to my office? I should be there in about an hour."

"Sure, but I don't think I have your fax number."

"Of course you don't. What am I thinking?" She shook her head, her hair gently swaying across her face, and she looked into the mirror on the dresser across from her bed. "Um, it's..." and she gave him the number. She stared into the mirror and wondered what Rick was thinking about as he spoke to her. *Did he find her attractive? But why would she care, anyway?* "Why don't you call me about seven o'clock my time? I should have the coordinates plotted by then."

"Seven o'clock. I won't be late." Rick smiled as he hung up. Marly's voice had been soft, sensual. He closed his eyes and imagined her tanned skin and dark hair. *Maybe Joe's right. Maybe I should have delivered the coordinates in person.*

Marly put the phone heavily back into its cradle. She took a deep breath and held it. She exhaled, tilted her head back, and lifted her arms out straight, moving her fingers to stimulate her circulation. *The trawler. The Navy intercepted it. Good. No, not just good. Great. Yes, great.*

***

Rupert Budowski shook his head. No sign of Doctor Chen. No sign of anyone of Asian descent in the entire airport complex. He laughed to himself. He knew they'd never find them now.

***

Kam Fong slid out of bed and stretched. He leaned over and bent at the waist, keeping his knees locked, and touched his toes. He could feel his muscles were tired, but his mind was racing, so fast that he could barely keep up with the thoughts that seemed to ricochet all around his head.

Picking up the briefcase that had been waiting in the room and placing it on the bed, Fong opened it. He held up the green vest hidden inside, laden with plastic explosive. The lanyard that would ignite chaos when pulled, hung loosely. He slipped it on over his pajamas to test the fit. *Perfect.* He removed the vest and carefully laid it down.

He headed for the bathroom, a smile lighting his face. Hot running water had been a luxury in his home, and sponge baths were the rule of the day. Showers were rare and only for the most special of occasions. Today would make one more, the last. He decided to stand under a hot shower until he could tolerate it no more.

***

Benny yelped for joy when Marly appeared in the hallway. Next to him was a yellow puddle. *Now why at 5:30 in the morning would Benny relieve himself in the house?* She leaned up against the wall, her body protesting the time of day. "Benny, Benny, Benny…"

***

"Charlie!" yelled the pilot. "Bob! What are you guys doing back there? What's all the ruckus? You guys need some help?"

There was no reply.

"Charlie! Bob!" Jimmy Blase turned around vainly in his seat to look at the gunner, but he could not see. "Chief, maybe you need to go down there."

An exhausted voice echoed into the interphone. "Bob's cut himself, real bad."

"Whattaya mean he cut himself? How'd he do that?" asked the pilot.

"He fell on the crash axe, and it stabbed him in the leg."

"He fell on the crash axe? How could Bob fall on the crash axe?"

"I don't know. He just snapped. He attacked me with the crash axe, and he fell on it when I pushed him. Now he's bleeding pretty bad."

"He attacked you with the crash axe? Why would he do that?"

"How do I know why he did it? He went psycho, that's all I know." The wizzo mumbled the last part. "He went crazy, like a loon."

He shook his head and disconnected his headset from the interphone cord. He walked over to the bulkhead behind his seat, and pulled the emergency first aid kit from the wall once more. Opening it, he pulled out a large roll of gauze.

***

Kam Fong waited for the hot water. Thirty seconds. A minute. Two minutes. Three. Although he was the first person awake in the hotel, there was no hot water coming from the faucet.

***

Marly pushed away from the wall and took a step. She felt something soft and warm and lifted her bare foot to look. *What now? Dog crap, too?* "Benny, what has gotten into you?" The smell of dog feces filled the air with an impressive stench. Marly hopped on one foot into the kitchen to get a paper towel to clean up the mess, when her foot landed on the dog's water bowl, spilling it and sending water everywhere. Marly almost fell and caught herself on the kitchen counter with her hand. She stood paralyzed, her foot screaming with pain. She began to laugh, and Benny began to bark. The harder Marly laughed, the louder he barked. She leaned against the counter and let herself slide into a sitting position, her bottom feeling the damp cold of the dog's spilled water. Benny leapt into her lap, his paws soaking wet.

***

Think, Jimmy Blase told himself. *Think!* He blinked his eyes. He thought that he could make out the round shape of the gauges on the plane's instrument panel. He blinked hard again.

There are only three of us left. No missiles. No tankers. That's it! We have to call the tankers. "Charlie, the tankers. You've got to get a message to Colonel Rader and tell him that we need the tankers to meet us a lot farther west than planned."

Charlie Macklin sat in a daze. Robert Mueller's blood covered the entire floor of the navigator station. The bandage he tied just above the injury to stem the blood loss had turned crimson.

"Charlie, did you hear me?"

The wizzo seemed to wake up. "Yeah, I heard you, Pilot. You want me to send a SATCOM message to get the tankers out over the ocean to meet us?"

"Right."

"When did you want me to do it?"

"Now, Charlie, now."

"OK. Got it." He fumbled for a moment and then looked at the equipment on his weapons station, which held the SATCOM radio box. The box was sliced in two, a clean blow from the crash axe having ended its usefulness.

***

Poised at the side of the bathtub, shower curtain pulled back, Kam Fong's body trembled. Extremely superstitious, he stood paralyzed, afraid. Could this be a sign? Cold water flowed out of the tap, and there would be no hot water this day. He stepped into the cold stream and started shaking violently. He took the soap and began to wash.

***

"Pilot, this is the Weapons Systems Officer."

Jimmy Blase was puzzled by Charlie Macklin's formal manner. "Yeah, Charlie, what's up?"

"The navigator's destroyed the SATCOM box. We can't talk to anybody, and they can't talk to us."

Jimmy Blase considered the wizzo's words and turned them over slowly. *No tankers? We can't tell anybody to send the tankers? Do we break comm-out procedures and make a call in the clear? No, can't do that until we make the decision to abort.* "OK, so that means no refueling. We're back to where we were before, but now it's unlikely we'll make it back."

"Looks that way."

"OK. I'm willing to take another vote before we press on to the target."

"Now's a nice time to take another vote, after Bob practically killed me when he popped his circuit breakers."

"Before Bob hurt himself, we were gonna try to get refueled. But now we can't. So the circumstances have changed, and I'm willing to take another vote on whether or not we continue with the mission. I haven't changed my mind. I'm ready to do whatever it takes, but maybe you guys have decided something different."

"Not me, Cap'n," said the gunner. "It's still a go-er for me."

The wizzo's voice sounded strained and resigned to the fate that awaited them. "Guess it doesn't matter what I think. OK, I'm moving over to Bob's station to fly the waypoints. It'll take me a second to switch places." *Damn you, Bob*, Charlie Macklin said to himself. *Now we're all gonna drown for sure, unless we're lucky and get eaten by sharks first.*

***

Colonel Steve Rader grew impatient. "Have we got anything from the crew or air traffic control?"

"Nothing," said the major. "It looks like they went completely incommunicado after the second target."

"That wasn't the plan," said the Colonel. "Something's happened. Get me the wing commander in Washington."

"Sir, we might interrupt his breakfast with the chief of staff at the Pentagon."

"I don't care if we interrupt his morning constitutional on the crapper, I don't care if we interrupt him while he's making love to his wife, and I certainly don't care if we interrupt his breakfast! Now get him on the phone!"

***

"Pilot, what are you gonna miss the most?"

"Whattaya mean, Chief?"

"I mean, we're not gonna make it back. What do you think'll happen? You gonna miss anybody? Anybody gonna miss you?"

"Oh. Well, probably a few friends will miss me, and my mama is going to miss me a lot. I know that."

"What about your dad?"

"Never knew him, Chief. He left my mom before I was born. My granddad was my dad."

"Brothers? Sisters? They gonna miss you?"

Jimmy Blase shook his head. "No brothers or sisters. Just me. Mama never got married and never had any more children." He laughed. "But if I'll miss anything, I think it's gonna be Mama's fried chicken. Ain't nothin' better than fried chicken that's cooked right." He laughed again.

"Maybe there's fried chicken where we're going, you know, after we die," said the gunner.

"There's no fried chicken in Heaven, Chief," said the pilot.

"Do you believe you're going to Heaven?" asked the gunner.

"Of course."

"How about you, Chief, are you going to Heaven?" asked the wizzo, making no attempt to hide his sarcasm and anger.

"I don't think so, Cap'n." The gunner seemed to take no note of the wizzo's tone of voice. "I'd like to believe in Heaven, but I just don't see how somethin' like Heaven could be real. Besides, the way I lived my life, I have the feelin' that if I believed in anything, it'd be hell."

"Believing the Bible is the way to get to Heaven," said Jimmy Blase. "None of us deserve to go to Heaven."

"Don't preach to us about the Bible, Jimmy," said Charlie Macklin. "You think my wife and son are gonna believe in God when I don't come home from this mission? My wife knows that a good God doesn't do things like this. My kid's going to grow up without a father."

"I grew up without a dad, Charlie, so I know how your boy will feel. I just wish that my dad had died a hero instead of leaving my mama to fend for herself after he made her pregnant."

Charlie Macklin was quiet.

"How about you, Chief? I've never met your wife or family," said the pilot.

"That's 'cause I don't have one, Cap'n. My wife divorced me 'bout fifteen years ago."

"I'm sorry, Chief. I never knew that."

"No reason to be sorry, Cap'n. She was sick and tired of me bein' gone all the time on alert and flyin' and all, and she tole me if I left to go to the desert when we fought the Iraqis the first time that she'd be gone when I got back." He paused. "I tole her that bein' a sergeant, I couldn't do nothin' else but what I was told. Besides, bein' a gunner in a B-52 didn't exactly translate too good to the civilian world. What was I goin' to do if I got out? All I could do was kill people and break things."

"So you went to the Gulf?"

"'Course. And when I got back, she was gone. Just like she promised. Took our daughter and left. 'Course she'll be happy now when I die, 'cause she'll get survivor benefits. Was gonna get half my retirement pay, but I wasn't goin' to retire for awhile. Yep, I 'spect that she'll be real happy when I'm gone." He shook his head.

"What about your daughter? Won't she miss you?"

The gunner did not answer right away. "No. She and my wife pretty much feel the same way 'bout me. I guess I hafta admit I wasn't too good at being a husband or a father. Sorta struck out on both counts."

"You're breakin' my heart, Chief," said the wizzo with contempt in his voice. "Really breakin' my heart."

***

An army of small, black dinghies set out from the sides of the trawler Mao Tse-tung, which was treading slowly through the water. Each dinghy held two sailors, one armed with a handheld infrared missile-launcher capable of locking onto the exhaust emanating from a jet engine. When fired, the launcher's missile would home in on the heat, striking the engine with the intent of shooting down the plane.

The dinghies were tethered to the trawler and dropped back several thousand feet behind. The plan was for the sailors to fire their handheld missiles as the bomber roared by. With an airspeed of over mach six, the missiles would easily catch the bomber from behind and destroy it before it reached its target.

The captain watched the dinghies disappear into the early morning light. He doubted that the American bomber would ever get close enough for his sailors to take a shot. He expected the Americans to strike with a missile attack entirely out of range for handheld defenses, and that their adversary would only be visible after the damage was already done. But it was his duty to direct the ship and its crew to resist the attack, and he watched his executive officer organize the sailors under his command to do just that.

***

Kam Fong put on the vest filled with plastic explosive and buttoned it. He took his shirt and pulled it over his shoulders, the flat vest invisible underneath. The mirror finally convinced him that the vest could not be seen, and he departed the hotel after paying for three more days. Putting his hand to his abdomen, he felt for the lanyard that would birth China's new life. He wore a knowing smile and scoffed at the people around him, who were going through the routine of their daily lives unaware that today, this very day, once and forever the course of history would be irrevocably thrust in a new direction.

CHAPTER 14

Marly arrived to an empty office. Awaiting her on the fax machine was the page with the coordinates of the trawler, coordinates that she had chewed on for the last two days. She practically memorized the longitudinal line from the Panama Canal to the northwest panhandle of the Nazca plate and had estimated the coordinates she'd be getting from Rick. Her arms got goose bumps, and the paper shook in her hand.

Marly read the numbers, one pair at a time, and put her hand to her mouth. She turned and looked at the large computer monitor where she drew a line from the canal to the predicted destination. On the screen were written her estimated coordinates for the first two hours of the trawler's journey, and they almost exactly matched what was on the paper. She looked at the clock. It was 6:45AM.

***

John Renoir walked up to Rick. "The B-52 has disappeared. The crew hasn't contacted anyone since the second trawler. We've intercepted a MAYDAY from three of the trawlers, so it looks like they made it to the first three targets."

"Maybe they lost their SATCOM radio," said Rick.

"I hope you're right, but satellite imagery shows a pristine fourth trawler. The plane's flight plan says they should have hit the last trawler hours ago."

Rick nodded his head.

"So what options do we have to go after the trawler heading south if we don't dispatch another B-52?"

"What, you think they shot the plane down or something?"

Renoir shrugged. "I don't know. But like I said, it looks like they never made it to the fourth ship. We can't afford to lose another bomber, and if what you say is true, this last ship heading south and its load of nukes is a must-job. I don't think the president wants to use something that didn't succeed the first time."

Rick rested his arm on his chest to support his elbow. "Before the president decided to direct the Air Force to attack the trawlers, I called the Navy to see what they had." He could see the questioning look on John Renoir's face. "You know, to see if they had deep sea submersibles like the MIR-1 — the one salvagers used to get to the Titanic. Turns out the Navy has something called the Special Mission Program, and it has submersibles for rescuing crews from disabled submarines and for recovering stuff from the ocean floor.

"They have unmanned tethered vehicles for their deep sea missions, which they control remotely from the surface. They can go deeper than a manned submarine, and they're more compact and lighter — plus they don't put people at risk." He was quiet for a moment. "But I don't think an unmanned platform is going to work. This time the trawler will know we're coming so we're talking about intercepting, maybe even chasing the Chinese submersibles. That means we need manned submarines." Rick looked at his boss. "Unfortunately the Navy's manned subs don't go very deep. Everything they have in their inventory right now only goes down to about five thousand feet. I looked at a map of the Pacific Ocean, and I think we have to go all the way down to fifteen thousand."

"It sounds like the Navy doesn't have what we need."

"Not necessarily. I talked to a petty officer who works on the program. He said they used to have a pair of manned deep submergence vehicles and that even though the Navy phased them out a few years ago, they're in mothballs and could be made operational again virtually overnight. And those things can apparently go down to the depths we've been talking about."

"Go on."

"To begin with, we'll need to get the submersibles to South America."

"How do we do that?" Renoir asked. "Those things must be huge."

"That's the best part. They were built for emergencies, so the Navy designed them to be flown on top of a Boeing 747 — just like the space shuttle. You can ferry them wherever you want in a matter of hours."

"And then what? How do you get them out to the trawler?"

"I haven't figured that out."

Renoir sighed. "How long before we get these things into position if the president decides to go along with your plan?"

"We think we've got a day and a half until the trawler gets to the drop off point." Rick shrugged. "We need to start moving now, which means you've got to give the go ahead. I can work the logistics with my team and the Navy, but even a few hours could make all the difference."

Renoir sighed again. "OK, do it. I'll brief the president this afternoon, and he can stop the plan if he doesn't like it. You sure you know what you're doing? About what has to be done?"

Rick smiled. "No. I have no idea what I'm doing. But I've got friends who do, and..." Rick's smile turned into a grin. "...I've got the entire U.S. Navy at my disposal if I need it to turn this delusional fantasy into a genuine operation."

"What about the 747s to fly the subs? Where will you get them?"

Rick shook his head. "I don't think it's going to be a problem. I saw Wal-Mart's got a big sale, and I thought I'd start my search there."

Renoir shook his head. "You guys make me nervous when you start talking trash."

***

The phone rang. "Doctor Cooper."

"Marly, this is Rick. Did you get the fax?"

Marly Cooper was all business. "Yeah, and you're not going to like what they show. They track almost exactly on a straight line from the canal to the northwest corner of the Nazca plate."

"So it looks like your hypothesis was correct…" Rick could not finish the sentence. "This is all pretty crazy, isn't it?"

"It's more than crazy. I can't imagine that Doctor Chen is behind all this."

"I wish I could tell you something different, but I can't. We've been advised that he was a member of the Communist Party before he came to the states. He's disappeared, by the way. He was last seen in Mexico and is probably on his way back to China by now."

***

Kam Fong sipped his tea. He never noticed before how it left a flat taste in his mouth after each sup. He was always in such a hurry that he never noted the smaller pleasures of life. The destination was always more important than the journey. But today was different. As he went through the day, he found himself enjoying almost everything. Each sound, every smell, and colors that appeared to glisten. All were suddenly brilliant and alive as if he had lived in musty shadows of gray his entire life. Another sup of tea. The hot burned his mouth, but he knew that it did not matter. Nothing mattered today except, yes, except.

***

Marly Cooper sat down tiredly at her desk. The night was too short, the wine too abundant, and the stress of finding out she was right about the last trawler did not increase her energy level. Fatigue was rapidly consuming her.

***

Rick dialed his contact at the Special Missions Office.

"Petty Officer Lo-wan Washing-ton," came a voice.

"Lowan, this is Rick Starr. We talked a couple days ago."

"Oh, yeah, how ya doin', Mister Starr? How's it hangin'? Did you get those bad dudes you talked about?"

Rick laughed. "Not quite. We're going to need your help. We need to use the deep submergence vehicles that you said were in mothballs, the ones that can go down to ten thousand feet plus."

"OK, OK, we can handle that. 'Course now you gotta get the Navy to agree to let us use 'em. They're the ones that's got to get them out of the museum."

"Museum? I thought you said they were in mothballs."

"They are, Mister Starr. The politicians killed the program, and it was the only way the Navy could justify not turning them into scrap metal. We squids ain't stupid, you know."

"I have to admit it sounds ingenious. I wanted to give you a heads-up so that you could start pulling your team together."

"I wanted to talk to you 'bout that, Mister Starr. I tried to call my buddy who retired when they put the subs in mothballs, and I can't find him. He's up in Canada somewhere."

"You can't find him? What does that mean?"

"It means we don't got nobody to drive the other sub."

"Isn't there somebody else in the Navy who can pilot a submarine?"

"You gotta be outta your mind to drive a submarine several miles underwater, Mister Starr, and the world ain't exactly full of people willing to do that."

"So what are you saying? We can only use one sub?"

"No, we can use both of 'em. You just gotta find someone to drive the other one."

"How do I do that?"

"I don't know, Mister Starr. Oh, and there's one other little detail."

"What's that?"

"Each submarine holds three people, one driver and two to work the systems on-board. You and me make two. Who's gonna be the other people that'll be goin'?"

"The other people? And what do you mean, you and me?"

***

Taking time to stop and peer into every window, Kam Fong walked leisurely down the street, absorbing the various odds and ends that dressed the spaces behind the glass. He checked his reflection and stood up straight to see if the vest was still invisible. He impulsively touched his shirt.

A small food stand rested on the sidewalk. "*Señor, como ayudo?*" its young proprietor asked.

Fong pointed to a stale-looking hotdog bun. The girl obliged by pulling a dripping hotdog from a pot of boiling water and setting it on the bread. He pointed to a bottle, and the girl poured a generous stream of yellow mustard onto his order. He paid with the remainder of his money. He walked away before getting his change from the girl's outstretched hand. She shrugged her shoulders and dropped it back into her cash box.

Kam Fong held the mustard-laden hotdog up to his nose and drank in the pungent odor. He had not eaten a hotdog since he defected to the mainland, and he hungrily gulped it down. It would be his last meal. Suddenly, chills tickled the hair on his neck. Sirens. He pointed his ear toward the sound. Yes, sirens. And they were getting closer.

***

John Kale and his team were wedged into an old Volkswagen Beetle that sputtered along behind the Chinese president's entourage.

Despite his assurances, Miguel Gonzalez put the American team too far away from the president to have a role in his protection. Kale gazed out the window, his frown registering his displeasure.

The white stucco residence of Mexico City's mayor, surrounded by large palm trees, dominated the horizon. Men, armed with machine guns, lined the roof's edge. The entourage drove through the gate of the large iron fence that surrounded the home. The first limousine carried the "expendables", a shield for the second vehicle that carried both the Mexican and Chinese presidents. They were followed in a limo by Gonzalez's security detail, whose contents emptied before it stopped. They ran to the second car and pulled open its doors. Kale's Volkswagen was stopped at the gate, and they were told to remain outside the compound.

Meanwhile, a crowd gathered outside the fence, and police along the sidewalk encouraged people to approach the fence and wave. Television cameras, held by local media and national news teams, took shots from across the street. They were following the entourage and competed for the best filming locations. Reporters talked endlessly to cameras that seemed hungry for their every word about this historic visit. Only a meeting with the Pope could rival the attention.

Kam Fong panicked as he approached the mayor's residence. He found that he could not get through the thick crowd, and he was unable to reach the fence where he was supposed to meet the president. Moving laterally along the edge of the horde, he searched for a hole where he could squeeze through. But human flesh had merged into a single mass of amorphous tissue. His English appeals were ignored. He watched helplessly as the two presidents walked leisurely to the side of the mayor's house and then turned toward the crowd.

***

John Kale stepped out of the Volkswagen, ignoring the police officer who commanded him to stay in the car. He saw the two presidents walking toward the fence. "Let's go," he barked at his team. "The Chinese president is walking over to greet the crowd. I want to be there!"

His team got out of the small Volkswagen, and the four men walked briskly toward the edge of the tightly packed throng. John Kale held up a badge and in Spanish commanded the crowd to give way. The people pushed apart, making room for the determined man and the three agents behind him. They shoved their way through the crowd toward the fence. Kale and his team did not notice the small Asian man who fell in behind and followed them through the mob. They reached the fence as the Chinese president gazed at the gathering multitude as if he were looking for someone. He seemed to smile as if he recognized a familiar face, and Kale looked to his left. Standing there was a diminutive Asian man. The man appeared to return the president's smile. The Mexican president nodded at his counterpart, and the two began walking together toward the sea of people while talking in English, the one language in which they could communicate. Kale wondered at the presence of this Asian man by the fence in the middle of a crowd of Mexican citizens. He put his hand into his jacket to touch a holstered pistol, and he watched the man carefully in his peripheral vision.

***

Kam Fong saw the president's smile and returned it. He did not dare wave, lest he give their secret away. So he pressed up against the fence and joined with the others who were putting their hands through the metal bars toward the two men. Some of the beckoning hands held pencil and paper.

***

A group of Mexican security agents approached the fence ahead of the two presidents and carefully perused the people pressed into the barrier, a group which had grown from a few hundred into well over several thousand. For the first time, Miguel Gonzalez grew uncomfortable. He pointed to his left with his head and ordered his security crew to their positions.

***

The Mexican president walked aimlessly in the direction of the fence. But when he tried to deviate too far to the right or left, the Chinese president herded him so that they continued toward Kale and his team — and toward the small Asian man standing off to his side.

***

Kam Fong carefully placed his left hand on the thick bar of the steel black fence, directly in front of his abdomen. His face could not stop smiling. He looked up at the sky one last time, its beauty intoxicating. An omen, the sign he was waiting for. He looked back at the president, who was slowly, but incessantly, moving in his direction. The president did not try to catch Fong's attention anymore. But it did not matter. They already communicated their recognition of one another. History now waited patiently for its partners to rent the future.

***

Kale thought it odd that the Chinese president seemed to be coaxing his counterpart more or less directly toward the Asian man standing off to his left. He looked back into the group of faces, and there were now tens of Asians in the midst of the sea of Mexican nationals. He noticed that Miguel Gonzalez and his team set themselves up against the black metal fence, trying to screen the presidents from direct contact with the people, who were shouting enthusiastically.

***

The two presidents paused in front of the security team that blocked them from the crowd. They smiled widely at one another over an apparent joke made by the Chinese president, and the Mexican president gestured toward Gonzalez and his men to move aside. Gonzalez protested, but the president's unhappy look made him reconsider. He motioned to his team, and they stepped away. The crowd began to cheer wildly as the two men reached out and grabbed the extended hands, taking the papers and pencils offered to them and signing autographs.

***

Kam Fong was elated that the Chinese president was bringing his Mexican host over to where he was waiting. It would be so much more meaningful, so much more tragic if both presidents were to pass into eternity with him. The idea was so exhilarating, the move so bold, the inspiration so brilliant that he could hardly hide his eagerness for what was about to happen. The elation made him lightheaded.

John Kale noticed the changed demeanor of the Asian man, who suddenly seemed to be extremely animated, almost giddy at the approach of the two presidents. He watched in amazement as the Chinese president, as if on cue, took the arm of his Mexican colleague and pulled him over to his ethnic equal who stood grinning widely. The Chinese president guided his host's hand toward the small man, who took it and bowed slightly in a sign of respect. Kale no longer hid his stare, but looked directly at the scene playing out in front of him. *Maybe it makes sense for the Chinese president to be attracted to the one Asian face in the front of the crowd*, he thought. The Mexican president released his grip, and the Chinese president reached in to replace the hand with his own. He seemed to hold the young man's hand and wait. *What is he waiting for?* wondered John Kale.

Then he saw it. The Asian man, his hand firmly clasping that of the Chinese president, reached up under his shirt with his left hand and revealed a small lanyard attached to a rope-like cord. Without thinking, Kale lurched to his left and leapt in the direction of the fist that seemed to be moving in slow motion as it grasped the exposed lanyard. Kale tore the hand of the assassin from that of the president as he reached in vain for his target, knowing that it was too late. The man pulled the lanyard, and Kale could hear a scream coming from somewhere behind. He did not realize the sound was that of his own voice, the desperate cry of a dying man.

***

Miguel Gonzalez watched the two presidents walk to the steel bars and take the outstretched hands of the crowd. He caught sight of John Kale absorbed in the actions of a small man, who seemed to be waiting his turn to shake the hands of the dignitaries. He observed Kale's countenance suddenly transition from a look of intense interest to one of abject fear, and he instinctively moved in the direction of the Mexican president at the first sign of the change. Just as Gonzalez reached the president, Kale leapt. Gonzalez glanced in the direction where Kale seemed to be headed, when he saw the lanyard. He grabbed the Mexican president and threw him to the ground face first. He pressed the president into the hard earth, spread himself over his body, and waited for the inevitable.

***

Kam Fong took the hand of the Mexican president. *It's soft, like a woman's,* he thought. He smiled at the man in front of him, bowed, and released his hand. The Chinese president then took his hand and held it. He was waiting, Fong knew. He reached up under his shirt, and as he did so he heard a yell from the right. Turning his head he saw a man, an American, airborne and falling in his direction. Fong flashed a triumphant smile. The American grabbed Fong's wrist and yanked it from the president's hand, pulling Fong to the ground. Fong's smile grew wider as he pulled the lanyard. The fuse ignited, and the smell of burning flesh filled his nostrils. He knew that it was his own, but it did not matter. Nothing mattered now except, yes, except. He was the father of the new China, and he felt the forces of history embrace his soul.

CHAPTER 15

"Pilot, it's time to start scannin' for the target," said the wizzo, Charlie Macklin. He was caught up in the hunt, forgetting the blood at his feet and the likelihood of never returning home. "I've got the radar cookin', and once I find this baby, we're goin' to have to do some macho maneuverin'." He spoke to himself out loud. "Radar keeps fading in and out, probably the result of the laser hit we took." He spoke to the pilot again. "I don't think the trawler's gonna come up on radar till we're right at a hundred miles. We're about 200 miles out now, according to the coordinates we got."

"Roger, nav. Chief, you better get your guns."

"You gonna be OK, pilot? Can you fly without my help?" asked the Chief.

"Yeah, I think so. I can see the gauges, and I can make the numbers out on the compass now. I couldn't fly without the autopilot, but I can handle it."

"Roger, pilot. I'm unlockin' my guns and goin' through the checklist. They're showin' cocked and loaded to the max. I'll be dumpin' a thousand rounds a minute out the barrels, and I'll be aimin' for the rudder. My camera's workin' great. I can see like I'm lookin' out the window on a sunny day, so once I have the beast in my sites, he's gonna be eatin' titanium bullets a hell of a lot faster than he can swallow them. I've only shot real ammo a couple o' times, so I'm lookin' forward to this opportunity to excel."

"You think this'll work, Chief?" asked the pilot.

"Oh, it'll work all right. I have a real good feelin' 'bout it, if that's what's botherin' you. Titanium is known to be bad for your health."

***

"Lowan, you're going to have to say that again."

"What's a matter, Mister Starr? You got wax in yore ears? I said you gotta supply the crews for the submarines."

"But why? Can't you get the guys to man the subs?"

"Chief of Naval Operations won't allow it. I had to sign ten different pieces of paper so I could go with you, all in the presence of a whole bunch o' high-powered lawyers. CNO says this is CIA's boondoggle, so CIA can staff it. Ain't no sense arguin', Mister Starr. You just gotta come up with four guys besides yoreself. We need someone to pilot the other sub and a couple o' folks to run the hydraulic arms on each sub."

Rick knew the CNO was annoyed with him. After all, the Navy was not running the operation, the CIA was, and the CIA would get the credit if it was a success. "OK, I understand. What about the 747s?"

"That's no problem, Mister Starr. The subs should be ready to fly out in a couple o' hours once the Navy gets the go-ahead. You'll just have to tell 'em where you want 'em to go. Can't wait forever, though."

"We're working that, Lowan, we're working that. I should have the final coordinates for you by the time the boats are ready to fly. And authorization has already been given to the Navy."

"Speakin' o' flyin', who's gonna drive the other sub? Got anyone in mind?"

"I haven't talked to him in awhile, but I've got a colleague who used to fly fighters for the Air Force. I'm thinking that driving a sub in the water is a lot like flying a jet through the air."

"Sounds good to me, Mister Starr. I heard stories 'bout airplane pilots drivin' boats. They say boats is a lot slower but kind o' the same. So you're probably gonna be OK. Got any ideas for the other crew members?"

Rick thought about Marly Cooper. "Well, if I've got to get an entire crew for the submarines, it seems to me that each one should have a driver, a CIA representative, and a seismologist — you know, a specialist on earthquakes." He thought that Marly might be able to supply the names of a couple people, like Ralph Thiele.

"Earthquakes? What's earthquakes got to do with what we want to do?"

"Well, I've told you that we're going to be intercepting a couple of submersibles carrying nukes."

"Yeah, that's some really heavy guano, boss."

"The subs plan to put the nukes on the ocean floor where they can cause an earthquake, so we need someone who knows where that might be."

"Whoa. Is there a chance that those nukes might, well, you know? Not that it matters. I'm goin' along no matter what. But you know, I was just wonderin'."

"I won't kid you, Lowan. This could be a one way trip to the bottom of the sea."

There was a moment of silence. Rick wondered if he'd have to revert to plan B. Not that he had one.

"That's OK, Mister Starr. I tole you I'd help, so that's what I'm gonna do. I don't think you can do this mission without me, anyway."

"You're right about that, Lowan. If it's any comfort, I'll put in a good word about you to the president this afternoon."

"The president? Of the U-nited States?"

"None other, Lowan. Not that it'll make our mission any easier. But I want you to know that what you're doing is of great service to the nation." He knew that he was saying this to himself as much as he was telling Washington. "I better go. I've got to call that friend to see if he's interested in a one way ticket, too."

***

"Pilot, I've got the target. He's well off to the right. Start your turn. We're goin' sixty degrees right to heading…make that, uh…make it three-two-zero."

Jimmy Blase began his turn at the wizzo's first direction. He wrapped the plane into a thirty-degree bank turn and crosschecked the attitude indicator and altimeter to make sure the plane was maintaining altitude. He rolled out. "Heading three-two-zero, Mac."

The wizzo was glued to the radar, the trawler dead center in his scope. "Trawler's straight ahead, eighty miles."

Sunlight splashed the water as the sun greeted the morning, and the pilot scanned the brightened horizon for the ship. The gunner readjusted his camera for daylight conditions. "Three-two-five now, pilot. Boat is trackin' left to right. We're gonna fly smack dab over the top of this sucker," said the wizzo.

"Coming right five degrees, nav."

The gunner clicked off the safety on his weapon. "Pilot, slower's better. I'll have more time to find the target and more time to load it up with iron."

Jimmy Blase did not hesitate. He dropped the flaps to thirty degrees and lowered the landing gear. The plane slowed almost immediately. Jimmy let the airspeed fall to a hundred-seventy knots before pushing the throttles up again.

"Safety's off. Preparation to fire checklist complete. I'm ready to turn this cruise liner into a rowboat."

"Fifty miles to the target," said the wizzo.

Jimmy Blase peered out the windscreen. He thought he saw the trawler. Had his eyes been their usual keen selves, he might have noticed the armada of dinghies trailing the ship. "Got a visual, nav. It's gotta be the trawler. Get your stuff ready, Chief. This baby has your name engraved on the side of it."

***

Tom Bowman answered his mobile. "Bowman here."

"Tom, this is Rick."

Silence.

"Tom, this is Rick, Rick Starr."

Rick could hear someone breathing into the phone. Tom Bowman spoke slowly. "Are you OK? You don't have a problem, do you?"

Rick Starr laughed. "Well, as a matter of fact I do. But not like the last time. This time you get to decide whether you want to help me out, although I have to admit I'm pretty desperate."

Tom Bowman sighed. "Just like before. So what's up? I thought you were giving up field work."

"I am. I mean I did. But this is different. How'd you like to do some flying?"

"You know the doc says I can't. Says I could screw up my spine permanently. The compressed discs in my vertebrae can't handle another jolt."

"I'm not talking airplanes. How'd you like to fly a submarine?"

"A submarine?"

"Yeah, through the water like a plane. Only slower, and down instead of up."

"What's the catch and why me?"

"There's only one very small catch, and you're the only guy I could think of who might be able to fly a sub." Rick took a deep breath before continuing. "The catch is that you might not come back if you agree to do this."

Tom Bowman coughed. "I might not come back? What do you mean by that?"

"I mean it could be a permanent vacation to an underwater beach at the bottom of the Pacific Ocean."

Tom Bowman laughed to himself. Gulf War, shot down. CIA, almost killed in the line of duty. Submarine driver on a one way cruise? "Are you going?"

"There's two submarines. I'll be on the first. You'd drive the second, and you'd have two passengers with you to do the dirty work. All you have to do is get them to their destination."

"At the bottom of the Pacific Ocean? I didn't know submarines could go that deep."

"It's a deep sea submersible with the capability to go to a depth of ten thousand feet plus."

"So why is it a one way ticket — potentially, that is?"

"We're going to be chasing some bad guys. Guys carrying nukes. It's going to be cat and mouse, and we won't stop until we either take the cheese or kill the mouse."

Tom Bowman paused for only a second. "If I say yes, when do we go?"

"We'll be leaving in six hours to fly to California and from there down to Chile. We'll be flying in a plane equipped with a hyperbaric chamber so we can jump right into the subs after we land."

"Six hours? That's great planning, Rick. And Chile? Like in South American Chile?"

"Tom, yes or no. I don't have time to fool around. Say yes, and I'll fill you in on the rest of the story. Say no, and I'll talk to you about all this when I get back. But like I said, I'm desperate, and you'd be doing your country an invaluable service."

Tom Bowman shook his head. "OK, I'll go. Now tell me about Chile. I always wanted to see the Andes."

***

Jimmy Blase could see the trawler clearly now. He wondered at the line of dinghies behind the ship.

***

"Marly, this is Rick. I need your help."

"Again? Don't you ever call just to talk?"

Rick could feel himself turning red. *Am I really that way?*

Marly did not give him a chance to answer. "What do you need?"

"I need the names of a couple guys, maybe Ralph Thiele could be one of them — guys who could tell us exactly where the submarines from the fifth trawler might plant their nukes around the Nazca plate."

"Are you planning to chase them?" Marly's voice betrayed her eagerness.

"That's certainly an option now that we've destroyed three of the trawlers. The Navy has a couple of deep sea submersibles that we're hopefully going to drop in near the trawler."

"Why Ralph?"

"We'll be taking two submarines, and I think there should be a seismologist on each one."

"Why not take me? No one knows more about tectonic plates than I do. Not even Ralph."

"Oh. Well, I was thinking, you know, that, uh," Rick gave up trying to explain.

"That what? A girl shouldn't go? Why not both Bev and me?"

"No, it's not that. I just didn't, I mean I wouldn't want anything to happen to you."

"Are you going?"

"Of course."

"Then take me with you and let Beverly ride on the other one."

"I suppose that might work. But I think the sub's are pretty small, and Ralph might be a better choice. Aside from you, of course."

"You can be diplomatic when you need to, can't you? All right. I'll ask Ralph. Bev needs to be here to handle our conference planning while I'm gone, anyway. When do we leave?"

"We'll be arriving in California in about ten hours. We'll meet you at Travis Air Force Base, and from there we'll be flying to Chile. Probably to somewhere near Santiago."

"Ten hours? That's not much time to pack. What should I bring?"

Pack? Who said anything about packing? "I'm bringing myself and a toothbrush. You can bring whatever you want, I suppose. We'll plan our strategy on the flight, and once we land we'll be going directly into the subs and immediately to the expected intercept point."

"What should I wear? Jeans? A sweater? Is it going to be hot on the plane? Will it be cold underwater?"

"I don't know," said Rick. "I guess I never thought about it. I was going to wear jeans and a light jacket. The only thing I think I know is that you don't want to wear a dress and high heels."

***

Jimmy Blase blinked. He wondered if what his eyes were telling him was real. *Why would a fleet of rubber rafts be following the trawler? Have they abandoned ship?*

"Chief, you ready? The target is straight ahead. I estimate it's less than a minute away."

"Ready as I'll ever be, wizzo." He positioned his gun and steadied his weapon. He zoomed out to see a bigger area and set the red circle in the middle of the picture.

"Thirty seconds, Chief."

"Roger, thirty seconds. I'm lookin' for the target."

The pilot scanned the water, his eyes still too blurred to see the passengers in the small rafts clearly.

***

"You got a girl to go on our sub?"

"Well, she's not a girl, exactly. She's a woman."

"A woman? Mister Starr, deep sea submersibles ain't made for women. There ain't no toilet facilities on a deep sea submersible. We're gonna be yore-rinatin' into a hose if we gotta go. There ain't exactly no privacy, neither, and I don't plan to hang my you-know-what out in front of some girl I don't know. You're gonna need to get a different sized-mologist."

"The lady's a seismologist, Lowan, *not* a *sized*-mologist. And besides, it's too late. She insisted. It was the only way she'd help us find someone else for the other sub. I'll just have to warn her."

"Mister Starr, I ain't worried 'bout her. I'm worried 'bout me. When I gotta go, I gotta go." Rick could hear Washington swearing under his breath. "Women, you jus' can't make 'em mind their own business."

Rick shook his head. "Lowan, we'll just have to take the chance. She's a nice person, and I'll make sure that if you, you know, if you have to do it, that she closes her eyes. And if she has to really go and can't wait, then I guess we'll have to see."

"Ain't no closin' your eyes when you're drivin' a sub, Mister Starr. You need to tell her if she's gotta go, there ain't nothin' available. And if she tries anyway, she's gonna have an audience."

***

The B-52, flaps down and gear hanging, swooped toward the trawler as if it was going to land on the ship's deck. Less than two thousand feet above the water, the roar of its jet engines trailed behind. As the thunder of the engines enveloped the vessel below, the gunner unleashed a hail of death. Bullets encased in titanium and weighing nearly a pound each hurtled from the four barrels protruding from the B-52's turret. The bullets hit the water just behind the trawler, shredding the ropes that tied the dinghies to the ship and throwing up a thick spray as they slipped into the sea. Holding the trigger full down and finding his mark, the gunner moved the steady stream of bullets until the line of fire rested on the ship's rudder. He zoomed his camera in on the rear of the ship, and he held the red circle steady on the ship's controls. The gunner began to hum "America the Beautiful" as he watched the rudder disintegrate instantaneously. He adjusted his aimpoint to just behind the hull and below the water line where he thought the ship's propellers might be. Although firing doctrine called for intermittent bursts of fire, the gunner continued to hold the trigger tightly, pumping out the BUFF's fifteen hundred rounds in a minute and a half.

***

The young sailor looked to his right and caught sight of the large black dragon screaming silently across the water. Larger than any plane he'd ever seen, it looked alive. Water vapor streamed in a twirling motion off the ends of the plane's wings, the wing tip vortices pulling salt water from the ocean and spinning it into fine mist that skipped across the waves.

Kneeling and doing his best to maintain his balance in the bobbing raft, the sailor aimed his weapon at the bomber and followed its approach to the ship. Fingers stiff from hours in the cold, the young man shuddered involuntarily as he tried to adjust the heavy missile-launcher on his shoulder. As the giant plane crossed the stern of the trawler, he pointed the launcher at the exhaust plume of the closest engine and switched on the heat-seeking device. The infrared homing mechanism hummed excitedly, its intermittent high-pitched tone beeping rapidly as it locked onto its target. Just before it would have announced its readiness to spring from the launcher and attack the eagle-like plane, a volley of bullets from the plane's turret cut the lines that tethered the dinghies to their mother ship. The lines went limp, and the dinghy holding the young sailor lurched as it was severed from its mooring, its small bow catching a wave and stopping abruptly. The sailor taking aim at the aircraft was thrown unexpectedly to the floor of the raft, and the missile-launcher leapt from his shoulder and into the sea.

***

The situation room was nearly empty in contrast to the previous meetings Rick attended. Present were John Renoir, Rick, the vice president, secretary of defense, and the president's national security advisor. Noticeably absent were the chairman and his joint chiefs, other than the chief of naval operations. The atmosphere was informal and relaxed. The group stood as the president walked in.

"Sit down, gentlemen." The president took his seat, and the group sat with him. "All right, what's the latest?"

Christopher Bennett, the national security advisor, spoke. "Sir, the B-52 hit three of the planned targets. It looks like all three were disabled, with one suffering major damage. As far as the fourth trawler goes, and as far as we can tell, the bomber never got there. We've heard nothing from the bomber's crew since they attacked the second ship."

The president turned the palms of his hands up and then clasped them together. "And?"

"Well, we don't know. We think the bomber may have gone down, although we don't have any hard evidence."

"Do we know what happened? Where's the chairman? Why isn't he here to brief me?"

"Sir," said the SecDef, "there's nothing to brief. The mission was a success through the third target, and for unknown reasons the bomber never hit the last ship."

"OK, we'll address it later. What's next? Can we still hit the fourth ship?" asked the president.

John Renoir spoke up. "Sir, the bomber was our only hope to get to the four original targets, and we think that now we should concentrate on the fifth and last trawler."

"What do you mean by concentrate?"

"We need to intercept the submarines carried by that trawler and destroy them before they detonate any more nuclear weapons."

"With another B-52?"

Rick Starr spoke up. "Sir, we think that because we've attacked the other trawlers, the ship's captain will drop the submarines off as early as possible. And as John pointed out, the Chinese are no longer constrained by secrecy. That presents the possibility that these next detonations could be significantly larger than the others." The president fixed his gaze on Rick and said nothing.

Rick continued. "We believe we need to put something out there that can locate the subs once they leave the trawler and then neutralize them, possibly in very deep water. Of course, we also need a way to force the subs out of the ship's hold. We could use another B-52, but because the first one is lost the Air Force has proposed sending a B-2 instead. I suggest that under the circumstances, the B-2 should hit the trawler with overwhelming force with the intention of sinking it.

"To sum up our plan, we're proposing to fly two of the Navy's manned deep sea submersibles down to the coast of Chile and ferry them out over the water so they arrive at the trawler right after the B-2 destroys it. The Navy submersibles will be dropped into the water to either frustrate or eliminate the Chinese subs."

The president leaned forward and scanned the faces of the men at the table before he looked back at Rick. "OK, I approve the B-2 and agree with your assessment that it's necessary to sink the trawler. Who's taking the lead on neutralizing the subs? The Navy?"

Rick looked at John Renoir and knew that he was about to get his boss into hot water. "Well, sir, since the Agency is responsible for the operation, CIA will man the subs with the exception of one Navy pilot."

"Why CIA?"

John Renoir took over. "Because it's our idea. We did the research, found out the Navy had some retired deep submergence vehicles in mothballs, and we coordinated to have them flown down to South America."

"So we have rivalry now between CIA and the Navy? That puts in jeopardy the entire west coast of the United States?" The president's face became flushed. "What's going on, John? I thought you were smarter than that."

"Sir, it's not really rivalry. It's more a matter of who is responsible."

"What's your take, Charlie? You happy with this arrangement?" asked the president, directing his question to the Navy chief.

"Sir, if CIA wants this Chinese fire drill, they can have it."

Rick chimed in. "Sir, each submarine will have a seismologist and a CIA analyst on board in addition to the pilot. The mission may require intimate knowledge of tectonic plates and what the seams between two adjacent plates look like. The CIA agents will provide the corporate knowledge that's accumulated since we uncovered China's intentions. Since the subs retired a couple years ago, the Navy has only one pilot that's operationally current, and he'll drive one of the subs for us. The rest of the team are volunteers who acknowledge the risks associated with the mission."

The president leaned back, his complexion changing to normal. "Are you personally going on the mission?"

"Yes, sir. In addition to the Navy petty officer, it will be me, two CIA colleagues — one who's a former Air Force fighter pilot and will pilot the second submersible — and two seismologists. One is out of San Francisco State University and the other is from the U.S. Geological Survey."

"And you said they know the risks involved?"

"Yes, sir. All are aware that it could be a one way trip."

The president tapped his fingers on the table. He spoke quietly. "When do you plan to leave?"

"Sir," said Rick, "we will leave as soon as this meeting is over."

The president stood unexpectedly. The table struggled to join him. "Don't let me hold you up." He looked at John Renoir. "Get me the names of everyone who's going on this trip and the names of the B-52 crewmembers. I want to know who I'm eulogizing if and when the time comes." He walked around the table and stood directly in front of Rick. He reached out, and the two shook hands. "Your nation is counting on you to be successful." Rick nodded, and the president wore a thin smile. "Remember, the idea is to make the other guys die for their country."

***

The B-52 was gone as quickly as it arrived. The sailors in the dinghies were left gaping at the horizon. No longer attached to the mother ship and helpless against a growing weather system that was generating ever-larger waves, the small craft were rapidly disseminating in all directions behind and away from the trawler. The ship's captain was on the bridge and tried to bring order to chaos. "Report damage. Report casualties," he called into the ship's speaker system. In response to the order, his executive officer ran breathlessly onto the bridge.

"Request permission to address the captain," he said formally in front of the other members of the ship's crew. The captain nodded. "We have lost our rudder and one propeller has been destroyed. There is a fire in the rear hold, but it is under control. All injured men have been taken to sick bay." He paused. "The Americans cut the lines that held the dinghies to the ship." He looked down. "They are quickly being swept away, and we have no way to help the men." He looked back up, and the captain nodded.

"They are heroes," said the captain to his executive officer and the other sailors who were listening. "They have done their duty, and in respect for their efforts we must now see to the ship and the rest of the crew. Continue damage control, take care of the wounded, and send a MAYDAY." His executive officer waited to be dismissed. "We have followed orders. It is enough. Now go and do what you must so we can return home."

***

"OK, I'm climbing out. How'd you do, Chief? And what's my altitude going to be, Mac?"

"I kicked their hiney, pilot. Rudder's gone, and I'm pretty sure I beat hell out o' the props, too."

The weapon systems officer tiredly pulled out the flight plan that he so eagerly sought to look at when they first took off in what now seemed another lifetime. He ran his finger through the phases of flight until he came to the tab marked "recovery". "Flight level two-niner-zero, Jimmy. Think you can do the climbout?"

"I can see almost normally again, Mac. But we're down to just over twenty grand on the fuel. What we need are some tankers." He keyed his mike and broke radio silence. "This is Paydirt-zero-two, a B-52 military aircraft on guard frequency, passing five thousand feet for flight level two-niner-zero. Does anybody copy?"

There was an immediate reply. "Roger, Paydirt, this is Mug-five-seven. How can we help?"

Charlie Macklin screamed into the interphone. "Sonofagun, Jimmy, Mug is the tanker call sign for 135's out of March. The guy's a tanker! Now all we gotta do is find out how much gas he's got!"

"Roger, roger, Mug-fifty-seven," continued the pilot. "We're down to emergency fuel. I repeat, we're down to emergency fuel, and we're gonna have to ditch out here in the middle of the Pacific if we don't get refueled ASAP. You got any gas you can spare?"

There was a pause. "Roger, zero-two, it looks like we've got about fifty thousand pounds we can give you. I'm going to put my nav on the radio, and he'll coordinate to get us together."

The wizzo and the gunner began to whoop it up. "We're goin' home! Sonofagun, we're goin' home!" sang Charlie Macklin.

"Guess it wadn't our time," said the gunner.

"I'll take the radios, pilot." The wizzo keyed his radio. "Come in Mug-five-seven. Give me your location, and let's get hooked up." He went back to interphone. "In the meantime, pilot, turn northeast. We're headin' for dry tundra."

CHAPTER 16

Kam Fong felt his arms twisting behind his back. His head pressed into the ground by someone much larger, it took his every strength to turn his gaze toward the Chinese president. They exchanged looks, the president's face registering contempt. The burning sensation near Fong's stomach was intense. He could feel his skin melting, the failed device embedding itself deep into his abdominal muscles.

Where was the explosion? I had the vest on. I pulled the lanyard, but nothing happened. Yanked to his feet, hands from seemingly everywhere feeling like vices on his arms, his neck, his wrists. His head felt heavy.

***

Joe Craxton and Denise Carlson listened to Rick describe the mission. Craxton shook his head, Carlson was intrigued. "I don't know," said Craxton, "it sounds pretty dangerous."

Carlson, on the other hand, did not hesitate. "I'll go."

Rick looked at Craxton. "What about it, Joe? I can't order you to go, but Denise would be the better choice to take my place while I'm gone."

Craxton hung his head. "I don't know, Rick. I get claustrophobia. And going underwater in a really small submarine doesn't sound like it'd give me a chance to walk around and stretch my legs. I mean, I'd like to go with you, but in a three-man submarine?" He shuddered. "I'd go crazy."

Carlson traded looks with Rick. "Why not let me go?"

Rick's attention was locked on Craxton, who would not look up. "OK, Denise. We've got two hours till we leave to catch our plane at Andrews Air Force Base."

"Gotcha. I'm going to go home now so I can pack."

Pack? Where do these women think they're going?

***

John Kale released the captive to his three colleagues. As they took him away, Kale stripped off the assassin's shirt and removed the surprisingly heavy vest. It seemed to stick momentarily to the man's abdomen, but a hard pull freed it. Their captive groaned in pain. Kale held the vest at arm's length and ran his free hand over the material. C-4 explosive filled its every orifice. *Certain death for the occupant and anyone unfortunate enough to be near*, Kale knew.

The crowd had dispersed in panic, but the news reporters stayed and surrounded the failed assassin with their cameras. Lenses with large rubber cups on their ends were held inches from the Asian man's face, as reporters spoke rapid-fire and staccato-like into their microphones.

Kale walked to the black steel fence surrounding the mayor's residence and hung the vest carefully on one of the fence's pikes. *We were lucky. The fuse was obviously a dud.*

He turned his attention to the two presidents, who were by now under heavy escort at the door leading to the interior of the mayor's house. The Mexican president seemed to be unaware of the danger he narrowly escaped and was still angrily brushing the dirt from his clothes. The Chinese president appeared unshaken.

Kale watched the scene. Reporters called the man being carried away a suicide bomber, and he was surrounded by tens of Mexican police. The cops were trying to push the reporters away with little success. Kale knew that the Mexican authorities would soon kidnap his team's prey and that they could do nothing about it.

***

Rick looked at the older, narrow-bodied Boeing 707 Stratotanker that sat on the tarmac, a ladder protruding from beneath its nose. Equipped by the Navy with a hyperbaric chamber, the aircraft was designed to ferry the crews of deep sea submersibles to and from their destination. The plane was painted a dull, dirty white and looked as if it was an original 1955 model. Its four small compact Pratt and Whitney engines hanging off the wings were a throwback to the era of turbojets.

Standing in the window of the passenger terminal at Andrews Air Force Base, Rick searched for Tom Bowman and Denise Carlson. The three of them were flying to California to pick up Marly Cooper, Ralph Thiele and Lowan Washington. From there they would fly to Chile.

Already on their way to South America where they would be cabled to large helicopters configured as flying cranes were the submersibles. The plan was to haul them out over the ocean and lower them to the water's surface with their crews.

Rick thought about Marly and wondered if he was right to agree to her going along. While he was pleased that she would most likely be on the submarine with him, he found himself preoccupied with her safety. He could not shake the sense that bad things lurked just over the horizon. Really bad things. Waiting quietly. And waiting just for them.

***

Marly Cooper finished packing her small gym bag. Jeans, a sweater, two pairs of extra underwear, an athletic bra, and warm cotton socks. Tucked in amongst all the clothes were her makeup bag and a teddy bear — the Steif yellow bear she was given one Christmas when she was young. The one she could not part with now. The one that always brought her good luck.

She wore her best pair of tennis shoes, a pair of bright pink high tops. Equipped with anti-skid soles, they were her constant companions at aerobic classes.

Marly found herself feeling sentimental as she looked around her apartment. *This must be how soldiers feel when they go into battle*, she thought. *They don't know if they are coming back, so a last look at things familiar soothes the soul.* She sighed. Having dropped Benny off with Beverly yesterday, she found herself missing his constantly wagging tail.

***

Tom Bowman and Denise Carlson arrived at Andrews Air Force Base at the same time. Looking as if they coordinated their wardrobes, both wore jeans, a gray sweatshirt and tennis shoes. Carlson's shoes were white leather, Bowman's an old pair of Converse. Bowman carried a shaving kit, Carlson a large gym bag that was stuffed. Rick waved.

"Over here!" Rick called to his friends. He had not spent time with Tom Bowman since their time together in California. Bowman lost weight and dyed his hair a light brown. He looked much younger than Rick remembered. Rick walked over and shook his hand while giving another small wave to Carlson. "Tom, you look great!" Bowman returned the compliment. Rick pointed to the old 707. "There's our transportation. *Guarda bene.*"

"Wow, I haven't seen a jet like that since I first joined the Air Force," said Bowman.

Carlson grimaced. "Is it safe?"

Rick laughed. "It won't be long before we'll wish we were back on it."

"So, we ready to go?" asked Bowman.

"Just waiting for you guys."

"Well, you don't have to wait any longer. Let's fire that antique up and get airborne."

"You're awfully anxious for an old busted-up fighter pilot. I think you just want to go fly that submarine."

"Busted up? What do you mean busted up?" asked Carlson. "Are you guys not telling me something?"

***

Marly Cooper climbed into her car to drive to the Air Force base where Rick's plane was landing and where she would also meet Ralph Thiele. Fighting last minute doubts and a growing fear of what was ahead, she wondered if she made the right decision to go. *Maybe this is a job for a man, after all. Well, at least I'll be with Rick. And there does seem to be a guarantee of excitement.* She could feel the goose bumps on her arms and shivered.

***

Rick walked up to the plane where a Navy corpsman waited. "Is your crew ready for us?"

"Aye aye, sir. We're ready to get airborne as soon as you and the rest of your team arrive."

"This is it. Just the three of us." He pointed to Tom Bowman and Denise Carlson, who approached the front of the plane where Rick stood. Rick turned toward them. "OK, we're cleared to board."

"Cool," said Bowman. Without hesitation, he climbed onto the first rung of the ladder that led upward and into the crew entry chute. The ladder was a single piece of thick aluminum with a curved top that hooked onto the deck, just behind the cockpit.

Rick watched Bowman disappear from sight as he ascended the ladder. Carlson stepped onto the ladder next, her large bag barely fitting into the crew entry chute above her head. She rested it on her chest and tried to push it upward. She paused after every step, leaning back against the side of the entry chute and repositioning the bag. It kept tumbling back down, and she kept trying to push it up. Tom Bowman noticed her struggle and climbed part way down the ladder. He grabbed her bag and pulled it up behind him.

"Thanks," said Carlson, who followed him up.

When Rick arrived at the top of the ladder, he stepped onto the deck and walked to the back of the fuselage where Bowman and Carlson were now standing. The fuselage was dimly lit, and it took a moment for Rick's eyes to adjust. The deck was padded and covered with a carpet of thick, beaded rubber. A large chamber filled the entire rear of the fuselage.

"Guess this'll be our home for the next couple hours," said Rick.

"I was wondering why they didn't put the hyperbaric chamber into a P-3," said Bowman. "It's too darn big to fit into anything else the Navy's got."

***

Marly showed her driver's license to the guard at the gate and asked directions to the terminal. It was clear he was expecting her.

"Yes, ma'am," the guard said, "you just go straight ahead and turn right at the flashing yellow light. The passenger terminal is on the left. You can park your car in the visitors' area. There's a parking space with your name on it near the entrance to the terminal."

Marly followed the guard's directions. Sure enough, there was a space marked RESERVED: DR MARLY COOPER. Next to it was another marked RESERVED: DR RALPH THIELE. She pulled between the white lines and cut the engine. She sat back and relaxed for a moment. Rick was still hours away, but she wanted to make sure that she was on time. Having never been on a military installation before, she also thought she might want to savor the experience.

What's this? A man in uniform walked out of the terminal building and headed directly for her car.

Before she could open the door to get out, the man in uniform had her door open. "Here, ma'am, let me take that," he said as he took her bag. "If you'll give me your car keys, we'll keep them for you until you return." Marly got out of the car. The soldier was young, handsome, and professional. He smiled politely, not a grin or a leer. She was impressed. She handed him her keys.

"Thanks. You guys are on the ball, aren't you?" Marly asked.

The soldier nodded modestly, almost an 'aw, shucks,' response. "We aim to please, ma'am."

"You're certainly doing that."

The soldier closed the car door and locked it. "Ma'am, if you'll follow me, we have the VIP lounge open for you and the others."

***

The three climbed into the chamber. Made to hold up to twelve people, six plastic seats designed to conform to the human body lined each side. The low ceiling prevented the two men from standing up straight, and they both leaned over.

A Navy corpsman materialized and followed them in. "I'll be riding in the chamber with ya'll. Hope you don't mind."

"No problem. You can compress the cells of your body with us anytime," Rick replied as he sat down and made himself comfortable. Denise Carlson sat next to him. Tom Bowman settled himself across from the pair.

The crewman slammed shut the oval door leading into the chamber and cranked a large brass wheel to the right until it reached its stop. He grabbed it like a steering wheel in a car and gave it one last hard turn. Like the hatch on a ship, the door was lined with a large rubber gasket that created an airtight seal. The corpsman walked over to a large panel and turned a dial.

"We're going to start our descent now," he said. With a loud bang, air poured into the chamber. Tom Bowman felt pressure in his ears and grabbed his nose. He closed his mouth and blew gently, using the Valsalva technique to clear the pressure. Denise Carlson and Rick were clearly uncomfortable.

"Grab your nose, close your mouth, and push gently like you're blowing your nose. That'll clear your ears," said Bowman to the two of them. They followed his lead, the Valsalva opening their eustachian tubes, which let the air in their sinuses equalize with the air in the chamber. The discomfort was relieved immediately.

"Must be a pilot thing," said Rick.

"The air pressure will decrease to a pressure altitude equal to sea level," said the corpsman. "You'll need to strap in for takeoff."

Their seats were equipped with shoulder straps and a heavy, thick webbed lapbelt with a piece of leather undergirding a pair of metal phalanges to hook up the straps. The sound of a jet engine winding up could be heard. It was followed by three others. Bowman gave a thumbs-up. "Looks like we're on our way."

Rick nodded. He cleared his ears again, and the pressure subsided once more. The chamber made another loud bang.

"We're at sea level," said the corpsman.

A muffled voice came over a small loudspeaker. "Crew, we've been cleared to taxi. Prepare the passengers for takeoff."

The corpsman sat in a seat next to the chamber door and picked up a microphone. "We're strapped in and ready for takeoff here in the chamber."

There was a muffled "Roger".

***

Marly followed her military escort into a large room. Inside were several leather couches, a like number of leather chairs, and a large wet bar in one corner. Behind the wet bar was a small refrigerator. A thick, warm looking carpet covered the floor in dark forest green.

"May I get you something to drink, ma'am?" asked the airman.

"Do you have Coke or Pepsi?"

"Yes, ma'am. We've got both. Do you have a preference?"

"Not really, although I'm finding myself enjoying Coke as I get older."

"Ma'am, you don't look old enough to be getting older. You look like you're the same age as my big sister, and she's young."

Marly smiled. *Is everyone in the military this polite?*

***

A young, clean-shaven African-American man with close-cropped hair dressed in maroon straight-legged jeans, a white linen shirt, bright yellow high top tennis shoes, and a tall dark blue cap with a short bill walked into the VIP lounge. He was over six feet tall and pencil thin. He gave a loud whistle. "I always wondered what was in this room."

The young man's cell phone rang. "Whaddup, dog?" he called into his mobile.

"Is Clint there?" asked a voice.

"Clint? Didn't anyone tell you, man? Clint's dead. Died yesterday in a really bad car accident."

The voice went hysterical. "He's dead? Clint's dead? Oh, my God!"

"No, no, man. He ain't dead. I'm just playin' with you. Clint ain't dead. You got the wrong number."

"Oh, thank God, thank God. Wrong number? That's my bad."

"No, man, it's OK. You give Clint a call now."

Marly stared. The young man closed his cell phone and returned her look.

"Are you Mister Starr's woman?" he asked.

Marly blushed, not knowing quite how to reply. "I'm going to be accompanying Mister Starr on a mission, if that's what you mean. But I'm not his woman."

"I shoulda knowed you'd be a fine lookin' filly."

"I'm sorry?"

Washington gave Marly the once-over from top to bottom. "Love those sneakers. Used to have a pair like that myself." He whistled. "Mister Starr said you insisted on comin' on this mission with us, but I knowed there was another reason he didn't say 'no' to you." He walked over to Marly and stuck out his hand.

"Name's Petty Officer Lo-wan Washington, submarine driver and favorite object of affection for babies and beautiful women." Marly took his outstretched hand.

"I'm Doctor Cooper. College professor." Her instincts told her that Lowan Washington was harmless, and she smiled. "Please call me Marly." Her smile became a grin. "You're quite the snappy dresser, Mister Washington. Are you going to wear what you've got on in the submersible?"

"Sure will, Doc. You gotta understand. When you look good, you feel good. When you feel good, you do good. And when you do good, you make good things happen. And I'd say we want good things happenin' when we're huntin' 'round the bottom o' the Pacific Ocean. And please, Doc, all my good friends call me Lo-wan."

Marly nodded as she listened. "That's an interesting philosophy, Lo-wan."

"Mister Starr says you know all about earthquakes."

"That's right. He's asked me to come along because he thought it might be important to identify the areas between adjacent tectonic plates."

"Tec-tonic? What kinda plates'd you say?"

"Tectonic plates. He thought it could be important to identify where the earth's tectonic plates come together on the ocean floor. He thought…" Marly could see by his expression that Washington was not tracking with her words. "He just thought that it would be helpful if I came along, since I know something about earthquakes."

"Oh, yeah, o' course. Never know when you're goin' to run into an earthquake."

Marly nodded and laughed. "You're going to drive one of the submersibles?"

"That's right. By the way, did Mister Starr mention to you 'bout the facilities arrangements?"

Marly shook her head. "The facilities arrangements?"

"Yeah, namely that there ain't no facilities onboard the sub."

"Oh. No, he didn't mention there weren't any facilities on the submersible. But I think I'll be OK."

"I hope so. Well, I'm gonna go drop the kids off at the swimmin' pool. You better do the same, Doc. It's a long flight to Chile, and we'll be goin' right into the sub when we get there. Mister Starr said we're in a real hurry."

"Drop the kids off at the swimming pool?"

Washington winked. "You know. Drop the kids off at the porcelain pool?"

Marly shook her head. "No, I don't know."

***

The 707 leveled off at altitude for the flight across the continent to California. Rick unstrapped his seat belt and stood up as best he could, his body slightly bent at the waist. Carlson and Bowman did the same.

"What's the plan for California?" asked Bowman.

"We pick up our two seismologists and the other sub driver. Plane will probably have to take on more fuel. Then it's off to South America. Subs should be there a couple hours before us. They're being hooked up to helos that'll ferry us out to intercept the trawler."

"How far out will the helos take us?"

"That depends on our seismologists. Right now we don't think too far. I'll check with Joe to see where the trawler is, and they'll tell us where the subs will do their dirty work."

"So we're guessing?" asked Carlson.

Rick nodded. "Unfortunately. But it'll be an educated guess, so I'm optimistic. My hunch is that Chen chose the location. Doctor Cooper already has a theory about where the trawler's headed."

"So some guy named 'Chin' laid out the whole plan in advance from start to finish?" asked Bowman.

"The earthquake thing, for sure. Since we've got the time, want me to tell you the whole story?" Bowman nodded.

***

Joe Craxton walked into John Renoir's office. "Just got word that our third guy made an attempt on the Chinese president."

"What happened?" Renoir threw out his hands to either side.

"Nothin'. Suicide bomber was wearing a vest full of C-4, but the fuse was a dud."

Renoir laughed. "Maybe the fuse did exactly what it was supposed to do. What's the fallout? China trying to start something now?"

"Of course. They blame us for letting the guy into the United States. Taiwan says the guy defected to the mainland long ago. It looks like a stalemate for the moment. That could change, though, if California is hit by an earthquake or swamped by a tsunami."

"I don't even want to think about it. Is FEMA ready?"

"Homeland Security and FEMA have transportation lined up. FEMA also coordinated with the Army National Guard and has orders cut to fly them in to restore order. I think this mess is gonna make the Katrina response look like it was a complete success. There could be millions heading east with no place to go."

CHAPTER 17

Doctor Ralph Thiele entered the room. Marly Cooper smiled at her colleague and waved. "Ralph, over here!" Thiele heard Marly's call and returned her smile.

The young airman who met her outside followed him. "Sir," he said as Thiele sat down, "can I get you something to drink?"

"How about a beer?" Thiele asked.

"We only serve imported beer: Lone Star."

"Lone Star? From Texas?"

"Yes, sir. Our wing commander is from Texas, and he has it imported for all official functions and VIPs."

"Imported beer, huh? OK, I'll give it a try."

"Yes, sir, coming right up." He looked over at Marly. "Ma'am, do you need something else?"

"No, thanks." As the airman left, Marly leaned over to Ralph. "Isn't he cute? And he's so polite!"

Thiele looked at Marly and gave her a condescending shake of the head. "Is politeness suddenly such a virtue?" He turned to watch the airman as he opened a beer and poured it into a glass. "I suspect that when he's out of uniform, he reverts to behavior that would disappoint you."

Marly frowned and looked over Thiele's shoulder at the young man she admired. "Nah. You think so?"

"I thought you were a college professor. Do you really need me to tell you that?"

The airman came over and handed Thiele his beer. "Anything else, sir?"

"No, this should do it." He lifted the glass toward his host. "Here's to your wing commander." He took a sip and looked at the liquid gold. "This isn't too bad. Are you going to join us?"

The airman laughed politely. "No, sir. The Air Force doesn't let us drink on duty." He turned away to leave the room when Lowan Washington walked back in.

"Whaddup, dog?" he said to the young airman as he walked by, and he threw him a high-five as he passed. The airman absentmindedly raised his hand, and Washington slapped it. He walked over to where Marly and Ralph Thiele sat. He put out his hand out toward Thiele. "Whaddup?" Thiele shook his hand. "Name's Petty Officer Washington. Lo-wan Washington. I was recruited by Mister Starr to drive one o' the submersibles."

"Pleased to meet you, Lowan. My name's Thiele."

"Thiele? I've never heard that name before. Is that Polynesian or somethin'?"

"No, actually it's German."

"German? *Sprechen sie Deutsch?*" Washington asked, his pronunciation a catastrophe.

"*Ein bisschen*. Do you speak German?"

"You gotta be kiddin'. I never even been to Germany. Went to Oktoberfest once downtown, though. Had me some o' that German beer, but it weren't too good. Expensive, too." He nodded, paused and rested his chin on his hand, pretending to think. "I also speak a little bit o' Italian." He grinned at Marly and Thiele. "Ciao, baby."

Thiele nodded. "That's pretty impressive stuff, Lowan."

Washington pointed at Thiele and winked. "You sure you're not Polynesian? You got that Polynesian look 'bout you."

***

Washington was gone from the VIP lounge when Thiele finally returned from the men's room. "We've got about an hour until Rick gets here on a plane with his colleagues from Washington," said Marly. "He said we'll all be sitting in a hyperbaric chamber on the flight to Chile. Should be cozy."

"Why do we need to ride in a hyperbaric chamber? I've never heard of that before."

"Rick says you have to wait a couple days before flying again if you've been scuba diving. The hyperbaric chamber mitigates the effects of altitude. He said it has something to do with the bends."

"But we're flying first and then going into the water." Thiele shrugged. "It doesn't make sense to me, but since I'm just along for the ride, anyway, I won't ask questions."

He pulled a large map from his briefcase and unfolded it onto the carpet. Marly helped spread it out and flatten it. They kneeled next to each other. "Why don't you tell me a little more about what we're going to be doing? I've tried to look at this thing, but you need to give me some specifics now." Covered with curving ridgelines, deep trenches, and numbers showing the depth at various locations, the map provided a detailed view of the floor of the Pacific Ocean. A straight line that started just west of the Panama Canal and ended in the armpit of the Nazca tectonic plate's lower panhandle, was drawn in opaque yellow.

Marly ran her finger across the north-south contours that emanated from the corner of the panhandle. "The trawler is headed for here, where the Antarctic and Nazca plates come together and form a panhandle."

"Do we know where the trawler is now?"

Marly pointed to a spot on the yellow line north of the area. "It's up here somewhere. Rick is counting on us to tell him where the subs are going after they leave the trawler."

"How are we supposed to do that?"

Marly shrugged. "I thought that between the two of us we could figure out where they'd get the most torque on the Nazca."

"You think they'll actually try to turn the whole plate?"

"We think they plan to give the Nazca one hell of a nuclear kick."

Thiele shook his head. "Don't they realize what they're doing? Think of the tsunami. They could wipe out an entire section of the planet." He rubbed his chin and shook his head again. "So if they don't make it to their destination down here..." He pointed to where Marly indicated the panhandle. "...then you're saying they might try to put their nukes someplace else. Maybe somewhere along this east-west line between the two plates?"

"That's what you and I are supposed to figure out."

"How many bad guys are we chasing? Two? Three?"

"Two, I think."

"So if the depth is 14,000 feet in this area, they can get to the bottom in what — fifteen minutes maybe — and then they can take off in any direction? Plus it's black as Hades down there." Thiele looked at Marly. "We're still planning to make it back, aren't we?" Marly nodded unconvincingly. Thiele whistled and shook his head. "Maybe we need to split up if there's more than one sub."

"Rick was hoping we wouldn't have to. Lowan is Navy, but the guy who's driving the other submersible is an Air Force fighter pilot. I think Rick is hoping we find the subs before they submerge."

Thiele laughed and shook his head again. "A fighter pilot in a submarine?" His face wore a look of incredulity. "We've been given an impossible task."

Marly took the map and pulled it closer to her. "I don't think so. I think the subs have got to go for the area where the Antarctic and Nazca plates come together." She ran her finger along the contours of the ocean floor. "If they can't put the nukes here, then my guess is they'll try to put them somewhere along this line like you said."

Thiele nodded. "Could be. But the line you're pointing to is hundreds of miles long. And what if we don't guess right, like whether they go east or west when they leave the trawlers? They could be anywhere on this line, and that's if they're even on the line."

"Our arrival is going to be a surprise, and Rick is planning for us to be there when the subs are released. They won't have much of a head start."

Washington came strutting back into the VIP lounge. "What you guys got there?" He looked at the light gray map unfolded on the carpet. "Hey, that's a map o' the Pacific Ocean."

Ralph Thiele was surprised. "You're familiar with ocean maps?"

Washington laughed. "'Course. You can't drive no submersible and not know how to read an ocean map. I've studied them things 'til my eyes bugged outta my head."

Now Marly was surprised. "But you didn't know what a tectonic plate was when I tried to explain to you that I was a seismologist."

"Never heard o' no tectonic plates, Doc, but I do know ocean maps." Washington walked behind Marly. "You tell me where you want to go, and I'll get us there."

Thiele turned his head toward Washington and really looked at him. "How many times have you been down in a submersible?"

"Lots. Hundreds, maybe. Never down here, o' course." He pointed at the coast off South America. "But up here…" He pointed to the California coast and ran his finger to the west. "…I dived here so many times on the continental shelf I lost count."

Thiele looked at Marly and raised his eyebrows. "So if we make a good guess, then we've got a pretty good chance of getting there and finding the subs."

"Sure," said Washington. "A heckuva good chance if I'm drivin'. We got sonar and lights that'll burn out yore eyeballs if you're not careful." He pointed at Thiele again. "Did the doc here tell you there ain't no facilities onboard the submersible?"

***

Tom Bowman completed his twentieth mission in the Gulf when his plane took a hit and he was forced to eject. His flying career ended with that last flight, his back broken as he went through the canopy. He remembered how he wrote a letter to his family before every flight, confessing his sins and asking for their forgiveness, thanking his mother and father for all they did for him growing up — in case the flight was his last. He suddenly felt vulnerable, not having penned such a letter before leaving Washington, D.C.

He leaned toward Rick. "So what's going to happen to us once we're dropped into the ocean? Do we have a plan?"

"Well," said Rick. "Like I said, the seismologists going with us should have a pretty good idea where the Chinese subs will need to put their nukes to get the effect they want. The plan is to arrive at the trawlers the same time the subs are released, or at least right after. If we don't get to the subs before they submerge, I'm thinking they can at least get us started in the right direction."

"And if we find them? Then what?"

Rick frowned. "We sink 'em."

"Sink them? With what?"

"We had the submersibles retrofitted with underwater bazookas."

"Underwater bazookas? I've shot missiles and guns from a jet at five hundred miles an hour at altitude, but a water bazooka?" Bowman smiled. "Sounds kinda cool. What's its range? Do we guide the projectiles to the target? Do they have a homing device?"

"I was told the bazookas are fairly accurate out to a range of about twenty-five yards. The projectiles aren't guided, so we have to get in pretty close to hit the target. Each sub has two shots."

"So this is the cat and mouse stuff you talked about."

"Right."

"What if we're in too close when we shoot the bazooka?"

"I was told the force from the projectiles is designed to create a frontal effect. But they are experimental." Rick raised his eyebrows. "Depending on where we hit 'em, we might have to move the nukes."

"Move them? Is that even safe?" asked Bowman.

Rick shrugged his shoulders and winced. "We don't know. Hopefully they'll be inert. If not, then moving them may be moot."

Denise Carlson, who was talking with the corpsman, came over.

"So," said Rick, finishing his thought. "If the nukes are dropped anywhere along the edge of the Nazca tectonic plate, we'll probably be taking them on a road trip."

"Do you think we'll make it home?" asked Carlson. The magnitude of what they were doing was beginning to dawn on her.

"We were just talking about that. I wouldn't have asked you to go if I didn't believe we'd make it back. But we're messing with nuclear weapons, and they're not designed for people who want to live long and prosper." Rick paused. "We should discuss all this when we get together with the rest of the team. We don't really even know how many subs are with the trawler. We're thinking two because that seems to be all the ship can accommodate, but we don't know for sure." He paused again. "The only one of us who's ever been in a submersible is the Navy petty officer. We're going to be depending on his professional judgment and expertise to make this all work."

***

Lowan Washington pulled a bottle of beer from the small refrigerator in the VIP lounge. He looked at Thiele and Marly, who were leaning cross-legged as they mulled over the map. He twisted the cap off the beer and set it on the counter to his left. He leaned down and put his head into the refrigerator. "Um hmm, look at all this food. We got crackers, chocolate bars. And raisins? We don't want no raisins." He continued to fumble with the refrigerator's contents, pulled the cellophane off a package of crackers, and stuffed them into his mouth. "If this is all the government has to offer, we're goin' to starve to death."

***

The modified Boeing 707 Stratotanker softly touched down onto the concrete runway. Smoke from the eight main tires under the fuselage, when they accelerated from zero to over a hundred knots in an instant, was the only evidence that contact had been made with the ground. The nose slowly dropped, speed brakes leapt up from the top of the plane's wings, and the aircraft slowed as the pilot applied the wheel brakes. Designed without thrust reversers, the plane took the entire runway to reach taxi speed.

"I'll be bringing us up to ambient pressure now," said the young Navy corpsman standing at the pressure controller inside the chamber, as he pulled a lever. By the time the plane parked, the corpsman was opening the compartment door.

"You and your team can leave your bags on the plane, sir," the corpsman said to Rick as he prepared to step out of the chamber. "We'll be refueling for the next hour. Commander says we'll be ready for takeoff as soon as we have fuel on board."

"Sounds good. Hopefully, the rest of the team is already here." Rick looked at his wrist like he was wearing a watch, but being Italian and adopting the family tradition of never wearing one, there was nothing to look at. "We'll be back in an hour."

"Aye, aye, sir," said the corpsman, pretending not to notice Rick's strange routine.

The three team members, faces grim, each lost in thought, climbed down the ladder leading from the crew entry chute. Rick came down last, and they walked together in silence toward the passenger terminal. Pulling a cell phone from his pocket, Rick dialed in Joe Craxton's work number.

"Craxton."

"Joe, this is Rick. We've arrived in California, and we're at the passenger terminal. Plan is to take off in an hour. Can you make sure that everything is copasetic in Santiago? We expect to board the subs as soon as we get there."

"Gotcha. We'll have everything waiting. Just to let you know, the B-2 is already airborne. We're still on track to have it arrive at the trawler before you're dropped. The pilot will pass you the coordinates so you can plan your intercept. Hopefully, the subs will be with the trawler when the B-2 takes it out."

"Thanks, Joe. That would be best case, but I'm not counting on it. I just wanted to let you know that we're on the ground."

Craxton did not answer. He was embarrassed that he was not with Rick and that Denise Carlson was there in his place. Rick waited for him to say something, but nothing was forthcoming.

"OK, Joe, I guess that's it. I'll call you when we hit Santiago."

"Have a good trip." There was a pause. "And say 'hi' to Denise for me, will you?"

Rick thought he detected a tone in Joe Craxton's voice he had not heard before. "Sure. I'll tell her good luck for you."

"Thanks. And one more thing. We've got a Navy sub on the way that'll be picking you guys up after you complete your mission."

Denise Carlson gave Rick a questioning look as he closed his cell phone. "Joe says to tell you good luck and that he misses you," said Rick.

"He misses us? We just left. How could he miss us?"

"I didn't say us. I said he misses you."

"I know you did. I was ignoring it." Rick thought he saw Carlson's face soften for a moment.

***

Rick walked into the passenger terminal. A young airman approached the three of them. "Sir, the others are waiting for you in the VIP lounge. If you'll go ahead and wait with them, I'll call you when the plane's ready. There's also a bathroom if you need it. And some refreshments in the refrigerator at the bar."

"Thanks," said Rick. Bowman nodded at the airman and Carlson smiled. The three walked to the lounge.

***

As Rick walked in, Marly looked up. She surprised herself at how glad she was to see him. She stared at Rick's face. His eyes were searching, and when they finally gazed in her direction, she gave him her best smile.

***

Rick was the first through the door and took in the large room. He scanned the faces until his eyes rested on Marly Cooper. She was dressed in jeans, pink tennis shoes and a sweatshirt. Her black hair was swept back like she was standing in an eternal wind, and her lips were full and revealed the most beautiful smile he had ever seen. He let his eyes travel lazily up to hers, and her look of recognition brought a wide smile that he could barely keep from turning into a grin. He felt self-conscious as Marly walked over and took his hand to say hello.

"Ah hmm." Carlson cleared her throat.

"Sorry," said Rick. "Doctor Cooper, this is Miz Carlson who works with me in Washington."

"Pleased to meet you," said Carlson. "Call me Denise."

"I'm Marly. Pleased to meet you, too, Denise."

"And this," Rick continued, "is my old friend Tom Bowman, ex-fighter pilot and soon to be submarine driver."

"Hello. It's a pleasure to meet you."

"The pleasure is mine, I assure you," said Bowman.

Thiele and Washington walked up to the group. "Thiele," said Ralph. He shook hands with both Carlson and Bowman. He nodded at Rick.

"I'm Lo-wan," said Washington. Carlson and Bowman both shook his hand.

"It's good to finally meet you, Lowan," said Rick, also shaking his hand. "Your hat's a little crooked."

Washington fixed his hat. "Yeah, well, I had a little accident over there by the fridge. We got the whole crew here, huh, Mister Starr?"

"Yeah, this should be it unless someone's coming I don't know about."

Washington winked at Rick, and Rick gave him a questioning look. Washington pointed at Marly and held his hand off to the side of his mouth so that only Rick could see his lips. "I knew she was gonna be a looker when you told me 'bout her."

Rick nodded, not quite knowing how to respond. He turned his attention to Marly. "You haven't changed your mind about going with us?"

"No. I'm glad you brought Denise along, though. It makes me feel like it's OK that I'm here. I was beginning to believe this was a man thing." She smiled at Carlson, who returned the gesture.

***

Denise Carlson continued to smile at Marly Cooper, her eyes sad. Here was a complete woman. Smart, attractive, and she had Rick wrapped around her cute little seismograph. In contrast, Rick never once looked in her direction, despite the many hints she thought she dropped over the years.

"Which submarine will you be going on?" Carlson looked over at the man asking the question. Ralph Thiele smiled at her.

She shrugged her shoulders. "I don't know. Rick hasn't told us who's doing what yet."

Thiele laughed and nodded his head at Rick and Marly, who were now walking over to the map that was spread on the floor. "I think they're in cahoots. Coop told me that she and Rick will be on the same submersible."

"Coop?"

"Marly. She's been Coop to me for so long, I don't think I could ever call her by her real name."

Carlson smiled again. *Funny that Marly did not ask Rick to call her Coop like her other friends.* She looked at Rick as he walked and noticed he was not wearing his wedding band on his left ring finger. She had never seen him without it.

***

Marly led Rick to the map and sat on the floor. Rick followed suit. "I like your shoes."

Marly laughed. "These guys are my best friends. They go everywhere with me."

"I can see why," Rick teased.

Marly's smile left her face as she pointed to the corner where the Antarctic and Nazca plates came together. "Here's the armpit of the panhandle of the Nazca plate. Anywhere below this 'V' would work. It'd do the most damage in terms of applying torque."

"They won't make it that far south. We've got a B-2 bomber intercepting them in about eleven hours, just before we're dropped in.

They should be somewhere up in here." He put his finger on the map almost two hundred miles north of where Marly pointed. "We'll know their exact coordinates before we go in, but for planning purposes, this is the location that you and Ralph should use."

Marly considered Rick's words. "So they won't get anywhere near the edge of the plate." She stared at the map. She could feel goose bumps on her forearms and rubbed them.

Rick noticed her panicked look. "What's wrong?"

"If I knew that I couldn't make it to the panhandle of the Nazca plate?" Marly stopped and continued to stare at the map.

"Yeah?" Rick prodded.

"I'd turn west and head for the Pacific Rise."

"The Pacific Rise? What's that?"

"It's a north-south ridge that expands out from where the Pacific and Nazca plates border each other." Marly looked at Rick. "It rises straight up from the ocean floor, and in some places it's almost two thousand miles wide." She turned and pointed to the Nazca plate on the map. "The trawler is probably within a couple hundred miles of its east side."

"So it'd be a good place to get some great torque on the plate with a couple of nuclear bombs."

"Exactly."

"The helicopters that we're using to get to the trawler won't make it that far. They were already at max range and then some." Rick looked back at Marly. "Do we need to ask Ralph what he thinks?"

"We can. After all, it's just a hunch." Marly shook her head. "I could be wrong."

"How are we going to know what to do?" It was Rick's turn to shake his head. "We've got to know exactly where that trawler's going to be."

"How will we get out to the trawler if I'm right?"

Rick pulled his cell phone from his pocket and hit redial.

"Craxton."

"Joe, it's Rick. We've got a problem, and I don't know how you're going to fix it."

CHAPTER 18

The team of six gathered around Rick Starr. He looked at everyone in turn and waited until each returned his smile. "Well," Rick said, "we're here, and it's time to make some decisions." He looked at each person again, his eyes lingering on Marly.

"We analyzed the structure of the trawlers and believe that their holds can only accommodate a pair of submersibles. We also believe that each submersible has the capacity to carry only a single nuclear weapon. And because we've lost the element of surprise, we think the submersibles will launch at the first sign of trouble — if not sooner.

"The biggest unknown, of course, is where the submersibles plan to put their weapons. We thought we had a pretty good idea of where that might be, but now that the trawler isn't going to reach its planned destination, we have to do some speculating. That speculation depends not only on where the trawler might go, but where the subs go after they launch. Hopefully, though, we're going to be doing some educated guesswork." He looked at Thiele and Marly, who nodded at him.

"We're going to be riding in two Navy deep submergence vehicles. The first is Sea Cliff, which can dive to a depth of 20,000 feet. Turtle is the second and can dive to a depth of 10,000 feet. Where we're going the depth is well over 10,000 feet, which means Sea Cliff could be doing most of the work.

"Both submersibles were de-commissioned a couple years ago. We had them put back into service, but there's only one Navy sub driver who's still on active duty and that's Lowan, here, who all of you met." The group looked at Lowan, and he gave a thumbs-up. "He's piloted both Sea Cliff and Turtle, so he's our expert. The other submersible is going to be piloted by Tom Bowman. He's an ex-fighter pilot, and we think he can fly the submersible like a jet — only a lot slower, of course."

"And at a lot lower," said Bowman. The group laughed. Bowman grinned.

"The first decision we need to make as a team is who's going to drive which submersible."

Lowan Washington did not hesitate. "I should pilot Sea Cliff, since I have the most experience. Plus I was the deep guy on the team before we broke up, and Sea Cliff was my baby. If we're gonna chase down those subs and get those bombs where they need to go, then you probably need me to do it."

"I don't have a problem with that," said Bowman.

"OK," said Rick, "Lowan pilots Sea Cliff, and Tom drives the Turtle." Everyone nodded their agreement. "Now for the harder part. Who's going to go with Lowan, and who's going with Tom?"

***

On the phone for over an hour, Joe Craxton finally threw the receiver down in frustration and walked toward John Renoir's office. Renoir's secretary tried to stop him with her finger to indicate that someone was already in there, but Craxton ignored her. His lack of protocol was out of character. He opened the door without hesitating.

Renoir looked up. "Joe, Donna should have told you that I have Senator Moriarity here with me."

"Hi, Senator," said Craxton. "Sir," he said to his boss, ignoring the senator, "we've got a big time problem, and it's gonna take the president to fix it."

Renoir knew immediately that Rick and his team were involved. "Senator, I'm sorry to have to end our meeting so suddenly, but an ongoing, important national security matter that can't wait has flared up." Renoir abruptly stood up and walked out of his office without another word. He grabbed Craxton's arm and pulled him along as he walked out the door. "Are you crazy? The president briefed only the leadership of the Congress, and the first thing Moriarity will do when he leaves is to start nosing around. I hope the president has put as tight a lid on this operation as he seems to think."

Renoir waved to his secretary as he walked by. "Donna, please take care of the senator."

The senator left Renoir's office in a huff. "I have never been treated like this by anyone during my fifteen years in the U.S. Senate. I'll be talking to the president about his CIA director." Renoir's secretary started to say something, but the senator gave her a look that told her she should keep her thoughts to herself. "I'll see myself out."

***

"So what are the options?" asked Thiele, as the group turned into a loose circle.

"You can go with Denise or me," said Rick, "and Marly will go with the other crew."

"And what about the submersibles?"

"I'm going with Lowan since he's driving Sea Cliff. Whoever goes with me goes on Sea Cliff."

Thiele looked at Marly and then Carlson. "Why don't you take Coop — I mean Marly, and I'll go with Tom and Denise?"

Bowman nodded. Marly spoke up almost too quickly. "That was going to be my suggestion since I'm the only one who seems to know anything about the Pacific Rise, and Sea Cliff will be doing the deep work." She felt her face turning warm when she realized everyone was staring at her. "What? Doesn't that make sense?"

"Makes perfect sense to me," said Thiele, smiling at his colleague.

"C'mon," said Washington. "Why don't we three guys go together?" He pointed to Rick, Thiele and himself. "Let the girls go with Mister Bowman."

"Girls? Isn't that a little sexist?" asked Carlson.

"Sexist? What's sex got to do with what I said? I'm just tryin' to get the best team on my boat."

"What if I decided I didn't want to go with you because you're black?" asked Carlson.

"Sister, that wouldn't bother me a bit 'cause I don't want you with me."

"Decision's made," said Rick interrupting, stepping between the pair and moving his arm up and down with his palm out sideways. "Marly and I will go with Lowan, Denise and Ralph will go with Tom." He looked at his wrist, but there was still no watch. "We'll be leaving in fifteen minutes, so if you need to use the facilities, take advantage of them now. We'll be flying in a hyperbaric chamber for the trip to Chile and then going directly into the submersibles when we get there. We've got box lunches waiting for us onboard the plane."

***

"So what's the problem?" asked Renoir.

"It's Rick. He says they need to be dropped a thousand miles off the coast of Chile, and the choppers we've got lined up are good for a lot less. We need an airplane, like a C-130. We've contacted the Chilean Air Force, 'cause we know they've got Herky birds, but they say only a request directly from the president and some U.S. dollars…" He rolled his eyes. "…can make it happen."

"Of course. OK, I thought it was something serious. I'll go see the president personally on this one. I'm sure he'll be able to oblige the egos and avarice of our southern neighbors, under the circumstances."

***

The two teams of three boarded the Navy's Boeing 707 Stratotanker. Rick was first up the crew entry chute and led the way into the chamber. Tom Bowman was next, and the rest filed in after. Marly was last and positioned herself next to Rick when he sat down. Lowan Washington sat on Rick's other side, closest to the entrance. Carlson, Bowman and Thiele sat directly across from them. The corpsman closed the hatch and gave it a last hard tug to make sure it was locked tight.

"Tell me again why we need to ride in this thing," said Thiele.

"Bends," said Bowman. "Flying regulations say you can't scuba dive and then fly on a plane until you've waited forty-eight hours."

Thiele put a questioning look on his face. "Aren't we doing it the other way round? Flying and then scuba diving?"

"Right," said Bowman. He shrugged his shoulders.

"Procedures," interrupted Washington.

"Procedures?" asked Thiele.

"Procedures," repeated Washington. "Anytime we're airlifted, we fly in a chamber where they keep us at sea level. Makes it possible to do more diving and go deeper."

"But we're not stepping outside the submersibles, are we?" Thiele asked, hoping his sarcasm registered.

"Certainly don't plan, too," said Washington.

The sound of the first engine winding up ended the conversation.

***

Navy Captain Chung Phan sat with his officers in the dining room of the trawler China Rose. He smoked a cigarette as did everyone else at the table. White smoke curled from the end of his cigarette and drifted slowly to the ceiling where a six-inch thick cloud, the evidence of ubiquitous burning tobacco, hung below its summit. None of the young officers at the table spoke as they watched their commander's every move. When he finally put his cigarette out in the ashtray in front of him, they followed his lead. When he leaned back to look at his young protégés, they leaned back to return his gaze.

The captain seemed to peer idly around the room for a brief moment, but his mind was racing. "Gentlemen," he began, "we have eleven hours until we reach our destination."

One officer wrinkled his brow. "But sir, I thought that we were still more than twenty-four hours from our objective."

"Had we kept our original objective, you would be right. But in thirty minutes, we will turn due west and proceed to the Pacific Rise." Although no one said a word, every face wore the same question.

"We believe," the captain continued, "that the Americans are sending bomber aircraft to intercept our ship, and that they will try to sink us." The faces of his men became expressionless. "So we must find a new home for our cargo. The closest appropriate site, according to our scientists, is the Pacific Rise."

"But why would the Americans attack us?" ventured the oldest officer among the men. He sailed with Captain Phan numerous times, and his mentor's words perplexed him. "We are doing nothing wrong. We are only conducting seismic experiments. Why should the Americans try to sink us?"

"The Americans believe that they can attack with impunity and that no one will know."

"But that still doesn't explain why they would want to attack us."

"Why would we deliver our cargo if we're going to be attacked? Should we not be heading for a safe harbor?" asked another officer.

"You are asking too many questions," said the captain. "We have been ordered to deliver the equipment we have on board, regardless of the circumstances. The seismographs we are carrying are the only means that we have to monitor the actions of the Americans, and the Americans don't like it." He took a full thirty seconds, without saying a word, to take in the face of each his officers. "It is not our right to question the orders of our superiors. Our duty is to act in accordance with their wishes. Nothing more. Nothing less. Nothing else."

The group remained silent. "Good," said the captain. "Begin to prepare the submersibles. We will launch them both when we arrive at the Pacific Rise, ten minutes apart."

***

Onboard the jet, the Navy corpsman handed box lunches to the group. Marly and Denise, having never eaten a military box lunch before, were fascinated.

Marly carefully inventoried the white cardboard box's contents: a cellophane package containing a plastic spoon, fork, knife, and salt and pepper, all wrapped in a single thin paper napkin; a carton of white milk and a carton of chocolate milk; a hoagie with too little ham and cheese on a soft white bun that was much too large; a packet of mayonnaise and a packet of mustard; two small chocolate candy bars; a soft cookie; and an apple. *A veritable goodie feast. Do people really eat this stuff?*

"This would kill me if I ate it," said Marly, dropping the contents back into the box.

"I was thinking the same thing," said Carlson. "There's nothing in here but carbohydrates and sugar. This is unhealthy."

"I'll take yore candy bars if you don't want 'em," volunteered Washington. Both women threw him their candy bars.

"I'll take your sandwich," said Thiele. Both women threw their hoagies at him. He caught one, but the other fell to the floor. He leaned over and picked it up. "I don't need both."

"I'll take the cookies," said Rick. They threw their cookies at him.

Marly held up her carton of chocolate milk and gave a questioning look to the rest of the group. Washington grabbed it. When Carlson held up hers, Thiele took it.

Marly opened her remaining carton of white milk and took a swallow from the diamond-shaped opening. Denise Carlson took a bite of her apple and smiled as she chewed.

Washington opened up the chocolate milk he got from Marly and gulped it in a single swallow. He opened the two candy bars and shoved them into his mouth. The women gave him a disgusted look at his gluttonous display, and he gave them a caramel filled smile that could have turned the stomach of a Bull Mastiff.

Thiele and Rick laughed at Washington, and Bowman shook his head. The women turned their faces away with a verbal reprimand that Washington should learn some manners.

***

Major Tom "Aggie" Aguilar and his crew climbed into the bat-like plane. At two point four billion dollars a copy, the B-2 stealth bomber was by far the most expensive airplane ever built in aviation history. Its outer surfaces were engineered so precisely and fitted together with such exactness that its shape was impervious to radar. Its visual and auditory signatures were minimal. Tens of millions of lines of computer code directed its flight controls and guided its electronics. Even if the U.S. were to publish its blueprints on the Internet, the B-2 could not be duplicated. The technology embodied within its engines, its outer skin, its flight control system, its aerodynamics, its electronics, and its software was extraordinarily complex. The B-2 exceeded the capacity of any known entity, person or otherwise, to reproduce and construct a similar plane. It was a one-of-a-kind technological, aeronautical marvel.

Major Aguilar climbed into the aircraft commander's seat. The weapons system officer sat in the jump seat, and the pilot climbed into the right seat. The B-2's every system was automated, and the crewmembers' job was more one of monitoring and supervising systems than providing motor skills. Normally flown by a crew of two, this special mission called for the addition of a weapon systems officer.

The three men worked in silence, preparing their aerospace vehicle for flight. They knew that they were to take off and head to the southwest, destination unknown. A flight tape provided by their wing commander would be injected into their mission planning software once airborne, directing them to their destination and ultimate target. The plane's bomb bay contained a single, highly classified smart weapon. The crew was briefed that they would be seeking out and destroying a nautical vessel, preventing it from delivering a deadly payload.

Within a matter of hours they expected to be in combat, and the men executed their checklists with serious looks on their faces. They were briefed on the fate of the B-52 crew that preceded them, and they were determined to avoid the same end. They were granted license to strike decisively and with crushing force — shock and awe the military called it — and the deliberate way they performed their preparatory actions indicated that was exactly what they intended.

***

Captain Phan sat in his cabin alone in the upper decks of the trawler China Rose. *This Is sheer madness*, he thought. He knew that he had blinded himself to this trip's true purpose, his ambition for higher command so intense. Even though rumors were strong in the officer ranks of a secret mission on the perimeter of the United States, this trip through the Panama Canal and then to South America in a vessel filled with electronics expressly developed to collect intelligence while pretending to fish in the southern hemisphere, was unforeseen.

The submersibles he ferried were designed to gather debris off the ocean floor. Delivering listening devices deep in the canyons, although something new, sounded reasonable. Why near the southern continent and not North America did not necessarily trouble him, either. After all, the Americans were everywhere. *But to deliver them in the face of an attack by an American bomber?* He knew that the devices were cover for something more sinister. *Do not ask*, he repeated to himself. *Do not ask, why this madness?* It was his duty to obey, and obey he would. *But then? If I lose my crew or my ship? Die with honor. On the bridge. Yes, on the bridge.* He stood and pulled his dress cap from the small closet adorning one wall and set it upon his head. He left the cabin and began the short climb to the captain's seat and its master panel that controlled the ship. Unable to rest or sleep, he would spend the wait where he could see events from beginning to end. *Fewer than a dozen hours. A dozen hours until Fate arrives to do her work. Who will she favor?* He knew the answer and did not like it.

The bridge came to attention when the captain arrived, no one moving. He waved his hand, and the busy activity required to commandeer a large ocean-going vessel continued. He sat heavily into his seat.

"Sir," said the navigator sitting in the chair next to him. "It is time to turn west."

The captain took a deep breath and let it out slowly. He felt a great fatigue tugging at his soul as he nodded.

***

The B-2 bomber, its fuselage emblazoned with "The Spirit of America" in large, Air Force blue letters, began its long journey. With enough fuel to fly over nine thousand miles, its destination could be anywhere in the western hemisphere. Or with refueling, virtually anywhere in the world. The weapons system officer inserted the tape into the tape reader. The mission slowly unfolded while the crew watched. They turned the furtive jet southwest and would eventually be directed to turn south — headings that led only to open ocean.

***

Washington, Thiele and Bowman leaned their heads back after consuming their sugar-infested box lunches, and as if on cue they all fell asleep. Even the Navy corpsman leaned his head against the chamber's closed hatch and drifted off. Rick remained awake, hoping to talk with Marly.

The women were uncomfortable in the unfamiliar environment. Every bump, every alien sound meant that disaster lurked ahead. Without the sound insulation found in commercial jetliners, the plane's fuselage was noisy. The constant clear-air turbulence caused by the day's heat did not help their perception that the plane was a catastrophe waiting to happen. How could men sleep in the face of such uncertainty? Lowan Washington's loud snore spoke the answer: While his body was in mortal danger, his dream-swept mind had him lying on a deserted beach somewhere on a distant shore. Carlson tried to nod off, but the attempt was fitful.

"Don't be nervous," Rick said to Marly. "It feels a lot worse than it really is."

Marly nodded. "I'm happiest with my feet on the ground, even if it's quaking."

"Yeah, I've never been a big fan of flying unless it's absolutely necessary. And I've never been in a submarine, either, unless you count Disneyland."

Marly laughed. "I can't even claim that." She turned her body squarely toward Rick so that she could read his body language. "How did you end up as a CIA analyst?"

"Oh, that's a long story. I really wanted to be a field agent with the Agency, but my background check ruled me out — Italian mafia on my mother's side — so I took what they offered and became an analyst."

"You seem to like it."

"I do. Probably more than if I was working in the field. So things seem to work out for the best." He also turned and leaned against the side of his seat. "And how did you end up in the earthquake business?"

"It's something I wanted to do since I was a kid. My uncle was caught in the great Alaska earthquake, and he could tell one heck of a riveting story. Got me hooked, and I never looked back."

Rick laughed and smiled.

"Can I ask something personal?" Marly asked.

Rick pressed his lips together. "Sure, I guess."

"Why did you get divorced?"

Rick took a deep breath and sighed. "Kids."

"Kids? I don't know what that means."

"Pretty simple, really. I wanted kids, my wife did not. We talked about it before we got married, but I was young and naïve, and I convinced myself that I could persuade my wife to change her mind once she learned just how wonderful her new husband really was. My grandmother — you have to understand Italian families; in the old country the grandmother is probably the most influential member of the extended family — advised against the marriage, but it's hard to turn your back on a beautiful full-blooded Italian woman, especially when you have so much already invested in the relationship. 'If it is not in her heart to have children,' my grandmother said, 'it is not in your power to put it there.' I didn't listen, but of course she was right."

Marly shook her head. "Why didn't your wife want kids?"

"Didn't need 'em. Wanted to work. We argued almost daily the last couple years. She was mad because I didn't think she was enough to make a happy marriage. I was mad because she didn't want to create a legacy with me for future generations. It was a pretty typical Mediterranean standoff with lots of emotional conflict and no resolution."

"Was it a man thing with you? You know, that you needed to keep your line intact? Did you want your firstborn to be a son?"

"We never got far enough along in our discussions for me to even think about having a preference one way or the other. And I never really analyzed the psychological motivations of either one of us. I just wanted kids. Still do."

"Did your wife remarry?"

"Oh, yeah. Another American, a year after we divorced."

"Any kids?"

"No. She and her husband both work, live in a big house out in California, travel a lot. They live *la dolce vita* and seem happy. We parted good friends, although we've seen each other only once since the divorce."

"Does it make you sad? The divorce, I mean?"

"Used to. I was pretty miserable for awhile and buried myself in work. Now it's something I don't really think much about. I can't even tell you anymore why I've been avoiding a new relationship for so long. I'm trying to think about all that now."

"Have you ever been married?"

"No. Haven't had a serious relationship that was even close."

"I'm surprised," Rick said. "Attractive women like you usually don't make it to thirty."

Marly ignored Rick's compliment. "You know, I vowed that I would never marry a divorced man. I always wanted to begin life with someone just like me, with a clean slate. No emotional baggage. No hard feelings. Never having walked out of a lifetime commitment. I wanted it to be perfect."

Rick gave Marly a sad look. "That's very admirable, and I think you should hang onto that goal for all you're worth. Life sometimes has a way of overcoming our ideals, pressing us into situations that we never expected or wanted. At least it's been that way for me."

"Kind of like now?" Marly asked.

Rick managed a smile. "Yeah, like now. Of course, it's how you deal with the unexpected and unwanted that makes all the difference."

Their words were worlds apart.

***

The China Rose completed its turn. "Captain," said the navigator, "we will be at the Pacific Rise in approximately ten hours."

"We will stop when we reach the east side," said the captain.

CHAPTER 19

Tom Bowman sat across from Lowan Washington. Both leaned forward with their hands folded and elbows resting on the tops of their knees. "So tell me how a submersible handles. Is it smooth? Do I have a stick or will I be driving with a wheel?"

"Water's smooth, real smooth. You got a stick, a small one. You push it forward to go down, pull it to go up. Left for port, right for starboard. It's like a joystick on a computer. In fact, we trained on a computer before we took our first ride."

"OK. Sounds like the stick in a fighter jet, except I'm flying underwater."

"Don't get too excited, Mister Bowman. You ain't gonna fly this thing. It's more like crawlin' through the water."

Bowman laughed. "So what's the visibility like? How do we see outside? How do I know where we're going?"

"You got a double-paned window made outta real thick glass. There's a couple 'o big headlights you can turn on once you get 'bout fifty feet down, 'cause where we're goin' it's blacker than squid ink." He rested his chin on one hand. "You also got sonar that looks out about a thousand yards."

"What do you know about this underwater bazooka we've got?"

"We tested some kind o' underwater shoot-'em-ups a couple o' years ago. Weren't too accurate. Pretty nasty things, though."

"You know we're carrying them with us?"

"Yeah, I'm the one who suggested to Mister Starr that we get 'em." They both turned and looked at Rick Starr, who was sleeping. The women finally fell asleep, too. They had unbuckled their shoulder straps and seat belts, and that freedom allowed a comfortable enough angle and position so they could nod off. Bowman and Washington seemed alone in their conversation.

"Is the bazooka hard to aim?"

"Can't really aim it," said Washington. "That was the problem. There weren't no way to aim the bazooka or guide the projectile to the target once you shot it. You just kinda pointed your sub in the direction you wanted it to go and pulled the trigger." He folded his hands again. "I thought it was more like shootin' a depth charge than a bazooka shell. You didn't have to hit the target to do some major damage. You just needed to get pretty close. I tole Mister Starr all that."

Bowman nodded. "Sounds like I'm going to have to find my target before it goes below 10,000 feet."

It was Washington's turn to nod. "Yeah, you're gonna have to get 'em on their way down for sure." He paused. "You know, there's supposed to be 'bout thirty percent slop built into the subs' specifications." He looked at Bowman to see if he understood his meaning. "'Course, we never tested it. Guess I'm sayin' you might have a little extra room to play with if you need it."

"It's the same for airplanes," said Bowman. "If the specs said the limit was three times the force of gravity, you knew there was a pad if something bad happened. I once talked to an old KC-135 tanker pilot who flew in Vietnam, and he saved an F-4 Phantom that was shot up over the north and was going down. He dove the tanker to get in front of the Phantom. Went supersonic, plugged his boom into the F-4's refueling receptacle, and pulled him all the way home. Saved the pilot from a stay at the Hanoi Hilton. Said the tanker was designed for point-eight-five mach, but that it did fine going through the sound barrier. Trim control reversed on him, though." Bowman looked down at the floor and then back up at Washington. "So you're telling me I've really got about 13,000 feet."

"We talked a lot about the subs with the engineers. They said you could exceed the max depth for a short time, but it better be a momentary deviation."

"So you've got to be smart about it."

"Smartness don't help when you're outta bounds."

"A momentary deviation beyond the limits in a jet could cause your plane to disintegrate. It sounds like driving a submersible is a lot more forgiving."

"I ain't sayin' there's forgiveness for exceedin' the limits, Mister Bowman. You need to be prayin' for mercy if you wanna bust the specifications and get away with it."

***

Pretending to nap, Rick listened to Bowman and Washington. He could hear only bits and pieces of their conversation, but he was not much interested. He and Washington spent hours having the identical discussion. Instead, he peered through closed eyes at Marly, who was sleeping to his left. She looked as if someone had gently closed her eyelids and laid her eyelashes carefully out across her cheeks. Her skin was a light brown, her nose pleasantly pointed, her lips full and light pink. Her cheekbones were high, but not protrusive. He let his eyes follow the contours of her body. Her breasts were full and round, her waist slight, her legs supple. He looked back at her face, her dark hair parted across her ears. He sighed and turned away.

***

Denise Carlson watched Rick Starr look through partially open eyes at the woman next to him. Carlson, too, heard the conversation and wondered at the future. *If only someone would look at me the way that Rick looks at Marly.* She could see that his eyes were devouring her.

***

"Talk to me," said Renoir to Joe Craxton. "What's up with Rick and Denise?"

"They're three hours out of Chile. Submersibles are set to be loaded up in a pair of U.S. C-130s that are standing by. We've got our people on scene and Rick, Denise and the others will go directly into the subs when they get to Santiago. Then it's a thousand miles out to the trawler. The C-130s will get the location of the target from the B-2."

"U.S. 130s? I thought we were using the Chilean Air Force."

"We are," said Craxton, "but all they've got are the older E models, and I was told they don't have the payload or range to do the mission. Fortunately, we had a couple of new J models in Columbia. But even with their longer range and bigger payload, engineers had to strip out the insides, plus they had to cut out some of the fuselage so the subs would fit. We'll have a U.S. pilot onboard each plane. The Chilean pilots will take the right seat, mostly going along for the ride."

"Has Rick figured out where the subs will put the nukes?"

"That's the reason for the C-130s. Something about a massive lava mountain in the middle of the Pacific Ocean. I think Rick called it the Pacific Rise."

"The Pacific Rise?" Renoir shook his head slowly. "How can it be that the lives of millions of Americans depend on what happens in a place I've never even heard of?"

***

Rick Starr finally let himself drift off to sleep. His mind was full of images of the young woman resting next to him, the scent of her hair discernible even in the thin atmosphere of the cabin of a Boeing 707 flying at 35,000 feet. His subconscious mind pretended that Marly never said his divorce made him ineligible for her affection.

***

Lowan Washington found a comfortable position, but could not doze off. He had been on numerous missions in the submersibles, but never anything operational. That was why the Navy finally mothballed the subs — it was a great capability, but it was a capability looking for a mission. *Well, there's a mission now. I knew this day was comin'. Even when they said they were puttin' these babies in the boneyard for good, I knew it was comin'.*

***

The plane's engines whined quietly through the night air. More than minus sixty degrees centigrade ambient air temperature, the outside skin of the aircraft frosted over. Inside, the heat from the engines made the aircraft cabin warm enough for short sleeves. The crew worked quietly, monitoring the aircraft's altitude and airspeed, the engine instruments, and navigation waypoints. The stars shone brightly, a few lonely vessels on the water appearing as small dots of light resting on the top of the dark vast body of liquid below. It was a typical night out over the Pacific, quiet and secluded and full of solitude.

***

Marly Cooper felt a jolt. Outside air turbulence, which was light, increased to moderate and shook her awake. She resisted the urge to open her eyes and tried to become more comfortable by shifting her weight and leaning to the right. Her head found Rick's shoulder and a smile crossed her lips, the smell of his body noticeable through his shirt. She drifted back to sleep.

The moderate turbulence continued to increase steadily in frequency, with an occasional heavy spike. The bumps from the heavy turbulence were like hitting large potholes in the road at high speed, and Marly was again pulled from her slumber. The jostling continued to increase.

The plane suddenly lurched as if it struck an invisible object. Marly's head was tossed to the side, and her face came crashing down on Rick's shoulder. *That hurts.* She reluctantly opened her eyes, rolling to her left. A numbness engulfed her, and alarm bells began ringing in her head. *Something isn't right.* Eyes now wide open, Marly tried to look around the chamber. But her pupils would not focus, and she was forced to close her eyes. Sitting up with great effort and looking around once more, she could see that a thin wisp of white smoke permeated the air. She breathed in and smelled — *what, an electrical fire?* Instant headache. Eyes watering, stinging. The aircraft started shaking violently. Everyone else was still sleeping. *How could they possibly sleep?*

Marly managed to get to her feet and looked around in a panic. She was thrown back into her seat, but pushed herself up again into a standing position. No one moved. *Were they unconscious?* She stumbled over to the Navy corpsman who had locked them inside the chamber, but when she pushed him to get his attention, he fell lifelessly to his side. She looked back at Rick, and he shifted his body as if he were in a deep sleep. Marly tried to turn the large brass wheel that held them prisoner. *My God, it won't move.* She looked back at the chamber's control panel that held information she knew was vital to their escape from the metal tomb. Its dials and switches were indecipherable. Between the smoke and the fog that saturated her mind, she could not concentrate on what the panel seemed to want to tell her. She pushed the interphone button she saw the corpsman use to talk to the crew and shouted into the small microphone. Her voice sounded strange, her words slightly slurred.

"Help, help, we can't breathe. There's a fire, and smoke." She quit speaking, her lungs burning from the effort, her voice hoarse. There was no answer. The turbulence threw her to the side of the chamber, and she struggled to pull herself upright once more.

Frightened and hardly able to stand because the turbulence was so severe, Marly practically fell on top of Rick. The plane continued to shake violently. A momentary zero-G dive nearly lifted her off her feet. Marly grabbed Rick's collar and began to pull it as hard as she could.

"Rick! Rick! You have to wake up!" But Rick did not move. The turbulence became more violent. Lowan Washington fell to the floor, but the fall did not wake him. "Rick! My God, Rick, I don't want us to die in the middle of the Pacific Ocean! We didn't even get married or have a family!" Her words surprised her. "Wake up! Please, please, wake up," Marly sobbed, collapsing onto Rick's chest. She gave Rick one last hard shake.

***

The B-52 sent to disable the other four trawlers had suddenly reappeared out of nowhere, and they relayed their belief that they were attacked with a powerful laser, blinding the pilots. To avoid the same fate, the B-2 windows were covered with "blast curtains". Designed originally to resist the flash emanating from a nuclear explosion, the curtains were coated with bright reflective silver.

Flying at an altitude of 45,000 feet, the B-2 bomber was invisible as it sailed south through the night at almost 700 miles per hour. Hidden in the belly of the stealthy plane this night was a weapon from the

Pentagon's black world, a weapon whose capabilities were known only to the select few responsible for its development and kept secret until pulled from the depths of the compartmentalized shadows of the Department of Defense. The object carried by the B-2 was a smart weapon possessing powers never-before-seen in the light of combat. Its lethality would bring a new dimension to the art of war, the trawler they were tracking via satellite subject to a force that the Chinese, and anyone else for that matter, could not have anticipated.

***

"Marly! Marly!" Marly opened her eyes, and Rick stood over her, his outstretched arm pressing against her shoulder. She looked up into his face and realized that both her hands tightly gripped his shirt collar. She let go.

"You were having a nightmare," he said. Marly looked around. Everyone was on their feet, and the looks on their faces told Marly that she woke them all.

"You scared the cornbread right out o' us," said Washington. "Somethin' 'bout the plane crashing."

Marly held her hands to her eyes. "I'm sorry. I guess I was dreaming. The turbulence was terrible. There was smoke, and the plane was in a dive."

Rick kept his right hand on her left shoulder. Marly looked around the chamber. The air was clear, the plane quiet, turbulence non-existent.

"It's OK," Rick said. "The crew says it's time to prepare for landing, anyway. We're almost to Santiago."

Marly's expression told Rick that she was still disoriented. She rubbed her hands on her arms, and they were covered with goose bumps.

Marly looked at Rick intently. "It was horrible. You wouldn't wake up, and I didn't know what to do, so I grabbed your shirt and started shaking as hard as I could."

"Well, it worked. You woke me up."

"But in my dream, you didn't wake up. Lowan fell on the floor, and he just laid there." Marly managed a sheepish smile as everyone found their seats again.

"Sister," said Washington. "Don't try no stunt like that on the sub. There ain't no room for panic once we're underwater. There ain't no place to go."

"I'm OK now," said Marly. She brushed her hand through her hair.

Rick sat down next to her and pulled her head to his shoulder. "Why don't you rest for a few more minutes?"

Marly laid her head on Rick's shoulder. His muscles were firm, the warmth of his body comforting. With surprising ease, she fell back asleep. This time, she did not dream.

***

Tom Bowman pulled out from his pocket a small bag of peanuts he bought from one of the vending machines at base operations in California. He tore the bag open and began eating.

"Whattaya eatin'?" asked Washington.

"Peanuts," said Bowman. He held up the plastic bag.

Washington shook his head. "Don't you know that peanuts is a lay-gume?"

Bowman shook his head and furrowed his brow. "A legume?"

"Yeah, you know, beans. Peanuts ain't nuts. They's beans. Peanuts and beans are the same thing. You're gonna be sorry when you get down under the water and the gas from them beans decides it's time to come out. You're gonna die from tryin' to hold it in, or you're gonna kill everybody when you let it out."

Bowman laughed, but Washington's expression told him he was serious.

"So these are beans?" asked Bowman. Washington nodded. "And you're saying that eating peanuts has the same effect as eating what, Mexican food?"

Washington nodded again. "You got it, Mister Bowman. You eat that bag o' peanuts, and you're gonna regret it. You ain't gonna be in a nice big airplane cockpit with air conditioning to freshify your surroundings. You're gonna be ridin' in a real small, closed-in space where every smell is magnified a hunnerd times. 'Specially the bad ones."

Bowman laughed again, shaking his head. "OK, Lowan, you got my attention." He folded the small bag and put it back into his pocket. He looked at the young black man sitting across from him and smiled. Washington grinned back.

***

Marly no more sat up when a loud 'thunk' told her the plane landed. She looked at Rick with a questioning look.

"Yep," he said, "we're here. Chile this morning, sandwiched in a hot sub in the middle of the ocean by this afternoon."

"How do you propose we get to the middle of the ocean?"

Rick shook his head. "My buddy Joe is supposed to be taking care of that problem. He promised me transportation, and that's all I know."

"Depressurizing the chamber," called the corpsman to no one in particular. A loud bang and a rush of air filled the compartment. A minute later the corpsman turned the large brass wheel and pulled the heavy door open. "Welcome to Santiago, Chile."

The plane halted its taxi, and Rick unfastened his lapbelt and threw off the shoulder straps that held him in his seat for landing. Marly struggled with her belt.

"Can I help?" Rick offered, reaching out before Marly could answer. He popped the lanyard and gently lifted the straps from her shoulders. He took her hands and helped her stand. It took a moment for her to gain her balance, and she leaned on Rick. His body felt good, and she looked up into his face.

"You gonna be OK?" he asked.

"I think so," Marly nodded. "I feel drugged from sleeping so long. It takes me a minute to wake up."

"Take a couple," Rick said. The others were beginning to stand, and the Navy corpsman left the chamber. "You may want to stretch a little, because Joe said we'd be going directly into the submersibles."

"I don't think I could be a pilot," said Marly. "Too many ups and downs."

Washington heard Marly and laughed. "That's pretty good, Doc. You got a good sense 'o humor." He laughed again. "Too many ups and downs. Yeah, that's pretty funny."

Marly could not tell if Lowan was making fun of her. She decided to take his comment at face value and laughed, too. Her head was clearing rapidly now. The cool sea air from outside the aircraft was replacing the stale atmosphere inside. "OK," she said to Rick. "I'm ready. Let's go and get on the subs before I lose my courage."

Everyone was waiting for Rick to lead the way. He stepped confidently out of the chamber, Marly falling in directly behind. *Gotta find out what Craxton's arranged and who's in charge down here.*

"Watch your step," Rick called. "We don't want to lose anyone this late in the game. It's not like there's a whole gang of crazy people waiting to volunteer to take your place."

***

Rick blinked as he stepped from the crew entry chute onto the tarmac and into the bright sun. He was surprised to find a Washington, D.C., colleague waiting for him.

"Hey, Rick!" said Quentin Parker, grabbing Rick's hand. "You look surprised to find me here!" Parker was the CIA analyst in Rick's office responsible for South American affairs. "I was in Santiago for a quick visit when Joe Craxton called. He almost blew an aneurysm when I told him the president was going to have to call down here personally to get you guys transportation." The rest of the team got off the plane and was listening.

"So you got us a flight?"

"Sure did. A couple of herky-birds."

"Great," said Rick. "Joe say anything? Any words from Renoir?"

"Only that for what this thing is costing the taxpayer, you guys better make it work."

"A herky-bird? What's that?" asked Thiele.

"C-130 Hercules," said Washington. "Good airplane. Flown on 'em before. Reliable and safe."

"When do we leave?" asked Rick.

"You got enough time to unload your bladders, and that's about it," said Parker.

"Have you heard from the B-2?"

"Not yet, but we think we've got a SATLOC on your target."

"Really?"

"Could be. Satellite showed a ship on the course you guys gave us, and it turned dead west a couple hours ago."

"How far out?"

"Could be twelve hundred miles by the time you get to her."

"What's the plan?"

"No plan except to get you guys on the planes and in the air."

"Do I know you?" Washington interrupted Rick and Parker. "You look awful familiar."

Parker laughed. "I get that a lot. I think I just have a familiar face. Don't think we've ever met." He put out his hand. "Name's Quentin Parker. Friends call me Parker."

"I'm Lo-wan." He shook his head. "You sure do look familiar. Probably just my Presbyterianism."

"Presbyterianism?"

"Yeah, you know — near-sightedness. I'm a little near-sighted." Washington turned and walked away.

Parker looked at Rick. "Is he making a religious joke?"

Rick shrugged as the team moved toward base operations. "Maybe he meant presbyopia." Parker stared blankly.

"Presbyopia. You know, near-sighted," said Rick.

CHAPTER 20

Walking into base operations, Rick looked around. It appeared as if some odd force transported them back in time to the sixties. The chairs in the large concourse were formed of thick, brightly colored molded plastic, backs and seats riveted to stout aluminum supports fitted with large flat coasters that sat on the floor underneath each leg. The carpet was a dense, peroxide-orange shag. The tables matched the chairs in style, with bright blue, orange and white plastic dotting the room. It all seemed strangely familiar.

Rick spoke to everyone on the team individually, reassuring each member that everything was going according to plan. "We'll be boarding a small blue van outside in ten minutes. Don't be late. We need to get underway as quickly as possible. Your bag is already loaded." He went to Marly last.

"Are you better?" he asked. Marly nodded, unconvincingly. "It's going to be a long ride." She nodded again.

"You know," said Marly. "On the airplane, while I was dreaming I wasn't afraid of dying." She looked to the floor and then let her eyes slowly meet Rick's. "But I was afraid that I'd never really get to know you, that our relationship would end when this is over. I'd like to have a chance to get to know you better."

"What about your vow not to get involved with someone who's been divorced?"

"I'm trying to think about all that now."

Rick could only smile.

"You look like a Cheshire cat."

"I was thinking." Rick looked around the room, and everyone was gathering and getting ready to head out the door. He let his right arm swing forward toward the others. "It looks like we have to go."

"What were you thinking?" Marly asked, walking up behind Rick and trying to get his attention as he walked. She hit him on the back of his shoulder.

But Rick was off, pushing everyone toward the door. "Let's go, everybody. Time to go. One last chance if you need to visit the toilets."

"Never pass up an opportunity, I always say," Washington said to no one as he walked to the men's room.

***

The group squeezed into the van. Quinten Parker boarded last. He found a seat near the front and turned toward the group as the driver pulled away from the curb.

"Hi, everyone. In case you didn't hear, my name is Parker, and I'm a colleague of Rick and Denise." He smiled. "We've got a pair of C-130 airplanes to ferry you and the submersibles out to sea. The plan is to put you inside the subs, fly you out to where you can intercept your targets, and then drop you into the water."

Marly, Carlson, Thiele and Washington looked horrified. "That don't sound too cool to me, Mister Parker," said Washington. "We're supposed to be lowered gently into the water, not dropped. You seen the insides of those subs? They's made outta steel, and they don't got much padding."

"I don't know if my back can take a drop," said Bowman.

"It won't be your back that's in trouble, Mister Bowman. It's your face and the family jewels. You and I will be lying on our stomachs on something 'bout as wide as an ironing board when this thing hits the water." Washington's expression showed his displeasure.

"It's the best we can do under the circumstances," said Parker. "A parachute will deploy to pull you out of the airplane, and hopefully the chute will give you a soft landing." The reaction of the group made him wonder if he was giving too much information. "Once you hit the water, a salinity mechanism will activate and release your parachutes so you can make your dive."

"I ain't never heard o' no salinity mechanism," said Washington.

"It means the salt water will react with whatever's holding the chute onto the sub so that it releases," offered Thiele.

"Precisely," said Parker.

"What if it's rainin' when we get pulled outta the airplane? Is the salinity mechanism gonna release the parachute so we hit the water like some kind o' steel turd?"

"The idea," said Parker, "is that the salinity of fresh water isn't sufficient to activate the mechanism."

"What if someone spills somethin' salty in the back of the plane? Like Mister Bowman, here. He was eatin' peanuts. Maybe the mechanism will release."

"Right," said Parker, groping for words. "I'll make sure that we throw away all the salty food before we board the planes."

Washington's frown grew into a grin. "You're playin' with me now, aren't ya?"

Parker returned Washington's grin.

Carlson shook her head. "I thought he was serious."

The van slowed as it approached the C-130s. Parked behind the aircraft were the two submersibles, which were clearly too large to fit inside. Rick looked at the two aircraft and was astonished to see a gaping hole in the top of each fuselage that was easily four feet wide and thirty feet long. Large arching aluminum bands were wrapped around the fuselage.

"I thought you said these planes were safe and reliable, Lowan," said Thiele.

"Ain't never seen no C-130s like these," Washington replied.

"Before you comment," Parker said, "the large cutouts you see were made by Lockheed Martin engineers. The only way the subs could be loaded into the planes was to cut out the tops of the fuselages." The entire team was now gawking at the sight. "I've been assured the planes can be flown this way and are absolutely safe."

"Where did you find Lockheed Martin engineers down here?" asked Rick.

"They work for the Chilean Air Force. They had their C-130 division do a complete structural analysis, and I can assure you that we did this with Lockheed Martin's blessing." Parker continued. "It's the only way we could get you guys out to where you need to go and down into the water. If you've got a better idea, I'm listening."

"I was gonna suggest that we climb into the subs just before we're dropped into the water, but I guess that ain't possible flyin' in a convertible," said Washington.

"I'll say it again," said Parker, the van now stopped. "It's the best we could do on such short notice. If there was any other possibility, we'd have tried it."

"Are you sure the planes will hold together like that?" asked Marly.

"Me? Heck, no," said Parker with a shrug. "They look like death traps to me. But the engineers say this will work."

Rick laughed.

"That doesn't sound too funny," said Carlson.

"I'm not laughing because it's funny," Rick said. "I'm laughing because it's going to take a string of minor miracles if we're going to have the slightest chance of making this operation a success."

Tom Bowman spoke. "More like a string of major miracles. But I've seen worse, and the planes always seem to hold together."

"That's what we need," Rick said, "some optimism."

"Optimist, hell," said Bowman. "I'm a realist. Optimists in combat tend to have short life spans, and pessimists do even worse."

"Let's quit talking and just do it," said Marly.

"We better start prayin'," said Washington. "I think we got a good chance o' becomin' canned tuna if we don't get the good Lord behind us."

"Going to practice your Presbyterianism, Lowan?" asked Parker.

"Don't matter if you're near-sighted or far-sighted in a case like this, Mister Parker. It's all the same when you can't predict what's ahead."

Rick laughed. The rest of the team looked confused.

***

"One last thing," Parker said as the new arrivals unloaded their bags. "We've had a satellite report on the location of the trawler. You've got about three and a half hours flying time 'til reaching them."

"We'll use that time to develop a strategy," said Rick. "I'm assuming we can talk over the submersibles' communications systems to share ideas?" He gave a questioning look at Washington.

"Comms work underwater, so I don't know why they shouldn't work in the air. We can talk a couple miles apart, usually," said Washington.

"The plan is for the planes to fly in close formation," said Parker.

"Good. We'll put something together and talk options."

"Sounds OK to me," said Bowman.

"This is it, team. Time to board these tin cans." Rick looked at the Turtle's crew, which was now standing together in a separate group. "Talk to you when we're airborne."

"Roger that," said Bowman, switching to the aviator vernacular.

The two teams of three headed for their respective subs — Rick, Marly and Washington going to Sea Cliff, and Carlson, Thiele and

Bowman heading for the Turtle. Each submersible had its name and a matching picture emblazoned on its side.

A third C-130 was parked in front of and between the modified aircraft.

"The submersibles look like sharks," said Carlson. "I thought they'd be round and fat."

"It's not what I imagined, either, although I guess the round guys are called bathyspheres," said Bowman. "This thing may be easier to fly than I thought."

"I never thought that flying a plane and a submarine would be the same," said Thiele, "but I guess it makes sense, since both move in a three dimensional space."

"The only thing that's different is altitude, speed and visibility," said Bowman. "Other than that, I don't expect any big surprises." He suddenly got a puzzled look on his face.

"What's the matter?" asked Carlson, sensitive to anything that appeared out of the ordinary.

"You've got a speedometer in a car and an airspeed indicator in a plane. I wonder what we've got in the sub that'll tell us how fast we're going."

Carlson shrugged. "Maybe it's a water-o-meter, or a water speed indicator."

"Maybe it's knot important," Thiele said, putting emphasis on the word "knot". He waited a moment to see if anyone got his joke. Satisfied they did not, he dropped it.

***

The Turtle and Sea Cliff were sisters. Turtle was a foot taller and wider than Sea Cliff, and four feet shorter. It weighed four tons less. Despite the similarities in their size and shape, and the fact that their electronics and hydraulics were virtually identical, Turtle's maximum depth of ten thousand feet was only half that of its younger sibling.

Electric Boat built both submersibles, four years apart. The Turtle could lift three hundred pounds with one hydraulic arm, sixty-five pounds with the other. Sea Cliff could lift three hundred pounds with either arm. Each submersible cradled a small bazooka in its left craw.

Water intakes on each lower front side and large round lights on either side near the top combined to give the subs an exotic, bug-eyed look.

The team members climbed ladders to the top of the submersibles and slowly stepped down into their hollow bellies.

Dropping into Sea Cliff first was Lowan Washington. He climbed into the pilot's position and settled onto his stomach on a padded platform covered with vinyl, resting his chin on a small chinrest. A black stick made of heavy plastic sat below and slightly forward of the chinrest, and Washington stretched his legs and rested his feet on top of a pair of leather straps attached to two large metal rudder pedals that were perpendicular to the ground. When he pushed on the right rudder pedal, the left pedal moved forward and vice versa. Pushing the control stick to its stops, a grin covered his face.

Rick settled into a small chair to Washington's left, and Marly settled into a chair on his right. Controls for their respective hydraulic arms were in easy reach of them both.

"What are you grinning about?" asked Rick.

"I'm home, Mister Starr. I've come home."

Marly pulled her yellow Steif teddy bear from her bag. Both Rick and Washington gave her a questioning look.

"It's my good luck bear." She folded her arms around the bear and held it to her chest.

"I don't believe in good luck, Doc," said Washington. "There's only one kinda luck, and that's bad luck. You gotta make good stuff happen, which means it ain't really luck. Instead, it's what we do that counts."

"Which is why you dress the way you do." Marly smiled. "'Cause when you look good, you feel good. And when you feel good, you do good."

Washington grinned again. "And when you do good, good stuff happens. You's smart, Doc, and got a real good memory, too. Mister Starr, you got yoreself one fine lady here."

***

Tom Bowman lowered himself gently into the Turtle. Inside were two seats on either side of a thin, padded vinyl-covered board. The quarters were small, and Bowman had to bend over in order to stand. "Guess this is my place," he said aloud.

"What's that?" asked Thiele, who followed him in.

"Just said that it looks like I'll be spending the rest of the day lying on my stomach." He knelt down and flattened himself out on the thin board. He moved the controls from side to side and front to back. "Feels like the flight controls on the jets I used to fly. This should be no problem."

Thiele slipped into the seat left of Bowman's. "Lowan was right. This thing isn't built for comfort."

Bowman laughed. "Actually, it's a lot like an airplane cockpit."

Denise Carlson stumbled into the small area, almost landing on top of Bowman. "Sorry!" She pushed herself into a bent position, straddling Bowman's backside. "Wow. Joe would have gone nuts in here."

"Who?" asked Thiele.

"A colleague of mine back at the office," Carlson replied as she slid into the empty seat. "He has claustrophobia. He was supposed to come, but he was afraid he'd go crazy because the sub might be too small."

"Sounds like he made the right decision," said Bowman. "But since we can see the outside, maybe it's not too bad."

A large glass window, over two feet in height, spanned the entire width of the Turtle and offered a clear view of what was directly in front of them.

Bowman scanned the instrument panel. There was an indicator labeled "speed in knots", a depth meter, vertical velocity indicator, battery status gauge, and a dial registering the oxygen quantity. A radio, oxygen regulator, sonar panel and GPS display completed the instrumentation. A small throttle sat on the display panel next to a rocker switch labeled "on/off", which Bowman assumed was for the motor that powered the propeller.

"Simple and efficient," he said to his two shipmates, turning his head toward one and then the other. "On another day, this would be fun."

"If it were another day, I wouldn't be here," said Carlson.

***

There was movement above their heads. Rick watched the last glimpse of sunlight disappear as the hatch slammed into place. "Guess this is it," he said.

Marly looked at Rick and gave a "I'm trying my best to be brave" smile. Rick returned her smile, doing his best to look confident and encouraging. Washington threw a switch to activate the oxygen regulator. He turned a knob, and the radio came to life.

"Sure hope Mister Bowman knows he needs to switch on the O-2," said Washington. "Shoulda mentioned it to him before we split up."

"Didn't you say we have radios so we could talk to each other?" asked Rick.

"Sure," said Washington. "Do you think he's on frequency already? Shoulda tole him to turn on his radio, too. Man, I messed up." He keyed the microphone switch on the control stick. "Turtle, this is Sea Cliff. You on?"

"Roger, Sea Cliff. Turtle's up."

Washington gave Rick a thumbs-up. "Good thing you got a pilot who knows what he's doin'." Rick nodded. "You got your oxygen on, Turtle?"

"Roger that," said Bowman. "Oxygen's on, showing a full load. Figured since this baby was watertight, I better give us some air to breathe. Let me ask you a couple questions, though, Lowan."

"Go ahead. What's on yore mind?"

"This one guarded switch labeled GPS. What's that for?"

"Once we're in the water, you hit that switch, and it deploys your GPS receiver so you know where you're at. It'll float on the surface, no matter how deep you go. So you got to keep that cable in mind, otherwise it could get tangled and broken off — which is OK in an emergency."

"How about the one marked "emergency ballast release"? Does that switch shoot us to the surface if we get into trouble?"

"Yeah. You want to use that switch only if you absolutely got to. You'll pop to the surface like the cork off a champagne bottle."

Bowman laughed. "Anything else I need to power up right now? The only thing I'm running is the radio."

"You'll need the outside lights after we're dropped in. You can leave the inside lights on now if you want. It's the outside lights that eat up the system battery. There's a bank of separate batteries for the motor. We should have plenty o' juice for our plane trip. Other than that, everything is apple pie a la mode with vanilla ice cream on top."

There was a bump, and Rick could feel the submersible moving forward. He looked out the front window and watched as the sub was pushed toward the yawning entryway awaiting them in the back of the C-130. He looked over at Marly, who seemed to be relaxed, her heels pulled up on her seat. A lapbelt hung loosely to either side. Marly turned her head and looked toward Rick. He reached out, and she took his hand.

"Don't get any romantic ideas. This ain't the Love Boat, you know," said Washington.

Washington's comment broke the tension, and Marly was able to laugh easily. She dropped Rick's hand and gave a clap. "When we gonna get this tugboat underway, anyhow?"

"Tugboat? Doc, you obviously don't know nothin' 'bout nautical de-vices."

"Nautical devices?" laughed Marly. "Lowan, you're killin' me."

***

The Turtle paused when it struck the base of the ramp leading into the plane. The front rose upward, assuming a twenty-degree nose-up attitude as it ascended into the fuselage. The light pouring through the cutouts in the top of the plane's fuselage and into the sub's large front window slowly dimmed as they were pushed inside. The hunk of steel came to an abrupt halt just behind the cockpit bulkhead.

"I think we're in," said Bowman into the radio microphone.

"We's in, too," replied Washington over the radio. "Talk to you after we're airborne."

"Roger that," said Bowman. "See you in the atmosphere."

***

The C-130s started their engines. The lead plane was at the front of the strange parade, the aircraft with Turtle fell in second, and the C-130 carrying Sea Cliff ended the procession. The only indication that this mission was extraordinary was the modified fuselages of the second two airplanes.

Wearing a headset and occupying the jump seat between the two pilots of the lead aircraft was Quentin Parker. "Rick, Tom, this is Parker. Do you read me?"

"Five-by-five here," said Bowman.

"Loud and clear," said Washington for Rick.

"Renoir called and directed me to go with you guys, and I jumped on the lead one-thirty. I'll call you once we have the final coordinates for the target."

"Roger," said Bowman.

"Gotcha," said Washington.

***

Aggie Aguilar and his crew put the satellite coordinates they received for the trawler into the B-2's GPS equipment. The autopilot turned the plane slightly more west. The knife-like fuselage, more flying saucer than aircraft, sliced through the air. Fewer than 2,000 miles remained to the target.

***

Marly reached back and pulled a large map of the ocean floor from her bag. She spread it out across the instrument panel, covering the gauges and the world outside. Rick helped her to smooth it out.

"For the sake of context," Rick said, "we're going to end up about twelve hundred miles out when we reach the trawler." He pulled a piece of paper from his pocket. "These are the preliminary coordinates Parker gave us for the target."

Marly took the paper from Rick and quickly found the location. Washington took a grease pencil from his pocket and marked where she was pointing.

"Is this out by the Pacific Rise?" asked Rick.

"Could be," said Marly. "Like I said, the Rise is almost two thousand miles wide in some places, and it can be as much as two miles high." She sighed audibly. "To be honest, it's only in the last decade that anyone has studied it in detail. But the Rise could definitely be in the neighborhood of these coordinates." A frown suddenly adorned her face.

"What's the matter?" asked Rick.

"I was just thinking. If the trawler is still sailing west when we intercept it, does that mean it hasn't gotten to the rise yet?"

"Maybe it means that they passed the edge of the rise, dropped the subs off, and are just trying to fake us out," said Washington.

"Maybe. But if the trawler turns north or south, that probably means they found the edge and are looking for the right location to drop the submersibles." She looked at Rick and Washington. "So I guess I'm suggesting that we should be dropped off behind the trawler going in the same direction."

"Sounds reasonable to me," said Rick. "What do you think, Lowan?"

"If I knew someone was comin' after me like these guys do," said Washington. "I mean really comin'? I'd throw 'em a curve ball for sure. No way would I show 'em which way my subs were gonna go."

Marly sighed again. "Lowan, I liked it better when you were trying to be funny."

CHAPTER 21

Another quake hit California, this time north of San Francisco. Registering 6.5 on the Richter Scale, it rocked the city for over two minutes, and the metropolitan area was roiled by pounding aftershocks for hours afterward.

***

If anyone in the Bay Area had doubt that something might happen soon, there was little now. The airways were filled with speculation. Even the mayor appeared shaken by the force of this second earthquake on the heels of the seven-pointer just a week earlier. Again the city survived with relatively little damage, and there was only a single casualty, perhaps in part because so many people left and those remaining had curtailed their activities.

But the constant airtime given to events leading up to the quake and the widespread feeling that the city was lucky this time, pushed the population's fears beyond the tipping point. Within an hour of the quake's end, thousands more people abandoned their workplaces, headed home, and packed up their cars. Many handed in their resignations at work without notice. But the effects did not end in the Bay Area. The quake was felt as far south as Baja California and as far north as Seattle. The entire west coast was suddenly abloom with nervous activity, and states to the east of California, Oregon and Washington were inundated with calls for extended hotel reservations. The already overloaded air transportation system became a quagmire, with passengers reserving the remaining seats on flights that would take them anywhere away from the west coast.

Fisherman's Wharf in San Francisco was a ghost town. Its businesses were mostly closed with the exception of a couple bars. A few young and adventurous tourists looking for excitement were the only people left. The remaining homeless drifted aimlessly, an occasional police car passing through the empty streets. The scene would be repeated in Monterey, Carmel, and other nearby coastal areas.

The phones to the offices of Marly Cooper and Beverly Duncan began to ring with cancellations. Their earthquake conference would have to be postponed. "We're canceling our earthquake conference because of earthquakes?" Beverly asked sadly. "Now how ironic is that?"

But no one was coming to San Francisco. No one.

***

"I've just received a call from Washington," Quentin Parker called into his radio. "There's been a major earthquake in San Francisco."

Marly turned toward Washington. "Ask him what the magnitude of the quake was."

"Mister Parker, this is Sea Cliff. Copy on the earthquake. Did they pass you the magnitude?"

"I think it was six plus," Parker said.

Marly's face reacted to the number with a deep frown. "Sea Cliff copies. Six plus," said Washington.

"Turtle copies," said Bowman. "Major earthquake in San Francisco."

"What do you think?" asked Rick, turning toward Marly.

Marly shrugged and shook her head. "To have a seven followed a week later by a six is scary. This one is probably due to accumulated stress."

Rick nodded. "Coulomb stress transfer?"

Marly nodded. "For sure. But it's the potential for elastic rebound that has me worried."

***

"Bingo on the target," said the B-2's right-seater. "Twelve o'clock, two hundred miles."

"Roger," said Major Aggie Aguilar, the aircraft commander. "Prepare for weapons release. The checklist on this thing is two feet long, and we don't want to screw it up."

"Copy, pilot," said the weapons system officer. "Starting weapon prep for our drop. You have any idea what this sucker is gonna do?"

"No clue," said the major. "But I have the feeling we're going to unleash hell."

"I'm calling home base," said the pilot. "I'll let 'em know we've got a bingo and pass them the coordinates."

"Roger," said Aguilar.

***

"Got a call from the B-2," said Parker into the radio. "Says the target is off to our northwest, about a hundred miles and heading due west. You got a plan, Sea Cliff? How do you want to do the drop?"

Marly looked at Washington. "My guess is they haven't reached the Pacific Rise if they're heading west, and I still say we should drop in behind the trawler going in the same direction."

Washington pressed his cheeks with his fingers. "The doc's got a point. Until they turn north or south, we won't know for sure. Is the bomber gonna hit the trawler before we go in?"

"That's the plan," Rick said.

"Then I definitely agree with the doc."

Rick glanced at Marly with a questioning look for one last word.

"OK," said Marly. "Let's go in from behind, same direction."

Rick nodded. "OK, Lowan, tell everyone that's the plan."

***

The captain of the China Rose scowled. *Where is it?* He'd seen the Pacific Rise once before on an excursion to the western hemisphere, and they should be there by now. *It has to be here.*

"Captain!" A young sailor ran up to him breathlessly. "We have radar contact with a plane off our starboard, less than two hundred miles."

"Captain!" called the navigator. "Sonar shows the Pacific Rise directly off our bow, a thousand yards."

The captain managed a smile. Fate was with them, at least for now. "Turn to the north. Tell the submersibles to prepare for immediate release. I want them to exit toward the stern of the ship."

"Aye aye, Captain!" replied the navigator. He began his turn and pulled the throttle for the ship's engines to quarter speed to slow the vessel.

"Do not slow down. We need to distance ourselves from the submersibles as quickly as possible."

"But sir, I thought…"

"I didn't tell you to think! I will do the thinking on this ship. Full speed ahead!" The navigator pushed the throttles back to full ahead.

The young sailor continued to hold his salute. The captain returned it, and the youngster dropped his hand, his chest heaving from the importance of his mission.

"There is nothing we can do to protect ourselves," said the captain. "Tell your superior that the crew is to man emergency evacuation stations. The gunners should stay in position and fire if they see the plane."

Another sailor came running up.

"What now?" The captain directed his question to the new arrival, annoyed by all the activity.

"Three planes flying at low altitude have been detected at a hundred miles off our stern."

The captain was surprised. "What is the altitude of the other plane?" he asked the first sailor.

"Ten thousand feet, sir."

The captain did not know what to make of the conflicting reports. Two attacks? The alarm sounded, and crewmembers began dashing to their stations.

"Return to your positions," the captain ordered.

He leaned his elbow on the arm of the chair and rested his chin on his fist.

***

"Thirty-five miles, crew," called the B-2 wizzo into the interphone. "Level at ten thousand feet, speed should be two fifty."

"Two fifty, ten thousand feet," said the aircraft commander.

"Release in seven minutes. Open the bomb bay doors, pilot."

"Bomb bay doors open," called the pilot, raising the spring-loaded red switch guard and moving the silver lever under it to the up position. The doors on the bottom of the plane parted and exposed a trio of weapons connected by a single cable.

***

"Submersibles have been ordered to launch, Captain," said the ship's executive officer.

The captain nodded. "Good. The Americans cannot stop us now."

The executive officer furrowed his brow. "Sir, I do not understand."

"It is not necessary that you understand," the captain answered tiredly.

***

"Radar has the trawler heading north," said Parker. "Do you still want us to drop you off behind it?"

"Yes. We want to come at the trawler from the south and drop in behind," Rick said. Washington repeated Rick's words. The planes banked sharply left.

"It's almost time. You ready?" Rick asked Marly.

"No, but does it matter?"

"We're dropping our altitude to fifty feet," called Parker. "You guys'll want to strap in. It could be a rough ride."

"Strappin' in," Washington called into the radio.

"Ditto here," replied Bowman.

Rick watched Marly buckle her lapbelt. She turned her head toward him and smiled.

Washington looked up at Rick first and then Marly. "Better hang on tight. This thing ain't got wings, and no parachute is gonna make it fly."

***

The Chinese trawler rocked to the side as it drove north, the waves moving west to east under its hull.

"The captain has given the launch order!" shouted a sailor to the others. A small group stood on the deck overlooking the trawler's interior hold, where two submersibles, the Nimble Monkey and the Iron Dolphin, floated in the water.

"Are you sure? I thought that we would be given proper notice," said one.

"We have received the launch order," the senior petty officer spoke into his headset in response to the sailor's words. The headset was connected to a box with a pair of cables attached to the subs.

The crews in the submersibles responded immediately. "The ship is moving much too fast. We cannot launch."

"The captain has given the launch order," the petty officer said again. "You are to exit the hold under the stern of the ship." He pulled his headset off and pointed to the tethers. "Cut them loose!" he shouted.

The sailors scrambled to pull the communication cables from their sockets and release the slipknots that held the submersibles in place. The subs were rapidly filling their ballasts, and as the last rope was removed, they slipped away under the ocean.

***

The crews watched helplessly as the sailors began pulling away the ropes. The pilot of the Iron Dolphin hit the switch for the pumps that would open the ballasts. "Prepare to launch," he ordered.

"But lieutenant," protested the navigator, strapping himself into his seat. "The ship's propellers. They should be silenced before we take any action."

"There must be an emergency. The captain would stop the ship if he could." He moved a switch that started the submersible's propellers turning. Their forward speed would be only a fraction of the trawler's, but it might keep their heading stable as they dropped out from under the ship.

"What are they doing?" screamed the navigator of the Nimble Monkey. "Why haven't they halted the trawler? This is not in accordance with proper procedure!"

The pilot of the Nimble Monkey was not as experienced as his colleague in the Iron Dolphin. He opened the ballast doors, but he did not direct full power to the propellers. As his submersible dropped out from under the trawler, it was tossed off to the side of the ship's wake and spun around like a top. The crew became disoriented, their instruments useless.

The Iron Dolphin managed to maintain its heading, but as it went under the ship's stern it was sucked into the churning water generated by the trawler's huge propellers. Its antennas, vulnerable and in easy reach on top of the submersible, were shredded.

Hanging off the bottom of both submersibles was a single slender tube that measured ten feet long. The crews believed they held listening devices that would be part of a network to monitor America's compliance with the nuclear test ban treaty. Their task was to place them on the ocean floor and to activate them electronically after their release. Upon activation, the crews were to return to the trawler.

***

Three weaponized cylindrical objects plummeted from the B-2's bomb bay in unison. The first was heaviest, the second less so, the third less still. The first cylinder received an infrared lock on the smokestack of the trawler from the avionics of the B-2. The weapon aimed its seeker at the heat source, and its internal electronics assumed control as it fell away from the bomb bay.

With gravity pulling the three projectiles toward the earth below, the separation between them speedily increased. A cable provided the means for the first weapon to pass guidance information to the others, and the cable stretched for hundreds of yards as the three siblings continued their downward plunge.

When it passed through two thousand feet above the water, the first cylinder detonated into a burst of electromagnetic pulse that destroyed virtually all the ship's electronics. Radars, radios and sonar died, instrument dials froze, and the navigation equipment stopped functioning. No MAYDAY from the China Rose would be sent this day informing the world that the trawler was under attack.

The second weapon followed in the wake of the first, and it exploded into a brilliant flash of light that enveloped the vessel below it. Everyone onboard the deck or in line of sight of the weapon was blinded by the dazzling burst. The ship's captain stumbled out of his chair. Could he have seen, he would have observed that everyone around him was also helpless and disabled.

The third weapon lit up and transformed into a missile, piercing the center of the trawler's smokestack as it broke through the sound barrier with an explosive scream. It drove down through the ship's many decks and erupted through the keel. The trawler rolled violently left and then right, water pouring into its holds. The ballast pumps no longer worked, the electronics that would drive them no longer functional. The crew, many of them blind, limped toward the deck as best they could to begin the futile task of evacuating the ship.

***

"Fifty miles to the drop zone," said the C-130 pilot. Parker echoed his words into the radio.

"Looks like the drop will be in about eight minutes," Parker said.

"Eight minutes," acknowledged Sea Cliff and Turtle.

***

The Iron Dolphin leveled at a depth of fifty feet and established a speed of five knots.

"Lieutenant," said the navigator, "we have lost communications, and we have neither visual nor sonar contact with the Nimble Monkey. We must find them to coordinate the placement of our cargo. What are your orders?"

"Begin a circling maneuver, maintain a depth of fifty feet, and start a sonar scan. They are close by. We will find them."

***

The Nimble Monkey and its crew were in a slow spin, bobbing at the surface. The pilot fought to stabilize the vessel, without success. In frustration, he slammed the throttle to the full-on position, and as the propellers spun up the vessel responded to his direction. The sub began to submerge, its ballast tanks still full, and the pilot adjusted the pumps to stabilize their depth. The planned rendezvous procedures called for a depth of fifty feet.

The sub's navigator called vainly into the radio, receiving no rejoinder.

***

"One minute to the drop zone. Godspeed and good luck," said Parker into his radio.

"He's got that right," said Washington. "We're gonna need dee-vine intervention so we don't get hurt. Specially Mister Bowman."

His words were cut short by a loud whirring sound followed by a loud thump. No sooner did they look at each other than the submersible began a rapid movement to the rear.

"That weren't no minute!" yelped Washington.

The submersible dropped suddenly, and the panicked look on all three of their faces told them they weren't imagining the fall. With a jerk, their rapid descent was arrested, and the sub began swaying front to back as if it were suspended like a swing on a playground. They felt the downward motion continue, until with a hard thud the sub smacked into the water. All three gave a loud "oomph," as the air was forced from their lungs. Washington's legs were lifted vertically into the air, and the force thrust him into the instrument panel. The submersible's downward motion continued and then quickly reversed itself. Washington was thrown again, this time toward the back of the small compartment. Marly and Rick were safely strapped into their chairs.

Washington was able to reorient himself quickly and climbed back into position on the small padded board. "We seem to have survived the drop," Washington said after catching his breath.

"Are you OK, Lowan?" asked Marly, her voice full of concern.

"Yeah, I'm fine. Just wanted to do a little somersault to show how happy I am 'bout parachutin' into the water."

***

Turtle also swung back and forth from its parachute, but it was luckier. The crew landed just as the sub was at the peak of its forward swing, and they settled gently into the water.

"That wasn't so bad," said Thiele. "What was everyone so worried about?"

***

"Turtle, this is Sea Cliff," the radio called.

"Roger, Sea Cliff, this is Turtle. We got you loud and clear."

"We're heading three-six-zero. Say heading."

"Roger, Sea Cliff," said Bowman. He switched on the sonar and picked up not one, but two targets. "Sea Cliff, this is Turtle. I have two bogeys on my sonar. We're presently heading two-niner-zero. We've got one bogey at twelve o'clock at about five hundred yards, and another at two o'clock." Bowman watched the sonar for a moment. "It looks like you're at our twelve o'clock. Do you have the other bogey in sight? He's a couple hundred yards off to your right heading two-five-zero."

Washington turned on his sonar. Rick and Marly leaned over from their seats to look. Just as Bowman had said, there was an object to their right, less than two hundred yards away and moving in their direction.

"We have the bogey at our two o'clock," said Washington. "He's below the surface. We're submerging to match his depth."

"This is good," said Rick. "They were still with the trawler, and they haven't gone deep yet."

"Roger on the submerging," said Bowman into his radio. "He looks like he's coming right for you!"

"I thought they'd be running in the other direction when they saw us," said Rick.

"Maybe he thinks we're his partner," suggested Marly.

"They should be talkin' to each other," said Washington.

"Maybe they've got communication problems," Rick said. "They barely got out of the trawler alive, and maybe they damaged something on the way out. Or maybe they're just disoriented."

"I'd be awful surprised if they was this bad o' navigators. Somethin' else is goin' on. I think they're comin' after us."

"I'm taking the safety off the bazooka," said Rick.

"Turtle, this is Sea Cliff. We're gonna take a shot at this guy if we can," said Washington.

"Roger," said Bowman. "We'll hang back and stay out of your way."

Suddenly, another bogey came into view on Bowman's sonar at his five o'clock. "We've got another visitor, this time at our five o'clock, about six hundred yards."

The object was too far away for Sea Cliff to pick it up.

"Tell Tom to take him," said Rick.

"Mister Bowman, Mister Starr says for you guys to take 'em," Washington relayed into the radio.

"Roger that," said Bowman, starting a right turn toward the bogey. He looked at Ralph Thiele, who controlled the bazooka in Turtle's metal claw. "You ready to fire that thing?"

***

"Lieutenant," said the Iron Dolphin's navigator. "We have our comrades at nine o'clock, six hundred yards. Turn left ninety degrees to intercept. We'll get within visual range and coordinate our drops using visual signals if we cannot establish radio contact."

"Turning left ninety degrees to intercept," said the pilot.

***

Lowan Washington pushed the throttle to full forward and descended until the sonar indicated the two submersibles were at the same depth. He leveled at fifty feet below the surface and kept the unidentified object directly in the twelve o'clock position.

"That's strange. They're slowin' down," said Washington. "It's like they're settin' up for a rendezvous." He looked over at Marly. "You could be right, Doc. Maybe they are searchin' for their partner." He looked back at Rick. "You better shoot that bazoo-ker as soon as we get into range, Mister Starr, and before they recognize we're not one o' their bro's."

"That's my plan," said Rick. "Instead of a friendly handshake, they'll get a big, ugly bazooka shell shoved up their noses."

***

"Pilot," said the navigator of the Nimble Monkey, "our sister ship is off the nose at two hundred yards. I'm setting the sonar for close-in contact."

"Going half power," said the pilot. "Reducing velocity for the join-up. Do we have radio contact yet?"

The navigator watched his scope. "We still do not have radio contact." He shook his head. "The Iron Dolphin is not following procedures, pilot. They are approaching us at full speed."

"Perhaps they are having problems with their equipment. I'm turning ten degrees left to give them a better visual."

The pilot turned ten degrees left. A moment later, their sonar showed that the oncoming submersible turned ten degrees right to keep the two vessels nose to nose.

"The Iron Dolphin has turned with us, so they have working sonar. But you are right. She does not appear to be slowing for the rendezvous."

"Something is wrong," replied the navigator. "She is not following procedures."

"One hundred yards. Pulling off power to compensate. Going to idle," said the pilot.

***

"Lieutenant!" cried the navigator of the Iron Dolphin.

"What is it?" asked the pilot.

"A second target has appeared on sonar at less than a thousand yards! Do you think it's another submersible? Or a whale, perhaps?"

"A whale?" The pilot thought for only an instant. "This is why the captain did not stop the ship. The Americans have sent their forces to intercept us!"

"But where would they have come from? And which of these is ours? Surely the captain would have told us that another vessel was in close proximity."

"What matters is that they are here. And if we can see them, then they can surely see us. I am turning back one hundred eighty degrees and beginning an emergency descent to the ocean floor." The pilot opened his ballast tanks. Water filled the empty spaces, driving the submersible downward.

"Where is our planned drop zone?" asked the pilot.

"It will be in front of us after you complete your turn. Our only guidance is to drop our cargo near the Pacific Rise."

"Roger," said the pilot, as the sub rolled fully into its turn.

The Iron Dolphin continued its sharp turn, and the Turtle entered its sonar's cone of silence, five hundred yards behind.

"The second target's descending and turning," said Bowman into the radio. "I think he's seen us."

"You gotta get 'em, Mister Bowman," replied Washington. "We're busy here. Our guy's barely fifty yards away."

"Wilco." Bowman hit the switch that opened the ballast doors. Water poured in, the downward motion surprisingly rapid. "We're going after him."

CHAPTER 22

"Fifty yards," said Lowan Washington over interphone. "I'm maintaining our speed at five knots. Looks like they's stopped dead. You should be in firing range any second, Mister Starr."

"I'm looking, Lowan. As soon as I see the bad guys, I'll shoot."

"That'll be too late, Mister Starr. When I tell you to fire, you better shoot that thing. They'll be right off our nose at twelve o'clock and twenty-five yards. If you wait 'til you see the whites 'o their eyes, they'll run before you ever get your shot off."

"Whatever you say, Lowan. Just tell me when to pull the trigger."

***

"Pilot, their closing speed has not changed," said the navigator. "The Iron Dolphin should be slowing. Something is not right. We must initiate evasive action immediately."

The Nimble Monkey had stopped its forward motion and sat suspended in the water. "You are too nervous," said the pilot. "You are referring to procedures, not regulations. Variances are permitted."

"Pilot," said the navigator, "I am suggesting very strongly that we take evasive action. If I am wrong, then nothing has been lost. But if I am right, it may make the difference between survival and catastrophe. Our sister ship's crew has always followed rendezvous procedures precisely in the past. Their navigator and I have talked many times about how to conduct a proper comm-out rejoin."

The young pilot nodded resentfully. The navigator was older and more experienced, and the pilot was annoyed at the unsolicited advice.

We are in the middle of the Pacific Ocean. Who else could this be? He slammed the power to full ahead, and the sub's propellers spun up and began pushing the submersible forward. "Taking evasive action," the pilot said, his voice reflecting his annoyance. He turned the submarine sharply left and then back right again until it was on a course paralleling the object displayed on the sonar.

***

"Get ready, Mister Starr." The sudden increase in closing speed, in conjunction with the other submersible's maneuver, caught Washington by surprise. He veered right to match the turn. "What's he doin'?"

No sooner did Washington speak than a behemoth nearly twice the size of their submersible appeared in the window, approaching rapidly from the right, a long tube hanging loosely underneath.

"My God!" yelled Marly. "Get out of the way, Lowan! He's going to ram us!"

But Washington turned abruptly into the other sub, the front of the two vessels colliding with each other. Through their respective windows, the crewmembers looked directly into the surprised eyes of their adversaries.

"I couldn't run," said Washington, fighting the controls to keep Sea Cliff nose-to-nose with its rival. "He mighta hit us broadside, and that coulda been fatal."

The Chinese submarine tried to reverse course upon discovering that its sister ship was really an American vessel. But Washington continued to push Sea Cliff forward. Marly clamped her hydraulic arm onto the metal claw protruding from the front of the other vessel. "I got him!"

The Chinese sub veered sharply to the left as Washington continued to drive ahead, and its appendage was torn from its roost. Marly dropped the metal limb as quickly as she grabbed it.

"Back up!" yelled Rick. "Back off and keep him directly off the nose. As soon as they get twenty-five yards away, I'll fire."

Washington reversed course. "They're turning, Mister Starr. I'll keep 'em at twelve o'clock, but you better take yore shot while you can. I can't promise they'll stay off our nose or that they'll be in firing range if you wait. They're big and they're probably lots faster than us. And if they submerge, you may never get 'em."

"They seem awfully close," Rick protested, but he hesitated for only a moment. He aimed the bazooka as best he could at the fleeing submarine and pulled the trigger. There was a loud thump, and a raft of bubbles obscured his view as the projectile left the barrel.

Time seemed to drift and somersault into slow motion. Rick gazed over at Marly. He consciously confessed to himself how much he liked this woman. He turned his eyes back to the window and squinted. The turquoise of the water, light dancing through its rolling layers, struck him as surreal.

***

Tom Bowman closed the gap between Turtle and its prey to less than five hundred yards, but he found he could not get closer. He watched the depth meter pass through two thousand feet, their descent increasing rapidly. Florescent green flashes from luminescent biological organisms were suddenly visible in the dark water. Nothing else was discernible out the front window, the water becoming completely devoid of light as they descended ever deeper. Turtle's headlights, bright as they were, provided little illumination without something to reflect their brilliance.

"Do you think they'll go all the way to the bottom?" asked Thiele.

"Sure looks like it. They're dropping like a rock."

"I wonder how deep the water is here."

Bowman shrugged. "I don't know. Let's hope it's not much more than ten thousand feet."

"Why's that?" asked Carlson, trying to recall what Washington and Bowman talked about back on the plane.

Bowman only shook his head. "It makes me nervous to think that I might be more than two miles below the surface." Five thousand feet. The Turtle began to make metal sounds as if it were flexing its muscles in preparation to go still deeper.

***

"It is your fault that we are now in danger, pilot," scolded the navigator. "You should have taken evasive action as soon as it became apparent the other vessel was not following procedures."

Ignoring the comment, the Nimble Monkey's young pilot continued his turn away from the Americans. He threw the switch that opened their ballasts to "full open" so they would fill with water and push the sub into a rapid dive. But the timing was unfortunate. As the valves leading to the ballasts reached the full open position, an explosion pierced the water. Overpressure from the detonation entered the mostly empty ballasts, with the effect of increasing the blast's force. The left side of the submersible ruptured and split open, fatally injuring the navigator.

Water spewed in through the gaping hole in the side. The sub began to rotate slowly to the right, water rapidly displacing the remaining air in the vessel. The pilot and systems engineer unbuckled their seatbelts as the water engulfed them, and the pilot hit a large flat piece of metal that would open a way of escape. The wheel that held the hatch in place turned, and the hatch burst open. The pilot was sucked out and upward. The systems engineer followed, and the two of them struggled toward the surface. Waiting for them on top of the waves was a small three-man rubber raft that deployed and inflated as part of the emergency evacuation.

***

"We've got movement." It was Larry Davis, sticking his head into the office of John Renoir, where he was mulling over options with Joe Craxton.

"What do you mean?" asked Renoir.

"Since the quake earlier this morning, the Chinese have begun flying transport aircraft to an airbase less than twenty miles out of Xiamen." Neither Renoir nor Craxton spoke, so Davis continued. "There aren't any trucks full of paratroopers leaving Xiamen for the airport yet. But if that were to happen, I'd say the Chinese were all but committed to an invasion. Do we have a plan?"

"Yeah," said Renoir. "It's called 'cope.' It's gonna be another couple days before we even get our forces fully into position, much less able to respond to an attack with any real effect."

"Maybe the president needs to say something again about our resolve to defend Taiwan," suggested Craxton.

"The Chinese seem to be expecting something big to happen in California," said Davis. "What will the president do if there's another earthquake and it does some real damage? Fox News is suggesting that we'll call everybody home and that Taiwan could find itself on its own."

Renoir could not hide his frustration. "One more quake, and life may get interesting. *Way* too interesting."

***

When the bazooka round exploded, the inside of Sea Cliff sounded as if a hundred massive sledgehammers struck it, all at the same time. The outer pane of Sea Cliff's double-paned front window cracked and split from top to bottom with a loud snap.

"What was that?" asked Marly, sure that the sub would fill with water at any moment.

"Outer pane of the window's cracked!" said Washington, fighting the controls to maintain equilibrium. "We can't descend below a thousand feet with a broken window." He looked at Rick, who was straining to see what happened to the other submersible. "That means we can't help Mister Bowman and the Turtle!"

Rick looked at Washington and winced. "OK. A thousand feet." He looked back out the window again. "Go find that Chinese sub so we can get the nuke before it sinks to the bottom where we can't get to it." He opened his hydraulic claw and dropped the bazooka.

"You lost our only weapon, Mister Starr," whined Washington.

"You're stating the obvious, Lowan. I want that nuke. Let's get going!"

Slamming the power full forward, Washington headed for where they last saw the Chinese vessel. When it came into view, the sub was rolling slowly over onto its back and beginning a leisurely descent. The cables that held the long slender tube to its belly had extended their full length, and the tube attached to the cables drifted lazily over the top of the craft and followed its downward spiral.

"That's it!" said Rick.

"That's what?" asked Washington.

"The tube there, that's what we want!"

Washington aimed for the slender cylinder, driving Sea Cliff downward. He monitored the depth and kept pace with the now increasing rate of descent of the other submarine. As they approached the cylinder, Rick grabbed the cable at its front. "Grab the other cable!" he shouted at Marly. She reached out with her hydraulic arm and snatched it.

The larger vessel, full of water, pulled Sea Cliff behind it. "Full power, Lowan. Full power!" shouted Rick.

But Washington was already at full power with full-up elevator. Sea Cliff's nose pointed at the surface, but its movement continued downward. "It ain't workin', Mister Starr. It's either gonna be us or the nuke. And you better decide real quick. We're goin' through five hundred feet."

The disabled vessel seemed determined to take Sea Cliff with it to the depths of the crushing waters. The downward motion continued.

"Seven hundred. Eight hundred. Lord-ee, Mister Starr, whattaya want me to do?"

Rick began moving the Sea Cliff's hydraulic arm back and forth as rapidly as the system would allow. "Try to yank on it!" he shouted to Marly, who was already following his lead.

"I can't believe this!" mumbled Rick. "Every metal tool I buy from China breaks. How come this stupid cable won't?"

As if on cue, the ring securing the front cable to the container holding the nuclear weapon snapped. The second cable could not support the Nimble Monkey's weight by itself and also broke free. The long slender tube fell gently into Sea Cliff's extended claws. The Chinese submersible continued its descent and disappeared into the black.

"Good catch," said Rick, "good catch." He smiled triumphantly at Marly, and she returned his smile with a grin.

Washington rolled Sea Cliff to the west and headed toward the surface. Rick felt a great release of tension and was suddenly tired. The three of them sat in silence, staring out the front window.

***

Bowman scanned his instruments. Eight thousand feet, no sign of the bottom, and their prey was heading ever deeper. The sonar showed the ocean bottom was still at least a thousand yards away — or more than three thousand feet. Even if they hit bottom soon, the depth would exceed ten thousand. Turtle groaned noisily, the loud sounds the protest of metal straining against great weight.

"Is all this noise normal?" asked Carlson.

"I sure hope so," replied Bowman. He remembered his conversation with Washington. *A thirty percent buffer.*

"If it's any consolation," said Thiele, "it's a normal part of Hollywood submarine movies. There's always creaking and moaning. But of course the sounds get loudest just before the hull of the vessel collapses and everyone dies."

Carlson shot Thiele an unappreciative look. "Thanks for the reassuring comment. I feel much better now."

"Sea Cliff, this is Turtle," Bowman called into the radio. "We're passing eight thousand feet with no sign of the bottom. You guys OK? What's your status?"

Bowman's voice pierced the silence and snapped the Sea Cliff back to reality. Washington handed the microphone to Rick. "Hey, Tom, this is Rick. The subs are carrying the nukes under their bellies in a long black tube. The tube is your target. If you can't kill the mouse, you've got to steal the cheese." He paused. "We have a broken window, so you're on your own."

Through the crackling sound of static, Bowman heard the bad news. "Roger. Understand you can't help, a broken window. Our bogey's straight ahead off our nose. We're still in trail. We're gonna go as deep as we have to. See you at the surface."

The transmission was comprehensible, but garbled. "He's almost out of range, Mister Starr. Any last words?" Rick handed the microphone back to Washington.

"Tell him to check six." Washington repeated the words into the radio. Bowman heard only static.

***

"What do we do now?" asked Washington.

Rick shook his head. "Well, we can't help the others." He looked back out the window. "And we don't know if this nuke's got a timing fuse, or a depth fuse, or all of the above, or none of the above."

"So what do we do with it?" asked Marly.

"You're supposed to tell me. How about if we find the Pacific Rise and then we drop it on top where it can't get any torque?"

Marly nodded. "Not a perfect plan," she said. "But if this thing has any chance of going off, I think it's the best option."

"Do you see the Pacific Rise in the sonar?" asked Rick.

"I'm lookin', Mister Starr. If it's out there, I'll find it."

"While you're looking, can you give Bowman another try?"

Washington called out for Turtle. Quiet was the only reply.

"He's out of range," said Washington.

Rick nodded slowly.

***

At ten thousand feet, the sonar showed the ocean bottom a thousand yards away. *We'll be at thirteen thousand feet.* Bowman laughed to himself. "I'm beginning to believe in miracles," he said into the interphone.

Thiele and Carlson looked at him, and Bowman pointed to the sonar. "We're almost at the bottom."

As the Chinese sub changed its attitude to break its descent, Bowman closed the remaining gap rapidly. Two hundred yards. One ninety. One eighty. Turtle passed through twelve thousand feet, its structure suddenly deathly quiet as if it was afraid the massive pressure might crush its outer hull at any moment. *Twenty-five yards. Fire at twenty-five yards.*

The gap between Turtle and the Iron Dolphin continued to decrease rapidly. It was as if the Chinese submersible suddenly stopped.

"Seventy five yards to target," Bowman said. "Get ready to fire the bazooka."

Thiele removed the safety. "Safety's off. Ready to fire. Just give me the word."

"Fifty yards," said Bowman. The other vessel was moving again, but not fast enough to get away. "Forty yards." Thiele looked out the window, straining to see his target.

Turtle was now skirting the sand on the ocean floor, its headlights illuminating the light brown earth beneath. Bowman was flying the Turtle like he would an Air Force jet to take out a target: low and fast and with death in his sights. *Huh? What was that?* A long slender black tube was illuminated for a brief second as it lay in the sand, a cable strung out at each end. Thirty yards. *There's the sub, up ahead in the dark.*

"Fire!" yelled Bowman into the interphone, the loudness of his voice surprising even himself.

***

"Device is released," said the navigator.

"Copy," said Iron Dolphin's pilot. "Prepare to activate."

"Ready," said the navigator.

"Activate."

"Initiating activation."

No sooner did the navigator hit the switch than the submersible's sides collapsed from the force of a huge explosion. None of the crewmembers felt it, knocked unconscious as the water enveloped and then crushed them.

***

Sea Cliff glided through the water, the top of the Pacific Rise several hundred feet below.

***

Turtle felt the explosion of the bazooka shell, a loud ka-thump echoing on its insides. Bowman continued to drive the Turtle forward until they reached the Chinese vessel resting on the ocean floor, gulps of air pouring from its interior.

"Good shot, Ralph. You hit 'em dead center."

"Where's the nuke these guys were supposed to be carrying?" asked Carlson. "I don't see the tube Rick talked about."

"I think I saw it about a hundred yards back lying on the sand."

"You mean they just dropped it?"

"Looks that way. Let's go get it and get to the surface. We need to let Rick know we've recovered it." He tried to keep his voice calm, a sense of urgency now taking over to get them and the Turtle above a depth of ten thousand feet.

Bowman turned Turtle around to where the bomb lay resting on the ocean bottom. The avionics embedded in the nuclear weapon were still awaiting the command to detonate, a signal that never came, the antenna that could have relayed it sheared off when the Iron Dolphin slipped through the churning propellers of the China Rose.

Thiele and Carlson picked the nuke up with Turtle's claws, and they headed for the surface. Bowman paralleled the east side of the Pacific Rise. Black smokers expelled dark sulfurous liquid into the ocean. Crabs and starfish and sea anemones could be seen in the coral growing on the side of the lava mountain. Eels hovered near active volcanic vents.

Bowman turned directly to the south and continued the ascent. Turtle creaked again in a sigh of relief as if a great weight was lifted from its straining shoulders. When the depth meter indicated they were passing through ten thousand feet, Bowman found himself whispering a prayer of thanks. The last time he prayed was just before he was picked up by friendlies after ejecting from his jet aircraft when he was shot down over Iraq.

Thiele and Carlson laughed and talked now that they were safe, all the while cradling the long slender tube in Turtle's hydraulic arms as they continued their upward climb to daylight.

"Sea Cliff, this is Turtle," called Bowman into the radio.

"Go ahead Turtle, we've got you five-by."

EPILOGUE

"The U.S. president has given me a letter that he wants you to read to your authorities immediately," said the U.S. vice president to the Chinese ambassador. The two sat in the large receiving room of the Chinese embassy in Washington, D.C. Large red curtains hung on the windows. Pictures of the Politburo, men in various poses conducting important business, decorated the walls.

"The letter says that we sank the last of your trawlers in the Pacific, putting an end to all explosions and earthquakes. We are prepared to defend Taiwan with our full military might, and should China attack Taiwan or attempt to destabilize the North American continent in any way in the future, we are prepared to take whatever actions are necessary to show our displeasure, including the gravest action imaginable."

The Chinese ambassador said nothing, his face expressionless.

"Does the United States make its position clear?"

The Chinese ambassador nodded.

"Call now."

The ambassador stood and left the room holding the letter. He could be heard yelling for an assistant.

***

"Are you going to reschedule your conference?" asked Rick.

Marly shrugged. "I don't know. I'm considering leaving California. I've been thinking it'd be nice to live in Colorado again.

There's a position open at the university where I graduated, and they've invited me to apply." She smiled at Rick. "I would miss Beverly, but I think I'm going to take them up on the offer. She and I have already talked about collaborating long distance."

"Are there any earthquakes in Colorado? Can you still be a seismologist?"

"Today you can be a seismologist from just about anywhere with all the technology available. I'll travel to the earthquakes if they don't come to me."

"It certainly sounds a lot safer." Rick returned Marly's smile. "Of course, Colorado's not Washington, D.C., but you are a thousand miles closer." His smile became a grin.

"I've got some vacation time. And I've never really visited the nation's capital before."

"There's no time like the present, I always say. And I know a great place with an extra room that you could rent for a few weeks."

"Rent?"

"Of course, it's not as comfortable as a submersible, but it's close."

"Rent?"

"Well, it's certainly not for sale."

Marly slugged Rick's arm. "What were you thinking about in Chile when I asked and you wouldn't tell me?"

"When was that?" Rick teased.

"OK, don't tell me. Tell me about Italy. I've always wanted to visit Rome. I'd love to see the Roman Forum and the Coliseum."

***

John Renoir sat in his chair smoking a cigar, his feet resting on top of his desk. The ceremony in the Rose Garden with the president had been a thirst-quenching rain at the end of a long and severe drought. The president acknowledged the heroism of everyone involved, including the Navy crews that recovered the nuclear weapons from the top of the Pacific Rise. The operation was a complete success, and the president's popularity reflected that.

Fox News had just reported that Taiwan's armed forces were coming off high alert. China declared it was in fact conducting military exercises.

Renoir's secretary came in, her expression displaying alarm. "Sir, are you all right?" She paused before speaking again. "You know, Doctor Renoir, you can't smoke in this building."

Renoir continued to puff on the cigar, smoke billowing out from between his lips. "I know. And the stinkin' Chinese leadership wasn't supposed to try to start World War Three." He puffed again. "But that didn't stop them from trying."

He took the cigar from his mouth and pounded the lit end in the ashtray. "I'm feelin' good, and a good cigar makes me feel even better."

His secretary sighed and shook her head. Renoir was a good boss, and she was glad he was sticking around. She turned to hide her smile and stepped out of the office.

***

"How was it?" asked Joe Craxton.

"You wouldn't have liked it," said Denise Carlson. "The inside of the submarine was pretty small, just like you thought."

"Were you scared?"

"There wasn't time to be scared, really. Everything happened so fast. I wondered a couple times if we were going to make it." Carlson nodded her head. "But here I am."

"You know," said Craxton. "I've taken some time to think while you were away. I'd like to give our relationship another try."

Carlson kept nodding. "I've had time to think, too, Joe. If you had said that before I went away, I would have considered it." She looked directly into his eyes. "But now, I don't think so. Something's changed. I feel more alive, and it feels good. I want something different."

***

Rick Starr entered the Agency for the first time in weeks. It felt good to be back in the office. But it was certainly quieter. And it seemed emptier than before.

Had he really fallen in love with a beautiful college professor? And together, had they truly saved the world? He felt the bare space on his finger, the wedding band gone. A smile captured his lips. With a laugh, an exaggerated "*amore*" rolled off his tongue.

So Marly wants to visit Roma? The eternal city? Una città bella!

It's time for a real vacation.